NONE OTH[

BY

Robert Hugh Benson

NONE OTHER GODS

Published by Yurita Press

New York City, NY

First published circa 1940

Copyright © Yurita Press, 2015

ABOUT YURITA PRESS

Yurita Press is a boutique publishing company run by people who are passionate about history's greatest works. We strive to republish the best books ever written across every conceivable genre and making them easily and cheaply available to readers across the world.

PART I: CHAPTER I: (I)

"I think you're behaving like an absolute idiot," said Jack Kirkby indignantly.

Frank grinned pleasantly, and added his left foot to his right one in the broad window-seat.

These two young men were sitting in one of the most pleasant places in all the world in which to sit on a summer evening—in a ground-floor room looking out upon the Great Court of Trinity College, Cambridge. It was in that short space of time, between six and seven, during which the Great Court is largely deserted. The athletes and the dawdlers have not yet returned from field and river; and Fellows and other persons, young enough to know better, who think that a summer evening was created for the reading of books, have not yet emerged from their retreats. A white-aproned cook or two moves across the cobbled spaces with trays upon their heads; a tradesman's boy comes out of the corner entrance from the hostel; a cat or two stretches himself on the grass; but, for the rest, the court lies in broad sunshine; the shadows slope eastwards, and the fitful splash and trickle of the fountain asserts itself clearly above the gentle rumble of Trinity Street.

Within, the room in which these two sat was much like other rooms of the same standing; only, in this one case the walls were paneled with white-painted deal. Three doors led out of it—two into a tiny bedroom and a tinier dining-room respectively; the third on to the passage leading to the lecture-rooms. Frank found it very convenient, since he thus was enabled, at every hour of the morning when the lectures broke up, to have the best possible excuse for conversing with his friends through the window.

The room was furnished really well. Above the mantelpiece, where rested an array of smoking-materials and a large silver cigarette-box, hung an ancestral-looking portrait, in a dull gilded frame, of an aged man, with a ruff round his neck, purchased for one guinea; there was a sofa and a set of chairs upholstered in a good damask: a black piano by Broadwood; a large oval gate-leg table; a bureau; shelves filled with very indiscriminate literature—law books, novels, Badminton, magazines and ancient school editions of the classics; a mahogany glass-fronted bookcase packed with volumes of esthetic appearance—green-backed poetry books with white labels; old leather tomes, and all the rest of the specimens usual to a man who has once thought himself literary. Then there were engravings, well framed, round the walls; a black iron-work lamp, fitted for electric light, hung from the ceiling; there were a couple of oak chests, curiously carved. On the stained floor lay three or four mellow rugs, and the window-boxes outside blazed with geraniums. The débris of tea rested on the window-seat nearest the outer door.

Frank Guiseley, too, lolling in the window-seat in a white silk shirt, unbuttoned at the throat, and gray flannel trousers, and one white shoe, was very pleasant to look upon. His hair was as black and curly as a Neapolitan's; he had a smiling, humorous mouth, and black eyes—of an extraordinary twinkling alertness. His clean-shaven face, brown in its proper complexion as well as with healthy sunburning (he had played very vigorous lawn-tennis for the last two months), looked like a boy's, except for the very determined mouth and the short, straight nose. He was a little below middle height—well-knit and active; and though, properly speaking, he was not exactly handsome, he was quite exceptionally delightful to look at.

Jack Kirkby, sitting in an arm-chair a yard away, and in the same sort of costume—except that he wore both his shoes and a Third Trinity blazer—was a complete contrast in appearance. The other had something of a Southern Europe look; Jack was obviously English—wholesome red cheeks, fair hair and a small mustache resembling spun silk. He was, also, closely on six feet in height.

He was anxious just now, and, therefore, looked rather cross, fingering the very minute hairs of his mustache whenever he could spare the time from smoking, and looking determinedly away from Frank upon the floor. For the last week he had talked over this affair, ever since the amazing announcement; and had come to the conclusion that once more, in this preposterous scheme, Frank really meant what he said.

Frank had a terrible way of meaning what he said—he reflected with dismay. There was the affair of the bread and butter three years ago, before either of them had learned manners. This had consisted in the fastening up in separate brown-paper parcels innumerable pieces of bread and butter, addressing each with the name of the Reverend Junior Dean (who had annoyed Frank in some way), and the leaving of the parcels about in every corner of Cambridge, in hansom cabs, on seats, on shop-counters and on the pavements—with the result that for the next two or three days the dean's staircase was crowded with messenger boys and unemployables, anxious to return apparently lost property.

Then there had been the matter of the flagging of a fast Northern train in the middle of the fens with a red pocket-handkerchief, to find out if it were really true that the train would stop, followed by a rapid retreat on bicycles so soon as it had been ascertained that it was true; the Affair of the German Prince traveling incognito, into which the Mayor himself had been drawn; and the Affair of the Nun who smoked a short black pipe in the Great Court shortly before midnight, before gathering up her skirts and vanishing on noiseless india-rubber-shod feet round the kitchen quarters into the gloom of Neville's Court, as the horrified porter descended from his signal-box.

Now many minds could have conceived these things; a smaller number of people would have announced their intention of doing them: but there were very few persons who would actually carry them all out to the very end: in fact, Jack reflected, Frank Guiseley was about the only man of his acquaintance who could possibly have done them. And he had done them all on his own sole responsibility.

He had remembered, too, during the past week, certain incidents of the same nature at Eton. There was the master who had rashly inquired, with deep sarcasm, on the fourth or fifth occasion in one week when Frank had come in a little late for five-o'clock school, whether "Guiseley would not like to have tea before pursuing his studies." Frank, with a radiant smile of gratitude, and extraordinary rapidity, had answered that he would like it very much indeed, and had vanished through the still half-open door before another word could be uttered, returning with a look of childlike innocence at about five-and-twenty minutes to six.

"Please, sir," he had said, "I thought you said I might go?"

"And have you had tea?"

"Why, certainly, sir; at Webber's."

Now all this kind of thing was a little disconcerting to remember now. Truly, the things in themselves had been admirably conceived and faithfully executed, but they seemed to show that Frank was the kind of person who really carried through what other people only talked about—and especially if he announced beforehand that he intended to do it.

It was a little dismaying, therefore, for his friend to reflect that upon the arrival of the famous letter from Lord Talgarth—Frank's father—six days previously, in which all the well-worn phrases occurred as to "darkening doors" and "roof" and "disgrace to the family," Frank had announced that he proposed to take his father at his word, sell up his property and set out like a prince in a fairy-tale to make his fortune.

Jack had argued till he was sick of it, and to no avail. Frank had a parry for every thrust. Why wouldn't he wait a bit until the governor had had time to cool down? Because the governor must learn, sooner or later, that words really meant something, and that he—Frank—was not going to stand it for one instant.

Why wouldn't he come and stay at Barham till further notice? They'd all be delighted to have him: It was only ten miles off Merefield, and perhaps—Because Frank was not going to sponge upon his friends. Neither was he going to skulk about near home. Well, if he was so damned obstinate, why didn't he go into the City—or even to the Bar? Because (1) he hadn't any money; and (2) he would infinitely sooner go on the tramp than sit on a stool. Well, why didn't he enlist, like a gentleman? Frank dared say he would some time, but he wanted to stand by himself a bit first and see the world.

"Let's see the letter again," said Jack at last. "Where is it?"

Frank reflected.

"I think it's in that tobacco-jar just behind your head," he said. "No, it isn't; it's in the pouch on the floor. I know I associated it somehow with smoking. And, by the way, give me a cigarette."

Jack tossed him his case, opened the pouch, took out the letter, and read it slowly through again.

"Merefield Court, "near Harrogate. "May 28th, Thursday.

"I am ashamed of you, sir. When you first told me of your intention, I warned you what would happen if you persisted, and I repeat it now. Since you have deliberately chosen, in spite of all that I have said, to go your own way, and to become a Papist, I will have no more to do with you. From this moment you cease to be my son. You shall not, while I live, darken my doors again, or sleep under my roof. I say nothing of what you have had from me in the past—your education and all the rest. And, since I do not wish to be unduly hard upon you, you can keep the remainder of your allowance up to July and the furniture of your rooms. But, after that, not one penny shall you have from me. You can go to your priests and get them to support you.

"I am only thankful that your poor mother has been spared this blow.

"T."

Jack made a small murmurous sound as he finished. Frank chuckled aloud.

"Pitches it in all right, doesn't he?" he observed dispassionately.

"If it had been my governor—" began Jack slowly.

"My dear man, it isn't your governor; it's mine. And I'm dashed if there's another man in the world who'd write such a letter as that nowadays. It's—it's too early-Victorian. They'd hardly stand it at the Adelphi! I could have put it so much better myself.... Poor old governor!"

"Have you answered it?"

"I ... I forget. I know I meant to.... No, I haven't. I remember now. And I shan't till I'm just off."

"Well, I shall," remarked Jack.

Frank turned a swift face upon him.

"If you do," he said, with sudden fierce gravity, "I'll never speak to you again. I mean it. It's my affair, and I shall run it my own way."

"But—"

"I mean it. Now! give me your word of honor—"

"I—"

"Your word of honor, this instant, or get out of my room!"

There was a pause. Then:

"All right," said Jack.

Then there fell a silence once more.

(II)

The news began to be rumored about, soon after the auction that Frank held of his effects a couple of days later. He carried out the scene admirably, entirely unassisted, even by Jack.

First, there appeared suddenly all over Cambridge, the evening before the sale, just as the crowds of undergraduates and female relations began to circulate about after tea and iced strawberries, a quantity of sandwich-men, bearing the following announcement, back and front:

TRINITY COLLEGE, CAMBRIDGE. The Hon. Frank Guiseley

has pleasure in announcing that on

June 7th (Saturday)

at half-past ten a.m. precisely

in Rooms 1, Letter J, Great Court, Trinity College,

he will positively offer for

SALE BY AUCTION

The household effects, furniture, books, etc., of the Hon. Frank Guiseley, including—

A piano by Broadwood (slightly out of tune); a magnificent suite of drawing-room furniture, upholstered in damask, the sofa only slightly stained with tea; one oak table and another; a bed; a chest of drawers (imitation walnut, and not a very good imitation); a mahogany glass-fronted bookcase, containing a set of suggestive-looking volumes bound in faint colors, with white labels; four oriental mats; a portrait of a gentleman (warranted a perfectly respectable ancestor); dining-room suite (odd chairs); numerous engravings of places of interest and noblemen's seats; a Silver Cigarette-box and fifteen Cigarettes in it (Melachrino and Mixed American); a cuckoo-clock (without cuckoo); five walking-sticks; numerous suits of clothes (one lot suitable for Charitable Purposes); some books—all very curious indeed—comprising the works of an Eminent Cambridge Professor, and other scholastic luminaries, as well as many other articles.

At Half-past Ten a.m. Precisely

All friends, and strangers, cordially invited.

No Reserve Price.

It served its purpose admirably, for by soon after ten o'clock quite a considerable crowd had begun to assemble; and it was only after a very serious conversation with the Dean that the sale was allowed to proceed. But it proceeded, with the distinct understanding that a college porter be present; that no riotous behavior should be allowed; that the sale was a genuine one, and that Mr. Guiseley would call upon the Dean with further explanations before leaving Cambridge.

The scene itself was most impressive.

Frank, in a structure resembling an auctioneer's box, erected on the hearth-rug, presided, with extraordinary gravity, hammer in hand, robed in a bachelor's gown and hood. Beneath him the room seethed with the company, male and female, all in an excellent humor, and quite tolerable prices were obtained. No public explanations were given of the need for the sale, and Jack, in the deepest dismay, looked in again that afternoon, about lunch-time, to find the room completely stripped, and Frank, very cheerful, still in his hood and gown, smoking a cigarette in the window-seat.

"Come in," he said. "And kindly ask me to lunch. The last porter's just gone."

Jack looked at him.

He seemed amazingly genial and natural, though just a little flushed, and such an air of drama as there was about him was obviously deliberate.

"Very well; come to lunch," said Jack. "Where are you going to dine and sleep?"

"I'm dining in hall, and I'm sleeping in a hammock. Go and look at my bedroom."

Jack went across the bare floor and looked in. A hammock was slung across from a couple of pegs, and there lay a small carpet-bag beneath it. A basin on an upturned box and a bath completed the furniture.

"You mad ass!" said Jack. "And is that all you have left?"

"Certainly. I'm going to leave the clothes I've got on to you, and you can fetch the hammock when I've gone."

"When do you start?"

"Mr. Guiseley will have his last interview and obtain his exeat from the Dean at half-past six this evening. He proposes to leave Cambridge in the early hours of to-morrow morning."

"You don't mean that!"

"Certainly I do."

"What are you going to wear?"

Frank extended two flanneled legs, ending in solid boots.

"These—a flannel shirt, no tie, a cap, a gray jacket."

Jack stood again in silence, looking at him.

"How much money did your sale make?"

"That's immaterial. Besides, I forget. The important fact is that when I've paid all my bills I shall have thirteen pounds eleven shillings and eightpence."

"What?"

"Thirteen pounds eleven shillings and eightpence."

Jack burst into a mirthless laugh.

"Well, come along to lunch," he said.

It seemed to Jack that he moved in a dreary kind of dream that afternoon as he went about with Frank from shop to shop, paying bills. Frank's trouser-pockets bulged and jingled a good deal as they started—he had drawn all his remaining money in gold from the bank—and they bulged and jingled considerably less as the two returned to tea in Jesus Lane. There, on the table, he spread out the coins. He had bought some tobacco, and two or three other things that afternoon, and the total amounted now but to twelve pounds nineteen shillings and fourpence.

"Call it thirteen pounds," said Frank. "There's many a poor man—"

"Don't be a damned fool!" said Jack.

"I'm being simply prudent," said Frank. "A contented heart—"

Jack thrust a cup of tea and the buttered buns before him.

These two were as nearly brothers as possible, in everything but blood. Their homes lay within ten miles of one another. They had gone to a private school together, to Eton, and to Trinity. They had ridden together in the holidays, shot, dawdled, bathed, skated, and all the rest. They were considerably more brothers to one another than were Frank and Archie, his actual elder brother, known to the world as Viscount Merefield. Jack did not particularly approve of Archie; he thought him a pompous ass, and occasionally said so.

For Frank he had quite an extraordinary affection, though he would not have expressed it so, to himself, for all the world, and a very real admiration of a quite indefinable kind. It was impossible to say why he admired him. Frank did nothing very well, but everything rather well; he played Rugby football just not well enough to represent his college; he had been in the Lower Boats at Eton, and the Lent Boat of his first year at Cambridge; then he had given up rowing and played lawn-tennis in the summer and fives in the Lent Term just well enough to make a brisk and interesting game. He was not at all learned; he had reached the First Hundred at Eton, and had read Law at Cambridge—that convenient branch of study which for the most part fills the vacuum for intelligent persons who have no particular bent and are heartily sick of classics; and he had taken a Third Class and his degree a day or two before. He was remarkably averaged, therefore; and yet, somehow or another, there was that in him which compelled Jack's admiration. I suppose it was that which is conveniently labeled "character." Certainly, nearly everybody who came into contact with him felt the same in some degree.

His becoming a Catholic had been an amazing shock to Jack, who had always supposed that Frank, like himself, took the ordinary sensible English view of religion. To be a professed unbeliever was bad form—it was like being a Little Englander or a Radical; to be pious was equally bad form—it resembled a violent devotion to the Union Jack. No; religion to Jack (and he had always hitherto supposed, to Frank) was a department of life in which one did not express any particular views: one did not say one's prayers; one attended chapel at the proper times; if one was musical, one occasionally went to King's on Sunday afternoon; in the country one went to church on Sunday morning as one went to the stables in the afternoon, and that was about all.

Frank had been, too, so extremely secretive about the whole thing. He had marched into Jack's rooms in Jesus Lane one morning nearly a fortnight ago.

"Come to mass at the Catholic Church," he said.

"Why, the—" began Jack.

"I've got to go. I'm a Catholic."

"What!"

"I became one last week."

Jack had stared at him, suddenly convinced that someone was mad. When he had verified that it was really a fact; that Frank had placed himself under instruction three months before, and had made his confession—(his confession!)—on Friday, and had been conditionally baptized; when he had certified himself of all these things, and had begun to find coherent language once more, he had demanded why Frank had done this.

"Because it's the true religion," said Frank. "Are you coming to mass or are you not?"

Jack had gone then, and had come away more bewildered than ever as to what it was all about.

He had attempted to make a few inquiries, but Frank had waved his hands at him, and repeated that obviously the Catholic religion was the true one, and that he couldn't be bothered. And now here they were at tea in Jesus Lane for the last time.

Of course, there was a little suppressed excitement about Frank. He drank three cups of tea and took the last (and the under) piece of buttered bun without apologies, and he talked a good deal, rather fast. It seemed that he had really no particular plans as to what he was going to do after he had walked out of Cambridge with his carpet-bag early next morning. He just meant, he said, to go along and see what happened. He had had a belt made, which pleased him exceedingly, into which his money could be put (it lay on the table between them during tea), and he proposed, naturally, to spend as little of that money as possible.... No; he would not take one penny piece from Jack; it would be simply scandalous if he—a public-school boy and an University man—couldn't keep body and soul together by his own labor. There would be hay-making presently, he supposed, and fruit-picking, and small jobs on farms. He would just go along and see what happened. Besides there were always casual wards, weren't there? if the worst came to the worst; and he'd meet other men, he supposed, who'd put him in the way of things. Oh! he'd get on all right.

Would he ever come to Barham? Well, if it came in the day's work he would. Yes: certainly he'd be most obliged if his letters might be sent there, and he could write for them when he wanted, or even call for them, if, as he said, it came in the day's work.

What was he going to do in the winter? He hadn't the slightest idea. He supposed, what other people did in the winter. Perhaps he'd have got a place by then—gamekeeper, perhaps—he'd like to be a gamekeeper.

At this Jack, mentally, threw up the sponge.

"You really mean to go on at this rotten idea of yours?"

Frank opened his eyes wide.

"Why, of course. Good Lord! did you think I was bluffing?"

"But ... but it's perfectly mad. Why on earth don't you get a proper situation somewhere—land-agent or something?"

"My dear man," said Frank, "if you will have it, it's because I want to do exactly what I'm going to do. No—I'm being perfectly serious. I've thought for ages that we're all wrong somehow. We're all so beastly artificial. I don't want to preach, but I want to test things for myself. My religion tells me—" He broke off. "No; this is fooling. I'm going to do it because I'm going to do it. And I'm really going to do it. I'm not going to be an amateur—like slumming. I'm going to find out things for myself."

"But on the roads—" expostulated Jack.

"Exactly. That's the very point. Back to the land."

Jack sat up.

"Good Lord!" he said. "Why, I never thought of it."

"What?"

"It's your old grandmother coming out."

Frank stared.

"Grandmother?"

"Yes—old Mrs. Kelly."

Frank laughed suddenly and loudly.

"By George!" he said, "I daresay it is. Old Grandmamma Kelly! She was a gipsy—so she was. I believe you've hit it, Jack. Let's see: she was my grandfather's second wife, wasn't she?"

Jack nodded.

"And he picked her up off the roads on his own estate. Wasn't she trespassing, or something?"

Jack nodded again.

"Yes," he said, "and he was a magistrate and ought to have committed her: And he married her instead. She was a girl, traveling with her parents."

Frank sat smiling genially.

"That's it," he said. "Then I'm bound to make a success of it."

And he took another cigarette.

Then one more thought came to Jack: he had determined already to make use of it if necessary, and somehow this seemed to be the moment.

"And Jenny Launton," he said "I suppose you've thought of her?"

A curious look came into Frank's eyes—a look of great gravity and tenderness—and the humor died out. He said nothing for an instant. Then he drew out of his breast-pocket a letter in an envelope, and tossed it gently over to Jack.

"I'm telling her in that," he said. "I'm going to post it to-night, after I've seen the Dean."

Jack glanced down at it.

"Miss Launton, "The Rectory, "Merefield, Yorks."

ran the inscription. He turned it over; it was fastened and sealed.

"I've told her we must wait a bit," said Frank, "and that I'll write again in a few weeks."

Jack was silent.

"And you think it's fair on her?" he asked deliberately.

Frank's face broke up into humor.

"That's for her to say," he observed. "And, to tell the truth, I'm not at all afraid."

"But a gamekeeper's wife! And you a Catholic!"

"Ah! you don't know Jenny," smiled Frank. "Jenny and I quite understand one another, thank you very much."

"But is it quite fair?"

"Good Lord!" shouted Frank, suddenly roused. "Fair! What the devil does it matter? Don't you know that all's fair—under certain circumstances? I do bar that rotten conventionalism. We're all rotten—rotten, I tell you; and I'm going to start fresh. So's Jenny. Kindly don't talk of what you don't understand."

He stood up, stretching. Then he threw the end of his cigarette away.

"I must go to the Dean," he said. "It's close on the half-hour."

(III)

The Reverend James Mackintosh was an excellent official of his college, and performed his duties with care and punctilium. He rose about half-past seven o'clock every morning, drank a cup of tea and went to chapel. After chapel he breakfasted, on Tuesdays and Thursdays with two undergraduates in their first year, selected in alphabetical order, seated at his table; on the other days of the week in solitude. At ten o'clock he lectured, usually on one of St. Paul's Epistles, on which subjects he possessed note-books filled with every conceivable piece of information that could be gathered together—grammatical, philological, topographical, industrial, social, biographical—with a few remarks on the fauna, flora, imports, characteristics and geological features of those countries to which those epistles were written, and in which they were composed. These notes, guaranteed to guide any student who really mastered them to success, and even distinction, in his examinations, were the result of a lifetime of loving labor, and some day, no doubt, will be issued in the neat blue covers of the "Cambridge Bible for Schools." From eleven to twelve he lectured on Church history of the first five centuries—after which period, it will be remembered by all historical students, Church history practically ceased. At one he lunched; from two to four he walked rapidly (sometimes again in company with a serious theological student), along the course known as the Grantchester Grind, or to Coton and back. At four he had tea; at five he settled down to administer discipline to the college, by summoning and remonstrating with such undergraduates as had failed to comply with the various regulations; at half-past seven he dined in hall—a meek figure, clean shaven and spectacled, seated between an infidel philosopher and a socialist: he drank a single glass of wine afterwards in the Combination Room, smoked one cigarette, and retired again to his rooms to write letters to parents (if necessary), and to run over his notes for next day.

And he did this, with the usual mild variations of a University life, every weekday, for two-thirds of the year. Of the other third, he spent part in Switzerland, dressed in a neat gray Norfolk suit with knickerbockers, and the rest with clerical friends of the scholastic type. It was a very solemn thought to him how great were his responsibilities, and what a privilege it was to live in the whirl and stir of one of the intellectual centers of England!

Frank Guiseley was to Mr. Mackintosh a very great puzzle. He had certainly been insubordinate in his first year (Mr. Mackintosh gravely suspected him of the Bread-and-Butter affair, which had so annoyed his colleague), but he certainly had been very steady and even deferential ever since. (He always took off his hat, for example, to Mr. Mackintosh, with great politeness.) Certainly he was not very regular at chapel, and he did not dine in hall nearly so often as Mr. Mackintosh would have wished (for was it not part of the University idea that men of all grades of society should meet as equals under the college roof?). But, then, he had never been summoned for any very grave or disgraceful breach of the rules, and was never insolent or offensive to any of the Fellows. Finally, he came of a very distinguished family; and Mr. Mackintosh had the keenest remembrance still of his own single interview, three years ago, with the Earl of Talgarth.

Mr. Mackintosh wondered, then, exactly what he would have to say to Mr. Guiseley, and what Mr. Guiseley would have to say to him. He thought, if the young man were really going down for good, as he had understood this morning, it was only his plain duty to say a few tactful words about responsibility and steadiness. That ridiculous auction would serve as his text.

Mr. Mackintosh paused an instant, as he always did, before saying "Come in!" to the knock on the door (I think he thought it helped to create a little impression of importance). Then he said it; and Frank walked in.

"Good evening, Mr. Guiseley.... Yes; please sit down. I understood from you this morning that you wished for your exeat."

"Please," said Frank.

"Just so," said Mr. Mackintosh, drawing the exeat book—resembling the butt of a check-book—towards him. "And you are going down to-morrow?"

"Yes," said Frank.

"Going home?" murmured the Dean, inscribing Frank's name in his neat little handwriting.

"No," said Frank.

"Not?... To London, perhaps?"

"Well, not exactly," said Frank; "at least, not just yet."

Mr. Mackintosh blotted the book carefully, and extracted the exeat. He pushed it gently towards Frank.

"About that auction!" he said, smiling indulgently; "I did want to have a word with you about that. It was very unusual; and I wondered.... But I am happy to think that there was no disturbance.... But can you tell me exactly why you chose that form of ... of ..."

"I wanted to make as much money as ever I could," said Frank.

"Indeed!... Yes.... And ... and you were successful?"

"I cleared all my debts, anyhow," said Frank serenely. "I thought that very important."

Mr. Mackintosh smiled again. Certainly this young man was very well behaved and deferential.

"Well, that's satisfactory. And you are going to read at the Bar now? If you will let me say so, Mr. Guiseley, even at this late hour, I must say that I think that a Third Class might have been bettered. But no doubt your tutor has said all that?"

"Yes, I think so."

"Well, then, a little more application and energy now may perhaps make up for lost time. I suppose you will go to the Temple in October?"

Frank looked at him pensively a moment.

"No, Mr. Mackintosh," he said suddenly; "I'm going on the roads. I mean it, quite seriously. My father's disowned me. I'm starting out to-morrow to make my own living."

There was dead silence for an instant. The Dean's face was stricken, as though by horror. Yet Frank saw he had not in the least taken it in.

"Yes; that's really so," he said. "Please don't argue with me about it. I'm perfectly determined."

"Your father ... Lord Talgarth ... the roads ... your own living ... the college authorities ...

responsibility!"

Words of this sort burst from Mr. Mackintosh's mouth.

"Yes ... it's because I've become a Catholic! I expect you've heard that, sir."

Mr. Mackintosh threw himself back (if so fierce a word may be used of so mild a manner)—threw himself back in his chair.

"Mr. Guiseley, kindly tell me all about it. I had not heard one word—not one word."

Frank made a great effort, and told the story, quite fairly and quite politely. He described his convictions as well as he could, the various steps he had taken, and the climax of the letter from his father. Then he braced himself, to hear what would be said; or, rather, he retired within himself, and, so to speak, shut the door and pulled down the blinds.

It was all said exactly as he knew it would be. Mr. Mackintosh touched upon a loving father's impatience, the son's youth and impetuosity, the shock to an ancient family, the responsibilities of membership in that family, the dangers of rash decisions, and, finally, the obvious errors of the Church of Rome. He began several sentences with the phrase: "No thinking man at the present day ..."

In fact, Mr. Mackintosh was, so soon as he had recovered from the first shock, extraordinarily sensible and reasonable. He said all the proper things, all the sensible and reasonable and common-sense things, and he said them, not offensively or contemptuously, but tactfully and persuasively. And he put into it the whole of his personality, such as it was. He even quoted St. Paul.

He perspired a little, gently, towards the end: so he took off his glasses and wiped them, looking, still with a smile, through kind, short-sighted eyes, at this young man who sat so still. For Frank was so quiet that the Dean thought him already half persuaded. Then once more he summed up, when his glasses were fixed again; he ran through his arguments lightly and efficiently, and ended by a quiet little assumption that Frank was going to be reasonable, to write to his father once more, and to wait at least a week. He even called him "my dear boy!"

"Thanks very much," said Frank.

"Then you'll think it over quietly, my dear boy. Come and talk to me again. I've given you your exeat, but you needn't use it. Come in to-morrow evening after hall."

Frank stood up.

"Thanks, very much, Mr. Mackintosh. I'll ... I'll certainly remember what you've said." He took up his exeat as if mechanically.

"Then you can leave that for the present," smiled the Dean, pointing at it. "I can write you another, you know."

Frank put it down quickly.

"Oh, certainly!" he said.

"Well, good-night, Mr. Guiseley.... I ... I can't tell you how glad I am that you confided in me. Young men are a little unwise and impetuous sometimes, you know. Good-night ... good-night. I shall expect you to-morrow."

When Frank reached the court below he stood waiting a moment. Then a large smile broke out on his face, and he hurried across to a passage opposite, found a friend's door open, and rushed in. The room was empty. He flew across to the window and crouched down, peeping over the sill at the opening on the other side of the court leading to Mr. Mackintosh's staircase.

He was rewarded almost instantly. Even as he settled himself on the window seat a black figure, with gown ballooning behind, hurried out and whisked through the archway leading towards the street. He gave him twenty seconds, and then ran out himself, and went in pursuit. Half-way up the lane he sighted him once more, and, following cautiously on tiptoe, with a handkerchief up to his face, was in time to behold Mr. Mackintosh disappear into the little telegraph office on the left of Trinity Street.

"That settles it, then," observed Frank, almost aloud. "Poor Jack—I'm afraid I shan't be able to breakfast with him after all!"

(IV)

It was a little after four o'clock on the following morning that a policeman, pacing with slow, flat feet along the little lane that leads from Trinity Hall to Trinity College, yawning as he went, and entirely unconscious of the divine morning air, bright as wine and clear as water, beheld a remarkable spectacle.

There first appeared, suddenly tossed on to the spikes that top the gate that guards the hostel, a species of pad that hung over on both sides of the formidable array of points. Upon this, more cautiously, was placed by invisible hands a very old saddle without any stirrups.

The policeman stepped back a little, and flattened himself—comparatively speaking—against the outer wall of the hostel itself. There followed a silence.

Suddenly, without any warning, a heavy body, discernible a moment later as a small carpet-bag, filled to bursting, fell abruptly on to the pavement; and, again, a moment later, two capable-looking hands made their appearance, grasping with extreme care the central rod on which the spikes were supposed to revolve, on either side of the saddle.

Still the policeman did not make any sign; he only sidled a step or two nearer and stood waiting.

When he looked up again, a young gentleman, in flannel trousers, gray jacket, boots, and an old deerstalker, was seated astride of the saddle, with his back to the observer. There was a pause while the rider looked to this side and that; and then, with a sudden movement, he had dropped clear of the wall, and come down on feet and hands to the pavement.

"Good morning, officer!" said the young gentleman, rising and dusting his hands, "it's all right. Like to see my exeat? Or perhaps half a crown—"

(V)

About six o'clock in the morning, Jack Kirkby awoke suddenly in his bedroom in Jesus Lane. This was very unusual, and he wondered what it was all about. He thought of Frank almost instantly, with a jerk, and after looking at his watch, very properly turned over and tried to go to sleep again. But the attempt was useless; there were far too many things to think about; and he framed so many speeches to be delivered with convincing force at breakfast to his misguided friend, that by seven o'clock he made up his mind that he would get up, go and take Frank to bathe, and have breakfast with him at half-past eight instead of nine. He would have longer time, too, for his speeches. He got out of bed and pulled up his blind, and the sight of the towers of Sidney Sussex College, gilded with sunshine, determined him finally.

When you go to bathe before breakfast at Cambridge you naturally put on as few clothes as possible and do not—even if you do so at other times—say your prayers. So Jack put on a sweater, trousers, socks, canvas shoes, and a blazer, and went immediately down the oilcloth-covered stairs. As he undid the door he noticed a white thing lying beneath it, and took it up. It was a note addressed to himself in Frank's handwriting; and there, standing on the steps, he read it through; and his heart turned suddenly sick.

There is all the difference in the world between knowing that a catastrophe is going to happen, and knowing that it has happened. Jack knew—at least, with all his reasonable part—that Frank was going to leave Cambridge in the preposterous manner described, after breakfast with himself; and it was partly because of this very knowledge that he had got up earlier in order to have an extra hour with Frank before the final severance came. Yet there was something in him—the same thing that had urged him to rehearse little speeches in bed just now—that told him that until it had actually happened, it had not happened, and, just conceivably, might not happen after all. And he had had no idea how strong this hopeful strain had been in him—nor, for that matter, how very deeply and almost romantically he was attached to Frank—until he felt his throat hammering and his head becoming stupid, as he read the terse little note in the fresh morning air of Jesus Lane.

It ran as follows:

"Dear Jack,

"It's no good, and I'm off early! That ass Mackintosh went and wired to my people directly I left him. I tracked him down. And there'll be the devil to pay unless I clear out. So I can't come to breakfast. Sorry.

"Yours, "F.G.

"P.S.—By the way, you might as well go round to the little man and try to keep him quiet. Tell him it'll make a scandal for Trinity College, Cambridge, if he makes a fuss. That'll stop him, perhaps. And you might try to rescue my saddle from the porter. He's probably got it by now."

Three minutes later a figure in a sweater, gray trousers, canvas shoes, Third Trinity blazer and no cap, stood, very inarticulate with breathlessness, at the door of the Senior Dean's rooms, demanding of a scandalized bed-maker to see the official in question.

"'E's in his barth, sir!" expostulated the old woman.

"Then he must come out of it!" panted Jack.

"—That is, if 'e's out o' bed."

"Then he can stop in it, if he isn't.... I tell you—"

Jack gave up arguing. He took the old lady firmly by the shoulders, and placed her in the doorway of the audience-room; then he was up the inner stairs in three strides, through the sitting-room, and was tapping at the door of the bedroom. A faint sound of splashing ceased.

"Who's there? Don't—"

"It's me, sir—Kirkby! I'm sorry to disturb you, but—"

"Don't come in!" cried an agitated voice, with a renewed sound of water, as if someone had hastily scrambled out of the bath.

Jack cautiously turned the handle and opened the door a crack. A cry of dismay answered his move, followed by a tremendous commotion and swishing of linen.

"I'm coming in, sir," said Jack, struggling between agitation and laughter. It was obvious from the sounds that the clergyman had got into bed again, wet, and as God made him. There was no answer, and Jack pushed the door wider and went in.

It was as he had thought. His unwilling host had climbed back into bed as hastily as possible, and the bed-clothes, wildly disordered, were gathered round his person. A face, with wet hair, looking very odd and childlike without his glasses, regarded him with the look of one who sees sacrilege done. A long flannel nightgown lay on the ground between the steaming bath and the bed, and a quantity of water lay about on the floor, in footprints and otherwise.

"May I ask what is the meaning of this disgraceful—"

"I'm sorry, sir," said Jack briefly, "but Frank Guiseley's bolted. I've just found this note." It did not occur to him, as he handed the note to a bare arm, coyly protruded from the tangled bed-clothes, that this very officer of the college was referred to in it as "that ass" and "the little man."

... All his attention, not occupied with Frank, was fixed on the surprising new discovery that deans had bodies and used real baths like other people. Somehow that had never occurred to him he had never imagined them except in smooth, black clothes and white linen. His discovery seemed to make Mr. Mackintosh more human, somehow.

The Dean read the note through as modestly as possible, holding it very close to his nose, as his glasses were unattainable, with an arm of which not more than the wrist appeared. He swallowed in his throat once or twice, and seemed to taste something with his lips, as his manner was.

"This is terrible!" said the Dean. "Had you any idea—"

"I knew he was going some time to-day," said Jack, "and understood that you knew too."

"But I had no idea—"

"You did telegraph, didn't you, sir?"

"I certainly telegraphed. Yes; to Lord Talgarth. It was my duty. But—"

"Well; he spotted it. That's all. And now he's gone. What's to be done?"

Mr. Mackintosh considered a moment or two. Jack made an impatient movement.

"I must telegraph again," said the Dean, with the air of one who has exhausted the resources of civilization.

"But, good Lord! sir—"

"Yes. I must telegraph again. As soon as I'm dressed. Or perhaps you would—"

"Office doesn't open till eight. That's no good. He'll be miles away by then."

"It's the only thing to be done," said the Dean with sudden energy. "I forbid you to take any other steps, Mr. Kirkby. I am responsible—"

"But—"

"We must not make a scandal.... What else did you propose?"

"Why—fifty things. Motor-cars; police—"

"Certainly not. We must make no scandal as he ... as he very properly says." (The Dean swallowed in his throat again. Jack thought afterwards that it must have been the memory of certain other phrases in the letter.) "So if you will be good enough to leave me instantly, Mr. Kirkby, I will finish my dressing and deal with the matter."

Jack wheeled and went out of the room.

It was a miserable breakfast to which he sat down half an hour later—still in flannels, and without his bath. Frank's place was laid, in accordance with the instructions he had given his landlady last night, and he had not the heart to push the things aside. There were soles for two, and four boiled eggs; there was coffee and marmalade and toast and rolls and fruit; and the comfortable appearance of the table simply mocked him.

He had had very confused ideas just now as to what was possible with regard to the pursuit of Frank; a general vision of twenty motor-cars, each with a keen-eyed chauffeur and an observant policeman, was all that had presented itself to his imagination; but he had begun to realize by now that you cannot, after all, abduct a young man who has committed no crime, and carry him back unwillingly, even to Cambridge! Neither the Dean of Trinity nor a father possesses quite unlimited power over the freedom of a pupil and a son. And, after all, Frank had only taken his father at his word!

These reflections, however, did not improve the situation. He felt quite certain, in theory, that something more could be done than feebly to send another telegram or two; the only difficulty was to identify that something. He had vague ideas, himself, of hiring a motor-car by the day, and proceeding to scour the country round Cambridge. But even this did not stand scrutiny. If he had failed to persuade Frank to remain in Cambridge, it was improbable that he could succeed in persuading him to return—even if he found him. About eight important roads run out of Cambridge, and he had not a glimmer of an idea as to which of these he had taken. It was possible, even, that he had not taken any of them, and was walking across country. That would be quite characteristic of Frank.

He finished breakfast dismally, and blew through an empty pipe, staring lackadaisically out of the window at the wall of Sidney Sussex for two or three minutes before lighting up. Cambridge seemed an extraordinary flat and stupid place now that Frank was no longer within it. Really there was nothing particular to do. It had become almost a regular engagement for him to step round to the Great Court about eleven, and see what was to be done. Sometimes Frank wanted lawn-tennis—sometimes a canoe on the Backs—at any rate, they would either lunch or dine together. And if they didn't—well, at any rate, Frank was there!

He tried to picture to himself what Frank was doing; he had visions of a sunlit road running across a fen, with a figure tramping up it; of a little wayside inn, and Frank drinking beer in the shade. But it seemed an amazing waste of company that the figure should always be alone. Why hadn't he proposed to go with him himself? He didn't know; except, that it certainly would not have been accepted. And yet they could have had quite a pleasant time for a couple of months; and, after a couple of months, surely Frank would have had enough of it!

But, again—would he?... Frank seemed really in earnest about making his living permanently; and when Frank said that he was going do a thing, he usually did it! And Jack Kirkby did not see himself leaving his own mother and sisters indefinitely until Frank had learned not to be a fool.

He lit his pipe at last; and then remembered the commission with regard to the saddle— whatever that might mean. He would stroll round presently and talk to the porter about it ... Yes, he would go at once; and he would just look in at Frank's rooms again. There was the hammock to fetch, too.

But it was a dreary little visit. He went round as he was, his hands deep in his pockets, trying to whistle between his teeth and smoke simultaneously; and he had to hold his pipe in his hand out of respect for rules, as he conversed with the stately Mr. Hoppett in Trinity gateway. Mr. Hoppett knew nothing about any saddle—at least, not for public communication—but his air of deep and diplomatic suspiciousness belied his words.

"It's all right," said Jack pleasantly, "I had nothing to do with the elopement. The Dean knows all about it."

"I know nothing about that, sir," said Mr. Hoppett judicially.

"Then you've not got the saddle?"

"I have not, sir."

Frank's outer door was open as Jack came to the familiar staircase, and his heart leaped in spite of himself, as he peered in and heard footsteps in the bedroom beyond. But it was the bed-maker with a mop, and a disapproving countenance, who looked out presently.

"He's gone, Mrs. Jillings," said Jack.

Mrs. Jillings sniffed. She had heard tales of the auction and thought it a very improper thing for so pleasant a young gentleman to do.

"Yes, sir."

"There isn't a saddle here, is there?"

"Saddle, sir? No, sir. What should there be a saddle here for?"

"Oh, well," said Jack vaguely. "I've come to fetch away the hammock, anyhow."

Certainly the rooms looked desolate. Even the carpets were gone, and the unstained boards in the middle seemed suggestive of peculiar dreariness. It was really very difficult to believe that these were the rooms where he and Frank had had such pleasant times—little friendly bridge-parties, and dinners, and absurd theatricals, in which Frank had sustained, with extreme rapidity, with the aid of hardly any properties except a rouge-pot, a burnt cork and three or four wisps of hair of various shades, the part of almost any eminent authority in the University of Cambridge that you cared to name. There were long histories, invented by Frank himself, of the darker sides of the lives of the more respectable members of the Senate—histories that grew, like legends, term by term—in which the most desperate deeds were done. The Master of Trinity, for example, in these Sagas, would pass through extraordinary love adventures, or discover the North Pole, or give a lecture, with practical examples, of the art of flying; the Provost of King's would conspire with the President of Queen's College, to murder the Vice-Chancellor and usurp his dignities. And these histories would be enacted with astonishing realism, chiefly by Frank himself, with the help of a zealous friend or two who were content to obey.

And these were all over now; and that was the very door through which the Vice-Chancellor was accustomed to escape from his assassins!

Jack sighed again; passed through, picked up the parcel of clothes that lay in the window-seat, unhitched the hammock in which Frank had slept last night (he noticed the ends of three cigarettes placed on the cover of a convenient biscuit-tin), and went off resembling a retiarius. Mrs. Jillings sniffed again as she looked after him up the court. She didn't understand those young gentlemen at all; and frequently said so.

(VI)

At half-past six o'clock that morning—about the time that Jack awoke in Cambridge—John Harris, laborer, emerged, very sleepy and frowsy—for he had sat up late last night at the "Spotted Dog"—from the door of a small cottage on the Ely road, in the middle of Grunty Fen. He looked this way and that, wondering whether it were as late as his kitchen-clock informed him, and observing the sun, that hung now lamentably high up in that enormous dome of summer sky that sat on the fenland like a dish-cover on a dish. And as he turned southwards he became aware of a young gentleman carrying a carpet-bag in one hand, and a gray jacket over his other arm, coming up to him, not twenty yards away. As he came nearer, Mr. Harris noticed that his face was badly bruised as by a blow.

"Good morning," said the young gentleman. "Hot work."

John Harris made some observation.

"I want some work to do," said the young gentleman, disregarding the observation. "I'm willing and capable. Do you know of any? I mean, work that I shall be paid for. Or perhaps some breakfast would do as a beginning."

John Harris regarded the young gentleman in silence.

CHAPTER II: (I)

Merefield Court, as every tourist knows may be viewed from ten to five on Tuesdays and Thursdays, when the family are not in residence, and on Tuesdays only, from two to four, when they are. It is unnecessary, therefore, to describe it very closely.

It stands very nearly on the top of a hill, protected by woods from the north winds of Yorkshire; and its towers and pinnacles can be seen from ten miles away down the valley. It is built, architecturally considered, in the form of an irregular triangular court—quite unique—with the old barbican at the lower end; the chapel wing directly opposite; the ruins of the old castle on the left, keep and all, and the new house that is actually lived in on the right. It is of every conceivable date (the housekeeper will supply details) from the British mound on which the keep stands, to the Georgian smoking-room built by the grandfather of the present earl; but the main body of the house, with which we are principally concerned—the long gray pile facing south down to the lake, and northwards into the court—is Jacobean down to the smallest detail, and extremely good at that. It was on the end of this that the thirteenth earl the fifteenth baron and the fourteenth viscount (one man, not three) thought it proper to build on a Palladian kind of smoking-room of red sandstone, brought at enormous cost from half across England. Fortunately, however, ivy has since covered the greater part of its exterior.

It was in this room—also used as a billiard-room—that Archie Guiseley (Viscount Merefield), and Dick Guiseley, his first cousin, first heard the news of Frank's intentions.

They were both dressed for dinner, and were knocking the balls about for ten minutes, waiting for the gong, and they were talking in that incoherent way characteristic of billiard-players.

"The governor's not very well again," observed Archie, "and the doctor won't let him go up to town. That's why we're here."

Dick missed a difficult cannon (he had only arrived from town himself by the 6.17), and began to chalk his cue very carefully.

"There's nothing whatever to do," continued Archie, "so I warn you."

Dick opened his mouth to speak and closed it again, pursing it up precisely as once more he addressed himself to the balls, and this time brought off a really brilliant stroke.

"And he's in a terrible way about Frank," continued the other. "You've heard all about that?" Dick nodded.

"And he swears he won't have him home again, and that he can go to the devil."

Dick arched his eyebrows interrogatively.

"Of course, he doesn't mean it.... But the gout, you know, and all that.... I think Frank had better keep out of the way, though, for a bit. Oh! by the way, the Rector and Jenny are coming to dinner."

"What does Jenny say to it all?" asked Dick gently.

"Oh! Jenny laughs."

These two young men—for Archie was only twenty-five, and Dick a year or two older—were quite remarkably like one another in manner and general bearing. Each, though their faces were entirely different, wore that same particular form of mask that is fashionable just now. Each had a look in his eyes as if the blinds were down—rather insolent and yet rather pleasant. Each moved in the same kind of way, slow and deliberate; each spoke quietly on rather a low note, and used as few words as possible. Each, just now, wore a short braided dinner-jacket of precisely the same cut.

For the rest, they were quite unlike. Archie was clean-shaven, of a medium sort of complexion, with a big chin and rather loosely built; Dick wore a small, pointed brown beard, and was neat and alert. Neither of them did anything particular in the world. Archie was more or less tied to his father, except in the autumn—for Archie drew the line at Homburg, and went about for short visits, returning continually to look after the estate; Dick lived in a flat in town on six hundred a year, allowed him by his mother, and was supposed to be a sort of solicitor. They saw a good deal of one another, off and on, and got on together rather better than most brothers; certainly better than did Archie and Frank. It was thought a pity by a good many people that they were only cousins.

Then, as they gossiped gently, the door suddenly opened and a girl came in.

She was a very striking girl indeed, and her beauty was increased just now by obvious excitement held well in check. She was tall and very fair, and carried herself superbly, looking taller than she really was. Her eyes, particularly bright just now, were of a vivid blue, wide-open and well set in her face; her mouth was strong and sensible; and there was a glorious air of breeziness and health about her altogether. She was in evening dress, and wore a light cloak over her white shoulders.

"I'm sorry to interrupt," she said—"Oh! good evening, Mr. Dick!—but there's something wrong. Clarkson ran out to tell us that Lord Talgarth—it's a telegram or something. Father sent me to tell you."

Archie looked at her a second; then he was gone, swiftly, but not hurriedly. The girl turned to Dick.

"I'm afraid it's something about Frank," she said. "I heard Clarkson mention his name to father. Is there any more news?"

Dick laid down his cue across the table.

"I only came an hour ago," he said. "Archie was telling me just now."

Jenny went across to the deep chair on the hearth, threw off her cloak and sat down.

"Lord Talgarth's—well—if he was my father I should say he was in a passion. I heard his voice." She smiled a little.

Dick leaned against the table, looking at her.

"Poor Frank!" he said.

She smiled again, more freely.

"Yes ... poor, dear Frank! He's always in hot water, isn't he?"

"I'm afraid it's serious this time," observed Dick. "What did he want to become a Catholic for?"

"Oh, Frank's always unexpected!"

"Yes, I know; but this happens to be just the one very thing—"

She looked at him humorously.

"Do you know, I'd no notion that Lord Talgarth was so deeply religious until Frank became a Catholic."

"Yes, I know," said Dick. "But it is just his one obsession. Frank must have known that."

"And I've not the slightest doubt," said Jenny, "that that was an additional reason for his doing it."

"Well, what'll happen?"

She jerked her head a little.

"Oh! it'll pass off. You'll see. Frank'll find out, and then we shall all be happy ever afterwards."

"But meantime?"

"Oh! Frank'll go and stay with friends a month or two. I daresay he'll come to the Kirkbys', and I can go and see him."

"Suppose he does something violent? He's quite capable of it."

"Oh! I shall talk to him. It'll be all right. I'm very sensible indeed, you know. All my friends tell me that."

Dick was silent.

"Don't you think so?"

"Think what?"

"That I'm very sensible."

Dick made a little movement with his head.

"Oh! I suppose so. Yes, I daresay.... And suppose my uncle cuts him off with a shilling? He's quite capable of it. He's a very heavy father, you know."

"He won't. I shall talk to him too."

"Yes; but suppose he does?"

She threw him a swift glance.

"Frank'll put the shilling on his watch-chain, after it's been shown with all the other wedding-presents. What are you going to give me, Mr. Dick?"

"I shall design a piece of emblematic jewelry," said Dick very gravely. "When's the wedding to be?"

"Well, we hadn't settled. Lord Talgarth wouldn't make up his mind. I suppose next summer some time."

"Miss Jenny—"

"Yes?"

"Tell me—quite seriously—what you'd do if there was a real row—a permanent one, I mean—between Frank and my uncle?"

"Dear Mr. Dick—don't talk so absurdly. I tell you there's not going to be a row. I'm going to see to that myself."

"But suppose there was?"

Jenny stood up abruptly.

"I tell you I'm a very sensible person, and I'm not going to imagine absurdities. What do you want me to say? Do you want me to strike an attitude and talk about love in a cottage?"

"Well, that would be one answer."

"Very well, then. That'll do, won't it? You can take it as said.... I'm going to see what's happening."

But as she went to the door there came footsteps and voices outside; and the next moment the door opened suddenly, and Lord Talgarth, followed by his son and the Rector, burst into the room.

I am very sorry to have to say it, but the thirteenth Earl of Talgarth was exactly like a man in a book—and not a very good book. His character was, so to speak, cut out of cardboard—stiff cardboard, and highly colored, with gilt edges showing here and there. He also, as has been said, resembled a nobleman on the stage of the Adelphi. He had a handsome inflamed face, with an aquiline nose and white eyebrows that moved up and down, and all the other things; he was stout and tall, suffered from the gout, and carried with him in the house a black stick with an india-rubber pad on the end. There were no shades about him at all. Construct a conventionally theatrical heavy father, of noble family, and you have Lord Talgarth to the life. There really are people like this in the world—of whom, too, one can prophesy, with tolerable certainty, how they will behave in any given situation.

Certainly, Lord Talgarth was behaving in character now. He had received meek Mr. Mackintosh's deferential telegram, occupying several sheets, informing him that his son had held an auction of all his belongings, and had proposed to take to the roads; asking, also, for instructions as to how to deal with him. And the hint of defiant obstinacy on the part of Frank— the fact, indeed, that he had taken his father at his word—had thrown that father into a yet more violent fit of passion. Jenny had heard him spluttering and exclamatory with anger as she came into the hall (the telegram had but that instant been put into his hands), and even now the footmen, still a little pale, were exchanging winks in the hall outside; while Clarkson, his valet, and the butler stood in high and subdued conference a little way off.

What Lord Talgarth would really have wished was that Frank should have written to him a submissive—even though a disobedient—letter, telling him that he could not forego his convictions, and preparing to assume the rôle of a Christian martyr. For he could have sneered at this, and after suitable discipline forgiven its writer more or less. Of course, he had never intended for one instant that his threats should really be carried out; but the situation—to one of Lord Talgarth's temperament—demanded that the threats should be made, and that Frank should pretend to be crushed by them. That the boy should have behaved like this brought a reality of passion into the affair—disconcerting and infuriating—as if an actor should find his enemy on the stage was armed with a real sword. There was but one possibility left—which Lord Talgarth instinctively rather than consciously grasped at—namely, that an increased fury on his part should once more bring realities back again to a melodramatic level, and leave himself, as father, master both of the situation and of his most disconcerting son. Frank had behaved like this in minor matters once or twice before, and Lord Talgarth had always come off victor. After all, he commanded all the accessories.

When the speeches had been made—Frank cut off with a shilling, driven to the Colonies, brought back again, and finally starved to death at his father's gates—Lord Talgarth found himself in a chair, with Jenny seated opposite, and the rest of the company gone to dinner. He did not quite realize how it had all been brought about, nor by whose arrangement it was that a plate of soup and some fish were to come presently, and Jenny and he to dine together.

He pulled himself together a little, however, and began to use phrases again about his "graceless son," and "the young villain," and "not a penny of his." (He was, of course, genuinely angry; that must be understood.)

Then Jenny began to talk.

"I think, you know," she said quietly, "that you aren't going the right way to work. (It's very impertinent of me, isn't it?—but you did say just now you wanted to hear what I thought.)"

"Of course I do; of course I do. You're a sensible girl, my dear. I've always said that. But as for this young—"

"Well, let me say what I think. (Yes, put the soup down here, will you. Is that right, Lord Talgarth?)." She waited till the man was gone again and the old man had taken up his spoon. Then she took up her own. "Well, I think what you've done is exactly the thing to make Frank more obstinate than ever. You see, I know him very well. Now, if you'd only laughed at him and patted his head, so to speak, from the beginning, and told him you thought it an excellent thing for a boy of his character, who wants looking after—"

Lord Talgarth glared at her. He was still breathing rather heavily, and was making something of a noise over his soup.

"But how can I say that, when I think—"

"Oh! you can't say it now, of course; it's too late. No; that would never do. You must keep it up—only you mustn't be really angry. Why not try a little cold severity?"

She looked so charming and humorous that the old man began to melt a little. He glanced up at her once or twice under his heavy eyebrows.

"I wonder what you'll do," he said with a kind of gruffness, "when you find you've got to marry a pauper?"

"I shan't have to marry a pauper," said Jenny. "That wouldn't do either."

"Oh! you're counting on that eight hundred a year still, are you?"

Jenny allowed a little coldness to appear on her face. Rude banter was all very well, but it mustn't go too far. (Secretly she allowed to herself sometimes that this old man had elements of the cad in his character.)

"That's entirely my own affair," she said, "and Frank's."

Lord Talgarth blazed up a little.

"And the eight hundred a year is mine," he said.

Jenny laid down her spoon as the servant reappeared with the fish and the menu-card. He came very opportunely. And while her host was considering what he would eat next, she was pondering her next move.

Jenny, as has been said, was an exceedingly sensible girl. She had grown up in the Rectory, down at the park gates; and since her mother's death, three years previously, had managed her father's house, including her father, with great success. She had begun to extend her influence, for the last year or two, even over the formidable lord of the manor himself, and, as has been seen, was engaged to his son. Her judgment was usually very sound and very sane, and the two men, with the Rector, had been perfectly right just now in leaving the old man to her care for an hour or so. If anything could quiet him it would be this girl. She was quite fearless, quite dignified, and quite able to hold her own. And her father perceived that she rather enjoyed it.

When the man had gone out again, she resumed:

"Well, let's leave it," she said, "for a day or two. There's no hurry, and—"

"But I must answer this—this telegram," he growled. "What am I to say to the feller?"

"Tell him to follow his discretion, and that you have complete confidence—"

"But—"

"Yes; I know you haven't, really. But it'll do no harm, and it'll make him feel important."

"And what if the boy does take to the roads?"

"Let him," said Jenny coolly. "It won't kill him."

He looked up at her again in silence.

Jenny herself was very far from comfortable, though she was conscious of real pleasure, too, in the situation. She had seen this old man in a passion pretty often, but she had never seen him in a passion with any real excuse. No one ever thwarted him. He even decided where his doctor should send him for his cure, and in what month, and for how long. And she was not, therefore, quite certain what would happen, for she knew Frank well enough to be quite sure that he meant what he said. However, she reflected, the main thing at present was to smooth things down all round as far as possible. Then she could judge.

"Can't make out why you ever consented to marry such a chap at all!" he growled presently.

"Oh, well—" said Jenny.

(III)

It was a delicious evening, and the three men, after dinner, strolled out on to the broad terrace that ran, looking over the lake, straight up and down the long side of the house. They had not had the advantage, since the servants were in the room, of talking over the situation as they wished, and there was no knowing when Lord Talgarth and Jenny might emerge. So they sat down at a little stone table at the end furthest from the smoking-room, and Archie and Dick lit their cigarettes.

There is not a great deal to say about the Rector. The most effective fact about him was that he was the father of Jenny. It was a case, here, of "Averill following Averill": his father and grandfather, both second sons, as was the Rector himself, had held the living before him, and had performed the duties of it in the traditional and perfectly respectable way. This one was a quiet middle-aged man, clean-shaven except for two small whiskers. He wore a white tie, and a small gold stud was visible in the long slit of his white shirt-front. He was on very easy terms in this house, in an unintimate manner, and dined here once a fortnight or so, without saying or hearing anything of particular interest. He had been secretly delighted at his daughter's engagement, and had given his consent with gentle and reserved cordiality. He was a Tory, not exactly by choice, but simply—for the same reason as he was Church of England—because he was unable, in the fiber of him, to imagine anything else. Of course, Lord Talgarth was the principal personage in his world, simply because he was Lord Talgarth and owned practically the whole parish and two-thirds of the next. He regarded his daughter with the greatest respect, and left in her hands everything that he decently could. And, to do her justice, Jenny was a very benevolent, as well as capable, despot. In short, the Rector plays no great part in this drama beyond that of a discreet, and mostly silent, Greek chorus of unimpeachable character. He disapproved deeply, of course, of Frank's change of religion—but he disapproved with that same part of him that appreciated Lord Talgarth. It seemed to him that Catholicism, in his daughter's future husband, was a defect of the same kind as would be a wooden leg or an unpleasant habit of sniffing—a drawback, yet not insuperable. He would be considerably relieved if it could be cured.

The three men sat there for some while without interruption from the smoking-room, while the evening breeze died, the rosy sky paled, and the stars came out one by one, like diamonds in the clear blue. They said, of course, all the proper things, and Dick heard a little more than he had previously known.

Dick was always conscious of a faint, almost impersonal, resentment against destiny when he stayed at Merefield. It was obvious to him that the position of heir there was one which would exactly have suited his tastes and temperament. He was extremely pleased to belong to the family—and it was, indeed, a very exceptional family as regards history: it had been represented in nearly every catastrophe since the Norman Conquest, and always on the winning side, except once—but it was difficult to enjoy the distinction as it deserved, living, as he did, in a flat in London all by himself. When his name was mentioned to a well-informed stranger, it was always greeted by the question as to whether he was one of the Guiseleys of Merefield, and it seemed to him singularly annoying that he could only answer "First cousin." Archie, of course, was a satisfactory heir; there was no question of that—he was completely of Dick's own school of manner—but it seemed a kind of outrage that Frank, with his violent convictions and his escapades, should be Archie's only brother. There was little of that repose about him that a Guiseley needed.

It would be about half-past nine that the sound of an opening door, and voices, from the further end of the terrace, told them that the smoking-room conference was over, and they stood up as Jenny, very upright and pale in the twilight, with her host at her side, came up towards them. Dick noticed that the cigar his uncle carried was smoked down almost to the butt, and augured well from that detail. The old man's arm was in the girl's, and he supported himself on the other side, limping a little, on his black stick.

He sat down with a grunt and laid his stick across the table.

"Well, boys, we've settled it," he said. "Jenny's to write the telegram."

"No one need be anxious any more," announced Jenny imperturbably. "Lord Talgarth's extremely angry still, as he has every right to be, and Frank's going to be allowed to go on the tramp if he wants to."

The Rector waited, in deferential silence, for corroboration.

"Jenny's a very sensible girl," observed Lord Talgarth. "And what she says is quite right."

"Do you mean to say—" began Archie.

The old man frowned round at him.

"All that I've said holds good," he said.

"Frank's made his bed and he must lie on it. I warned him. And Jenny sees that, too."

Archie glanced at the girl, and Dick looked hard at her, straight into her face. But there was absolutely no sign there of any perturbation. Certainly she looked white in the falling dusk, but her eyes were merry and steadfast, and her voice perfectly natural.

"That's how we've settled it," she said. "And if I'm satisfied, I imagine everyone else ought to be. And I'm going to write Frank a good long letter all by myself. Come along, father, we must be going. Lord Talgarth isn't well, and we mustn't keep him up."

(IV)

When the last game of billiards had been played, and whisky had been drunk, and Archie had taken up his candle, Dick stood still, with his own in his hand.

"Aren't you coming?" said Archie.

Dick paused.

"I think I'll smoke one more cigarette on the terrace," he said. "It's a heavenly night, and I want to get the taste of the train out of my mouth."

"All right, then. Lock up, will you, when you come in? I'm off."

It was, indeed, a heavenly night. Behind him as he sat at the table where they had had coffee the great house shimmered pale in the summer twilight, broken here by a line or two of yellow light behind shuttered windows, here with the big oriel window of the hall, blazing with coats, fully illuminated. (He must remember, he thought, to put out the lights there as he went to bed.)

And about him was the great soft, sweet-smelling darkness, roofed in by the far-off sky alight with stars; and beneath him in the valley he could catch the glimmer of the big lake and the blotted masses of pine and cypress black against it.

It was here, then, under these circumstances, that Dick confessed to himself, frankly and openly for the first time, that he was in love with Jenny Launton.

He had known her for years, off and on, and had thought of her as a pretty girl and a pleasant companion. He had skated with her, ridden with her, danced with her, and had only understood, with a sense of mild shock, at the time of her engagement to Frank six months before, that she was of an age to become a wife to someone.

That had been the beginning of a process which culminated to-night, as he now understood perfectly. Its next step had been a vague wonder why Archie hadn't fallen in love with her himself; and he had explained it by saying that Archie had too great a sense of his own importance to permit himself to marry a rector's daughter with only a couple of hundred a year of her own. (And in this explanation I think he was quite correct.) Then he had begun to think of her himself a good deal—dramatically, rather than realistically—wondering what it would feel like to be engaged to her. If a younger son could marry her, surely a first cousin could—even of the Guiseleys. So it had gone on, little by little. He had danced with her here at Christmas—just after the engagement—and had stayed on a week longer than he had intended. He had come up again at Easter, and again at Whitsuntide, though he always protested to his friends that there was nothing to do at Merefield in the summer. And now here he was again, and the thing had happened.

At first, as he sat here, he tried to analyze his attitude to Frank.

He had never approved of Frank altogether; he didn't quite like the queer kinds of things that Frank did; for Frank's reputation at Merefield was very much what it was at Cambridge. He did ridiculous and undignified things. As a small boy, he had fought at least three pitched battles in the village, and that was not a proper thing for a Guiseley to do. He liked to go out with the keepers after poachers, and Dick, very properly, asked himself what keepers were for except to do that kind of thing for you? There had been a bad row here, too, scarcely eighteen months ago; it had been something to do with a horse that was ill-treated, and Frank had cut a very absurd and ridiculous figure, getting hot and angry, and finally thrashing a groom, or somebody, with his own hands, and there had been uncomfortable talk about police-courts and actions for assault. Finally, he had fallen in love with, proposed to, and become engaged to, Jenny Launton. That was an improper thing for a younger son to do, anyhow, at his age, and Dick now perceived that the fact that Jenny was Jenny aggravated the offense a hundredfold. And, last of all, he had become a Catholic—an act of enthusiasm which seemed to Dick really vulgar.

Altogether, then, Frank was not a satisfactory person, and it would do him no harm to have a little real discipline at last....

It was the striking of midnight from the stable clock that woke Dick up from his deep reverie, and was the occasion of his perceiving that he had come to no conclusion about anything, except that Frank was an ass, that Jenny was—well—Jenny, and that he, Dick, was an ill-used person.

I do not like to set down here, even if I could, all the considerations that had passed through Dick's mind since a quarter-past eleven, simply because the very statement of them would give a false impression. Dick was not a knave, and he did not deceive himself about himself more than most of us do. Yet he had considered a number of points that, strictly speaking, he ought not to have considered. He had wondered whether Frank would die; he had wondered whether, if he did not, Lord Talgarth would really be as good as his word; and, if so, what effect that would have on Jenny. Finally, he had wondered, with a good deal of intellectual application, what exactly Jenny had meant when she had announced all that about the telegram she was going to send in Lord Talgarth's name, and the letter she was going to send in her own. (He had asked Archie just now in the smoking-room, and he, too, had confessed himself beaten. Only, he had been quite sure that jenny would get her way and obtain Frank's forgiveness.)

Also, in the course of his three-quarters of an hour he had considered, for perhaps the hundredth time since he had come to the age of discretion, what exactly three lives between a man and a title stood for. Lord Talgarth was old and gouty; Archie was not married, and showed no signs of it; and Frank—well, Frank was always adventurous and always in trouble.

Well, I have set down the points, after all. But it must not be thought that the gentleman with the pointed brown beard and thoughtful eyes, who at five minutes past twelve went up the two steps into the smoking-room, locked the doors, as he had been directed, took up his candle and went to bed, went with an uneasy conscience, or, in fact, was a villain in any way whatever.

CHAPTER III: (I)

The first spot in Frank's pilgrimage which I have been able to visit and identify in such a way that I am able to form to myself a picture of his adventure more or less complete in all its parts, lies about ten miles north-west of Doncaster, in a little valley, where curiously enough another pilgrim named Richard lived for a little while nearly six hundred years ago.

Up to the time of Frank's coming there, in the season of hay-making, numberless little incidents of his experience stand out, vivid, indeed, but fragmentary, yet they do not form to my mind a coherent whole. I think I understand to some extent the process by which he became accustomed to ordinary physical hard living, into which the initiation began with his series of almost wholly sleepless nights and heavy sleep-burdened days. Night was too strange—in barns, beneath hay-ricks, in little oppressive rooms, in stable-lofts—for him to sleep easily at first; and between his tramps, or in the dinner-hour, when he managed to get work, he would drop off in the hot sunshine down into depths of that kind of rest that is like the sea itself—glimmering gulfs, lit by glimpses of consciousness of the grass beneath his cheek, the bubble of bird-song in the copses, stretching down into profound and utter darkness.

Of how the little happenings of every day wore themselves into a coherent whole, and modified, not indeed himself, but his manner of life and his experience and knowledge, I can make no real picture at all. The first of these took place within ten miles of Cambridge on his first morning, and resulted in the bruised face which Mr. Harris noticed; it concerned a piece of brutality to a dog in which Frank interfered.... (He was extraordinarily tender to animals.) Then there was the learning as to how work was obtained, and, even more considerable, the doing of the work. The amateur, as Frank pointed out later, began too vigorously and became exhausted; the professional set out with the same deliberation with which he ended. One must not run at one's spade, or hoe, or whatever it was; one must exercise a wearisome self-control ... survey the work to be done, turn slowly, spit on one's hands, and after a pause begin, remembering that the same activity must show itself, if the work was to be renewed next day, up to the moment of leaving off.

Then there was the need of becoming accustomed to an entirely different kind of food, eaten in an entirely different way, and under entirely different circumstances. There was experience to be gained as to washing clothes—I can almost see Frank now by a certain kind of stream, stripped to the waist, waiting while his shirt dried, smoking an ill-rolled cigarette, yet alert for the gamekeeper. Above all, there was an immense volume of learning—or, rather, a training of instinct—to be gained respecting human nature: a knowledge of the kind of man who would give work, the kind of man who meant what he said, and the kind of man who did not; the kind of woman who would threaten the police if milk or bread were asked for—Frank learned to beg very quickly—the kind of woman who would add twopence and tell him to be off, and the kind of woman who, after a pause and a slow scrutiny, would deliberately refuse to supply a glass of water. Then there was the atmosphere of the little towns to be learned—the intolerable weariness of pavements, and the patient persistence of policemen who would not allow you to sit down. He discovered, also, during his wanderings, the universal fact that policemen are usually good-hearted, but with absolutely no sense of humor whatever; he learned this through various attempts to feign that the policeman was in fancy-dress costume and had no real authority. He learned, too, that all crimes pale before "resisting the police in the execution of their duty"; then, he had to learn, to, the way in which other tramps must be approached—the silences necessary, the sort of questions which were useless, the jokes that must be laughed at and the jokes that must be resented.

All this is beyond me altogether; it was beyond even Frank's own powers of description. A boy, coming home for the holidays for the first time, cannot make clear to his mother, or even to himself, what it is that has so utterly changed his point of view, and his relations towards familiar things.

So with Frank.

He could draw countless little vignettes of his experiences and emotions—the particular sensation elicited, for example, by seeing through iron gates happy people on a lawn at tea—the white china, the silver, the dresses, the flannels, the lawn-tennis net—as he went past, with string tied below his knees to keep off the drag of the trousers, and a sore heel; the emotion of being passed by a boy and a girl on horseback; the flood of indescribable associations roused by walking for half a day past the split-oak paling of a great park, with lodge-gates here and there, the cooing of wood-pigeons, and the big house, among its lawns and cedars and geranium-beds, seen now and then, far off in the midst. But what he could not describe, or understand, was the inner alchemy by which this new relation to things modified his own soul, and gave him a point of view utterly new and bewildering. Curiously enough, however (as it seems to me), he never seriously considered the possibility of abandoning this way of life, and capitulating to his father. A number of things, I suppose—inconceivable to myself—contributed to his purpose; his gipsy blood, his extraordinary passion for romance, the attraction of a thing simply because it was daring and unusual, and finally, a very exceptionally strong will that, for myself, I should call obstinacy.

The silence—as regards his old world—was absolute and unbroken. He knew perfectly well that by now letters and telegrams must be waiting for him at Jack's home, including at least one from Jenny, and probably a dozen; but as to Jenny, he knew she would understand, and as to the rest, he honestly did not care at all. He sent her a picture postcard once or twice—from Ely, Peterborough, Sleaford and Newark—towns where he stayed for a Sunday (I have seen in Sleaford the little room where he treated himself to a bed for two nights)—and was content. He made no particular plans for the future; he supposed something would turn up; and he settled with himself, by the help of that same will which I have mentioned before, that he would precipitate no conclusions till he reached Barham later on in the early autumn.

His faith and morals during these weeks are a little difficult to describe. As regards his morals, at least in one particular point, he had formulated the doctrine that, when he was very hungry, game might not be touched, but that rabbits and birds were permissible if they could be snared in the hedges of the high-road. He became an expert at this kind of thing, and Jack has described to me, as taught by Frank, a few devices of which I was entirely ignorant. Frank tramped for a couple of days with a gamekeeper out of work, and learned these things from him, as well as one or two simple methods of out-of-door cookery. As regards his religion, I think I had better not say much just now; very curious influences were at work upon him: I can only say that Frank himself has described more than once, when he could be induced to talk, the extraordinary, and indeed indescribable, thrill with which he saw, now and again, in town or country, a priest in his vestments go to the altar—for he heard mass when he could....

So much, then, is all that I can say of the small, detached experiences that he passed through, up to the point when he came out one evening at sunset from one of the fields of Hampole where he had made hay all day, when his job was finished, and where he met, for the first time, the Major and Gertie Trustcott.

(II)

They were standing with the sunset light behind them, as a glory—two disreputable figures, such as one sees in countless thousands along all the high-roads of England in the summer. The Major himself was a lean man, with a red mustache turning gray, deep-set, narrow, blood-shot eyes, a chin and very square jaw shaved about two days previously. He had an old cricketing cap on his head, trousers tied up with string, like Frank's, and one of those long, square-tailed, yellowish coats with broad side-pockets such as a gamekeeper might have worn twenty years ago. One of his boots was badly burst, and he, seemed to rest his weight by preference on the other foot. He was not prepossessing; but Frank saw, with his newly-gained experience, that he was different from other tramps. He glanced at the girl and saw that she too was not quite of the regular type, though less peculiar than her companion; and he noticed with an odd touch at his heart that she had certain characteristics in common with Jenny. She was not so tall, but she had the same colored hair under a filthy white sun-bonnet and the same kind of blue eyes: but her oval face again was weak and rather miserable. They were both deeply sunburned.

Frank had learned the discretion of the roads by now, and did no more than jerk his head almost imperceptibly as he went past. (He proposed to go back to the farm to get his dwindled belongings, as the job was over, and to move on a few miles northward before sleeping.)

As he went, however, he knew that the man had turned and was looking after him: but he made no sign. He had no particular desire for company. He also knew by instinct, practically for certain, that these two were neither husband and wife, nor father and daughter. The type was obvious.

"I say, sir!"

Frank turned as bucolically as he could.

"I say, sir—can you direct this lady and myself to a lodging?"

Frank had tried to cultivate a low and characterless kind of voice, as of a servant or a groom out of work. He knew he could never learn the proper accent.

"Depends on what kind of lodging you want, sir."

"What'd suit you 'ud suit us," said the Major genially, dropping the "sir."

"I'm going further, sir," said Frank. "I've done my job here."

The Major turned to the girl, and Frank caught the words, "What d'you say, Gertie?" There was a murmur of talk; and then the man turned to him again:

"If you've no objection, sir, we'll come with you. My good lady here is good for a mile or two more, she says, and we'd like some company."

Frank hesitated. He did not in the least wish for company himself. He glanced at the girl again.

"Very good, sir," he said. "Then if you'll wait here I'll be back in five minutes—I've got to get my belongings."

He nodded to the low farm buildings in the valley just below the village.

"We will await you here, sir," said the Major magnificently, stroking his mustache.

As Frank came back up the little hill a few minutes later, he had made up his mind as to what to say and do. It was his first experience of a gentleman-tramp, and it was obvious that under the circumstances he could not pretend to be anything else himself. But he was perfectly determined not to tell his name. None of his belongings had anything more than his initials upon them, and he decided to use the name he had already given more than once. Probably they would not go far together; but it was worth while to be on the safe side.

He came straight up to the two as they sat side by side with their feet in the ditch.

"I'm ready, sir," he said. "Yes; you've spotted me all right."

"University man and public school boy," said the Major without moving.

"Eton and Cambridge," said Frank.

The Major sprang up.

"Harrow and the Army," he said. "Shake hands."

This was done.

"Name?" said the Major.

Frank grinned.

"I haven't my card with me," he said. "But Frank Gregory will do."

"I understand," said the Major. "And 'The Major' will do for me. It has the advantage of being true. And this lady?—well, we'll call her my wife."

Frank bowed. He felt he was acting in some ridiculous dream; but his sense of humor saved him. The girl gave a little awkward bow in response, and dropped her eyes. Certainly she was very like Jenny, and very unlike.

"And a name?" asked Frank. "We may as well have one in case of difficulties."

The Major considered.

"What do you say to Trustcott?" he asked. "Will that do?"

"Perfectly," said Frank. "Major and Mrs. Trustcott.... Well, shall we be going?"

Frank had no particular views as to lodgings, or even to roads, so long as the direction was more or less northward. He was aiming, generally speaking, at Selby and York; and it seemed that this would suit the Major as well as anything else. There is, I believe, some kind of routine amongst the roadsters; and about that time of the year most of them are as far afield as at any time from their winter quarters. The Major and Mrs. Trustcott, he soon learned, were Southerners; but they would not turn homewards for another three months yet, at least. For himself, he had no ideas beyond a general intention to reach Barham some time in the autumn, before Jack went back to Cambridge for his fourth year.

"The country is not prepossessing about here," observed the Major presently; "Hampole is an exception."

Frank glanced back at the valley they were leaving. It had, indeed, an extraordinarily retired and rural air; it was a fertile little tract of ground, very limited and circumscribed, and the rail that ran through it was the only sign of the century. But the bright air was a little dimmed with smoke; and already from the point they had reached tall chimneys began to prick against the horizon.

"You have been here before?" he said.

"Why, yes; and about this time last year, wasn't it, Gertie? I understand a hermit lived here once."

"A hermit might almost live here to-day," said Frank.

"You are right, sir," said the Major.

Frank began to wonder, as he walked, as to why this man was on the roads. Curiously enough, he believed his statement that he had been in the army. The air of him seemed the right thing. A militia captain would have swaggered more; a complete impostor would have given more details. Frank began to fish for information.

"You have been long on the roads?" he said.

The Major did not appear to hear him.

"You have been long on the roads?" persisted Frank.

The other glanced at him furtively and rather insolently. "The younger man first, please."

Frank smiled.

"Oh, certainly!" he said. "Well, I have left Cambridge at the end of June only."

"Ah! Anything disgraceful?"

"You won't believe me, I suppose, if I say 'No'?"

"Oh! I daresay I shall."

"Well, then, 'No.'"

"Then may I ask—?"

"Oh, yes! I was kicked out by my father—I needn't go into details. I sold up my things and came out. That's all!"

"And you mean to stick to it?"

"Certainly—at least for a year or two."

"That's all right. Well, then—Major—what did we say? Trustcott? Ah, yes, Trustcott. Well, then, I think we might add 'Eleventh Hussars'; that's near enough. The final catastrophe was, I think, cards. Not that I cheated, you understand. I will allow no man to say that of me. But that was what was said. A gentleman of spirit, you understand, could not remain in a regiment when such things could be said. Then we tumbled downhill; and I've been at this for four years. And, you know, sir, it might be worse!"

Frank nodded.

Naturally he did not believe as necessarily true this terse little story, and he was absolutely certain that if cards were mixed up in it at all, obviously the Major had cheated. So he just took the story and put it away, so to speak. It was to form, he perceived, the understanding on which they consorted together. Then he began to wonder about the girl. The Major soon supplied a further form.

"And Mrs. Trustcott, here? Well, she joined me, let us say, rather more than eighteen months ago. We had been acquainted before that, however. That was when I was consenting to serve as groom to some—er—some Jewish bounder in town. Mrs. Trustcott's parents live in town."

The girl, who had been trudging patiently a foot or two behind them, just glanced up at Frank and down again. He wondered exactly what her own attitude was to all this. But she made no comment.

"And now we know one another," finished the Major in a tone of genial finality. "So where are you taking us—er—Mr. Gregory?"

(III)

They were fortunate that night.

The part of Yorkshire where they were traveling consists chiefly of an innumerable quantity of little cottages, gathered for the most part round collieries. One has the impression—at any rate, from a motor—that there is nothing but villages. But that is not a fact. There are stretches of road, quite solitary at certain hours; and in one of these they noticed presently a little house, not twenty yards from the road, once obviously forming part of a row of colliers' cottages, of which the rest were demolished.

It was not far off from ruin itself, and was very plainly uninhabited. Across the front door were nailed deal props, originally, perhaps, for the purpose of keeping it barred, and useful for holding it in its place. The Major and Gertie kept watch on the road while Frank pushed open the crazy little gate and went round to the back. A minute later he called to them softly.

He had wrenched open the back door, and within in the darkness they could make out a little kitchen, stripped of everything—table, furniture, and even the range itself. The Major kicked something presently in the gloom, swore softly, and announced he had found a kettle. They decided that all this would do very well.

Tramps do not demand very much, and these were completely contented when they had made a small fire, damped down with a turf to prevent it smoking, had boiled a little water, stewed some tea, and eaten what they had. Even this was not luxurious. The Major produced the heel of a cheese and two crushed-looking bananas, and Frank a half-eaten tin of sardines and a small, stale loaf. The Major announced presently that he would make a savory; and, indeed, with cheese melted on to the bread, and sardines on the top, he did very well. Gertie moved silently about; and Frank, in the intervals of rather abrupt conversation with the Major, found his eyes following her as she spread out their small possessions, vanished up the stairs and reappeared. Certainly she was very like Jenny, even in odd little details—the line of her eyebrows, the angle of her chin and so forth—perhaps more in these details than in anything else. He began to wonder a little about her—to imagine her past, to forecast her future. It seemed all rather sordid. She disappeared finally without a word: he heard her steps overhead, and then silence.

Then he had to attend to the Major a little more.

"It was easy enough to tell you," said that gentleman.

"How?"

"Oh, well, if nothing else, your clothes."

"Aren't they shabby enough?"

The Major eyed him with half-closed lids, by the light of the single candle-end, stuck in its own wax on the mantelshelf.

"They're shabby enough, but they're the wrong sort. There's the cut, first—though that doesn't settle it. But these are gray flannel trousers, for one thing, and then the coat's not stout enough."

"They might have been given me," said Frank, smiling.

"They fit you too well for that."

"I'll change them when I get a chance," observed Frank.

"It would be as well," assented the Major.

Somehow or another the sense of sordidness, which presently began to affect Frank so profoundly, descended on him for the first time that night. He had managed, by his very solitariness hitherto, to escape it so far. It had been possible to keep up a kind of pose so far; to imagine the adventure in the light of a very much prolonged and very realistic picnic. But with this other man the thing became impossible. It was tolerable to wash one's own socks; it was not so tolerable to see another man's socks hung up on the peeling mantelpiece a foot away from his own head, and to see two dirty ankles, not his own, emerging from crazy boots.

The Major, too, presently, when he grew a trifle maudlin over his own sorrows, began to call him "Frankie," and "my boy," and somehow it mattered, from a man with the Major's obvious record. Frank pulled himself up only just in time to prevent a retort when it first happened, but it was not the slightest use to be resentful. The thing had to be borne. And it became easier when it occurred to him to regard the Major as a study; it was even interesting to hear him give himself away, yet all with a pompous appearance of self-respect, and to recount his first meeting with Gertie, now asleep upstairs.

The man was, in fact, exactly what Frank, in his prosperous days, would have labeled "Bounder." He had a number of meaningless little mannerisms—a way of passing his hand over his mustache, a trick of bringing a look of veiled insolence into his eyes; there were subjects he could not keep away from—among them Harrow School, the Universities (which he called 'Varsity), the regiment he had belonged to, and a certain type of adventure connected with women and champagne. And underneath the whole crust of what the Major took to be breeding, there was a piteous revelation of a feeble, vindictive, and rather nasty character. It became more and more evident that the cheating incident—or, rather, the accusation, as he persisted in calling it—was merely the last straw in his fall, and that the whole thing had been the result of a crumbly unprincipled kind of will underneath, rather than of any particular strain of vice. He appeared, even now, to think that his traveling about with a woman who was not his wife was a sort of remnant of fallen splendor—as a man might keep a couple of silver spoons out of the ruin of his house.

"I recommend you to pick up with one," remarked the Major. "There are plenty to be had, if you go about it the right way."

"Thanks," said Frank, "but it's not my line."

(IV)

The morning, too, was a little trying.

Frank had passed a tolerable night. The Major had retired upstairs about ten o'clock, taking his socks with him, presumably to sleep in them, and Frank had heard him creaking about upstairs for a minute or two; there had followed two clumps as the boots were thrown off; a board suddenly spoke loudly; there was a little talking—obviously the Major had awakened Gertie in order to make a remark or two—and then silence.

Frank had not slept for half an hour; he was thinking, with some depression, of the dreary affair into which he had been initiated, of the Major, and of Gertie, for whom he was beginning to be sorry. He did not suppose that the man actually bullied her; probably he had done this sufficiently for the present—she was certainly very quiet and subdued—or perhaps she really admired him, and thought it rather magnificent to travel about with an ex-officer. Anyhow, it was rather deplorable....

When he awoke next morning, the depression was on him still; and it was not lifted by the apparition of Gertie on which he opened his eyes from his corner, in an amazingly dirty petticoat, bare-armed, with her hair in a thick untidy pig-tail, trying to blow the fire into warmth again.

Frank jumped up—he was in his trousers and shirt.

"Let me do that," he said.

"I'll do it," said Gertie passionlessly.

The Major came down ten minutes later, considerably the worse for his night's rest. Yesterday he had had a day's beard on him; to-day he had two, and there was a silvery sort of growth in the stubble that made it look wet. His eyes, too, were red and sunken, and he began almost instantly to talk about a drink. Frank stood it for a few minutes, then he understood and capitulated.

"I'll stand you one," he said, "if you'll get me two packets of Cinderellas."

"What's the good of that?" said the Major. "Pubs aren't open yet. It's only just gone five."

"You'll have to wait, then," said Frank shortly.

Presently the Major did begin to bully Gertie. He asked her what the devil was the good of her if she couldn't make a fire burn better than that. He elbowed her out of the way and set to work at it himself. She said nothing at all. Yet there was not the faintest use in Frank's interfering, and, indeed, there was nothing to interfere in.

Food, too, this morning, seemed disgusting; and again Frank learned the difference between a kind of game played by oneself and a reality in which two others joined. There had been something almost pleasing about unrolling the food wrapped up at supper on the previous night, and eating it, with or without cooking, all alone; but there was something astonishingly unpleasant in observing sardines that were now common property lying in greasy newspaper, a lump of bread from which their hands tore pieces, and a tin bowl of warmish cocoa from which all must drink. This last detail was a contribution on the part of Major and Mrs. Trustcott, and it would have been ungracious to refuse. The Major, too, was sullen and resentful this morning, and growled at Gertie more than once.

Even the weather seemed unpropitious as they set out together again soon after six. Rain had fallen in the night, yet not all the rain that there was overhead. There were still clouds hanging, mixed with the smoke from the chimneys; the hedges seemed dulled and black in spite of their green; the cinder path they walked on was depressing, the rain-fed road even more so. They passed a dozen men on their way to the pits, who made remarks on the three, and retaliation was out of the question.

It was very disconcerting to Frank to find the difference that his new circumstances made; and yet he did not seriously consider changing them. It seemed to him, somehow or other, in that strange fashion in which such feelings come, that the whole matter was pre-arranged, and that the company in which he found himself was as inevitably his—at least for the present—as the family to a child born into it. And there was, of course, too, a certain element of relief in feeling himself no longer completely alone; and there was also, as Frank said later, a curious sense of attraction towards, and pity for, Gertie that held him there.

At the first public-house that was open the Major stopped.

"I'll get your Cinderellas now, if you like," he said.

This had not been Frank's idea, but he hardly hesitated.

"All right," he said. "Here's fourpence."

The Major vanished through the swing-doors as a miner came out, and a gush of sweet and sickly scent—beer, spirits, tobacco—poured upon the fresh air. And there was a vision of a sawdusted floor and spittoons within.

Frank looked at Gertie, who had stopped like a patient donkey, and, like a prudent one, had let her bundle instantly down beside the Major's.

"Like one, too?" he said.

She shook her head.

"Not for me." ... And no more.

In a couple of minutes the Major was out again.

"Only had one packet left," he said, and with an air of extreme punctiliousness and magnanimity replaced one penny in Frank's hand. He had the air of one who is insistent on the little honesties of life. There was also a faintly spirituous atmosphere about him, and his eyes looked a little less sunken.

Then he handed over the cigarettes.

"Shouldn't mind one myself," he said genially.

Frank gave him one before lighting his own.

"You're a good sort," said the Major, "and I wish I could give you one of my old cigars I used to give my friends."

"Ah! well, when your ship comes home," observed Frank, throwing away his match.

The Major nodded his head as with an air of fallen grandeur.

"Well," he said, "vorwärts. That means 'forward,' my dear," he explained to Gertie.

Gertie said nothing. They took up their bundles and went on.

(V)

It was not till a week later that Gertie did that which was to effect so much in Frank—she confided in him.

The week had consisted of the kind of thing that might be expected—small negligible adventures; work now and then—the Major and Frank working side by side—a digging job on one day, the carrying of rather dingy smoke-stained hay on another, the scraping of garden-paths that ran round the small pink house of a retired tradesman, who observed them magnificently though a plate-glass window all the while, with a cigar in his teeth, and ultimately gave them ninepence between them. They slept here and there—once, on a rainy night, in real lodgings, once below a haystack. Frank said hardly a word to Gertie, and did little more than listen to the Major, who was already beginning to repeat himself; but he was aware that the girl was watching him.

The crisis came about under circumstances that might be expected—on a rather sentimental kind of Sunday evening, in a village whose name I forget (perhaps it was Escrick) between Selby and York. Frank had made a small excursion by himself in the morning and had managed to hear mass; they had dined well off cold bacon and beans, and had walked on in the afternoon some miles further; and they came to the village a little after six o'clock. The Major had a blister, which he had exhibited at least four times to the company, and had refused to go further; and as they came to the outskirts of the village, volunteered to go and look for shelter, if the two would wait for him at a stile that led across fields to the old church.

The scene was rather like the setting of the last act in a melodrama of a theater on the Surrey side of the Thames—the act in which the injured heroine, with her child, sinks down fainting as the folk are going to church in the old village on a June evening among the trees—leading up to moonlight effects and reunion. There was no organ to play "off," but the bells were an excellent substitute, and it was these that presently melted the heart of Gertie.

When the Major had disappeared, limping, the two climbed over the stile and sat down with their bundles under the hedge, but they presently found that they had chosen something of a thoroughfare. Voices came along presently, grew louder, and stopped as the speakers climbed the stile. The first pair was of a boy and girl, who instantly clasped again mutual waists, and went off up the path across the field to the churchyard without noticing the two tramps; their heads were very near together.

Then other couples came along, old and young, and twice a trio—one, two young men in black, who skirmished on either side of a very sedate girl in white; one, two girls who shoved one another, and giggled, walking in step three yards behind another young man with his hat on one side, who gloried in being talked at and pretended to be rapt in abstraction. Then some children came; then a family—papa walking severely apart in a silk hat, and mamma, stout and scarlet-faced, in the midst of the throng. Finally there came along a very old Darby and Joan, who with many Yorkshire ejaculations helped one another over the stile, and moved on with bent heads, scolding one another affectionately. It was as this last couple reached the spot where the path ran into the corn that the peal of four bells broke out, and Gertie broke down.

Frank had not been noticing her particularly. He was gloomy himself; the novelty of the whole affair had gone; the Major was becoming intolerable, and Frank's religion was beginning to ebb from his emotions. Mass this morning had not been a success from an emotional point of view; he had had an uncomfortable seat on a pitch-pine bench in a tin church with an American organ; the very young priest had been tiresome and antipathetic.... Frank had done his best, but he was tired and bored; the little church had been very hot, and it was no longer any fun to be stared at superciliously by a stout tradesman as he came out into the hot sunshine afterwards.

Just now he had been watching the figures make their appearance from the stile, re-form groups and dwindle slowly down to the corn, and their heads and shoulders bob along above it— all with a kind of resentment. These people had found their life; he was still looking for his. He was watching, too, the strangely unreal appearance of the sunlit fields, the long shadows, the golden smoky light, and the church tower, set among cypresses half a mile away—yet without any conscious sentiment. He had not said a word to Gertie, nor she to him, and he was totally taken by surprise when, after the first soft crash of bells for evening service, she had suddenly thrown herself round face forward among the grasses and burst out sobbing.

"My dear girl!" said Frank, "whatever's the matter?" Then he stopped.

Fortunately, the procession of worshipers had run dry, and the two were quite alone. He sat upright, utterly ignorant of what to say. He thought perhaps she was in pain ... should he run for the Major or a doctor?... Then, as after a minute or two of violent sobbing she began a few incoherent words, he understood.

"Oh! I'm a wicked girl ... a wicked girl ... it's all so beautiful ... the church bells ... my mother!"

He understood, then, what had precipitated this crisis and broken down the girl's reserve. It was, in fact, exactly that same appeal which holds a gallery breathless and tearful in the last act of a Surrey-side melodrama—the combination of Sunday quiet, a sunset, church bells, associations and human relationships; and Gertie's little suburban soul responded to it as a bell to a bell-rope. It was this kind of thing that stood to her for holiness and peace and purity, and it had gone clean through her heart. And he understood, too, that it was his presence that had allowed her to break down. The Major's atmosphere had held her taut so far. Frank was conscious of a lump in his own throat as he stared out, helpless, first at the peaceful Sunday fields and then down at the shaking shoulders and the slender, ill-clad, writhed form of Gertie.... He did not know what to do ... he hoped the Major would not be back just yet. Then he understood he must say something.

"Don't cry," he said. "The Major—"

She sat up on the instant in sudden consternation, her pretty, weak, sunburned face disfigured with tears, but braced for the moment by fear.

"No, no," said Frank; "he isn't coming yet; but—"

Then she was down again, moaning and talking. "Oh!... Oh!... I'm a wicked girl.... My mother!... and I never thought I should come to this!"

"Well, why don't you chuck it?" said Frank practically.

"I can't!... I can't! I ... I love him!"

That had not occurred to this young man as a conceivable possibility, and he sat silenced. The church-bells pealed on; the sun sank a little lower; Gertie sobbed more and more gently; and Frank's mind worked like a mill, revolving developments. Finally, she grew quiet, lay still, and, as the bells gave place to one of their number, sat up. She dabbed at her eyes with a handful of wet grass, passed her sleeve across them once or twice, and began to talk.

"I ... I'm very silly, Frankie," she said, "but I can't help it. I'm better now. Don't tell George."

"Of course I shan't!" said Frank indignantly.

"You're a gentleman too," said Gertie. (Frank winced a little, interiorly, at the "too.") "I can see that you're polite to a lady. And I don't know however I came to tell you. But there it is, and no harm's done."

"Why don't you leave him?" said Frank courageously. A little wave of feeling went over her face.

"He's a gentleman," she said.... "No, I can't leave him. But it does come over you sometimes; doesn't it?" (Her face wavered again.) "It was them bells, and the people and all."

"Where's your home?"

She jerked her head in a vague direction.

"Down Londonwards," she said. "But that's all done with. I've made my bed, and—"

"Tell me plainly: does he bully you?"

"Not to say bully," she said. "He struck me once, but never again."

"Tell me if he does it again."

A small, sly, admirative look came into her eyes. "We'll see," she said.

Frank was conscious of a considerable sense of disappointment. The thing had been almost touching just now, as the reserve first broke up, but it was a very poor little soul, it seemed to him, that had at last made its appearance. (He did not yet see that that made it all the more touching.) He did not quite see what to do next. He was Christian enough to resent the whole affair; but he was aristocratic enough in his fastidiousness to think at this moment that perhaps it did not matter much for people of this sort. Perhaps it was the highest ideal that persons resembling the Major and Gertie could conceive. But her next remark helped to break up his complacency.

"You're a Catholic," she said. "People say that you Catholics don't mind this kind of thing—me and the Major, I mean."

There was a dreadful sort of sly suggestiveness about this remark that stung him. He exploded: and his wounded pride gave him bitterness.

"My good girl," he said, "Catholics simply loathe it. And even, personally, I think it's beastly."

"Well—I ..."

"I think it's beastly," said Frank didactically. "A good girl like you, well-brought-up, good parents, nice home, religious—instead of which "—he ended in a burst of ironical reminiscence—"you go traveling about with a—" he checked himself—"a man who isn't your husband. Why don't you marry him?"

"I can't!" wailed Gertie, suddenly stricken again with remorse; "his wife's alive."

Frank jumped. Somehow that had never occurred to him. And yet how amazingly characteristic of the Major!

"Well—leave him, then!"

"I can't!" cried poor Gertie. "I can't!... I can't!"

CHAPTER IV: (I)

Frank awoke with a start and opened his eyes.

But it was still dark and he could see nothing. So he turned over on the other side and tried to go to sleep.

The three of them had come to this little town last night after two or three days' regular employment; they had sufficient money between them; they had found a quite tolerable lodging; they had their programme, such as it was, for the next day or so; and—by the standard to which he had learned to adjust himself—there was no sort of palpable cause for the horror that presently fell on him. I can only conjecture that the origin lay within, not without, his personality.

The trouble began with the consciousness that on the one side he was really tired, and on the other that he could not sleep and, to clinch it, the knowledge that a twenty-mile walk lay before him. He began to tell himself that sleep was merely a question of will—of will deliberately relaxing attention. He rearranged his position a little; shifted his feet, fitted himself a little more closely into the outlines of the bed, thrust one hand under the pillow and bade himself let go.

Then the procession of thoughts began as orderly as if by signal.

He found himself presently, after enumerating all the minor physical points of discomfort—the soreness of his feet, the knobbiness of the bed, the stuffiness of the room in which the three were sleeping, the sound of the Major's slow snoring—beginning to consider the wisdom of the whole affair. This was a point that he had not consciously yet considered, from the day on which he had left Cambridge. The impetus of his first impulse and the extreme strength of his purpose had, up to the present—helped along by novelty—kept him going. Of course, the moment had to come sooner or later; but it seems a little hard that he was obliged to face it in that peculiarly dreary clarity of mind that falls upon the sleepless an hour or two before the dawn.

For, as he looked at it all now, he saw it as an outsider would see it, no longer from the point of view of his own personality. He perceived a young man, of excellent abilities and prospects, sacrificing these things for an idea that fell to pieces the instant it was touched. He touched it now with a critical finger, and it did so fall to pieces; there was, obviously, nothing in it at all. It was an impulse of silly pride, of obstinacy, of the sort of romance that effects nothing. There was Merefield waiting for him—for he knew perfectly well that terms could be arranged; there was all that leisureliness and comfort and distinction in which he had been brought up and which he knew well how to use; there was Jenny; there was his dog, his horse ... there was, in fact, everything for which Merefield stood. He saw it all now, visualized and clear in the dark; and he had exchanged all this—well—for this room, and the Major's company, and back-breaking toil.... And for no reason.

So he regarded all this for a good long while; with his eyes closed, with the darkness round him, with every detail visible and insistent, seen as in the cold light of morning before colors reassert themselves and reconcile all into a reasonable whole....

"... I must really go to sleep!" said Frank to himself, and screwed up his eyes tight.

There came, of course, a reaction presently, and he turned to his religion. He groped for his rosary under his pillow, placed before him (according to the instructions given in the little books) the "Mystery of the Annunciation to Mary," and began the "Our Father." ... Half-way through it he began all over again to think about Cambridge, and Merefield and Jack Kirkby, and the auction in his own rooms, and his last dinner-party and the design on the menu-cards, and what a fool he was; and when he became conscious of the rosary again he found that he held in his fingers the last bead but three in the fifth decade. He had repeated four and a half decades without even the faintest semblance of attention. He finished them hopelessly, and then savagely thrust the string of beads under his pillow again; turned over once more, rearranged his feet, wished the Major would learn how to sleep like a gentleman; and began to think about his religion in itself.

After all, he began to say to himself, what proof was there—real scientific proof—that the thing was true at all? Certainly there was a great deal of it that was, very convincing—there was the curious ring of assertion and confidence in it, there was its whole character, composed (like personality) of countless touches too small to be definable; there was the definite evidence adduced from history and philosophy and all the rest. But underneath all that—was there, after all, any human evidence in the world sufficient to establish the astounding dogmas that lay at the root? Was it conceivable that any such evidence could be forthcoming?

He proceeded to consider the series of ancient dilemmas which, I suppose, have presented themselves at some time or another to every reasonable being—Free-will and Predestination; Love and Pain; Foreknowledge and Sin; and their companions. And it appeared to him, in this cold, emotionless mood, when the personality shivers, naked, in the presence of monstrous and unsympathetic forces, that his own religion, as much as every other, was entirely powerless before them.

He advanced yet further: he began to reflect upon the innumerable little concrete devotions that he had recently learned—the repetition of certain words, the performance of certain actions—the rosary for instance; and he began to ask himself how it was credible that they could possibly make any difference to eternal issues.

These things had not yet surrounded themselves with the atmosphere of experience and association, and they had lost the romance of novelty; they lay before him detached, so to say, and unconvincing.

I do not mean to say that during this hour he consciously disbelieved; he honestly attempted to answer these questions; he threw himself back upon authority and attempted to reassure himself by reflecting that human brains a great deal more acute than his own found in the dilemmas no final obstacles to faith; he placed himself under the shelter of the Church and tried to say blindly that he believed what she believed. But, in a sense, he was powerless: the blade of his adversary was quicker than his own; his will was very nearly dormant; his heart was entirely lethargic, and his intellect was clear up to a certain point and extraordinarily swift....

Half an hour later he was in a pitiable state; and had begun even to question Jenny's loyalty. He had turned to the thought of her as a last resort for soothing and reassurance, and now, in the chilly dawn, even she seemed unsubstantial.

He began by remembering that Jenny would not live for ever; in fact, she might die at any moment; or he might; and he ended by wondering, firstly, whether human love was worth anything at all, and, secondly, whether he possessed Jenny's. He understood now, with absolute certitude, that there was nothing in him whatever which could possibly be loved by anyone; the whole thing had been a mistake, not so much on his part as on Jenny's. She had thought him to be something he was not. She was probably regretting already the engagement; she would certainly not fulfill it. And could she possibly care for anyone who had been such an indescribable fool as to give up Merefield, and his prospects and his past and his abilities, and set out on this absurd and childish adventure? So once more he came round in a circle and his misery was complete.

He sat up in bed with a sudden movement as the train of thought clicked back into its own beginning, clasped his hands round his knees and stared round the room.

The window showed a faint oblong of gray now, beyond where the Major breathed, and certain objects were dingily and coldly visible. He perceived the broken-backed chair on which his clothes were heaped—with the exception of his flannel shirt, which he still wore; he caught a glimmer of white where Gertie's blouse hung up for an airing.

He half expected that things would appear more hopeful if he sat up in bed. Yet they did not. The sight of the room, such as it was, brought the concrete and material even more forcibly upon him—the gross things that are called Facts. And it seemed to him that there were no facts beyond them. These were the bones of the Universe—a stuffy bedroom, a rasping flannel suit, a cold dawn, a snoring in the gloom, and three bodies, heavy with weariness.... There once had been other facts: Merefield and Cambridge and Eton had once existed; Jenny had once been a living person who loved him; once there had been a thing called Religion. But they existed no longer. He had touched reality at last.

Frank drew a long, dismal sigh; he lay down; he knew the worst now; and in five minutes he was asleep.

Of course, the thing wore away by midday, and matters had readjusted themselves. But the effect remained as a kind of bruise below the surface. He was conscious that it had once been possible for him to doubt the value of everything; he was aware that there was a certain mood in which nothing seemed worth while.

It was practically his first experience of the kind, and he did not understand it. But it did its work; and I date from that day a certain increased sort of obstinacy that showed itself even more plainly in his character. One thing or the other must be the effect of such a mood in which—even though only for an hour or two—all things other than physical take on themselves an appearance of illusiveness: either the standard is lowered and these things are treated as slightly doubtful; or the will sets its teeth and determines to live by them, whether they are doubtful or not. And the latter I take to be the most utter form of faith.

About midday the twine round Frank's bundle broke abruptly, and every several article fell on to the road. He repressed a violent feeling of irritation, and turned round to pick them up. The Major and Gertie instinctively made for a gate in the hedge, rested down their bundles and leaned against it.

Frank gathered the articles—a shirt, a pair of softer shoes, a razor and brush, a tin of potted meat, a rosary, a small round cracked looking-glass and a piece of lead piping—and packed them once more carefully together on the bank. He tested his string, knotted it, drew it tight, and it broke again. The tin of potted meat—like some small intelligent animal—ran hastily off the path and dived into a small drain.

A short cry of mirth broke from the Major, and Gertie smiled.

Frank said nothing at all. He lay down on the road, plunged his arm into the drain and drew up the potted meat; it had some disagreeable-looking moist substance adhering to it, which he wiped off on to his sleeve, and then regretted having done so. Again he packed his things; again he drew the string tight, and again it snapped.

"Lord! man, don't be so hard on it."

Frank looked up with a kind of patient fury. His instinct was to kick every single object that lay before him on the path as hard as possible in every direction.

"Have you any more string?" he said.

"No. Stick the things in your pocket and come on."

Frank made no answer. He went to the hedge and drew out a long supple twig of hazel, stripped it of its leaves, and once more tried, with it, to tie up his parcel. But the angle was too acute, and just as the twig tightened satisfactorily it snapped, and this time the razor slid out sideways into a single minute puddle that lay on the path.

The Major snorted in mirthful impatience.

"But—"

"Kindly let me alone," said Frank icily. "The thing's got to go like this, or not at all."

He drew out the razor from the puddle, opened it and dried the blade on his sleeve. During the process Gertie moved suddenly, and he looked up. When he looked down again be perceived that he had slit a neat slice into the cloth of his jacket.

He remained quite still for one moment. Then he sat down on the bank, and examined the twine once more.

The Major began to make slightly offensive comments. Then Frank looked up.

"You can go to hell!" he said quite softly, "or anywhere else you like. But I'm going to do up the bundle in my way and not yours."

Now that is a sort of parable. It really happened, for it was reported to a witness by Frank himself exactly as I have told it, and it seems to me a very good little symbol of his state of mind. It is quite indefensible, of course—and especially his regrettable language that closed the interview; but it gives a pleasant little glimpse, I think, of Frank's character just now, in section. The things had to go in a certain way: he saw no adequate reason to change that way, and ultimately, of course, the twine held. It must have been a great satisfaction to him.

(III)

It seems that Frank must have been allowed just now to sample several different kinds of moods, for he had a very different kind of awakening a day or two later.

They had come to some piece of open country that I am unable to identify, and for some reason or other determined to spend the night out of doors. There was a copse a hundred yards away from the road, and in the copse a couple of small shelters built, probably, for wood-pigeon shooting. The Major and Gertie took possession of one, and Frank of the other, after they had supped in the dark under the beeches.

Frank slept deeply and well, half waking once, however, at that strange moment of the night when the earth turns and sighs in her sleep, when every cow gets up and lies down again. He was conscious of a shrill crowing, thin as a bugle, from some farm-yard out of sight; then he turned over and slept again.

When he awoke it was daylight. He lay on his back looking at the network of twigs overhead, the beech leaves beyond, and the sky visible only in glimpses—feeling extremely awake and extremely content. Certainly he was a little stiff when he moved, but there was a kind of interior contentment that caused that not to matter.

After a minute or two he sat up, felt about for his shoes and slipped them on. Then he unwound the wrapping about his neck, and crept out of the shelter.

It was that strange pause before the dawn when the light has broadened so far as to extinguish the stars, and to bring out all the colors of earth into a cold deliberate kind of tint. Everything was absolutely motionless about him as he went under the trees and came out above the wide park-land of which the copse was a sort of barrier. The dew lay soaking and thick on the grass slopes, but there was not yet such light as to bring out its sparkle; and everywhere, dotted on the green before him, sat hundreds of rabbits, the nearest not twenty yards away.

The silence and the solemnity of the whole seemed to him extraordinary. There was not a leaf that stirred—each hung as if cut of steel; there was not a bird which chirped nor a distant cock that crew; the rabbits eyed him unafraid in this hour of truce.

It seemed to him like some vast stage on to which he had wandered unexpectedly. The performance of the day before had been played to an end, the night scene-shifting was finished, and the players of the new eternal drama were not yet come. An hour hence they would be all about: the sounds would begin again; men would cross the field-paths, birds would be busy; the wind would awake and the ceaseless whisper of leaves answer its talking. But at present the stage was clear-swept, washed, clean and silent.

It was the solemnity then that impressed him most—solemnity and an air of expectation. Yet it was not mere expectation. There was a suggestion of the fundamental and the normal, as if perhaps movement and sound were, after all, no better than interruptions; as if this fixed poise of nature were something complete in itself; as if these trees hung out their leaves to listen to something that they could actually hear, as if these motionless creatures of the woodland were looking upon something that they could actually see; as if there were some great secret actually present and displayed in dead silence and invisibility before those only who possessed the senses necessary to perceive it.

It was odd to regard life from this standpoint—to look back upon the days and their incidents that were past, forward upon the days and incidents to come. Again it was possible for Frank to look upon these things as an outsider and a deliberate critic—as he had done in the stuffy room of the lodging-house in the town. Yet now, though he was again an outsider, though he was again out of the whirl of actual living, he seemed to be looking at things—staring out, as he was, almost unseeingly at the grass slopes before him—from exactly the opposite side. Then, they had seemed to him the only realities, these tangible physical things, and all else illusion: now it was the physical things that were illusive, and something else that was real. Once again the two elements of life lay detached—matter and spirit; but it was as obviously now spirit that was the reality as it had been matter a day or two before. It was obviously absurd to regard these outward things on which he looked as anything but a frame of something completely different. They were too silent, too still, too little self-sufficient to be complete in themselves. Something solid lay embraced within them....

So, then, he stared and ruminated, scarcely perceiving that he thought, so intensely conscious was he of that of which he thought. It was not that he understood anything of that on which he looked; he was but aware that there was something to be understood. And the trees hung rigid above him, and the clear blue sky still a hard stone beyond them, not yet flushed with dawn; and the grass lay before him, contracted, it seemed, with cold, and every blade soaked in wet; and the silence was profound....

Then a cock crew, a mile away, a thin, brazen cry; a rabbit sat up, then crouched and bolted, and the spell faded like a mist.

Frank turned and walked back under the trees, to see if the Major was awake.

CHAPTER V: (I)

We are arrived now at one of those few deplorable incidents in Frank's career, against which there is no defense. And the painful thing about it is that Frank never seemed to think that it required any defense. He shows no penitence for it in his diary: and yet moralists are united in telling us that we must never do evil that good may come. It is only, paralleled by his rash action in leaving Cambridge in defiance of all advice and good sense; so far, that is to say, as a legally permissible act, however foolish, can be paralleled by one of actual crime. Moralists, probably, would tell us, in fact, that the first led inevitably to the second.

It fell out in this way.

Once or twice in his travels with the Major he had been haunted by an uncomfortable suspicion that this or that contribution that the warrior made to their common table had not been come by honestly. When a gentleman, known to possess no more than tenpence, and with a predilection to drink, leaves the shelter of a small copse; let us say, at seven o'clock, and reappears, rather breathless, forty minutes later with a newly-plucked fowl—or even with a fowl not plucked at all, and still warm, or with half a dozen eggs; and, in addition, issues out again later in the evening and returns with a strong smell of spirits and a watery eye—it seems a little doubtful as to whether he has been scrupulously honest. In cases of this kind Frank persevered in making some excuse for not joining in the festivity: he put it to himself as being a matter of pride; but it is hard to understand that it was simply that in a young man who made no scruple of begging in cases of necessity. However, there it was, and even the Major, who began by protesting, ended by acquiescing.

They were somewhere in the neighborhood of Market Weighton when the thing happened—I cannot identify the exact spot. The situation was as follows:

They had secured an excellent barn for their night's lodging—facing on the road on the outskirts of a village. Behind them were, the farm buildings, and the farmer's household gone to bed. The sun had set and it was dark. They had supped sparingly, of necessity, and had finished every morsel of food. (Frank had even found himself mechanically gathering up crumbs on a wet finger.) They had had a bad week of it; the corn was not yet ready for cutting, and there seemed no work anywhere for honest men. The Major's gloom had become terrible; he had even made remarks upon a choice between a workhouse and a razor. He had got up after supper and turned his waistcoat pockets inside out to secure the last possible grains of tobacco, and had smoked about a quarter of a pipeful gathered in this way without uttering one word. He had then uttered a short string of them, had seized his cap and disappeared.

Frank, too, was even more heavy and depressed than usual. The last shreds of romance were gone from his adventure long ago, and yet his obstinacy held firm. But he found he could not talk much. He watched Gertie listlessly as she, listless too, began to spread out nondescript garments to make a bed in the corner. He hardly spoke to her, nor she to him.

He was beginning to feel sleepy, when he heard rather hurried steps, as of one trying to run on tiptoe, coming up the lane, and an instant later in popped the Major.

"Put out that damned light!" he whispered sharply.

The candle end went out with the swiftness of thought.

"What's up?" Frank roused himself to ask. There had been a strenuous look about the face seen an instant before that interested him.

There was dead silence. Gertie seemed frozen into motionlessness in her corner, almost as if she had had experience of this kind of thing before. Frank listened with all his ears; it was useless to stare into the dark: here in this barn the blackness was complete.

At first there was no sound at all, except a very soft occasional scrape of a boot-nail that betokened that the Major was seeking cover somewhere. Then, so suddenly that he started all over, Frank felt a hand on his arm and smelt a tobacco-laden breath. (Alas! there had been no drink to-night.)

"See here, Frankie, my boy.... I ... I've got the thing on me.... What shall I do with it?... It's no good chucking it away: they'd find it."

"Got what?" whispered Frank.

"There was a kid coming along ... she had a tin of something ... I don't even know what it is.... And ... and she screamed out and someone ran out. But they couldn't spot me; it was too dark."

"Hush!" whispered Frank sharply, and the hand tightened on his arm. But it was only a rat somewhere in the roof.

"Well?" he said.

"Frankie ... I suppose you wouldn't take it from me ... and ... and be off somewhere. We could meet again later.... I ... I'm afraid someone may have spotted us coming through the village earlier. They'll ... they'll search, I expect."

"You can do your own dirty work," whispered Frank earnestly through the darkness.

"Frankie, my boy ... don't be hard on a poor devil.... I ... I can't leave Gertie."

"Well, hide it somewhere."

"No good—they'd ... Good God—!"

The voice was stricken into silence once more, as a light, hardly seen before it was gone again, shone through a crack in the side of the barn. Then there was unmistakable low talking somewhere.

Frank felt the man, crouched at his side, suddenly stand up noiselessly, and in that instant his own mind was made up.

"Give it here, you fool," he said. "Here!"

He felt a smooth flat and circular thing thrust suddenly into his hands with a whisper that he could not catch, and simultaneously he heard a rush of footsteps outside. He had just time to stuff the thing inside his coat and roll over as if asleep when the door flew open, and three or four men, with a policeman at their head, burst into the barn.

It would be charitable, I think, to suppress the name of the small market-town where the trial was held. The excellent magistrates who conducted it certainly did their best under very difficult circumstances; for what are you to do if a man accused of theft cordially pleads guilty? and yet, certainly it would distress them to hear of a very obvious miscarriage of justice executed at their hands.

On Friday morning at ten o'clock the vehicles began to arrive—the motor of the country gentleman, the dog-cart of the neighboring rector, and the brougham of the retired general. It was the General who presided.

The court-room was not more dismal than court-rooms usually are. When I visited it on my little pilgrimage, undertaken a few months ago, it had been repainted and the woodwork grained to represent oak. Even so, it was not cheering.

At the upper end, under one of the windows, were ranged five seats on a daïs, with a long baize-covered table before them. Then, on a lower level, stood the clerk's and solicitors' table, fenced by a rail from the vulgar crowd who pressed in, hot and excited, to see the criminals and hear justice done. There was a case arising from an ancient family feud, exploded at last into crime; one lady had thrown a clog at another as the last repartee in a little dialogue held at street doors; the clog had been well aimed, and the victim appeared now with a very large white bandage under her bonnet, to give her testimony. This swelled the crowd beyond its usual proportions, as both ladies were well known in society.

The General was a kindly-looking old man (Frank recognized his name as soon as he heard it that morning, though he had never met him before) and conversed cheerily with his brother magistrates as they took their seats. The Rector was—well, like other rectors, and the Squire like other squires.

It was a quarter to twelve before the ladies' claims were adjusted. They were both admonished in a paternal kind of way, and sent about their business, since there was disputed evidence as to whether or not the lady with the bandage had provoked the attack, not only by her language, but by throwing a banana-skin at the lady without the bandage. They were well talked to, their husbands were bidden to keep them in order, and they departed, both a little crestfallen, to discuss the whole matter over a pint of beer.

There was a little shifting about in court; a policeman, looking curiously human without his helmet, pushed forward from the door and took his place by the little barrier. The magistrates and the clerk and the inspector all conferred a little together, and after an order or two, the door near the back of the court leading from the police-cells opened, and Frank stepped forward into the dock, followed by another policeman who clicked the barrier behind the prisoner and stood, waiting, like Rhadamanthus. Through the hedge of the front row of the crowd peered the faces of Gertie and the Major.

We need not bother with the preliminaries—in fact, I forget how they ran—Frank gave his name of Frank Gregory, his age as twenty-two years, his occupation as casual laborer, and his domicile as no fixed abode.

The charge was read to him. It was to the effect that he, on the night of Tuesday, the twenty-third instant, had in the village (whose name I choose to forget, if I ever knew it), seized from Maggie Cooper, aged nine years, a tin of preserved salmon, with intent to steal. The question put to the prisoner was: Did he or did he not plead guilty?

"I plead guilty, sir," said Frank, without a tremor.

He had been two full days in the cells by now, and it had not improved his appearance. He was still deeply sunburned, but he was a little pale under the eyes, and he was unshaven. He had also deliberately rumpled his hair and pulled his clothes to make them look as untidy as possible. He answered in a low voice, so as to attract as little attention as possible. He had given one quick look at the magistrates as he came in, to make sure he had never met them out shooting or at dinner-parties, and he had been deeply relieved to find them total strangers.

"You plead guilty, eh?" said the General.

Frank nodded.

"Well, well! let's hear the whole story. Where is the complainant?"

A rather pale and awe-stricken child appeared somewhere in a little box opposite Frank, with a virtuous mother in black silk behind her. It appeared that this child was on her way to her aunt—her father was a grocer—with a tin of salmon that had been promised and forgotten (that was how she came to be out so late). As she reached the corner by Barker's Lane a man had jumped at her and seized the tin. (No; he had not used any other violence.) She had screamed at the top of her voice, and Mrs. Jennings' door had opened. Then the man had run away.

"Had she seen the man clearly?" No, she hadn't seen him at all; she had just seen that he was a man. ("Called himself one," put in a voice.) The witness here cast an indignant—almost vindictive—look at Frank.

Then a few corroborations were issued. Mrs. Jennings, a widow lady, keeping house for her brother who was a foreman in Marks' yard, ratified the statement about the door being opened. She was going to shut up for the night when she heard the child scream. Her brother, a severe-looking man, with a black beard, finished her story. He had heard his sister call out, as he was taking off his boots at the foot of the stairs; he had run out with his laces dangling, in time to see the man run past the public-house fifty yards up the street. No ... he, too, had not seen the man clearly, but he had seen him before, in company with another; the two had come to his yard that afternoon to ask for work and been refused, as they wanted no more hands.

"Well, what had happened then?"

He had hammered at two or three doors as he ran past, among them that of the police-constable, and himself had run on, in time to hear the prisoner's footsteps run up the lane leading to the barn. He had stopped then as he was out of breath, and as he thought they would have the man now, since there was no exit from the lane except through Mr. Patten's farm-yard, and if he'd gone that way they'd have heard the dogs.

Finally the police-constable corroborated the entire story, and added that he, in company with the foreman and two other men, had "proceeded" to the barn immediately, and there had found the prisoner, who was pretending to be asleep, with the tin of salmon (produced and laid on the table) hidden inside his jacket. He had then taken him into custody.

"Was there any one else in the barn?"

Yes—two persons, who gave the names of George and Gertie Trustcott. These were prepared to give evidence as to the prisoner's identity, and as to his leaving and returning to the barn on the evening in question, if the magistrate wished.... Yes; they were present in court.

The General began to turn a little testy as the constable finished. He seemed a magistrate who liked to be paternal, and he appeared to grow impatient under the extraordinarily correct language of the policeman.

He turned to Frank—seeming to forget all about the two witnesses not yet called—and spoke rather sharply:

"You don't deny all that? You plead guilty, eh?"

"Yes, sir," said Frank, gazing at the very pink salmon emblazoned on the tin.

"Why did you do it?"

"I was hungry, sir."

"Hungry, eh? An able-bodied lad like you? Can't you work, then?"

"When I can get it, sir," said Frank

"Eh?... eh? Well, that's true enough. You couldn't get it that day, anyhow. Mr. What's-his-name's told us that."

"Yes, sir."

Then the Rector leaned forward swiftly—to Frank's horror.

"You speak like an educated man."

"Do I, sir? I'm very pleased to hear it."

There was a faint snigger in court.

"Where were you educated?" persisted the Rector.

"Am I bound to incriminate myself, sir?"

"Incriminate?" said the General suddenly interested. "Eh? you mean, after a good education. I see. No, of course you're not, my lad."

"Thank you, sir."

"And you plead guilty? And you'd like the case dealt with now?"

"If you please, sir."

The clerk rose swiftly in his place and began to whisper to the magistrates behind his hand. Frank understood perfectly what was happening; he understood that it was doubtful whether or no his case could be dealt with in this court. He exploded within himself a violent adjuration to the Supreme Authorities, and the next instant the General sat back.

"Nonsense! nonsense! It isn't highway robbery at all within the meaning of the term. We'll deal with it now—eh, gentlemen?"

There was a little more whispering, and finally the General settled himself and took up a quill pen.

"Well, we'll deal with it now, my lad, as you wish. I'm sorry to see a fellow like you in this position—particularly if you've had a good education, as you seem to have had. Cowardly thing, you know, to attack a child like that, isn't it? even if you were hungry. You ought to be more hardy than that, you know—a great fellow like you—than to mind a bit of hunger. Boys like you ought to enlist; that'd make a man of you in no time. But no.... I know you; you won't.... You'd sooner loaf about and pick up what you can—sooner than serve His Majesty. Well, well, there's no compulsion—not yet; but you should think over it. Come and see me, if you like, when you've done your time, and we'll see what can be done. That'd be better than loafing about and picking up tins of salmon, eh?"

"Well, I've no more to say. But you just think over it. And we'll give you fourteen days."

Then as Frank went out he saw the three magistrates lean back in conversation.

I find it very hard to explain, even to myself, the extraordinary depression that fell upon Frank during his fourteen days. He could hardly bear even to speak of it afterwards, and I find in his diary no more than a line or two, and those as bald as possible. Apparently it was no kind of satisfaction to him to know that the whole thing was entirely his own doing, or that it was the thought of Gertie that had made him, in the first instance, take the tin from the Major. Yet it was not that there was any sense of guilt, or even of mistake. One would have thought that from everybody's point of view, and particularly Gertie's, it would be an excellent thing for the Major to go to prison for a bit. It would certainly do him no harm, and it would be a real opportunity to separate the girl from his company. As for any wrong in his pleading guilty, he defended it (I must say, with some adroitness) by saying that it was universally acknowledged that the plea of "Not Guilty" is merely formal, and in no way commits one to its intrinsic truth (and he is right there, at least according to Moral Theology as well as common sense) and, therefore, that the alternative plea is also merely formal.

And yet he was depressed by his fourteen days to the verge of melancholia.

There are several contributory causes that may be alleged.

First, there is the extreme ignominy of all the circumstances, beginning with the paternal scolding in court, in the presence of grocers and persons who threw clogs, continuing with the dreary journey by rail, in handcuffs, and the little crowds that gathered to laugh or stare, and culminating with the details of the prison life. It is not pleasant for a cleanly man to be suspected of dirt, to be bathed and examined all over by a man suffering himself apparently from some species of eczema; it is not pleasant to be ordered about peremptorily by uniformed men, who, three months before, would have touched their hats to you, and to have to do things instantly and promptly for the single reason that one is told to do them.

Secondly, there was the abrupt change of life—of diet, air and exercise....

Thirdly, there was the consideration, the more terrible because the more completely unverifiable, as to what difference all this would make, not only to the regard of his friends for him, but to his own regard for himself. Innocence of a fault does not entirely do away with the distress and stigma of its punishment. He imagined himself telling Jenny; he tried to see her laughing, and somehow he could not. It was wholly uncharacteristic of all that he knew of her, and yet somehow, night after night, as the hours dragged by, he seemed to see her looking at him a little contemptuously.

"At any rate," he almost heard her say, "if you didn't do it, you made a friend of a man who did. And you were in prison."

Oh! there are countless excellent explanations of his really terrible depression; and yet somehow it does not seem to me at all in line with what I know of Frank, to think that they explain it in the least. I prefer to believe, with a certain priest who will appear by and by, that the thing was just one stage of a process that had to be accomplished, and that if it had not come about in this way, it must have come about in another. As for his religion, all emotional grasp of that fled, it seemed finally, at the touch of real ignominy. He retained the intellectual reasons for which he had become a Catholic, but the thing seemed as apart from him as his knowledge of law—such as it was—acquired at Cambridge, or his proficiency in lawn-tennis. Certainly it was no kind of consolation to him to reflect on the sufferings of Christian martyrs!

It was a Friday evening when he came out and went quickly round the corner of the jail, in order to get away from any possibility of being identified with it.

He had had a short interview with the Governor—a very conscientious and religious man, who made a point of delivering what he called "a few earnest words" to every prisoner before his release. But, naturally enough, they were extraordinarily off the point. It was not helpful to Frank to have it urged upon him to set about an honest livelihood—it was what he had tried to do every day since June—and not to go about robbing innocent children of things like tins of salmon—it was the very last thing he had ever dreamed of doing.

He had also had more than one interview with the chaplain of the Established Church, in consequence of his resolute refusal to acknowledge any religious body at all (he had determined to scotch this possible clue to his identification); and those interviews had not been more helpful than any other. It is not of much use to be entreated to turn over a new leaf when you see no kind of reason for doing so; and little books left tactfully in your cell, directed to the same point, are equally useless. Frank read them drearily through. He did not actually kick them from side to side of his cell when he had finished; that would have been offensive to the excellent intentions of the reverend gentleman....

Altogether I do not quite like to picture Frank as he was when he came out of jail, and hurried away. It is such a very startling contrast with the gayety with which he had begun his pilgrimage.

He had had plenty of time to think over his plans during the last fortnight, and he went, first, straight to the post-office. The Governor had given him half-a-crown to start life with, and he proposed to squander fourpence of it at once in two stamps, two sheets of paper and two envelopes.

His first letter was to be to Jack; the second to Major Trustcott, who had thoughtfully given him the address where he might be found about that date.

But there were to be one or two additional difficulties first.

He arrived at the post-office, went up the steps and through the swing doors. The place had been newly decorated, with a mahogany counter and light brass lattice rails, behind which two young ladies of an inexpressibly aristocratic demeanor and appearance were engaged in conversation: their names, as he learned from a few sentences he listened to before daring to interrupt so high a colloquy, were Miss Mills and Miss Jamieson.

After a decent and respectful pause Frank ventured on his request.

"Two stamps, two sheets of paper and two envelopes, please ... miss." (He did manage that!)

Miss Mills continued her conversation:

"So I said to her that that would never do, that Harold would be sure to get hold of it, and that then—"

Frank shuffled his feet a little. Miss Mills cast him a high glance.

"—There'd be trouble, I said, Miss Jamieson."

"You did quite right, dear."

"Two stamps, two sheets of paper and two envelopes, please, miss." He clicked four pence together on the counter. Miss Mills rose slowly from her place, went a yard or two, and took down a large book. Frank watched her gratefully. Then she took a pen and began to make entries in it.

"Two stamps, two sheets of paper and two envelopes, please."

Frank's voice shook a little with anger. He had not learned his lesson yet.

Miss Mills finished her entry; looked at Frank with extreme disdain, and finally drew out a sheet of stamps.

"Pennies?" she inquired sharply.

"Please."

Two penny stamps were pushed across and two pennies taken up.

"And now two sheets of paper and two envelopes, please, miss," went on Frank, encouraged. He thought himself foolish to be angry. Miss Jamieson uttered a short laugh and glanced at Miss Mills. Miss Mills pursed her lips together and took up her pen once more.

"Will you be good enough to give me what I ask for, at once, please?"

The whole of Frank blazed in this small sentence: but Miss Mills was equal to it.

"You ought to know better," she said, "than to come asking for such things here! Taking up a lot of time like that."

"You don't keep them?"

Miss Mills uttered a small sound. Miss Jamieson tittered.

"Shops are the proper places for writing-paper. This is a post-office."

Words cannot picture the superb high breeding shown in this utterance. Frank should have understood that he had been guilty of gross impertinence in asking such things of Miss Mills; it was treating her almost as a shop-girl. But he was extremely angry by now.

"Then why couldn't you have the civility to tell me so at once?"

Miss Jamieson laid aside a little sewing she was engaged on.

"Look here, young man, you don't come bullying and threatening here. I'll have to call the policeman if you do.... I was at the railway station last Friday week, you know."

Frank stood still for one furious instant. Then his heart sank and he went out without a word.

The letters got written at last, late that evening, in the back room of a small lodging-house where he had secured a bed. I have the one he wrote to Jack before me as I write, and I copy it as it stands. It was without address or date.

"Dear Jack,

"I want you to do, something for me. I want you to go to Merefield and see, first, Jenny, and then my father; and tell them quite plainly and simply that I've been in prison for a fortnight. I want Jenny to know first, so that she can think of what to say to my father. The thing I was sent to prison for was that I pleaded guilty to stealing a tin of salmon from a child called Mary Cooper. You can see the account of the case in the County Gazette for last Saturday week, the twenty-seventh. The thing I really did was to take the tin from somebody else I was traveling with. He asked me to.

"Next, I want you to send on any letters that may have come for me to the address I enclose on a separate piece of paper. Please destroy the address at once; but you can show this letter to Jenny and give her my love. You are not to come and see me. If you don't, I'll come and see you soon.

"Things are pretty bad just now, but I'm going to go through with it.

"Yours,

"F.

"P.S.—By the way, please address me as Mr. F. Gregory when you write."

He was perfectly obstinate, you understand, still.

Frank's troubles as regards prison were by no means exhausted by his distressing conversation with the young ladies in the post office, and the next one fell on him as he was leaving the little town early on the Saturday morning.

He had just turned out of the main street and was going up a quiet side lane that looked as if it would lead to the York Road, when he noticed a disagreeable little scene proceeding up a narrow cul-de-sac across whose mouth he was passing.

A tall, loose-limbed young man, in his working-clothes, obviously slightly excited with drink, had hold of a miserable old man by the scruff of the neck with one hand, and was cuffing him with the other.

Now I do not wish to represent Frank as a sort of knight-errant, but the fact is that if anyone with respectable and humane ideas goes on the tramp (I have this from the mouth of experienced persons) he has to make up his mind fairly soon either to be a redresser of wrongs or to be conveniently short-sighted. Frank was not yet sufficiently experienced to have learned the wisdom of the second alternative.

He went straight up the cul-de-sac and without any words at all hit the young man as hard as possible under the ear nearest to him.

There seems to have been a moment of amazed silence; the young man dropped the old one, who fled out into the lane, and struck back at Frank, who parried. Simultaneously a woman screamed somewhere; and faces began to appear at windows and doors.

It is curious how the customs of the Middle Ages, as well as some of their oaths, seem to have descended to the ranks of the British working-man. In the old days—as also in prize-fights to-day—it was quite usual to assail your adversary with insults as well as with blows. This was done now. The young man, with a torrent of imprecations, demanded who Frank thought he was, asked where he was coming to, required of society in general an explanation of a stranger's interfering between a son and a qualified father. There was a murmur of applause and dissent, and Frank answered, with a few harmless expletives such as he had now learned to employ as a sort of verbal disguise, that he did not care how many sons or fathers were in question, that he did not propose to see a certain kind of bully abuse an old man, and that he would be happy to take the old man's place....

Then the battle was set.

Frank had learned to box in a certain small saloon in Market Street, Cambridge, and knew perfectly well how to take care of himself. He received about half the force of one extremely hard blow just on his left cheek-bone before he got warmed to his work; but after that he did the giving and the loose-limbed young man the receiving, Frank was even scientific; he boxed in the American manner, crouching, with both arms half extended (and this seems to have entirely bewildered his adversary) and he made no effort to reach the face. He just thumped away steadily below the spot where the ribs part, and where—a doctor informs me—a nerve-center, known as the solar plexus, is situated. He revolved, too, with considerable agility, round his opponent, and gradually drew the battle nearer and nearer to the side lane outside. He knew enough of slum-chivalry by now to be aware that if a sympathizer, or sycophant, of the young man happened to be present, he himself would quite possibly (if the friend happened to possess sufficient courage) suddenly collapse from a disabling blow on the back of the neck. Also, he was not sure whether there was any wife in the question; and in this case it would be a poker, or a broken bottle, held dagger-wise, that he would have to meet. And he wished therefore to have more room round him than the cul-de-sac afforded.

But there was no need for precaution.

The young man had begun to look rather sickly under the eyes and to hiccup three or four times in distressed manner; when suddenly the clamor round the fight ceased. Frank was aware of a shrill old voice calling out something behind him; and the next instant, simultaneously with the dropping of his adversary's hands, he himself was seized from behind by the arms, and, writhing, discerned is blue sleeve and a gloved hand holding him.

"Now, what's all this?" said a voice in his ear.

There was a chorus of explanation, declaring that "'Alb" had been set upon without provocation. There was a particularly voluble woman with red arms and an exceedingly persuasive manner, who advanced from a doorway and described the incident from her own point of view. She had been hanging out the children's things, she began, and so forth; and Frank was declared the aggressor and "'Alb" the innocent victim.

Then the chorus broke out again, and "'Alb," after another fit of hiccupping, corroborated the witnesses in a broken and pathetically indignant voice.

Frank tore himself from one embracing arm and faced round, still held by the other.

"All right; I shan't run away.... Look here; that's a black lie. He was hitting that old man. Where is he? Come on, uncle, and tell us all about it."

The old man advanced, his toothless face contorted with inexplicable emotion, and corroborated the red-armed woman, and the chorus generally, with astonishing volubility and emphasis.

"You old fool!" said Frank curtly. "What are you afraid of? Let's have the truth, now. Wasn't he hitting you?"

"He, he, he!" giggled the old man, torn by the desire of self-preservation on one side and, let us hope, by a wish for justice on the other. "He warn't hittin' of me. He's my son, he is.... 'Alb is....

We were just having—"

"There! get out of this," said the policeman, releasing Frank with a shove. "We don't want your sort here. Coming and making trouble.... Yes; my lad. You needn't look at me like that. I know you."

"Who the deuce are you talking to?" snapped Frank.

"I know who I'm talking to, well enough," pronounced the policeman judicially. "F. Gregory, ain't it? Now you be off out of this, or you'll be in trouble again."

There was something vaguely kindly about the man's manner, and Frank understood that he knew very tolerably where the truth lay, but wished to prevent further disturbance. He gulped down his fury. It was no good saying anything; but the dense of the injustice of the universe was very bitter. He turned away—

A murmur of indignation broke out from the crowd, bidding the policeman do his duty.

And as Frank went up the lane, he heard that zealous officer addressing the court with considerable vigor. But it was very little comfort to him. He walked out of the town with his anger and resentment still hot in his heart at the indignity of the whole affair.

(V)

By the Sunday afternoon Frank was well on his way to York.

It was a heavy, hot day, sunny, but with brooding clouds on the low horizons; and he was dispirited and tired as he came at last into a small, prim village street rather after two o'clock (its name, once more, I suppress).

His possessions by now were greatly reduced. His money had gone, little by little, all through his journey with the Major, and he had kept of other things only one extra flannel shirt, a pair of thick socks and a small saucepan he had bought one day. The half-crown that the Governor had given him was gone, all but fourpence, and he wanted, if possible, to arrive at York, where he was to meet the Major, at least with that sum in his possession. Twopence would pay for a bed and twopence more for supper.

Half-way up the street he stopped suddenly. Opposite him stood a small brick church, retired by a few yards of turf, crossed by a path, from the iron railings that abutted on the pavement: and a notice-board proclaimed that in this, church of the Sacred Heart mass was said on Sundays at eleven, on holidays of obligation at nine, and on weekdays at eight-thirty a.m. Confessions were heard on Saturday evenings and on Thursday evenings before the first Friday, from eight to nine p.m. Catechism was at three p.m. on Sundays; and rosary, sermon and benediction at seven p.m. A fat cat, looking as if it were dead, lay relaxed on the grass beneath this board.

The door was open and Frank considered an instant. But he thought that could wait for a few minutes as he glanced at the next house. This was obviously the presbytery.

Frank had never begged from a priest before, and he hesitated a little now. Then he went across the street into the shadow on the other side, leaned against the wall and looked. The street was perfectly empty and perfectly quiet, and the hot summer air and sunshine lay on all like a charm. There was another cat, he noticed, on a doorstep a few yards away, and he wondered how any living creature in this heat could possibly lie like that, face coiled round to the feet, and the tail laid neatly across the nose. A dreaming cock crooned heart-brokenly somewhere out of sight, and a little hot breeze scooped up a feather of dust in the middle of the road and dropped again.

Even the presbytery looked inviting on a day like this. He had walked a good twenty-five miles to-day, and the suggestion of a dark, cool room was delicious. It was a little pinched-looking house, of brick, like the church, squeezed between the church and a large grocery with a flamboyant inscription over its closed shutters. All the windows were open, hung inside with cheap lace curtains, and protected with dust-screens. He pictured the cold food probably laid out within, and his imagination struck into being a tall glass jug of something like claret-cup, still half-full. Frank had not dined to-day.

Then he limped boldly across the street, rapped with the cast-iron knocker, and waited. Nothing at all happened.

Presently the cat from the notice-board appeared round the corner, eyed Frank suspiciously, decided that he was not dangerous, came on, walking delicately, stepped up on to the further end of the brick stair, and began to arch itself about and rub its back against the warm angle of the

doorpost. Frank rapped again, interrupting the cat for an instant, and then stooped down to
scratch it under the ear. The cat crooned delightedly. Steps sounded inside the house; the cat
stopped writhing, and as the door opened, darted in noiselessly with tail erect past the woman
who held the door uninvitingly half open.

She had a thin, lined face and quick black eyes.

"What do you want?" she asked sharply, looking up and down Frank's figure with suspicion.
Her eyes dwelt for a moment on the bruise on his cheek-bone.

"I want to see the priest, please," said Frank.

"You can't see him."

"I am very sorry," said Frank, "but I must see him."

"Coming here begging!" exclaimed the woman bitterly. "I'd be ashamed! Be off with you!"
Frank's dignity asserted itself a little.

"Don't speak to me in that tone, please. I am a Catholic, and I wish to see the priest."

The woman snorted; but before she could speak there came the sound of an opening door and a
quick step on the linoleum of the little dark passage.

"What's all this?" said a voice, as the woman stepped back.

He was a big, florid young man, with yellow hair, flushed as if with sleep; his eyes were bright
and tired-looking, and his collar was plainly unbuttoned at the back. Also, his cassock was
unfastened at the throat and he bore a large red handkerchief in his hand. Obviously this had just
been over his face.

Now, I do not blame this priest in the slightest. He had sung a late mass—which never agreed
with him—and in his extreme hunger he had eaten two platefuls of hot beef, with Yorkshire
pudding, and drunk a glass and a half of solid beer. And he had just fallen into a deep sleep
before giving Catechism, when the footsteps and voices had awakened him. Further, every
wastrel Catholic that came along this road paid him a call, and he had not yet met with one
genuine case of want. When he had first come here he had helped beggars freely and generously,
and he lived on a stipend of ninety pounds a year, out of which he paid his housekeeper fifteen.

"What do you want?" he said.

"May I speak to you, father?" said Frank.

"Certainly. Say what you've got to say."

"Will you help me with sixpence, father?"

The priest was silent, eyeing Frank closely.

"Are you a Catholic?"

"Yes, father."

"I didn't see you at mass this morning."

"I wasn't here this morning. I was walking on the roads."

"Where did you hear mass?"

"I didn't hear it at all, father. I was on the roads."

"What's your work?"

"I haven't any."

"Why's that?"

Frank shrugged his shoulders a little.

"I do it when I can get it," he said.

"You speak like an educated man."

"I am pretty well educated."

The priest laughed shortly.

"What's that bruise on your cheek?"

"I was in a street fight, yesterday, father."

"Oh, this is ridiculous!" he said. "Where did you come from last?"

Frank paused a moment. He was very hot and very tired.... Then he spoke.

"I was in prison till Friday," he said. "I was given fourteen days on the charge of robbing a child, on the twenty-sixth. I pleaded guilty. Will you help me, father?"

If the priest had not been still half stupid with sleep and indigestion, and standing in the full blaze of this hot sun, he might have been rather struck by this last sentence. But he did have those disadvantages, and he saw in it nothing but insolence.

He laughed again, shortly and angrily.

"I'm amazed at your cheek," he said. "No, certainly not! And you'd better learn manners before you beg again."

Then he banged the door.

About ten minutes later he woke up from a doze, very wide awake indeed, and looked round. There lay on the table by him a Dutch cheese, a large crusty piece of bread and some very soft salt butter in a saucer. There was also a good glass of beer left—not claret-cup—in a glass jug, very much as Frank had pictured it.

He got up and went out to the street door, shading his eyes against the sun. But the street lay hot and dusty in the afternoon light, empty from end to end, except for a cat, nose in tail, coiled on the grocery door-step.

Then he saw two children, in white frocks, appear round a corner, and he remembered that it was close on time for Catechism.

CHAPTER VI: (I)

About the time that Frank was coming into the village where the priest lived, Jenny had just finished lunch with her father. She took a book, two cigarettes, a small silver matchbox and a Japanese fan, and went out into the garden. She had no duties this afternoon; she had played the organ admirably at the morning service, and would play it equally admirably at the evening service. The afternoon devotions in the little hot Sunday school—she had decided, in company with her father a year or two ago—and the management of the children, were far better left in the professional hands of the schoolmistress.

She went straight out of the drawing-room windows, set wide and shaded by awnings, and across the lawn to the seat below the ancient yews. There she disposed herself, with her feet up, lit a cigarette, buried the match and began to read.

She had not heard from Frank for nearly three weeks; his last communication had been a picture postcard of Selby Abbey, with the initial "F" neatly printed at the back. But she was not very greatly upset. She had written her letter as she had promised, and had heard from Jack Kirkby, to whose care she sent it, that he had no idea of Frank's whereabouts, and that he would send on the letter as soon as he knew more. She supposed that Frank would communicate with her again as soon as he thought proper.

Other circumstances to be noted were that Dick had gone back to town some while ago, but would return almost immediately now for the grouse-shooting; that Archie and Lord Talgarth were both up at the house—indeed, she had caught sight of them in the red-curtained chancel-pew this morning, and had exchanged five words with them both after the service—and that in all other respects other things were as they had been a month ago.

The Dean of Trinity had telegraphed in great dismay on the morning following his first communication that Frank had gone, and that no one had the slightest idea of his destination; he had asked whether he should put detectives on the track, and had been bidden, in return, politely but quite firmly, to mind his own business and leave Lord Talgarth's younger son to Lord Talgarth.

It was a sleepy afternoon, even up here among the hills, and Jenny had not read many pages before she became aware of it. The Rectory garden was an almost perfect place for a small doze; the yews about her made a grateful shade, and the limes behind them even further cooled the air, and, when the breeze awoke, as one talking in his sleep, the sound about her was as of gentle rain. The air was bright and dusty with insects; from the limes overhead, the geranium beds, and the orchard fifty yards away, came the steady murmur of bees and flies.

Jenny woke up twenty minutes later with a sudden start, and saw someone standing almost over her. She threw her feet down, still bewildered by the sudden change and the glare on which she opened her eyes, and perceived that it was Jack Kirkby, looking very dusty and hot.

"I am so sorry," said Jack apologetically, "but I was told you were out here."

She did not know Jack very well, though she had known him a long time. She looked upon him as a pleasant sort of boy whom she occasionally met at lawn-tennis parties and flower shows, and things like that, and she knew perfectly how to talk to young men.

"How nice of you to came over," she said. "Did you bicycle? Have something to drink?"

She made room for him on the seat and held out her second cigarette.

"It's your last," said Jack.

"I've lots more in the house."

She watched him as he lit it, and as the last shreds of sleep rolled away, put the obvious question.

"You've news of Frank?"

Jack threw away the match and drew two or three draughts of smoke before answering.

"Yes," he said.

"Where is he?"

"He gave an address at York, though he wasn't there when he wrote. I sent your letter on there yesterday."

"Oh I did he give any account of himself?"

Jack looked at her.

"Well, he did. I've come about that. It's not very pleasant."

"Is he ill?" asked Jenny sharply.

"Oh, no; not at all; at least, he didn't say so."

"What's the matter, then?"

Jack fumbled in his breast-pocket and drew out a letter, which he held a moment before unfolding.

"I think you'd better read what he says, Miss Launton. It isn't pleasant, but it's all over now. I thought I'd better tell you that first."

She held out her hand without speaking.

Jack gave it her, and addressed himself carefully to his cigarette. He didn't like this kind of thing at all, he wished Frank wouldn't give him unpleasant commissions. But, of course, it had to be done. He looked out at the lawn and the sleepy house, but was aware of nothing except the girl beside him in her white dress and the letter in her hands. When she had finished it, she turned back and read it again. Then she remained perfectly still, with the letter held on her knee.

"Poor, dear old boy!" she said suddenly and quietly.

An enormous wave of relief rolled up and enveloped Jack. He had been exceedingly uncomfortable this morning, ever since the letter had come. His first impulse had been to ride over instantly after breakfast; then he had postponed it till lunch; then he had eaten some cold beef about half-past twelve and come straight away. He told himself he must give her plenty of time to write by the late Sunday night post.

He had not exactly distrusted Jenny; Frank's confidence was too overwhelming and too infectious. But he had reflected that it was not a wholly pleasant errand to have to inform a girl that her lover had been in prison for a fortnight. But the tone in which she had just said those four words was so serene and so compassionate that he was completely reassured. This really was a fine creature, he said to himself.

"I'm extraordinarily glad you take it like that," he said.

Jenny looked at him out of her clear, direct eyes.

"You didn't suppose I should abuse him, did you?... How exactly like Frank! I suppose he did it to save some blackguard or other."

"I expect that was it," said Jack.

"Poor, dear old boy!" she said again.

There was a moment's silence. Then Jack began again:

"You see, I've got to go and tell Lord Talgarth. Miss Launton, I wish you'd come with me. Then we can both write by to-night's post."

Jenny said nothing for an instant. Then:

"I suppose that would be best," she said. "Shall we go up pretty soon? I expect we shall find him in the garden."

Jack winced a little. Jenny smiled at him openly.

"Best to get it over, Mr. Jack. I know it's like going to the dentist. But it can't be as bad as you think. It never is. Besides, you'll have somebody to hold your hand, so to speak."

"I hope I shan't scream out loud," observed Jack. "Yes, we'd better go—if you don't mind."

He stood up and waited. Jenny rose at once.

"I'll go and get a hat. Wait for me here, will you? I needn't tell father till this evening."

The park looked delicious as they walked slowly up the grass under the shade of the trees by the side of the drive. The great beeches and elms rose in towering masses, in clump after clump, into the distance, and beneath the nearest stood a great stag with half a dozen hinds about him, eyeing the walkers. The air was very still; only from over the hill came the sound of a single church bell, where some infatuated clergyman hoped to gather the lambs of his flock together for instruction in the Christian religion.

"That's a beauty," said Jack, waving a languid hand towards the stag. "Did you ever hear of the row Frank and I got into when we were boys?"

Jenny smiled. She had been quite silent since leaving the Rectory.

"I heard of a good many," she said. "Which was this?"

Jack recounted a story of Red Indians and ambuscades and a bow and arrows, ending in the flight of a frantic stag over the palings and among the garden beds; it was on a Sunday afternoon, too.

"Frank was caned by the butler, I remember; by Lord Talgarth's express orders. Certainly he richly deserved it. I was a guest, and got off clear."

"How old were you?"

"We were both about eleven, I think."

"Frank doesn't strike me as more than about twelve now," observed Jenny.

"There's something in that," admitted Jack.... "Oh! Lord! how hot it is!" He fanned himself with his hat.

There was no sign of life as they passed into the court and up to the pillared portico; and at last, when the butler appeared, the irregular state of his coat-collar showed plainly that he but that moment had put his coat on.

(This would be about the time that Frank left the village after his interview with the priest.)

Yes; it seemed that Lord Talgarth was probably in the garden; and, if so, almost certainly in the little square among the yews along the upper terrace. His lordship usually went there on hot days. Would Miss Launton and Mr. Kirkby kindly step this way?

No; he was not to trouble. They would find their own way. On the upper terrace?

"On the upper terrace, miss."

The upper terrace was the one part of the old Elizabethan garden left entirely unaltered. On either side rose up a giant wall of yew, shaped like a castle bastion, at least ten feet thick; and between the two ran a broad gravel path up to the sun-dial, bordered on either side by huge herbaceous beds, blazing with the color of late summer. In two or three places grass paths crossed these, leading by a few yards of turf to windows cut in the hedge to give a view of the long, dazzling lake below, and there was one gravel path, parallel to these, that led to the little yew-framed square built out on the slope of the hill.

Two very silent persons now came out from the house by the garden door on the south side, turned along the path, went up a dozen broad steps, passed up the yew walk and finally turned again down the short gravel way and stood abashed.

His lordship was indeed here!

A long wicker chair was set in one angle, facing them, in such a position that the movement of the sun would not affect the delightful shade in which the chair stood. A small table stood beside it, with the Times newspaper tumbled on to it, a box of cigars, a spirit-bottle of iridescent glass, a syphon, and a tall tumbler in which a little ice lay crumbled at the bottom. And in the wicker chair, with his mouth wide open, slept Lord Talgarth.

"Good gracious!" whispered Jenny.

There was a silence, and then like far-off thunder a slow meditative snore. It was not an object of beauty or dignity that they looked upon.

"In one second I shall laugh," asserted Jenny, still in a cautious whisper.

"I think we'd better—" began Jack; and stopped petrified, to see one vindictive-looking eye opened and regarding him, it seemed, with an expression of extraordinary malignity. Then the other eye opened, the mouth abruptly closed and Lord Talgarth sat up.

"God bless my soul!"

He rolled his eyes about a moment while intelligence came back.

"You needn't be ashamed of it," said Jenny. "Mr. Jack Kirkby caught me at it, too, half an hour ago."

His lordship's senses had not even now quite returned. He still stared at them innocently like a child, cleared his throat once or twice, and finally stood up.

"Jack Kirkby, so it is! How do, Jack? And Jenny?

"That's who we are," said Jenny. "Are you sure you're quite recovered?"

"Recovered! Eh—!" (He emitted a short laugh.) "Sit down. There's chairs somewhere."

Jack hooked out a couple that were leaning folded against the low wall of yew beneath the window and set them down.

"Have a cigar, Jack?"

"No, thanks."

They were on good terms—these two. Jack shot really well, and was smart and deferential. Lord Talgarth asked no more than this from a young man.

"Well—what's the matter?"

Jack left it thoughtfully for Jenny to open the campaign. She did so very adroitly.

"Mr. Jack came over to see me," she said, "and I thought I couldn't entertain him better than by bringing him up to see you. You haven't such a thing as a cigarette, Lord Talgarth?"

He felt about in his pockets, drew out a case and pushed it across the table.

"Thanks," said Jenny; and then, without the faintest change of tone: "We've some news of Frank at last."

"Frank, eh? Have you? And what's the young cub at, now?"

"He's in trouble, as usual, poor boy!" remarked Jenny, genially. "He's very well, thank you, and sends you his love."

Lord Talgarth cast her a pregnant glance.

"Well, if he didn't, I'm sure he meant to," went on Jenny; "but I expect he forgot. You see, he's been in prison."

The old man jerked such a face at her, that even her nerve failed for an instant. Jack saw her put her cigarette up to her mouth with a hand that shook ever so slightly. And yet before the other could say one word she recovered herself.

"Please let me say it right out to the end first," she said. "No; please don't interrupt! Mr. Jack, give me the letter ... oh! I've got it." (She drew it out and began to unfold it, talking all the while with astonishing smoothness and self-command.) "And I'll read you all the important part. It's written to Mr. Kirkby. He got it this morning and very kindly brought it straight over here at once."

Jack was watching like a terrier. On the one side he saw emotions so furious and so conflicting that they could find no expression, and on the other a restraint and a personality so complete and so compelling that they simply held the field and permitted no outburst. Her voice was cool and high and natural. Then he noticed her flick a glance at himself, sideways, and yet perfectly intelligible. He stood up.

"Yes, do just take a stroll, Mr. Kirkby.... Come back in ten minutes."

And as he passed out again through the thick archway on to the terrace he heard, in an incredibly matter-of-fact voice, the letter begin.

"Dear Jack...."

Then he began to wonder what, as a matter of interest, Lord Talgarth's first utterance would be. But he felt he could trust Jenny to manage him. She was an astonishingly sane and sensible girl.

(III)

He was at the further end of the terrace, close beneath the stable wall, when the stable clock struck the quarter for the second time. That would make, he calculated, about seventeen minutes, and he turned reluctantly to keep his appointment. But he was still thirty yards away from the opening when a white figure in a huge white hat came quickly out. She beckoned to him with her head, and he followed her down the steps. She gave him one glance as if to reassure him as he caught her up, but said not a word, good or bad, till they had passed through the house again, and were well on their way down the drive.

"Well?" said Jack.

Jenny hesitated a moment.

"I suppose anyone else would have called him violent," she said. "Poor old dear! But it seems to me he behaved rather well on the whole—considering all things."

"What's he going to do?"

"If one took anything he said as containing any truth at all, it would mean that he was going to flog Frank with his own hands, kick him first up the steps of the house then down again, and finally drown him in the lake with a stone round his neck. I think that was the sort of programme."

"But—"

"Oh! we needn't be frightened," said Jenny. "But if you ask me what he will do, I haven't the faintest idea."

"Did you suggest anything?"

"He knows what my views are," said jenny.

"And those?"

"Well—make him a decent allowance and let him alone."

"He won't do that!" said Jack. "That's far too sensible."

"You think so?"

"That would solve the whole problem, of course," went on Jack, "marriage and everything. I suppose it would have to be about eight hundred a year. And Talgarth must have at least thirty thousand."

"Oh! he's more than that," said Jenny. "He gives Mr. Dick twelve hundred."

There was a pause. Jack did not know what to think. He was only quite certain that the thing would have been far worse if he had attempted to manage it himself.

"Well, what shall I say to Frank?" he asked. Jenny paused again.

"It seems to me the best thing for you to do is not to write. I'll write myself this evening, if you'll give me his address, and explain—"

"I can't do that," said Jack. "I'm awfully sorry, but—"

"You can't give me his address?"

"No, I'm afraid I mustn't. You see, Frank's very particular in his letter...."

"Then how can I write to him? Mr. Kirkby, you're really rather—"

"By George! I've got it!" cried Jack. "If you don't mind my waiting at the Rectory. Why shouldn't you write to him now, and let me take the letter away and post it? It'll go all the quicker, too, from Barham."

He glanced at her, wondering whether she were displeased. Her answer reassured him.

"That'll do perfectly," she said, "if you're sure you don't mind waiting."

The Rectory garden seemed more than ever a harbor from storm as they turned into it. The sun was a little lower now, and the whole lawn lay in shadow. As they came to the door she stopped.

"I think I'd better go and get it over," she said. "I can tell father all about it after you've gone. Will you go now and wait there?" She nodded towards the seat where they had sat together earlier.

But it was nearly an hour before she came out again, and a neat maid, in apron and cap, had come discreetly out with the tea-things, set them down and retired.

Jack had been thinking of a hundred things, which all centered round one—Frank. He had had a real shock this morning. It had been intolerable to think of Frank in prison, for even Jack could guess something of what that meant to him; and the tone of the letter had been so utterly unlike what he had been accustomed to from his friend. He would have expected a bubbling torrent of remarks—wise and foolish—full of personal descriptions and unkind little sketches. And, indeed, there had come this sober narration of facts and requests....

But in all this there was one deep relief—that it should be a girl like Jenny who was the heart of the situation. If she had been in the least little bit disturbed, who could tell what it would mean to Frank? For Frank, as he knew perfectly well, had a very deep heart indeed, and had enshrined Jenny in the middle of it. Any wavering or hesitation on her part would have meant misery to his friend. But now all was perfectly right, he reflected; and really, after all, it did not matter very much what Lord Talgarth said or did. Frank was a free agent; he was very capable and very lovable; it couldn't possibly be long before something turned up, and then, with Jenny's own money the two could manage very well. And Lord Talgarth could not live for ever; and Archie would do the right thing, even if his father didn't.

It was after half-past four before he looked up at a glint of white and saw Jenny standing at the drawing-room window. She stood there an instant with a letter in her hand; then she stepped over the low sill and came towards him across the grass, serene and dignified and graceful. Her head was bare again, and the great coils of her hair flashed suddenly as they caught a long horizontal ray from the west.

"Here it is," she said. "Will you direct it? I've told him everything."

Jack nodded.

"That's excellent!" he said. "It shall go to-night."

He glanced up at her and saw her looking at him with just the faintest wistfulness. He understood perfectly, he said to himself: she was still a little unhappy at not being allowed to send the letter herself. What a good girl she was!

"Have some tea before you go?" she said.

"Thanks. I'd better not. They'll be wondering what's happened to me."

As he shook hands he tried to put something of his sympathy into his look. He knew exactly how she was feeling, and he thought her splendidly brave. But she hardly met his eyes, and again he felt he knew why.

As he opened the garden gate beyond the house he turned once more to wave. But she was busy with the tea-things, and a black figure was advancing briskly upon her from the direction of the study end of the house.

Life had been a little difficult for the Major for the last fortnight or so. Not only was Frank's material and moral support lacking to him, but the calls upon him, owing to Gertie's extreme unreasonableness, had considerably increased. He had explained to her, over and over again, with a rising intensity each time, how unselfishly he had acted throughout, how his sole thought had been for her in his recent course of action. It would never have done, he explained pacifically, for a young man like Frank to have the responsibility of a young girl like Gertie on his hands, while he (the Major) was spending a fortnight elsewhere. And, in fact, even on the most economical grounds he had acted for the best, since it had been himself who had been charged in the matter of the tin of salmon, it would not have been a fortnight, but more like two months, during which the little community would have been deprived of his labor. He reminded her that Frank had had a clean record up to that time with the police....

But explanation had been fruitless. Gertie had even threatened a revelation of the facts of the case at the nearest police-station, and the Major had been forced to more manly tactics with her. He had not used a stick; his hands had served him very well, and in the course of his argument he had made a few insincere remarks on the mutual relations of Frank and Gertie that the girl remembered.

He had obtained a frugal little lodging in one of the small streets of York, down by the river—indeed looking straight on to it; and, for a wonder, five days' regular work at the unloading of a string of barges. The five days expired on the Saturday before Frank was expected, but he had several shillings in hand on the Sunday morning when Frank's letter arrived, announcing that he hoped to be with them again on Sunday night or Monday morning. Two letters, also, had arrived for his friend on the Sunday morning—one in a feminine handwriting and re-directed, with an old postmark of June, as well as one of the day before—he had held it up to the light and crackled it between his fingers, of course, upon receiving it—and the other an obvious bill—one postmark was Cambridge and the other Barham. He decided to keep them both intact. Besides, Gertie had been present at their delivery.

The Major spent, on the whole, an enjoyable Sunday. He lay in bed till a little after twelve o'clock, with a second-hand copy of the Sporting Times, and a tin of tobacco beside him. They dined at about one o'clock, and he managed to get a little spirit to drink with his meal. He had walked out—not very far—with Gertie in the afternoon, and had managed by representing himself as having walked seven miles—he was determined not to risk anything by foolishly cutting it too fine—to obtain a little more. They had tea about six, and ate, each of them, a kippered herring and some watercress. Then about seven o'clock Frank suddenly walked in and sat down.

"Give me something to eat and drink," he said.

He looked, indeed, extraordinarily strained and tired, and sat back on the upturned box by the fireplace as if in exhaustion. He explained presently when Gertie had cooked another herring, and he had drunk a slop-basinful of tea, that he had walked fasting since breakfast, but he said nothing about the priest. The Major with an air of great preciseness measured out half a finger of whisky and insisted, with the air of a paternal doctor, upon his drinking it immediately.

"And now a cigarette, for God's sake," said Frank. "By the way, I've got some work for to-morrow."

"That's first-rate, my boy," said the Major. "I've been working myself this week."

Frank produced his fourpence and laid it on the corner of the table.

"That's for supper and bed to-night," he said.

"Nonsense, my boy; put it back in your pocket."

"Kindly take that fourpence," remarked Frank. "You can add some breakfast to-morrow, if you like."

He related his adventures presently—always excepting the priest—and described how he had met a man at the gate of a builder's yard this evening as he came through York, who had promised him a day's job, and if things were satisfactory, more to follow.

"He seemed a decent chap," said Frank.

The Major and Gertie had not much to relate. They had left the market-town immediately after Frank's little matter in the magistrates' court, and had done pretty well, arriving in York ten days ago. They hardly referred to Frank's detention, though he saw Gertie looking at him once or twice in a curiously shy kind of way, and understood what was in her mind. But for very decency's sake the Major had finally to say something.

"By the way, my boy, I won't forget what you did for me and for my little woman here. I'm not a man of many words, but—"

"Oh! that's all right," said Frank sleepily. "You'll do as much for me one day."

The Major assented with fervor and moist eyes. It was not till Frank stood up to go to bed that anyone remembered the letters.

"By the way, there are two letters come for you," said the Major, hunting in the drawer of the table. Frank's bearing changed. He whisked round in an instant.

"Where are they?"

They were put into his hand. He looked at them carefully, trying to make out the postmark—turned them upside down and round, but he made no motion to open them.

"Where am I to sleep?" he said suddenly. "And can you spare a bit of candle?"

(And as he went upstairs, it must have been just about the time that the letter-box at Barham was cleared for the late Sunday post.)

Frank lay a long time awake in the dark that night, holding tight in his hand Jenny's letter, written to him in June. The bill he had not even troubled to open.

For the letter said exactly and perfectly just all those things which he most wished to hear, in the manner in which he wished to hear them. It laughed at him gently and kindly; it called him an extraordinarily silly boy; it said that his leaving Cambridge, and, above all, his manner of leaving it—Frank had added a postscript describing his adventure with the saddle and the policeman—were precisely what the writer would have expected of him; it made delightful and humorous reflections upon the need of Frank's turning over a new leaf—there was quite a page of good advice; and finally it gave him a charming description—just not over the line of due respect—of his father's manner of receiving the news, with extracts from some of the choicest remarks made upon that notable occasion. It occupied four closely-written pages, and if there were, running underneath it all, just the faintest taint of strain and anxiety, loyally concealed—well—that made the letter no less pleasant.

I have not said a great deal about what Jenny meant to Frank, just because he said so very little about her himself. She was, in fact, almost the only element in his variegated life upon which he had not been in the habit of pouring out torrential comments and reflections. His father and Archie were not at all spared in his conversation with his most intimate friends; in fact, he had been known, more than once, in a very select circle at Cambridge, to have conducted imaginary dialogues between those two on himself as their subject, and he could imitate with remarkable fidelity his Cousin Dick over a billiard-table. But he practically never mentioned Jenny; he had not even a photograph of her on his mantelpiece. And it very soon became known among his friends, when the news of his engagement leaked out through Jack, that it was not to be spoken of in his presence. He had preserved the same reticence, it may be remembered, about his religion.

And so Frank at last fell asleep on a little iron bedstead, just remembering that it was quite possible he might have another letter from her to-morrow, if Jack had performed his commission immediately. But he hardly expected to hear till Tuesday.

Gertie was up soon after five next morning to get breakfast for her men, since the Major had announced that he would go with Frank to see whether possibly there might not be a job for him too; and as soon as they had gone, very properly went to sleep again on the bed in the sitting-room.

Gertie had a strenuous time of it, in spite of the Major's frequently expressed opinion that women had no idea what work was. For, first, there was the almost unending labor of providing food and cooking it as well as possible; there was almost a standing engagement of mending and washing clothes; there were numerous arguments to be conducted, on terms of comparative equality, if possible, with landladies or farmers' wives—Gertie always wore a brass wedding-ring and showed it sometimes a little ostentatiously; and, finally, when the company was on the march, it was only fair that she should carry the heavier half of the luggage, in order to compensate for her life of luxury and ease at other times. Gertie, then, was usually dog-tired, and slept whenever she could get a chance.

It was nearly eight o'clock before she was awakened again by sharp knocking on her door; and on opening it, found the landlady' standing there, examining a letter with great attention. (It had already been held up to the light against the kitchen window.)

"For one of your folks, isn't it, Mrs.—er—" Gertie took it. It was written on excellent paper, and directed in a man's handwriting to Mr. Gregory:

"Thank you, Mrs.—er—" said Gertie.

Then she went back into her room, put the letter carefully away in the drawer of the table and set about her household business.

About eleven o'clock she stepped out for a little refreshment. She had, of course, a small private exchequer of her own, amounting usually to only a few pence, of which the Major knew nothing. This did not strike her as at all unfair; she only wondered gently sometimes at masculine innocence in not recognizing that such an arrangement was perfectly certain. She got into conversation with some elder ladies, who also had stepped out for refreshment, and had occasion, at a certain point, to lay her wedding-ring on the bar-counter for exhibition. So it was not until a little after twelve that she remembered the time and fled. She was not expecting her men home to dinner; in fact, she had wrapped up provisions for them in fragments of the Major's Sporting Times before they had left; but it was safer to be at home. One never knew.

As she came into the room, for an instant her heart leaped into her mouth, but it was only Frank.

"Whatever's the matter?" she said.

"Turned off," said Frank shortly. He was sitting gloomily at the table with his hands in his pockets.

"Turned off?"

He nodded.

"What's up?"

"'Tecs," said Frank.

Gertie's mouth opened a little.

"One of them saw me going in and wired for instructions. He had seen the case in the police-news and thought I answered to the description. Then he came back at eleven and told the governor."

"And—"

"Yes."

There was a pause.

"And George?"

"Oh! he's all right," said Frank a little bitterly. "There's nothing against him. Got any dinner, Gertie? I can't pay for it ... oh, yes, I can; here's half a day." (He chucked ninepence upon the table; the sixpence rolled off again, but he made no movement to pick it up.)

Gertie looked at him a moment.

"Well—" she began emphatically, then she stooped to pick up the sixpence.

Frank sighed.

"Oh! don't begin all that—there's a good girl. I've said it all myself—quite adequately, I assure you."

Gertie's mouth opened again. She laid the sixpence on the table.

"I mean, there's nothing to be said," explained Frank. "The point is—what's to be done?"

Gertie had no suggestions. She began to scrape out the frying-pan in which the herrings had been cooked last night.

"There's a letter for you," she said suddenly.

Frank sat up.

"Where?"

"In the drawer there—by your hand. Frankie...."

Frank tore at the handle and it came off. He uttered a short exclamation. Then, with infinite craft he fitted the handle in again, wrapped in yet one more scrap of the Sporting Times, and drew out the drawer. His face fell abruptly as he saw the handwriting.

"That can wait," he muttered, and chucked the letter face downwards on to the table.

"Frankie," said the girl again, still intent on her frying-pan.

"Well?"

"It's all my fault," she said in a low voice.

"Your fault! How do you make that out?"

"If it hadn't been for me, you wouldn't have taken the tin from George, and...."

"Oh, Lord!" said Frank, "if we once begin on that!... And if it hadn't been for George, he wouldn't have taken the tin; and if it hadn't been for Maggie Cooper, there wouldn't have been the tin; and if it hadn't been for Maggie's father's sister, she wouldn't have gone out with it. It's all Maggie's father's sister's fault, my dear! It's nothing to do with you."

The words were brisk enough, but the manner was very heavy. It was like repeating a lesson learned in childhood.

"That's all right," began Gertie again, "but—"

"My dear girl, I shall be annoyed if you go back to all that. Why can't you let it alone? The point is, What's to happen? I can't go on sponging on you and the Major."

Gertie flushed under her tan.

"If you ever leave us," she said, "I'll—"

"Well?"

"I'll ... I'll never leave George."

Frank was puzzled for a moment. It seemed a non sequitur.

"Do you mean—"

"I've got me eyes," said Gertie emphatically, "and I know what you're thinking, though you don't say much. And I've been thinking, too."

Frank felt a faint warmth rise in his own heart. "You mean you've been thinking over what I said the other day?"

Gertie bent lower over her frying-pan and scraped harder than ever.

"Do stop that confounded row one second!" shouted Frank.

The noise stopped abruptly. Gertie glanced up and down again. Then she began again, more gently.

"That's better," said Frank.... "Well, I hope you have," he went on paternally. "You're a good girl, Gertie, and you know better. Go on thinking about it, and tell me when you've made up your mind. When'll dinner be ready?"

"Half an hour," said Gertie.

"Well, I'll go out for a bit and look round."

He took up the letter carelessly and went out.

As he passed the window Gertie glanced towards it with the corner of her eye. Then, frying-pan still in hand, she crept up to the angle and watched him go down the quay.

A very convenient barrel was set on the extreme edge of the embankment above the water, with another beside it, and Frank made for this immediately. She saw him sit on one of the barrels and put the letter, still unopened, on the top of the other. Then he fumbled in his pockets a little, and presently a small blue cloud of smoke went upwards like incense. Gertie watched him for an instant, but he did not move again. Then she went back to her frying-pan.

Twenty minutes later dinner was almost ready.

Gertie had spread upon the table, with great care, one of the Major's white pocket-handkerchiefs. He insisted upon those being, not only retained, but washed occasionally, and Gertie understood something of his reasons, since in the corner of each was embroidered a monogram, of which the letters were not "G.T." But she never could make out what they were.

Upon this tablecloth she had placed on one side a black-handled fork with two prongs, and a knife of the same pattern (this was for Frank) and on the other a small pewter tea-spoon and a knife, of which the only handle was a small iron spike from which the wood had fallen away. (This was for herself.) Then there was a tooth-glass for Frank, and a teacup—without a handle, but with a gold flower in the middle of it, to make up—for herself. In the center of the pocket-handkerchief stood a crockery jug, with a mauve design of York Minster, with a thundercloud behind it and a lady and gentleman with a child bowling a hoop in front of it. This was the landlady's property, and was half full of beer. Besides all this, there were two plates, one of a cold blue color, with a portrait of the Prince Consort, whiskers and hat complete, in a small medallion in the center, and the other white, with a representation of the Falls of Lodore. There was no possibility of mistaking any of the subjects treated upon these various pieces of table-ware, since the title of each was neatly printed, in various styles, just below the picture.

Gertie regarded this array with her head on one side. It was not often that they dined in such luxury. She wished she had a flower to put in the center. Then she stirred the contents of the frying-pan with an iron spoon, and went again to the window.

The figure on the barrel had not moved; but even as she looked she saw him put out his hand to the letter. She watched him. She saw him run a finger inside the envelope, and toss the envelope over the edge of the quay. Then she saw him unfold the paper inside and become absorbed.

This would never do. Gertie's idea of a letter was that it occupied at least several minutes to read through; so she went out quickly to the street door to call him in.

She called him, and he did not turn his head, nor even answer.

She called him again.

(IV)

The letter that Frank read lies, too, with a few other papers, before me as I write.
It runs as follows:

"My Dear Frank,

"I know you won't like what I have to say, but it has to be said. Believe me, it costs me as much to write as you to read—perhaps more.

"It is this: Our engagement must be at an end.

"You have a perfect right to ask me for reasons, so I will give them at once, as I don't want to open the subject again. It would do no kind of good. My mind is absolutely made up.

"My main reason is this: When I became engaged to you I did not know you properly. I thought you were quite different from what you are. I thought that underneath all your nice wildness, and so on, there was a very solid person. And I hinted that, you will remember, in my first letter, which I suppose you have received just before this. And now I simply can't think that any longer.

"I don't in the least blame you for being what you are: that's not my business. But I must just say this—that a man who can do what you've done, not only for a week or two, as I thought at first, as a sort of game, but for nearly three months, and during that time could leave me with only three or four postcards and no news; above all, a man who could get into such disgrace and trouble, and actually go to prison, and yet not seem to mind much—well, it isn't what I had thought of you.

"You see, there are a whole lot of things together. It isn't just this or that, but the whole thing.

"First you became a Catholic, without telling me anything until just before. I didn't like that, naturally, but I didn't say anything. It isn't nice for a husband and wife to be of different religions. Then you ran away from Cambridge; then you got mixed up with this man you speak of in your letter to Jack; and you must have been rather fond of him, you know, to go to prison for him, as I suppose you did. And yet, after all that, I expect you've gone to meet him again in York. And then there's the undeniable fact of prison.

"You see, it's all these things together—one after another. I have defended you to your father again and again; I haven't allowed anybody to abuse you without standing up for you; but it really has gone too far. You know I did half warn you in that other letter. I know you couldn't have got it till just now, but that wasn't my fault; and the letter shows what I was thinking, even three months ago.

"Don't be too angry with me, Frank. I'm very fond of you still, and I shall always stand up for you when I can. And please don't answer this in any way. Jack Kirkby isn't answering just yet. I asked him not, though he doesn't know why.

"Your father is going to send the news that the engagement is broken off to the newspapers.

"Yours sincerely, "Jenny Launton."

Barham, as all Yorkshire knows, lies at the foot of a long valley, where it emerges into the flatter district round Harrogate. It has a railway all to itself, which goes no further, for Barham is shut in on the north by tall hills and moors, and lies on the way to nowhere. It is almost wholly an agricultural town, and has a curious humped bridge, right in the middle of the town, where men stand about on market days and discuss the price of bullocks. It has two churches—one, disused, on a precipitous spur above the town, surrounded by an amazingly irregular sort of churchyard, full, literally, to bursting (the Kirkbys lie there, generation after generation of them, beneath pompous tombs), and the other church a hideous rectangular building, with flat walls and shallow, sham Gothic windows. It was thought extremely beautiful when it was built forty years ago. The town itself is an irregular and rather picturesque place, with a twisting steep High Street, looking as if a number of houses had been shot at random into this nook among the hills and left to find their own levels.

The big house where the Kirkbys have lived since the middle of the seventeenth century is close to the town, as the squire's house ought to be, and its park gates open right upon the northern end of the old bridge. There's nothing of great interest in the house (I believe there is an old doorway in the cellar, mentioned in guide-books), since it was rebuilt about the same time as the new church first rose. It is just a big, comfortable, warm, cool, shady sort of house, with a large hall and a fine oak staircase, surrounded by lawns and shrubberies, that adjoin on the west the lower slopes, first of the park and then of the moors that stretch away over the horizon.

There is a pleasant feudal air about the whole place—feudal, in a small and neighborly kind of way. Jack's father died just a year before his only son came of age; and Jack himself, surrounded by sisters and an excellent and beneficently-minded mother, has succeeded to all the immemorial rights and powers, written and unwritten, of the Squire of Barham. He entertained me delightfully for three or four days a few months ago, when I was traveling about after Frank's footsteps, and I noticed with pleasure as we drove through the town that there was hardly a living creature in the town whom he did not salute; and who did not salute him.

He took me first to the bridge and pulled up in the middle of it, to point out a small recess in it, over the central pier, intended, no doubt, to give shelter to foot-passengers before the bridge was widened, in case a large vehicle came through.

"There," he said. "That's the place I first saw Frank when he came."

We drove on up through the town, and at the foot of the almost precipitous hill leading up to the ruined church we got out, leaving the dog-cart in charge of the groom. We climbed the hill slowly, for it was a hot day, Jack uttering reminiscences at intervals (many of which are recorded in these pages) and turned in at the churchyard gate.

"And this was the place," said Jack, "where I said good-by to him."

(II)

It was on the twenty-fifth of September, a Monday, that Jack sat in the smoking-room, in Norfolk jacket and gaiters, drinking tea as fast as he possibly could. He had been out on the moors all day, and was as thirsty as the moors could make him, and he had been sensual enough to smoke a cigarette deliberately before beginning tea, in order to bring his thirst to an acute point.

Then, the instant he had finished he snatched for his case again, for this was to be the best cigarette of the whole day, and discovered that his sensuality had overreached itself for once, and that there were none left. He clutched at the silver box with a sinking heart, half-remembering that he had filled his case with the last of them this morning. It was a fact, and he knew that there were no others in the house.

This would never do, and he reflected that if he sent a man for some more, he would not get them for at least twenty minutes. (Jack never could understand why an able-bodied footman always occupied twenty minutes in a journey that ought to take eight.) So he put on his cap again, stepped out of the low window and set off down the drive.

It was getting a little dark as he passed out of the lodge-gates. The sun, of course, had set at least an hour before behind the great hill to the west, but the twilight proper was only just beginning. He was nearly at the place now, and as he breasted the steep ascent of the bridge, peered over it, at least with his mind's eye, at the tobacconist's shop—first on the left—where a store of "Mr. Jack's cigarettes" was always on hand.

He noticed in the little recess I have just spoken of a man leaning with his elbows on the parapet, and staring out up the long reach of the stream to the purple evening moors against the sky and the luminous glory itself; and as he came opposite him, wondered vaguely who it was and whether he knew him. Then, as he got just opposite him, he stopped, uneasy at heart.

Naturally Frank was never very far away from Jack's thoughts just now—ever since, indeed, he had heard the news in a very discreet letter from the Reverend James Launton a week or two ago. (I need not say he had answered this letter, not to the father, but to the daughter, but had received no reply.)

He had written a frantic letter to Frank himself then, but it had been returned, marked: "Unknown at this address." And ever since he had eyed all tramps on the road with an earnestness that elicited occasionally a salute, and occasionally an impolite remark.

The figure whose back he saw now certainly was not much like Frank; but then—again—it was rather like him. It was dressed in a jacket and trousers so stained with dust and wet as to have no color of their own at all, and a cloth cap of the same appearance. A bundle tied up in a red handkerchief, and a heavy stick, rested propped against an angle of the recess.

Jack cleared his throat rather loud and stood still, prepared to be admiring the view, in case of necessity; the figure turned an eye over its shoulder, then faced completely round; and it was Frank Guiseley.

Jack for the first instant said nothing at all, but stood transfixed, with his mouth a little open and his eyes staring. Frank's face was sunburned almost beyond recognition, his hair seemed cut shorter than usual, and the light was behind him.

Then Jack recovered.

"My dear man," he said, "why the—"

He seized him by the hands and held him, staring at him.

"Yes; it's me all right," said Frank. "I was just wondering—"

"Come along, instantly.... Damn! I've got to go to a tobacconist's; it's only just here. There isn't a cigarette in the house. Come with me?"

"I'll wait here," said Frank.

"Will you? I shan't be a second."

It was, as a matter of fact, scarcely one minute before Jack was back; he had darted in, snatched a box from the shelf and vanished, crying out to "put it down to him." He found Frank had faced round again and was staring at the water and sky and high moors. He snatched up his friend's bundle and stick.

"Come along," he said, "we shall have an hour or two before dinner."

Frank, in silence, took the bundle and stick from him again, firmly and irresistibly, and they did not speak again till they were out of ear-shot of the lodge. Then Jack began, taking Frank's arm—a custom for which he had often been rebuked.

"My dear old man!" he said. "I ... I can't say what I feel. I know the whole thing, of course, and I've expressed my mind plainly to Miss Jenny."

"Yes?"

"And to your father. Neither have answered, and naturally I haven't been over again.... Dick's been there, by the way."

Frank made no comment.

"You look simply awful, old chap," pursued Jack cheerily. "Where on earth have you been for the last month? I wrote to York and got the letter returned."

"Oh! I've been up and down," said Frank impassively.

"With the people you were with before—the man, I mean?"

"No. I've left them for the present. But I shall probably join them again later."

"Join...!" began the other aghast.

"Certainly! This thing's only just begun," said Frank, with that same odd impassivity. "We've seen the worst of it, I fancy."

"But you don't mean you're going back! Why, it's ridiculous!"

Frank stopped. They were within sight of the house now and the lights shone pleasantly out.

"By the way, Jack, I quite forgot. You will kindly give me your promise to make no sort of effort to detain me when I want to go again, or I shan't come any further."

"But, my dear chap—"

"Kindly promise at once, please."

"Oh, well! I promise, but—"

"That's all right," said Frank, and moved on.

"I say," said Jack, as they came up to the hall door. "Will you talk now or will you change, or what?"

"I should like a hot bath first. By the way, have you anyone staying in the house?"

"Not a soul; and only two sisters at home. And my mother, of course."

"What about clothes?"

"I'll see about that. Come on round to the smoking-room window. Then I'll get in Jackson and explain to him. I suppose you don't mind your name being known? He'll probably recognize you, anyhow."

"Not in the least, so long as no one interferes."

Jack rang the bell as soon as they came into the smoking-room, and Frank sat down in a deep chair. Then the butler came. He cast one long look at the astonishing figure in the chair.

"Oh!—er—Jackson, this is Mr. Frank Guiseley. He's going to stay here. He'll want some clothes and things. I rather think there are some suits of mine that might do. I wish you'd look them out."

"I beg your pardon, sir?"

"This is Mr. Frank Guiseley—of Merefield.... It is, really! But we don't want more people talking than are necessary. You understand? Please don't say anything about it, except that he's come on a walking-tour. And please tell the housekeeper to get the Blue Room ready, and let somebody turn on the hot water in the bath-room until further notice. That's all, Jackson ... and the clothes. You understand?"

"Yes, sir."

"And get the eau de lubin from my dressing-room and put it in the bath-room. Oh, yes; and the wooden bowl of soap."

"These clothes of mine are not to be thrown away, please, Jackson," said Frank gravely from the chair. "I shall want them again."

"Yes, sir."

"That's all, then," said Jack.

Mr. Jackson turned stiffly and left the room.

"It's all right," said Jack. "You remember old Jackson. He won't say a word. Lucky no one saw us as we came up."

"It doesn't matter much, does it?" said Frank.

There was a pause.

"I say, Frank, when will you tell me—"

"I'll answer any questions after dinner to-night. I simply can't talk now."

Dinner was a little difficult that night.

Mrs. Kirkby had been subjected to a long lecture from her son during the half hour in which she ought to have been dressing, in order to have it firmly implanted in her mind that Frank— whom she had known from a boy—was simply and solely in the middle of a walking-tour all by himself. She understood the situation perfectly in a minute and a half—(she was a very shrewd woman who did not say much)—but Jack was not content. He hovered about her room, fingering photographs and silver-handled brushes, explaining over and over again how important it was that Frank should be made to feel at his ease, and that Fanny and Jill—(who were just old enough to come to dinner in white high-necked frocks that came down to their very slender ankles, and thick pig-tails down their backs)—must not be allowed to bother him. Mrs. Kirkby said, "Yes, I understand," about a hundred and thirty times, and glanced at the clock. She stood with one finger on the electric button for at least five minutes before venturing to ring for her maid, and it was only that lady's discreet tap at one minute before eight that finally got Jack out of the room. He looked in on Frank in the middle of his dressing, found to his relief that an oldish suit of dress-clothes fitted him quite decently, and then went to put on his own. He came down to the drawing-room seven minutes after the gong with his ears very red and his hair in a plume, to find Frank talking to his mother, and eyed by his sisters who were pretending to look at photographs, with all the ease in the world.

But dinner itself was difficult. It was the obvious thing to talk about Frank's "walking-tour"; and yet this was exactly what Jack dared not do. The state of the moors, and the deplorable ravages made among the young grouse by the early rains, occupied them all to the end of fish; to the grouse succeeded the bullocks: to the bullocks, the sheep, and, by an obvious connection— obvious to all who knew that gentleman—from the sheep to the new curate.

But just before the chocolate soufflée there came a pause, and Jill, the younger of the two sisters, hastened to fill the gap.

"Did you have a nice walking-tour, Mr. Guiseley?"

Frank turned to her politely.

"Yes, very nice, considering," he said.

"Have you been alone all the time?" pursued Jill, conscious of a social success.

"Well, no," said Frank. "I was traveling with a ... well, with a man who was an officer in the army. He was a major."

"And did you—"

"That's enough, Jill," said her mother decidedly. "Don't bother Mr. Guiseley. He's tired with his walk."

The two young men sat quiet for a minute or two after the ladies had left the room. Then Jack spoke.

"Well?" he said.

Frank looked up. There was an odd, patient kind of look in his eyes that touched Jack a good deal. Frank had not been distinguished for submissiveness hitherto.

"Oh! a bit later, if you don't mind," he said. "We can talk in the smoking-room."

(IV)

"Well, I'll tell you the whole thing as far as I understand it," began Frank, as the door closed behind Jackson, who had brought whisky and candles. "And then I'll answer any questions you want."

He settled himself back in his chair, stretching out his legs and clasping his hands behind his head. Jack had a good view of him and could take notice of his own impressions, though he found them hard to put into words afterwards. The words he finally chose were "subdued" and "patient" again, and there are hardly two words that would have been less applicable to Frank three months before. At the same time his virility was more noticeable than ever; he had about him, Jack said, something of the air of a very good groom—a hard-featured and sharp, yet not at all unkindly look, very capable and, at the same time, very much restrained. There was no sentimental nonsense about him at all—his sorrow had not taken that form.

"Well, I needn't talk much about Jenny's last letter and what happened after that. I was entirely unprepared, of course. I hadn't the faintest idea—Well, she was the one person about whom I had no doubts at all! I actually left the letter unread for a few minutes (the envelope was in your handwriting, you know)—because I had to think over what I had to do next. The police had got me turned away from a builder's yard—"

Jack emitted a small sound. He was staring at Frank with all his eyes.

"Yes; that's their way," said Frank. "Well, when I read it, I simply couldn't think any more at all for a time. The girl we were traveling with—she had picked up with the man I had got into trouble over, you know—the girl was calling me to dinner, she told me afterwards. I didn't hear a sound. She came and touched me at last, and I woke up. But I couldn't say anything. They don't even now know what's the matter. I came away that afternoon. I couldn't even wait for the Major—"

"Eh?"

"The Major.... Oh! that's what the chap calls himself. I don't think he's lying, either. I simply couldn't stand him another minute just then. But I sent them a postcard that night—I forget where from; and—There aren't any letters for me, are there?"

"One or two bills."

"Oh! well, I shall hear soon, I expect. I must join them again in a day or two. They're somewhere in this direction, I know."

"And what did you do?"

Frank considered.

"I'm not quite sure. I know I walked a great deal. People were awfully good to me. One woman stopped her motor—and I hadn't begged, either—"

"You! Begged!"

"Lord, yes; lots of times.... Well, she gave me a quid, and I didn't even thank her. And that lasted me very well, and I did a little work too, here and there."

"But, good Lord! what did you do?"

"I walked. I couldn't bear towns or people or anything. I got somewhere outside of Ripon at last, and went out on to the moors. I found an old shepherd's hut for about a week or ten days—"

"And you—"

"Lived there? Yes. I mended the hut thoroughly before I came away. And then I thought I'd come on here."

"What were you doing on the bridge?"

"Waiting till dark. I was going to ask at the lodge then whether you were at home."

"And if I hadn't been?"

"Gone on somewhere else, I suppose."

Jack tried to help himself to a whisky and soda, but the soda flew out all over his shirt-front like a fountain, and he was forced to make a small remark. Then he made another.

"What about prison?"

Frank smiled.

"Oh! I've almost forgotten that. It was beastly at the time, though."

"And ... and the Major and the work! Lord! Frank, you do tell a story badly."

He smiled again much more completely.

"I'm too busy inside," he said. "Those things don't seem to matter much, somehow."

"Inside? What the deuce do you mean?"

Frank made a tiny deprecating gesture.

"Well, what it's all about, you know ... Jack."

"Yes."

"It's a frightfully priggish thing to say, but I'm extraordinarily interested as to what's going to happen next—inside, I mean. At least, sometimes; and then at other times I don't care a hang."

Jack looked bewildered, and said so tersely. Frank leaned forward a little.

"It's like this, you see. Something or other has taken me in hand: I'm blessed if I know what. All these things don't happen one on the top of the other just by a fluke. There's something going on, and I want to know what it is. And I suppose something's going to happen soon."

"For God's sake do say what you mean!"

"I can't more than that. I tell you I don't know. I only wish somebody could tell me."

"But what does it all amount to? What are you going to do next?"

"Oh! I know that all right. I'm going to join the Major and Gertie again."

"Frank!"

"Yes?... No, not a word, please. You promised you wouldn't. I'm going to join those two again and see what happens."

"But why?"

"That's my job. I know that much. I've got to get that girl back to her people again. She's not his wife, you know."

"But what the devil—"

"It seems to me to matter a good deal. Oh! she's a thoroughly stupid girl, and he's a proper cad; but that doesn't matter. It's got to be done; or, rather, I've got to try to do it. I daresay I shan't succeed, but that, again, doesn't matter. I've got to do my job, and then we'll see."

Jack threw up his hands.

"You're cracked!" he said.

"I daresay," said Frank solemnly.

There was a pause. It seemed to Jack that the whole thing must be a dream. This simply wasn't Frank at all. The wild idea came to him that the man who sat before him with Frank's features was some kind of changeling. Mentally he shook himself.

"And what about Jenny?" he said.

Frank sat perfectly silent and still for an instant. Then he spoke without heat.

"I'm not quite sure," he said. "Sometimes I'd like to ... well, to make her a little speech about what she's done, and sometimes I'd like to crawl to her and kiss her feet—but both those things are when I'm feeling bad. On the whole, I think—though I'm not sure—that is not my business any more; in fact, I'm pretty sure it's not. It's part of the whole campaign and out of my hands. It's no good talking about that any more. So please don't, Jack."

"One question?"

"Well?"

"Have you written to her or sent her a message?"

"No."

"And I want to say one other thing. I don't think it's against the bargain."

"Well?"

"Will you take five hundred pounds and go out to the colonies?"

Frank looked up with an amused smile.

"No, I won't—thanks very much.... Am I in such disgrace as all that, then?"

"You know I don't mean that," said Jack quietly.

"No, old chap. I oughtn't to have said that. I'm sorry."

Jack waved a hand.

"I thought perhaps you'd loathe England, and would like—And you don't seem absolutely bursting with pride, you know."

"Honestly, I don't think I am," said Frank. "But England suits me very well—and there are the other two, you know. But I'll tell you one thing you could do for me."

"Yes?"

"Pay those extra bills. I don't think they're much."

"That's all right," said Jack. "And you really mean to go on with it all?"

"Why, yes."

The moors had been pretty well shot over already since the twelfth of August, but the two had a very pleasant day, for all that, a couple of days later. They went but with a keeper and half a dozen beaters—Frank in an old homespun suit of Jack's, and his own powerful boots, and made a very tolerable bag. There was one dramatic moment, Jack told me, when they found that luncheon had been laid at a high point on the hills from which the great gray mass of Merefield and the shimmer of the lake in front of the house were plainly visible only eight miles away. The flag was flying, too, from the flagstaff on the old keep, showing, according to ancient custom, that Lord Talgarth was at home. Frank looked at it a minute or two with genial interest, and Jack wondered whether he had noticed, as he himself had, that even the Rectory roof could be made out, just by the church tower at the foot of the hill.

Neither said anything, but as the keeper came up to ask for orders as they finished lunch, he tactfully observed that there was a wonderful fine view of Merefield.

"Yes," said Frank, "you could almost make out people with a telescope."

The two were walking together alone as they dropped down, an hour before sunset, on to the upper end of Barham. They were both glowing with the splendid air and exercise, and were just in that state of weariness that is almost unmixed physical pleasure to an imaginative thinker who contemplates a hot bath, a quantity of tea, and a long evening in a deep chair. Frank still preserved his impassive kind of attitude towards things in general, but Jack noticed with gentle delight that he seemed more off his guard, and that he even walked with something more of an alert swing than he had on that first evening when they trudged up the drive together.

Their road led them past the gate of the old churchyard, and as they approached it, dropping their feet faster and faster down the steep slope, Jack noticed two figures sitting on the road-side, with their feet in the ditch—a man and a girl. He was going past them, just observing that the man had rather an unpleasant face, with a ragged mustache, and that the girl was sunburned, fair-haired and rather pretty, when he became aware that Frank had slipped behind him. The next instant he saw that Frank was speaking to them, and his heart dropped to zero.

"All right," he heard Frank say, "I was expecting you. This evening, then.... I say, Jack!"

Jack turned.

"Jack, this is Major and Mrs. Trustcott, I told you of. This is my friend, Mr.—er—Mr. Jack."

Jack bowed vaguely, overwhelmed with disgust.

"Very happy to make your acquaintance, sir," said the Major, straightening himself in a military manner. "My good lady and I were resting here. Very pleasant neighborhood."

"I'm glad you like it," said Jack.

"Then, this evening," said Frank again. "Can you wait an hour or two?"

"Certainly, my boy," said the Major. "Time's no consideration with us, as you know."

(Jack perceived that this was being said at him, to show the familiarity this man enjoyed with his friend.)

"Would nine o'clock be too late?"

"Nine o'clock it shall be," said the Major.

"And here?"

"Here."

"So long, then," said Frank. "Oh, by the way—" He moved a little closer to this appalling pair, and Jack stood off, to hear the sound of a sentence or two, and then the chink of money.

"So long, then," said Frank again. "Come along, Jack; we must make haste."

"Good-evening, sir," cried the Major, but Jack made no answer.

"Frank, you don't mean to tell me that those are the people?"

"That's the Major and Gertie—yes."

"And what was all that about this evening?"

"I must go, Jack. I'm sorry; but I told you it couldn't be more than a few days at the outside."

Jack was silent, but it was a hard struggle.

"By the way, how shall we arrange?" went on the other. "I can't take these clothes, you know; and I can't very well be seen leaving the house in my own."

"Do as you like," snapped Jack.

"Look here, old man, don't be stuffy. How would it do if I took a bag and changed up in that churchyard? It's locked up after dark, isn't it?"

"Yes."

"You've got a key, I suppose?"

"Yes."

"Well, then, that's it. And I'll leave the bag and the key in the hedge somewhere."

Jack was silent.

Jack held himself loyally in hand that evening, but he could not talk much. He consented to explain to his mother that Frank had to be off after dinner that night, and he also visited the housekeeper's room, and caused a small bundle, not much larger than a leg of mutton, including two small bottles which jingled together, to be wrapped up in brown paper—in which he inserted also a five-pound note (he knew Frank would not take more)—and the whole placed in the bag in which Frank's old clothes were already concealed. For the rest of the evening he sat, mostly silent, in one chair, trying not to watch Frank in another; pretending to read, but endeavoring to picture to his imagination what he himself would feel like if he were about to join the Major and Gertie in the churchyard at nine o'clock.... Frank sat quite quiet all the evening, reading old volumes of Punch.

They dined at half-past seven, by request—Frank still in his homespun suit. Fanny and Jill were rather difficult. It seemed to them both a most romantic thing that this black-eyed, sunburned young man, with whom they had played garden-golf the day before, should really be continuing his amazing walking-tour, in company with two friends, at nine o'clock that very night. They wondered innocently why the two friends had not been asked to join them at dinner. It was exciting, too, and unusual, that this young man should dine in an old homespun suit. They asked a quantity of questions. Where was Mr. Guiseley going first? Frank didn't quite know; Where would he sleep that night? Frank didn't quite know; he would have to see. When was the walking-tour going to end? Frank didn't quite know. Did he really like it? Oh, well, Frank thought it was a good thing to go on a walking tour, even if you were rather uncomfortable sometimes.

The leave-taking was unemotional. Jack had announced suddenly and loudly in the smoking-room before dinner that he was going to see the last of Frank, as far as the churchyard; Frank had protested, but had yielded. The rest had all said good-by to him in the hall, and at a quarter to nine the two young men went out into the darkness.

(VI)

It was a clear autumn night—a "wonderful night of stars"—and the skies blazed softly overhead down to the great blotted masses of the high moors that stood round Barham. It was perfectly still, too—the wind had dropped, and the only sound as the two walked down the park was the low talking of the stream over the stones beyond the belt of trees fifty yards away from the road.

Jack was sick at heart; but even so, he tells me, he was conscious that Frank's silence was of a peculiar sort. He felt somehow as if his friend were setting out to some great sacrifice in which he was to suffer, and was only partly conscious of it—or, at least, so buoyed by some kind of exaltation or fanaticism as not to realize what he was doing. (He reminded me of a certain kind of dream that most people have now and then, of accompanying some friend to death: the friend goes forward, silent and exultant, and we cannot explain nor hold him back.

"That was the sort of feeling," said Jack lamely.)

Jack had the grim satisfaction of carrying the bag in which, so to speak, the knife and fillet were hidden. He changed his mood half a dozen times even in that quarter of an hour's walk through the town. Now the thing seemed horrible, like a nightmare; now absurdly preposterous; now rather beautiful; now perfectly ordinary and commonplace. After all, Jack argued with himself, there are such people as tramps, and they survive. Why should not Frank? He had gipsy blood in him, too. What in the world was he—Jack—frightened of?

"Do you remember our talking about your grandmother?" he said suddenly, as they neared the lodge.

"Yes. Why?"

"Only I've just thought of something else. Wasn't one of your people executed under Elizabeth?"

"By gad, yes; so he was. I'd quite forgotten. It was being on the wrong side for once."

"How—the wrong side?"

There was amusement in Frank's voice as he answered.

"It was for religion," he said. "He was a Papist. All the rest of them conformed promptly. They were a most accommodating lot. They changed each time without making any difficulty. I remember my governor telling us about it once. He thought them very sensible. And so they were, by George! from one point of view."

"Has your religion anything to do with all this?"

"Oh, I suppose so," said Frank, with an indifferent air.

There were a good many doors open in the High Street as they went up it, and Jack saluted half a dozen people mechanically as they touched their hats to him as he passed in the light from the houses.

"What does it feel like being squire?" asked Frank.

"Oh, I don't know," said Jack.

"Rather good fun, I should think," said Frank.

They were nearing the steep part of the ascent presently, and the church clock struck nine.

"Bit late," said Frank.

"When will you come again?" asked the other suddenly. "I'm here another fortnight, you know, and then at Christmas again. Come for Christmas if you can."

"Ah! I don't know where I shall be. Give my love to Cambridge, though."

"Frank!"

"Yes?"

"Mayn't I say what I think?"

"No!"

Ah! there was the roof of the old church standing out against the stars, and there could be no more talking. They might come upon the other two at any moment now. They went five steps further, and there, in the shadow of the gate, burned a dull red spot of fire, that kindled up as they looked, and showed for an instant the heavy eyes of the Major with a pipe in his mouth.

"Good-evening, sir," came the military voice, and the girl rose to her feet beside him. "You're just in time."

"Good-evening," said Jack dully.

"We've had a pleasant evening of it up here, Mr. Kirkby, after we'd stepped down and had a bit of supper at the 'Crown.'"

"I suppose you heard my name there," said Jack.

"Quite right, sir."

"Give us the key," said Frank abruptly.

He unlocked the door and pushed it back over the grass-grown gravel.

"Wait for me here, will you?" he said to Jack.

"I'm coming in. I'll show you where to change."

Twenty yards of an irregular twisted path, over which they stumbled two or three times, led them down to the little ruined doorway at the west end of the old church. Jack's father had restored the place admirably, so far as restoration was possible, and there stood now, strong as ever, the old tower, roofed and floored throughout, abutting on the four roofless walls, within which ran the double row of column bases.

Jack struck a light, kindled a bicycle lamp he had brought with him, and led the way.

"Come in here," he said.

Frank followed him into the room at the base of the tower and looked round.

"This looks all right," he said. "It was a Catholic church once, I suppose?"

"Yes; the parson says this was the old sacristy. They've found things here, I think—cupboards in the wall, and so on."

"This'll do excellently," said Frank. "I shan't be five minutes."

Jack went out again without a word. He felt it was a little too much to expect him to see the change actually being made, and the garments of sacrifice put on. (It struck him with an unpleasant shock, considering the form of his previous metaphor, that he should have taken Frank into the old sacristy.)

He sat down on the low wall, built to hold the churchyard from slipping altogether down the hill-side, and looked out over the little town below.

The sky was more noticeable here; one was more conscious of the enormous silent vault, crowded with the steady stars, cool and aloof; and, beneath, of the feverish little town with sparks of red light dotted here and there, where men wrangled and planned and bargained, and carried on the little affairs of their little life with such astonishing zest. Jack was far from philosophical as a rule, but it is a fact that meditations of this nature did engross him for a minute or two while he sat and waited for Frank, and heard the low voices talking in the lane outside. It even occurred to him for an instant that it was just possible that what Frank had said in the smoking-room before dinner was true, and that Something really did have him in hand, and really, did intend a definite plan and result to emerge from this deplorable and quixotic nonsense. (I suppose the contrast of stars and human lights may have helped to suggest this sort of thing to him.)

Then he gave himself up again to dismal considerations of a more particular kind.

He heard Frank come out, and turned to see him in the dim light, bag in hand, dressed again as he had been three days ago. On his head once more was the indescribable cap; on his body the indescribable clothes. He wore on his feet the boots in which he had tramped the moors that day. (How far away seemed that afternoon now, and the cheerful lunch in the sunshine on the hill-top!)

"Here I am, Jack."

Then every promise went to the winds. Jack stood up and took a step towards him.

"Frank, I do implore you to give up this folly. I asked you not to do it at Cambridge, and I ask you again now. I don't care a damn what I promised. It's simple madness, and—"

Frank had wheeled without a word, and was half-way to the gate. Jack stumbled after him, calling under his breath; but the other had already passed through the gate and joined the Major and Gertie before Jack could reach him.

"And so you think up here is the right direction?" Frank was saying.

"I got some tips at the 'Crown,'" said the Major. "There are some farms up there, where—"

"Frank, may I speak to you a minute?"

"No.... All right, Major; I'm ready at once if you are."

He turned towards Jack.

"By the way," he said, "what's in this parcel?"

"Something to eat and drink," murmured Jack.

"Oh ... I shan't want that, thanks very much. Here's the bag with the clothes in it. I'm awfully grateful, old man, for all your kindness. Awfully sorry to have bothered you."

"By the way, Frankie," put in the hateful voice at his side, "I'll take charge of that parcel, if you don't want it."

"Catch hold, then," said Frank. "You're welcome to it, if you'll carry it. You all right, Gertie?"

The girl murmured something inaudible. As at their first meeting, she had said nothing at all.

The Major lifted a bundle out of the depths of the hedge, slung it on his stick, and stood waiting, his face again illuminated with the glow of his pipe. He had handed the new parcel to Gertie without a word.

"Well, good-by again, old man," said Frank, holding out his hand. He, too, Jack saw, had his small bundle wrapped up in the red handkerchief, as on the bridge when they had first met. Jack took his hand and shook it. He could say nothing.

Then the three turned and set their faces up the slope. He could see them, all silent together, pass up, more and more dim in the darkness of the hedge, the two men walking together, the girl a yard behind them. Then they turned the corner and were gone. But Jack still stood where Frank had left him, listening, until long after the sound of their footfalls had died away.

(VII)

Jack had a horrid dream that night.

He was wandering, he thought, gun in hand after grouse, alone on the high moors. It was one of those heavy days, so common in dreams, when the light is so dim that very little can be seen. He was aware of countless hill-tops round him, and valleys that ran down into profound darkness, where only the lights of far-off houses could be discerned. His sport was of that kind peculiar to sleep-imaginings. Enormous birds, larger than ostriches, rose occasionally by ones or twos with incredible swiftness, and soared like balloons against the heavy, glimmering sky. He fired at these and feathers sprang from them, but not a bird fell. Once he inflicted an indescribable wound ... and the bird sped across the sky, blotting out half of it, screaming. Then as the screaming died he became aware that there was a human note in it, and that Frank was crying to him, somewhere across the confines of the wold, and the horror that had been deepening with each shot he fired rose to an intolerable climax. Then began one of the regular nightmare chases: he set off to run; the screaming grew fainter each instant; he could not see his way in the gloom; he clambered over bowlders; he sank in bogs, and dragged his feet from them with infinite pains; his gun became an unbearable burden, yet he dared not throw it from him; he knew that he should need it presently.... The screaming had ceased now, yet he dared not stop running; Frank was in some urgent peril, and he knew it was not yet too late, if he could but find him soon. He ran and ran; the ground was knee-deep now in the feathers that had fallen from the wounded birds; it was darker than ever, yet he toiled on hopelessly, following, as he thought, the direction from which the cries had come. Then as at last he topped the rise of a hill, the screaming broke out again, shrill and frightful, close at hand, and the next instant he saw beneath him in the valley a hundred yards away that for which he had run so far. Running up the slope below, at right angles to his own path came Frank, in the dress-clothes he had borrowed, with pumps upon his feet; his hands were outstretched, his face white as ashes, and he screamed as he ran. Behind him ran a pack of persons whose faces he could not see; they ran like hounds, murmuring as they came in a terrible whining voice. Then Jack understood that he could save Frank; he brought his gun to the shoulder, aimed it at the brown of the pack and drew the trigger. A snap followed, and he discovered that he was unloaded; he groped in his cartridge-belt and found it empty.... He tore at his pockets, and found at last one cartridge; and as he dashed it into the open breach, his gun broke in half. Simultaneously the quarry vanished over an edge of hill, and the pack followed, the leaders now not ten yards behind the flying figure in front.

Jack stood there, helpless and maddened. Then he flung the broken pieces of his gun at the disappearing runners; sank down in the gloom, and broke out into that heart-shattering nightmare sobbing which shows that the limit has been reached.

He awoke, still sobbing—certain that Frank was in deadly peril, if not already dead, and it was a few minutes before he dared to go to sleep once more.

CHAPTER II: (I)

The Rectory garden at Merefield was, obviously, this summer, the proper place to spend most of the day. Certainly the house was cool—it was one of those long, low, creeper-covered places that somehow suggest William IV. and crinolines (if it is a fact that those two institutions flourished together, as I think), with large, darkish rooms and wide, low staircases and tranquil-looking windows through which roses peep; but the shadow of the limes and the yews was cooler still. A table stood almost permanently through those long, hot summer days in the place where Dick had sat with Jenny, and here the Rector and his daughter breakfasted, lunched and dined, day after day, for a really extraordinarily long period.

Jenny herself lived in the garden even more than her father; she got through the household business as quickly as possible after breakfast, and came out to do any small businesses that she could during the rest of the morning. She wrote a few letters, read a few books, sewed a little, and, on the whole, presented a very domestic and amiable picture. She visited poor people for an hour or so two or three days a week, and occasionally, when Lord Talgarth was well enough, rode out with him and her father after tea, through the woods, and sometimes with Lord Talgarth alone.

She suffered practically no pangs of conscience at all on the subject of Frank. Her letter had been perfectly sincere, and she believed herself to have been exceedingly sensible. (It is, perhaps, one may observe, one of the most dangerous things in the world to think oneself sensible; it is even more dangerous than to be told so.) For the worst of it all was that she was quite right. It was quite plain that she and Frank were not suited to one another; that she had looked upon that particular quality in him which burst out in the bread-and-butter incident, the leaving of Cambridge, the going to prison, and so forth, as accidental to his character, whereas it was essential. It was also quite certain that it was the apotheosis of common-sense for her to recognize that, to say so, and to break off the engagement.

Of course, she had moments of what I should call "grace," and she would call insanity, when she wondered for a little while whether to be sensible was the highest thing in life; but her general attitude to these was as it would be towards temptation of any other kind. To be sensible, she would say, was to be successful and effective; to be otherwise was to fail and to be ineffective.

Very well, then.

At the beginning of September Dick Guiseley came to Merefield to shoot grouse. The grouse, as I think I have already remarked, were backward this year, and, after a kind of ceremonial opening, to give warning as it were, on the twelfth of August, they were left in peace. Business was to begin on the third, and on the evening of the second Dick arrived.

He opened upon the subject that chiefly occupied his thoughts just now with Archie that night when Lord Talgarth had gone to bed. They were sitting in the smoking-room, with the outer door well open to admit the warm evening air. They had discussed the prospects of grouse next day with all proper solemnity, and Archie had enumerated the people who were to form their party.

The Rector was coming to shoot, and Jenny was to ride out and join them at lunch.

Then Archie yawned largely, finished his drink, and took up his candle.

"Oh! she's coming, is she?" said Dick meditatively.

Archie struck a match.

"How's Frank?" went on Dick.

"Haven't heard from him."

"Where is the poor devil?"

"Haven't an idea."

Dick emitted a monosyllabic laugh.

"And how's she behaving?"

"Jenny? Oh! just as usual. She's a sensible girl and knows her mind."

Dick pondered this an instant.

"I'm going to bed," said Archie. "Got to have a straight eye to-morrow."

"Oh! sit down a second.... I want to talk."

Archie, as a compromise, propped himself against the back of a chair.

"She doesn't regret it, then?" pursued Dick.

"Not she," said Archie. "It would never have done."

"I know," agreed Dick warmly. (It was a real pleasure to him that head and heart went together in this matter.) "But sometimes, you know, women regret that sort of thing. Wish they hadn't been quite so sensible, you know."

"Jenny doesn't," said Archie.

Dick took up his glass which he had filled with his third whisky-and-soda, hardly five minutes before, and drank half of it. He sucked his mustache, and in that instant confidentialism rose in his heart.

"Well, I'm going to have a shot myself," he said.

"What?"

"I'm going to have a shot. She can but say 'No.'"

Archie's extreme repose of manner vanished for a second. His jaw dropped a little.

"But, good Lord! I hadn't the faintest—"

"I know you hadn't. But I've had it for a long time.... What d'you think, Archie?"

"My good chap—"

"Yes, I know; leave all that out. We'll take that as read. What comes next?"

Archie looked at him a moment.

"How d'you mean? Do you mean, do I approve?"

"Well, I didn't mean that," admitted Dick. "I meant, how'd I better set about it?"

Archie's face froze ever so slightly. (It will be remembered that Jack Kirkby considered him pompous.)

"You must do it your own way," he said.

"Sorry, old man," said Dick. "Didn't mean to be rude."

Archie straightened himself from the chair-back.

"It's all rather surprising," he said. "It never entered my head. I must think about it. Good-night. Put the lights out when you come."

"Archie, old man, are you annoyed?"

"No, no; that's all right," said Archie.

And really and truly that was all that passed between these two that night on the subject of Jenny—so reposeful were they.

(II)

There was a glorious breeze blowing over the hills as Jenny rode slowly up about noon next day. The country is a curious mixture—miles of moor, as desolate and simple and beautiful as moors can be, and by glimpses, now and then in the valleys between, of entirely civilized villages, with even a town or two here and there, prick-up spires and roofs; and, even more ominous, in this direction and that, lie patches of smoke about the great chimneys.

Jenny was meditative as she rode up alone. It is very difficult to be otherwise when one has passed through one considerable crisis, and foresees a number of others that must be met, especially if one has not made up one's mind as to the proper line of action. It is all very well to be sensible, but a difficulty occasionally arises as to which of two or three courses is the more in accordance with that character. To be impulsive certainly leads to trouble sometimes, but also, sometimes it saves it.

Jenny looked charming in repose. She was in a delightful green habit; she wore a plumy kind of hat; she rode an almost perfect little mare belonging to Lord Talgarth, and her big blue, steady eyes roved slowly round her as she went, seeing nothing. It was, in fact, the almost perfect little mare who first gave warning of the approach to the sportsmen, by starting violently all over at the sound of a shot, fired about half a mile away. Jenny steadied her, pulled her up, and watched between the cocked and twitching ears.

Below her, converging slowly upwards, away from herself, moved a line of dots, each precisely like its neighbor in color (Lord Talgarth was very particular, indeed, about the uniform of his beaters), and by each moved a red spot, which Jenny understood to be a flag. The point towards which they were directed culminated in a low, rounded hill, and beneath the crown of this, in a half circle, were visible a series of low defenses, like fortifications, to command the face of the slope and the dips on either side. This was always the last beat—in this moor—before lunch; and lunch itself, she knew, would be waiting on the other side of the hill. Occasionally as she watched, she saw a slight movement behind this or that butt—no more—and the only evidence of human beings, beside the beaters, lay in the faint wreath of all but invisible smoke that followed the reports, coming now quicker and quicker, as the grouse took alarm. Once with a noise like a badly ignited rocket, there burst over the curve before her a flying brown thing, that, screaming with terrified exultation, whirred within twenty yards of her head and vanished into silence. (One cocked ear of the mare bent back to see if the rocket were returning or not.)

Jenny's meditations became more philosophical than ever as she looked. She found herself wondering how much free choice the grouse—if they were capable themselves of philosophizing—would imagine themselves to possess in the face of this noisy but insidious death. She reminded herself that every shred of instinct and experience that each furious little head contained bade the owner of it to fly as fast and straight as possible, in squawking company with as many friends as possible, away from those horrible personages in green and silver with the agitating red flags, and up that quiet slope which, at the worst, only emitted sudden noises. A reflective grouse would perhaps (and two out of three did) consider that he could fly faster and be sooner hidden from the green men with red flags, if he slid crosswise down the valleys on either side. But—Jenny observed—that was already calculated by these human enemies, and butts (like angels' swords) commanded even these approaches too.

It was obvious, then, that however great might be the illusion of free choice, in reality there was none: they were betrayed hopelessly by the very instincts intended to safeguard them; practical common-sense, in this case, at least, led them straight into the jaws of death. A little originality and impulsiveness would render them immortal so far as guns were concerned....

Yes; but there was one who had been original, who had actually preferred to fly straight past a monster in green on a gray mare rather than to face the peaceful but deathly slopes; and he had escaped. But obviously he was an exception. Originality in grouse—

At this point the mare breathed slowly and contemptuously and advanced a delicate, impatient foot, having quite satisfied herself that danger was no longer imminent; and Jenny became aware she was thinking nonsense.

There were a number of unimportant but well-dressed persons at lunch, with most of whom Jenny was acquainted. These extended themselves on the ground and said the right things one after another; and all began with long drinks, and all ended with heavy meals. There were two other women whom she knew slightly, who had driven up half an hour before. Everything was quite perfect—down even to hot grilled grouse that emerged from emblazoned silver boxes, and hot black coffee poured from "Thermos" flasks. Jenny asked intelligent questions and made herself agreeable.

At the close of lunch she found herself somehow sitting on a small rock beside Dick. Lord Talgarth was twenty yards away, his gaitered legs very wide apart, surveying the country and talking to the keeper. Her father was looking down the barrels of his rather ineffective gun, and Archie, with three or four other men and two women, a wife and a sister, was smoking with his back against a rock.

"Shall you be in to-morrow?" asked Dick casually.

Jenny paused an instant.

"I should think so!" she said. "I've got one or two things to do."

"Perhaps I may look in? I want to talk to you about something if I may."

"Shan't you be shooting again?"

"No; I'm not very fit and shall take a rest."

Jenny was silent.

"About what time?" pursued Dick.

Jenny roused herself with a little start. She had been staring out over the hills and wondering if that was the church above Barham that she could almost see against the horizon.

"Oh! any time up to lunch," she said vaguely.

Dick stood up slowly with a satisfied air and stretched himself. He looked very complete and trim, thought Jenny, from his flat cap to his beautifully-spatted shooting-boots. (It was twelve hundred a year, at least, wasn't it?)

"Well, I suppose we shall be moving directly," he said.

A beater came up bringing the mare just before the start was made.

"All right, you can leave her," said Jenny. "I won't mount yet. Just hitch the bridle on to something."

It was a pleasant and picturesque sight to see the beaters, like a file of medieval huntsmen, dwindle down the hill in their green and silver in one direction, and, five minutes later, the sportsmen in another. It looked like some mysterious military maneuver on a small scale; and again Jenny considered the illusion of free choice enjoyed by the grouse, who, perhaps, two miles away, crouched in hollows among the heather. And yet, practically speaking, there was hardly any choice at all....

Lady Richard, the wife of one of the men, interrupted her in a drawl.

"Looks jolly, doesn't it?" she said.

Jenny assented cordially.

(She hated this woman, somehow, without knowing why. She said to herself it was the drawl and the insolent cold eyes and the astonishing complacency; and she only half acknowledged that it was the beautiful lines of the dress and the figure and the assured social position.)

"We're driving," went on the tall girl. "You rode, didn't you?

"Yes."

"Lord Talgarth's mare, isn't it? I thought I recognized her."

"Yes. I haven't got a horse of my own, you know," said Jenny deliberately.

"Oh!"

Jenny suddenly felt her hatred rise almost to passion.

"I must be going," she said. "I've got to visit an old woman who's dying. A rector's daughter, you know—"

"Ah! yes."

Then Jenny mounted from a rock (Lady Richard held the mare's head and settled the habit), and rode slowly away downhill.

(III)

Dick approached the Rectory next day a little before twelve o'clock with as much excitement in his heart as he ever permitted to himself.

Dick is a good fellow—I haven't a word to say against him, except perhaps that he used to think that to be a Guiseley, and to have altogether sixteen hundred a year and to live in a flat in St. James's, and to possess a pointed brown beard and melancholy brown eyes and a reposeful manner, relieved him from all further effort. I have wronged him, however; he had made immense efforts to be proficient at billiards, and had really succeeded; and, since his ultimate change of fortune, has embraced even further responsibilities in a conscientious manner.

Of course, he had been in love before in a sort of way; but this was truly different. He wished to marry Jenny very much indeed.... That she was remarkably sensible, really beautiful and eminently presentable, of course, paved the way; but, if I understand the matter rightly, these were not the only elements in the case. It was the genuine thing. He did not quite know how he would face the future if she refused him; and he was sufficiently humble to be in doubt.

The neat maid told him at the door that Miss Launton had given directions that he was to be shown into the garden if he came.... No; Miss Launton was in the morning-room, but she should be told at once. So Dick strolled across the lawn and sat down by the garden table.

He looked at the solemn, dreaming house in the late summer sunshine; he observed a robin issue out from a lime tree and inspect him sideways; and then another robin issue from another lime tree and drive the first one away. Then he noticed a smear of dust on his own left boot, and flicked it off with a handkerchief. Then, as he put his handkerchief away again, he saw Jenny coming out from the drawing-room window.

She looked really extraordinarily beautiful as she came slowly across towards him and he stood to meet her. She was bare-headed, but her face was shadowed by the great coils of hair. She was in a perfectly plain pink dress, perfectly cut, and she carried herself superbly. She looked just a trifle paler than yesterday, he thought, and there was a very reserved, steady kind of question in her eyes. (I am sorry to be obliged to go on saying this sort of thing about Jenny every time she comes upon the scene; but it is the sort of thing that everyone is obliged to go on thinking whenever she makes her appearance.)

"I've got a good deal to say," said Dick, after they had sat a moment or two. "May I say it right out to the end?"

"Why, certainly," said Jenny.

Dick leaned back and crossed one knee over the other. His manner was exactly right—at any rate, it was exactly what he wished it to be, and all through his little speech he preserved it. It was quite restrained, extremely civilized, and not at all artificial. It was his method of presenting a fact—the fact that he really was in love with this girl—and was in his best manner. There was a lightness of touch about this method of his, but it was only on the surface.

"I daresay it's rather bad form my coming and saying all this so soon, but I can't help that. I know you must have gone through an awful lot in the last month or two—perhaps even longer—

but I don't know about that. And I want to begin by apologizing if I am doing what I shouldn't. The fact is that—well, that I daren't risk waiting."

He did not look at Jenny (he was observing the robin that had gone and come again since Jenny had appeared), but he was aware that at his first sentence she had suddenly settled down into complete motionlessness. He wondered whether that was a good omen or not.

"Well, now," he said, "let me give a little account of myself first. I'm just thirty-one; I've got four hundred a year of my own, and Lord Talgarth allows me twelve hundred a year more. Then I've got other expectations, as they say. My uncle gives me to understand that my allowance is secured to me in his will; and I'm the heir of my aunt, Lady Simon, whom you've probably met. I just mention that to show I'm not a pauper—"

"Mr. Guiseley—" began Jenny.

"Please wait. I've not done yet. Do you mind? ... I'm a decent living man. I'm not spotless, but I'll answer any questions you like to put—to your father. I've not got any profession, though I'm supposed to be a solicitor; but I'm perfectly willing to work if ... if it's wished, or to stand for Parliament, or anything like that—there hasn't, so far, seemed any real, particular reason why I should work. That's all. And I think you know the sort of person I am, all round.

"And now we come to the point." (Dick hesitated a fraction of a second. He was genuinely moved.) "The point is that I'm in love with you, and I have been for some time past. I ... I can't put it more plainly ... (One moment, please, I've nearly done.) ... I can't think of anything else; and I haven't been able to for the last two or three months. I ... I ... I'm fearfully sorry for poor old Frank; I'm very fond of him, you know, but I couldn't help finding it an extraordinary relief when I heard the news. And now I've come to ask you, perfectly straight, whether you'll consent to be my wife."

Dick looked at her for the first time since he had begun his little speech.

She still sat absolutely quiet (she had not even moved at the two words she had uttered), but she had gone paler still. Her mouth was in repose, without quiver or movement, and her beautiful eyes looked steadily on to the lawn before her. She said nothing.

"If you can't give me an answer quite at once," began Dick again presently, "I'm perfectly willing to—"

She turned and looked him courageously in the face.

"I can't say 'Yes,'" she said. "That would be absurd.... You have been quite straightforward with me, and I must be straightforward with you. That is what you wish, isn't it?"

Dick inclined his head. His heart was thumping furiously with exultation—in spite of her words.

"Then what I say is this: You must wait a long time. If you had insisted on an answer now, I should have said 'No.' I hate to keep you waiting, particularly when I do really think it will be 'No' in the long run; but as I'm not quite sure, and as you've been perfectly honest and courteous, if you really wish it I won't say 'No' at once. Will that do?"

"Whatever you say," said Dick.

"You mustn't forget I was engaged to Frank till quite lately. Don't you see how that obscures one's judgment? I simply can't judge now, and I know I can't.... You're willing to wait, then?—even though I tell you now that I think it will be 'No'?"

"Whatever you say," said Dick again; "and may I say thank you for not saying 'No' at once?"

A very slight look of pain came into the girl's eyes.

"I would sooner you didn't," she said. "I'm sorry you said that...."

"I'm sorry," said poor Dick.

There was a pause.

"One other thing," said Jenny. "Would you mind not saying anything to my father? I don't want him to be upset any more. Have you told anybody else you were—?"

"Yes," said Dick bravely, "I told Archie."

"I'm sorry you did that. Will you then just tell him exactly what I said—exactly, you know. That I thought it would be 'No'; but that I only didn't say so at once because you wished it."

"Very well," said Dick.

It was a minute or so before either spoke again. Jenny had that delightful and soothing gift which prevents silence from being empty. It is the same gift, in another form, as that which enables its possessor to put people at their ease. (It is, I suppose, one of the elements of tact.) Dick had a sense that they were still talking gently and reasonably, though he could not quite understand all that Jenny was meaning.

She interrupted it by a sudden sentence.

"I wonder if it's fair," she said. "You know I'm all but certain. I only don't say so because—"

"Let it be at that," said Dick. "It's my risk, isn't it?"

(III)

When he had left her at last, she sat on perfectly still in the same place. The robin had given it up in despair: this human creature was not going to scratch garden-paths as she sometimes did, and disclose rich worms and small fat maggots. But a cat had come out instead and was now pacing with stiff forelegs, lowered head and trailing tail, across the sunny grass, endeavoring to give an impression that he was bent on some completely remote business of his own.

He paused at the edge of the shadow and eyed the girl malignantly.

"Wow!" said the cat.

There was no response.

"Wow!" said the cat.

Jenny roused herself.

"Wow!" said Jenny meditatively.

"Wow!" said the cat, walking on.

"Wow!" said Jenny.

Again there was a long silence.

"Wow!" said Jenny indignantly.

The cat turned a slow head sideways as he began to cross the path, but said nothing. He waited for another entreaty, but Jenny paid no more attention. As he entered the yews he turned once more.

"Wow!" said the cat, almost below his breath.

But Jenny made no answer. The cat cast one venomous look and disappeared.

Then there came out a dog—a small brown and black animal, very sturdy on his legs, and earnest and independent in air and manner. He was the illegitimate offspring of a fox-terrier. He trotted briskly across from the direction of the orchard, diagonally past Jenny. As he crossed the trail of the cat he paused, smelt, and followed it up for a yard or two, till he identified for certain that it proceeded from an acquaintance; then he turned to resume his journey. The movement attracted the girl's attention.

"Lama!" called Jenny imperiously. "Come here this instant!"

Lama put his head on one side, nodded and smiled at her indulgently, and trotted on.

"Oh, dear me!" said Jenny, sighing out loud.

CHAPTER III: (I)

There lived (and still lives, I believe) in the small Yorkshire village of Tarfield a retired doctor, entirely alone except for his servants, in a large house. It is a very delightful house, only—when I stayed there not long ago—it seemed to me that the doctor did not know how to use it. It stands in its own grounds of two or three acres, on the right-hand side of the road to a traveler going north, separated by a row of pollarded limes from the village street, and approached—or, rather, supposed to be approached—by a Charles II. gate of iron-scroll work. I say "supposed to be approached" because the gate is invariably kept locked, and access can only be gained to the house through the side gate from the stable-yard. The grounds were abominably neglected when I saw them; grass was growing on every path, and as fine a crop of weeds surged up amongst the old autumn flowers as ever I have seen. The house, too, was a sad sight. There here two big rooms, one on either side of the little entrance-hall—one a dining-room, the other a sort of drawing-room—and both were dreary and neglected-looking places. In the one the doctor occasionally ate, in the other he never sat except when a rare visitor came to see him, and the little room supposed to be a study at the foot of the stairs in the inner hall that led through the kitchen was hardly any better. I was there, I say, last autumn, and the condition of the place must have been very much the same as that in which it was when Frank came to Tarfield in October.

For the fact was that the doctor—who was possessed of decent private means—devoted the whole of his fortune, the whole of his attention, and the whole of his life—such as it was—to the study of toxins upstairs.

Toxins, I understand, have something to do with germs. Their study involves, at any rate at present, a large stock of small animals, such as mice and frogs and snakes and guinea-pigs and rabbits, who are given various diseases and then studied with loving attention. I saw the doctor's menagerie when I went to see him about Frank; they were chiefly housed in a large room over the kitchen, communicating with the doctor's own room by a little old powder-closet with two doors, and the smell was indescribable. Ranks of cages and boxes rose almost to the ceiling, and in the middle of the room was a large business-like looking wooden kitchen-table with various appliances on it. I saw the doctor's room also—terribly shabby, but undoubtedly a place of activity. There were piles of books and unbound magazines standing about in corners, with more on the table, as well as a heap of note-books. An array of glass tubes and vary-colored bottles stood below the window, with a microscope, and small wooden boxes on one side. And there was, besides, something which I think he called an "incubator"—a metal affair, standing on four slender legs; a number of glass tubes emerged from this, each carefully stoppered with cotton wool, and a thermometer thrust itself up in one corner.

A really high degree of proficiency in any particular subject invariably leads to atrophy in other directions. A man who eats and breathes and dreams Toxins, for instance, who lives so much in Toxins that he corresponds almost daily with learned and unintelligible Germans; who knows so much about Toxins that when he enters, with shabby trousers and a small hand-bag, into the room of a polished specialist in Harley Street, he sees as in a dream the specialist rise and bow before him—who, when he can be persuaded to contribute a short and highly technical article to a medical magazine, receives a check for twenty-five guineas by return of post—a man of this kind is peculiarly open to the danger of thinking that anything which cannot be expressed in terms of Toxin is negligible nonsense. It is the characteristic danger of every specialist in every branch of knowledge; even theologians are not wholly immune.

It was so in the case of Dr. Whitty (I forget all the initials that should follow his name). He had never been married, he never took any exercise; occasionally, when a frog's temperature approached a crisis, he slept in his clothes, and forgot to change them in the morning. And he was the despair of the zealous vicar. He was perfectly convinced that, since the force that underlay the production of Toxins could accomplish so much, it could surely accomplish everything. He could reduce his roses, his own complexion, the grass on his garden-paths, the condition of his snakes', and frogs' skins, and the texture of his kitchen-table—if you gave him time—to terms of Toxin; therefore, argued Dr. Whitty, you could, if you had more time, reduce everything else to the same terms. There wasn't such a thing as a soul, of course—it was a manifestation of a combination of Toxins (or anti-Toxins, I forget which); there was no God— the idea of God was the result of another combination of Toxins, akin to a belief in the former illusion. Roughly speaking, I think his general position was that as Toxins are a secretion of microbes (I am certain of that phrase, anyhow), so thought and spiritual experiences and so forth are a secretion of the brain. I know it sounded all very brilliant and unanswerable and analogous to other things. He hardly ever took the trouble to say all this; he was far too much interested in what he already knew, or was just on the point of finding out, to treat of these extravagant and complicated ramifications of his subject. When he really got to know his mice and bats, as they deserved to be known, it might be possible to turn his attention to other things. Meanwhile, it was foolish and uneconomical. So here he lived, with a man-of-all-work and his man's wife, and daily went from strength to strength in the knowledge of Toxins.

It was to this household that there approached, in the month of October, a small and dismal procession of three.

The doctor was first roused to a sense of what was happening as he shuffled swiftly through his little powder-closet one morning soon after breakfast, bearing in his hand the corpse of a mouse which had at last, and most disappointingly, succumbed to a severe attack of some hybrid of leprosy. As he flew through to his microscope he became aware of an altercation in the stable-yard beneath.

"I tell you he ain't a proper doctor," he heard his man explaining; "he knows nothing about them things."

"My good fellow," began a high, superior voice out of sight; but Dr. Whitty swept on, and was presently deep in indescribable disgustingness of the highest possible value to the human race, especially in the South Seas. Time meant nothing at all to him, when this kind of work was in hand; and it was after what might be an hour or two hours, or ten minutes, that he heard a tap on his door.

He uttered a sound without moving his eye, and the door opened.

"Very sorry, sir," said his man, "but there's a party in the yard as won't—"

The doctor held up his hand for silence, gazed a few moments longer, poked some dreadful little object two or three times, sighed and sat back.

"Eh?"

"There's a party in the yard, sir, wants a doctor."

(This sort of thing had happened before.)

"Tell them to be off," he said sharply. He was not an unkindly man, but this sort of thing was impossible. "Tell them to go to Dr. Foster."

"I 'ave, sir," said the man.

"Tell them again," said the doctor.

"I 'ave, sir. 'Arf a dozen times."

The doctor sighed—he was paying practically no attention at all, of course. The leprous mouse had been discouraging; that was all.

"If you'd step down, sir, an instant—"

The doctor returned from soaring through a Toxined universe.

"Nonsense," he said sharply. "Tell them I'm not practicing. What do they want?"

"Please, sir, it's a young man as 'as poisoned 'is foot, 'e says. 'E looks very bad, and—"

"Eh? Poison?"

"Yes, sir."

The doctor appeared to reflect a moment (that mouse, you know—); then he recovered.

"I'll be down directly," he said almost mechanically. "Take 'em all into the study."

(II)

Dr. Whitty could hardly explain to me, even when he tried, exactly why he had made an exception in this particular instance. Of course, I understand perfectly myself why he did; but, for himself, all he could say was that he supposed the word Poison happened to meet his mood. He had honestly done with the mouse just now; he had no other very critical case, and he thought he might as well look at the poisoned young man for an instant, before finally despatching him to Dr. Foster, six miles further on.

When he came into the study ten minutes later he found the party ranged to meet him. A girl was sitting on a box in the corner by the window, and stood up to receive him; a young man was sitting back in a Windsor chair, with one boot off, jerking spasmodically; his eyes stared unmeaningly before him. A tallish, lean man of a particularly unprepossessing appearance was leaning over him with an air of immense solicitude. They were all three evidently of the tramp-class.

What they saw—with the exception of Frank, I expect, who was too far gone to notice anything—was a benignant-looking old man, very shabby, in an alpaca jacket, with a rusty velvet cap on his head, and very bright short-sighted eyes behind round spectacles. This figure appeared in the doorway, stood looking at them a moment, as if bewildered as to why he or they were there at all; and then, with a hasty shuffling movement, darted across the floor and down on his knees.

The following colloquy was held as soon as the last roll of defiled bandage had dropped to the floor, and Frank's foot was disclosed.

"How long's this been going on?" asked the doctor sharply, holding the discolored thing carefully in his two hands.

"Well, sir," said the Major reflectively, "he began to limp about—let's see—four days ago. We were coming through—"

The doctor, watching Frank's face curiously (the spasm was over for the present), cut the Major short by a question to the patient.

"Now, my boy, how d'you feel now?"

Frank's lips moved; he seemed to be trying to lick them; but he said nothing, and his eyes closed, and he grinned once or twice, as if sardonically.

"When did these spasms begin?" went on the doctor, abruptly turning to the Major again.

"Well, sir—if you mean that jerking—Frankie began to jerk about half an hour ago when we were sitting down a bit; but he's seemed queer since breakfast. And he didn't seem to be able to eat properly."

"How do you mean? D'you mean he couldn't open his mouth?"

"Well, sir, it was something like that."

The doctor began to make comments in a rapid undertone, as if talking to himself; he pressed his hand once or twice against Frank's stomach; he took up the filthy bandage and examined it. Then he looked at the boot.

"Where's the sock?" he asked sharply.

Gertie produced it from a bundle. He looked at it closely, and began to mumble again. Then he rose to his feet.

"What's the matter with him, doctor?" asked the Major, trying to look perturbed.

"We call it tetanus," said the doctor.

"Who are you, my man?" he said. "Any relation?"

The Major looked at him loftily.

"No, sir.... I am his friend."

"Ha! Then you must leave your friend in my charge. He shall be well in a week at the latest."

The Major was silent.

"Well?" snapped the doctor.

"I understood from your servant, sir—"

"You speak like an educated man."

"I am an educated man."

"Ha—well—no business of mine. What were you about to say?"

"I understood from your servant, sir, that this was not quite in your line; and since—"

The specialist smiled grimly. He snatched up a book from a pile on the table, thrust open the title-page and held it out.

"Read that, sir.... As it happens, it's my hobby. Go and ask Dr. Foster, if you like.... No, sir; I must have your friend; it's a good sound case."

The Major read the title-page in a superior manner. It purported to be by a James Whitty, and the name was followed by a series of distinctions and of the initials, which I have forgotten. F.R.S. were the first.

"My name," said the doctor.

The Major handed the book back with a bow.

"I am proud to make your acquaintance, Dr. Whitty. I have heard of you. May I present Mrs. Trustcott?"

Gertie looked confused. The doctor made a stiff obeisance. Then his face became animated again.

"We must move your friend upstairs," he said. "If you will help, Mr. Trustcott, I will call my servant."

(III)

It was about half-past nine that night that the doctor, having rung the bell in the spare bedroom, met his man at the threshold.

"I'll sleep in this room to-night," he said; "you can go to bed. Bring in a mattress, will you?"

The man looked at his master's face. (He looked queer-like, reported Thomas later to his wife.)

"Hope the young man's doing well, sir?"

A spasm went over the doctor's face.

"Most extraordinary young man in the world," he said.... Then he broke off. "Bring the mattress at once, Thomas. Then you can go to bed."

He went back and closed the door.

Thomas had seldom seen his master so perturbed over a human being before. He wondered what on earth was the matter. During the few minutes that he was in the room he looked at the patient curiously, and he noticed that the doctor was continually looking at him too. Thomas described to me Frank's appearance. He was very much flushed, he said, with very bright eyes, and he was talking incessantly. And it was evidently this delirious talking that had upset the doctor. I tried to get out of Doctor Whitty what it was that Frank had actually said, but the doctor shut up his face tight and would say nothing. Thomas was more communicative, though far from adequate.

It was about religion, he said, that Frank was talking—about religion.... And that was really about all that he could say of that incident.

Thomas awoke about one o'clock that night, and, still with the uneasiness that he had had earlier in the evening, climbed out of bed without disturbing his wife, put on his slippers and great-coat and made his way down the attic stairs. The October moon was up, and, shining through the staircase window, showed him the door of the spare bedroom with a line of light beneath it. From beyond that door came the steady murmur of a voice....

Now Thomas's nerves were strong: he was a little lean kind of man, very wiry and active, nearly fifty years old, and he had lived with his master, and the mice and the snakes, and disagreeable objects in bottles, for more than sixteen years. He had been a male nurse in an asylum before that. Yet there was something—he told me later—that gripped him suddenly as he was half-way down the stairs and held him in a kind of agony which he could in no way describe. It was connected with the room behind that lighted door. It was not that he feared for his master, nor for Frank. It was something else altogether. (What a pity it is that our system of education teaches neither self-analysis nor the art of narration!)

He stood there—he told me—he should think for the better part of ten minutes, unable to move either way, listening, always listening, to the voice that rose and sank and lapsed now and then into silences that were worse than all, and telling himself vigorously that he was not at all frightened.

It was a creak somewhere in the old house that disturbed him and snapped the thin, rigid little thread that seemed to paralyze his soul; and still in a sort of terror, though no longer in the same stiff agony, he made his way down the three or four further steps of the flight, laid hold of the handle, turned it and peered in.

Frank was lying quiet so far as he could see. A night-light burned by the bottles and syringes on the table at the foot of the bed, and, although shaded from the young man's face, still diffused enough light to shoes the servant the figure lying there, and his master, seated beyond the bed, very close to it, still in his day-clothes—still, even, in his velvet cap—his chin propped in his hand, staring down at his patient, utterly absorbed and attentive.

There was nothing particularly alarming in all that, and yet there was that in the room which once more seized the man at his heart and held him there, rigid again, terrified, and, above all, inexpressibly awed. (At least, that is how I should interpret his description.) He said that it wasn't like the spare bedroom at all, as he ordinarily knew it (and, indeed, it was a mean sort of room when I saw it, without a fireplace, though of tolerable size). It was like another room altogether, said Thomas.

He tried to listen to what Frank was saying, and I imagine he heard it all quite intelligently; yet, once more, all he could say afterwards was that it was about religion ... about religion....

So he stood, till he suddenly perceived that the doctor was looking at him with a frown and contorted features of eloquence. He understood that he was to go. He closed the door noiselessly; and, after another pause, sped upstairs without a sound in his red cloth slippers.

(IV)

When Frank awoke to normal consciousness again, he lay still, wondering what it was all about. He saw a table at the foot of his bed and noticed on it a small leather case, two green bottles stoppered with india-rubber, and a small covered bowl looking as if it contained beef-tea. He extended his explorations still further, and discovered an Hanoverian wardrobe against the left wall, a glare of light (which he presently discerned to be a window), a dingy wall-paper, and finally a door. As he reached this point the door opened and an old man with a velvet skull-cap, spectacles, and a kind, furrowed face, came in and stood over him.

"Well?" said the old man.

"I am a bit stiff," said Frank.

"Are you hungry?"

"I don't think so."

"Well, you're doing very well, if that's any satisfaction to you," observed the doctor, frowning on him doubtfully.

Frank said nothing.

The doctor sat down on a chair by the bed that Frank suddenly noticed for the first time.

"Well," said the doctor, "I suppose you want to know the facts. Here they are. My name is Whitty; I'm a doctor; you're in my house. This is Wednesday afternoon; your friends brought you here yesterday morning. I've given them some work in the garden. You were ill yesterday, but you're all right now."

"What was the matter?"

"We won't bother about names," said the doctor with a kind sharpness. "You had a blister; it broke and became a sore; then you wore one of those nasty cheap socks and it poisoned it. That's all."

"That's in those bottles?" asked Frank languidly. (He felt amazingly weak and stupid.)

"Well, it's an anti-toxin," said the doctor. "That doesn't tell you much, does it?"

"No," said Frank.... "By the way, who's going to pay you, doctor? I can't."

The doctor's face rumpled up into wrinkles. (Frank wished he wouldn't sit with his back to the window.)

"Don't you bother about that, my boy. You're a case—that's what you are."

Frank attempted a smile out of politeness.

"Now, how about some more beef-tea, and then going to sleep again?"

Frank assented.

It was not until the Thursday morning that things began to run really clear again in Frank's mind. He felt for his rosary under his pillow and it wasn't there. Then he thumped on the floor with a short stick which had been placed by him, remembering that in some previous existence he had been told to do this.

A small, lean man appeared at the door, it seemed, with the quickness of thought.

"My rosary, please," said Frank. "It's a string of beads. I expect it's in my trouser-pocket."

The man looked at him with extraordinary earnestness and vanished.

Then the doctor appeared holding the rosary.

"Is this what you want?" he asked.

"That's it! Thanks very much."

"You're a Catholic?" went on the other, giving it him.

"Yes."

The doctor sat down again.

"I thought so," he said.

Frank wondered why. Then a thought crossed his mind.

"Have I been talking?" he said. "I suppose I was delirious?"

The doctor made no answer for a moment; he was looking at him fixedly. Then he roused himself.

"Well, yes, you have," he said.

Frank felt rather uncomfortable.

"Hope I haven't said anything I shouldn't."

The old man laughed shortly and grimly.

"Oh, no," he said. "Far from it. At least, your friends wouldn't think so."

"What was it about?"

"We'll talk about that later, if you like," said the doctor. "Now I want you to get up a bit after you've had some food."

It was with a very strange sensation that Frank found himself out in the garden next day, in a sheltered corner, seated in a wicker chair in which, by the help of bamboo poles, he had been carried downstairs by Thomas and the Major, with the doctor leading the way and giving directions as to how to turn the corners. The chair was brought out through an irregularly-shaped little court at the back of the house and set down in the warm autumn noon, against an old wall, with a big kitchen garden, terribly neglected, spread before him. The smoke of burning went up in the middle distance, denoting the heap of weeds pulled by the Major and Gertie during the last three days. He saw Gertie in the distance once or twice, in a clean sun-bonnet, going about her business, but she made no sign. The smell of the burning weeds gave a pleasant, wholesome and acrid taste to his mouth.

"Now then," said the doctor, "we can have our little talk." And he sat down beside him on another chair.

Frank felt a little nervous, he scarcely knew why. It seemed to him that it would be far better not to refer to the past at all. And it appeared to him a little unusual that a doctor should be so anxious about it. Twice or three times since yesterday this old man had begun to ask him a question and had checked himself. There was a very curious eagerness about him now.

"I'm awfully grateful and all that," said Frank. "Is there anything special you want to know? I suppose I've been talking about my people?"

The doctor waved a wrinkled hand.

"No, no," he said, "not a word. You talked about a girl a little, of course—everybody does; but not much. No, it isn't that."

Frank felt relieved. He wasn't anxious about anything else.

"I'm glad of that. By the way, may I smoke?"

The doctor produced a leather case of cigarettes and held it out.

"Take one of these," he said.

"Because," continued Frank, "I'm afraid I mustn't talk about my people. The name I've got now is Gregory, you know." He lit his cigarette, noticing how his fingers still shook, and dropped the match.

"No, it's not about that," said the doctor; "it's not about that."

Frank glanced at him, astonished by his manner.

"Well, then—?" he began.

"I want to know first," said the doctor slowly, "where you've got all your ideas from. I've never heard such a jumble in my life. I know you were delirious; but ... but it hung together somehow; and it seemed much more real to you than anything else."

"What did?" asked Frank uncomfortably.

The doctor made no answer for a moment. He looked out across the untidy garden with its rich, faded finery of wild flowers and autumn leaves, and the yellowing foliage beyond the wall, and the moors behind—all transfigured in October sunshine. The smoke of the burning weeds drew heavenly lines and folds of ethereal lace-work across the dull splendors beyond.

"Well," he said at last, "everything. You know I've heard hundreds and hundreds of folks ..." he broke off again, "... and I know what people call religion about here—and such a pack of nonsense ..." (He turned on Frank again suddenly.) "Where d'you get your ideas from?"

"Do you mean the Catholic religion?" said Frank.

"Bah! don't call it that. I know what that is—" Frank interrupted him.

"Well, that's my religion," he said. "I haven't got any other."

"But ... but the way you hold it," cried the other; "the grip ... the grip it has of you. That's the point. D'you mean to tell me—"

"I mean that I don't care for anything else in the whole world," said Frank, stung with sudden enthusiasm.

"But ... but you're not mad! You're a very sensible, fellow. You don't mean to tell me you really believe all that—all that about pain and so on? We doctors know perfectly what all that is. It's a reaction of Nature ... a warning to look out ... it's often simply the effects of building up; and we're beginning to think—ah! that won't interest you! Listen to me! I'm what they call a specialist—an investigator. I can tell you, without conceit, that I probably know all that is to be known on a certain subject. Well, I can tell you as an authority—"

Frank lifted his head a little. He was keenly interested by the fire with which this other enthusiast spoke.

"I daresay you can," said Frank. "And I daresay it's all perfectly true; but what in the world has all that got to do with it—with the use made of it—the meaning of it? Now I—"

"Hush! hush!" said the doctor. "We mustn't get excited. That's no good."

He stopped and stared mournfully out again.

"I wish you could really tell me," he said more slowly. "But that's just what you can't. I know that. It's a personal thing."

"But my dear doctor—" said Frank.

"That's enough," said the other. "I was an old fool to think it possible—"

Frank interrupted again in his turn. (He was conscious of that extraordinary mental clearness that comes sometimes to convalescents, and he suddenly perceived there was something behind all this which had not yet made its appearance.)

"You've some reason for asking all this," he said. "I wish you'd tell me exactly what's in your mind."

The old man turned and looked at him with a kind of doubtful fixedness.

"Why do you say that, my boy?"

"People like you," said Frank smiling, "don't get excited over people like me, unless there's something.... I was at Cambridge, you know. I know the dons there, and—"

"Well, I'll tell you," said the doctor, drawing a long breath. "I hadn't meant to. I know it's mere nonsense; but—" He stopped an instant and called aloud: "Thomas! Thomas!"

Thomas's lean head, like a bird's, popped out from a window in the kitchen court behind.

"Come here a minute."

Thomas came and stood before them with a piece of wash-leather in one hand and a plated table-spoon in the other.

"I want you to tell this young gentleman," said the doctor deliberately, "what you told me on Wednesday morning."

Thomas looked doubtfully from one to the other.

"It was my fancy, sir," he said.

"Never mind about that. Tell us both."

"Well, sir, I didn't like it. Seemed to me when I looked in—"

("He looked in on us in the middle of the night," explained the doctor. "Yes, go on, Thomas.")

"Seemed to me there was something queer."

"Yes?" said the doctor encouragingly.

"Something queer," repeated Thomas musingly.... "And now if you'll excuse me, sir, I'll have to get back—"

The doctor waved his hands despairingly as Thomas scuttled back without another word.

"It's no good," he said, "no good. And yet he told me quite intelligibly—"

Frank was laughing quietly to himself.

"But you haven't told me one word—"

"Don't laugh," said the old man simply. "Look here, my boy, it's no laughing matter. I tell you I can't think of anything else. It's bothering me."

"But—"

The doctor waved his hands.

"Well," he said, "I can say it no better. It was the whole thing. The way you looked, the way you spoke. It was most unusual. But it affected me—it affected me in the same way; and I thought that perhaps you could explain."

(V)

It was not until the Monday afternoon that Frank persuaded the doctor to let him go. Dr. Whitty said everything possible, in his emphatic way, as to the risk of traveling again too soon; and there was one scene, actually conducted in the menagerie—the only occasion on which the doctor mentioned Frank's relations—during which he besought the young man to be sensible, and to allow him to communicate with his family. Frank flatly refused, without giving reasons.

The doctor seemed strangely shy of referring again to the conversation in the garden; and, for his part, Frank shut up like a box. They seem both to have been extraordinarily puzzled at one another—as such people occasionally are. They were as two persons, both intelligent and interested, entirely divided by the absence of any common language, or even of symbols. Words that each used meant different things to the other. (It strikes me sometimes that the curse of Babel was a deeper thing than appears on the surface.)

The Major and Gertie, all this while, were in clover. The doctor had no conception of what six hours' manual work could or could not do, and, in return for these hours, he made over to the two a small disused gardener's cottage at the end of his grounds, some bedding, their meals, and a shilling the day. It was wonderful how solicitous the Major was as to Frank's not traveling again until it was certain he was capable of it; but Frank had acquired a somewhat short and decisive way with his friend, and announced that Monday night must see them all cleared out.

The leave-taking—so far as I have been able to gather—was rather surprisingly emotional. The doctor took Frank apart into the study where he had first seen him, and had a short conversation, during which one sovereign finally passed from the doctor to the patient.

I have often tried to represent to myself exactly what elements there were in Frank that had such an effect upon this wise and positive old man. He had been a very upsetting visitor in many ways. He had distracted his benefactor from a very important mouse that had died of leprosy; he had interfered sadly with working hours; he had turned the house, comparatively speaking, upside down. Worse than all, he had—I will not say modified the doctor's theories—that would be far too strong a phrase; but he had, quite unconsciously, run full tilt against them; and finally, worst of all, he had done this right in the middle of the doctor's own private preserve. There was absolutely every element necessary to explain Frank's remarks during his delirium; he was a religiously-minded boy, poisoned by a toxin and treated by the anti-toxin. What in the world could be expected but that he should rave in the most fantastic way, and utter every mad conception and idea that his subjective self contained. As for that absurd fancy of the doctor himself, as well as of his servant that there was "something queer" in the room—the more he thought of it, the less he valued it. Obviously it was the result of a peculiar combination of psychological conditions, just as psychological conditions were themselves the result of an obscure combination of toxin—or anti-toxin—forces.

Yet for all that, argue as one may, the fact remained that this dry and rather misanthropic scientist was affected in an astonishing manner by Frank's personality. (It will appear later on in Frank's history that the effect was more or less permanent.)

Still more remarkable to my mind was the very strong affection that Frank conceived for the doctor. (There is no mystery coming: the doctor will not ultimately turn out to be Frank's father in disguise; Lord Talgarth still retains that distinction.) But it is plainly revealed by Frank's diary that he was drawn to this elderly man by very much the same kind of feelings as a son might have. And yet it is hardly possible to conceive two characters with less in common. The doctor was a dogmatic materialist—and remains so still—Frank was a Catholic. The doctor was scientific to his finger-tips—Frank romantic to the same extremities; the doctor was old and a confirmed stay-at-home—Frank was young, and an incorrigible gipsy. Yet so the matter was. I have certain ideas of my own, but there is no use in stating them, beyond saying perhaps that each recognized in the other—sub-consciously only, since each professed himself utterly unable to sympathize in the smallest degree with the views of the other—a certain fixity of devotion that was the driving-force in each life. Certainly, on the surface, there are not two theories less unlike than the one which finds the solution of all things in Toxin, and the other which finds it in God. But perhaps there is a reconciliation somewhere.

The Major and Gertie were waiting in the stable-yard when the two other men emerged. The Major had a large bag of apples—given him by Thomas at the doctor's orders—which he was proceeding to add to Gertie's load at the very moment when the two others came out. Frank took them, without a word, and slung them over his own back.

The doctor stood blinking a moment in the strong sunshine.

"Well, good-by, my boy," he said. "Good luck! Remember that if ever you come this way again—"

"Good-by, sir," said Frank.

He held out his disengaged hand.

Then an astonishing thing happened. The doctor took the hand, then dropped it; threw his arms round the boy's neck, kissed him on both cheeks, and hurried back through the garden gate, slamming it behind him. And I imagine he ran upstairs at once to see how the mice were.

Well, that is the whole of the incident. The two haven't met since, that I am aware. And I scarcely know why I have included it in this book. But I was able to put it together from various witnesses, documentary and personal, and it seemed a pity to leave it out.

CHAPTER IV: (I)

An enormous physical weariness settled down on Frank, as he trudged silently with the Major, towards evening, a week later.

He had worked all the previous day in a farm-yard—carting manure, and the like; and though he was perfectly well again, some of the spring had ebbed from his muscles during his week's rest. This day, too, the first of November, had been exhausting. They had walked since daybreak, after a wretched night in a barn, plodding almost in silence, mile after mile, against a wet south-west wind, over a discouraging kind of high-road that dipped and rose and dipped again, and never seemed to arrive anywhere.

It is true that Frank was no longer intensely depressed; quite another process had been at work upon him for the last two or three months, as will be seen presently; but his limbs seemed leaden, and the actual stiffness in his shoulders and loins made walking a little difficult.

They were all tired together. They did not say much to one another. They had, in fact, said all that there was to be said months ago; and they were reduced—as men always are reduced when a certain pitch is reached—to speak simply of the most elementary bodily things—food, tobacco and sleep. The Major droned on now and then—recalling luxuries of past days—actual roofs over the head, actual hot meat to put in the mouth, actual cigars—and Frank answered him. Gertie said nothing.

She made up for it, soon after dark had fallen, by quite suddenly collapsing into a hedge, and announcing that she would die if she didn't rest. The Major made the usual remarks, and she made no answer.

Frank interposed suddenly.

"Shut up," he said. "We can't stop here. I'll go on a bit and see what can be done."

And, as he went off into the darkness, leaving his bundle, he heard the scolding voice begin again, but it was on a lower key and he knew it would presently subside into a grumble, soothed by tobacco.

He had no idea as to the character of the road that lay before him. They had passed through a few villages that afternoon, whose names meant nothing to him, and he scarcely knew why, even, they were going along this particular road. They were moving southwards towards London—so much had been agreed—and they proposed to arrive there in another month or so. But the country was unfamiliar to him, and the people seemed grudging and uncouth. They had twice been refused the use of an outhouse for the night, that afternoon.

It seemed an extraordinarily deserted road. There were no lights from houses, so far as he could make out, and the four miles that had been declared at their last stopping-place to separate them from the next village appeared already more like five or six. Certainly the three of them had between two and three shillings, all told; there was no actual need of a workhouse just yet, but naturally it was wished to spend as little as possible.

Then on a sudden he caught a glimpse of a light burning somewhere, that appeared and vanished again as he moved, and fifty yards more brought him to a wide sweep, a pair of gateposts with the gate fastened back, and a lodge on the left-hand side. So much he could make out dimly through the November darkness; and as he stood there hesitating, he thought he could see somewhere below him a few other lights burning through the masses of leafless trees through which the drive went downhill.

He knew very well by experience that lodge-keepers were, taken altogether, perhaps the most unsympathetic class in the community. (They live, you see, right on the high road, and see human nature at its hottest and crossest as well as its most dishonest.) Servants at back doors were, as a rule, infinitely more obliging; and, as obviously this was the entrance to some big country house, the right thing to do would be to steal past the lodge on tiptoe and seek his fortune amongst the trees. Yet he hesitated; the house might be half a mile away, for all he knew; and, certainly there was a hospitable look about the fastened-back gate.

There came a gust of wind over the hills behind him, laden with wet.... He turned, went up to the lodge door and knocked.

He could hear someone moving about inside, and just as he was beginning to wonder whether his double tap had been audible, the door opened and disclosed a woman in an apron.

"Can you very kindly direct me—" began Frank politely.

The woman jerked her head sharply in the direction of the house.

"Straight down the hill," she said. "Them's the orders."

"But—"

It was no good; the door was shut again in his face, and he stood alone in the dark.

This was all very unusual. Lodge-keepers did not usually receive "orders" to send tramps, without credentials, on to the house which the lodge was supposed to guard.... That open gate, then, must have been intentional. Plainly, however, he must take her at her word; and as he tramped down the drive, he began to form theories. It must be a fanatic of some kind who lived here, and he inclined to consider the owner as probably an eccentric old lady with a fad, and a large number of lap-dogs.

As he came nearer, through the trees, he became still more astonished, for as the branches thinned, he became aware of lights burning at such enormous distances apart that the building seemed more like a village than a house.

Straight before him shone a row of lighted squares, high up, as if hung in air, receding in perspective, till blocked out by a black mass which seemed a roof of some kind; far on the left shone some kind of illuminated gateway, and to his right another window or two glimmered almost beneath his feet.

Another fifty yards down the winding drive disclosed a sight that made him seriously wonder whether the whole experience were real, for now only a few steps further on, and still lower than the level at which he was, stood, apparently, a porter's lodge, as of a great college. There was a Tudor archway, with rooms above it and rooms on either side; a lamp hung from the roof illuminated the dry stone pavement within, and huge barred gates at the further end, shut off all other view. It looked like the entrance to some vast feudal castle, and he thought again that if an eccentric old lady lived here, she must be very eccentric indeed. He began to wonder whether a seneschal in a belt hung with keys would presently make his appearance: he considered whether or not he could wind a horn, if there were no other way of summoning the retainers.

When at last he tapped at a small interior door, also studded and barred with iron, and the door opened, the figure he did see was hardly less of a shock to him than a seneschal would have been.

For there stood, as if straight out of a Christmas number, the figure of a monk, tall, lean, with gray hair, clean-shaven, with a pair of merry eyes and a brisk manner. He wore a broad leather band round his black frock, and carried his spare hand thrust deep into it.

The monk sighed humorously.

"Another of them," he said. "Well, my man?"

"Please, father—"

The monk closed his eyes as in resignation.

"You needn't try that on," he said. "Besides, I'm not a father. I'm a brother. Can you remember that?"

Frank smiled back.

"Very well, brother. I'm a Catholic myself."

"Ah! yes," sighed the monk briskly. "That's what they all say. Can you say the 'Divine Praises'? Do you know what they are?... However, that makes no difference, as—"

"But I can, brother. 'Blessed be God. Blessed be His—"

"But you're not Irish?"

"I know I'm not. But—"

"Are you an educated man? However, that's not my affair. What can I do for you, sir?"

The monk seemed to take a little more interest in him, and Frank took courage.

"Yes," he said, "I'm an educated man. My name's Frank Gregory. I've got two friends out on the road up there—a man and a woman. Their name's Trustcott—and the woman—"

"No good; no good," said the monk. "No women."

"But, brother, she really can't go any further. I'm very sorry, but we simply must have shelter. We've got two or three shillings, if necessary—"

"Oh, you have, have you?" said the monk keenly. "That's quite new. And when did you touch food last? Yesterday morning? (Don't say 'S'elp me!' It's not necessary.)"

"We last touched food about twelve o'clock to-day. We had beans and cold bacon," said Frank deliberately. "We're perfectly willing to pay for shelter and food, if we're obliged. But, of course, we don't want to."

The monk eyed him very keenly indeed a minute or two without speaking. This seemed a new type.

"Come in and sit down a minute," he said. "I'll fetch the guest-master."

It was a very plain little room in which Frank sat, and seemed designed, on purpose, to furnish no temptation to pilferers. There was a table, two chairs, a painted plaster statue of a gray-bearded man in black standing on a small bracket with a crook in his hand; a pious book, much thumb-marked, lay face downwards on the table beside the oil lamp. There was another door through which the monk had disappeared, and that was absolutely all. There was no carpet and no curtains, but a bright little coal fire burned on the hearth, and two windows looked, one up the drive down which Frank had come, and the other into some sort of courtyard on the opposite side.

About ten minutes passed away without anything at all happening. Frank heard more than one gust of rain-laden wind dash against the little barred window to the south, and he wondered how his friends were getting on. The Major, at any rate, he knew, would manage to keep himself tolerably dry. Then he began to think about this place, and was surprised that he was not surprised at running into it like this in the dark. He knew nothing at all about monasteries—he hardly knew that there were such things in England (one must remember that he had only been a Catholic for about five months), and yet somehow, now that he had come here, it all seemed inevitable. (I cannot put it better than that: it is what he himself says in his diary.)

Then, as he meditated, the door opened, and there came in a thin, eager-looking elderly man, dressed like the brother who followed him, except that over his frock he wore a broad strip of black stuff, something like a long loose apron, hanging from his throat to his feet, and his head was enveloped in a black hood.

Frank stood up and bowed with some difficulty. He was beginning to feel stiff.

"Well," said the priest sharply, with his bright gray eyes, puckered at the corners, running over and taking in the whole of Frank's figure from close-cut hair to earthy boots. "Brother James tells me you wish to see me."

"It was Brother James who said so, father," said Frank.

"What is it you want?"

"I've got two friends on the road who want shelter—man and woman. We'll pay, if necessary, but—"

"Never mind about that," interrupted the priest sharply. "Who are you?"

"The name I go by is Frank Gregory."

"The name you go by, eh?... Where were you educated?"

"Eton and Cambridge."

"How do you come to be on the roads?"

"That's a long story, father."

"Did you do anything you shouldn't?"

"No. But I've been in prison since."

"And your name's Frank Gregory.... F.G., eh?"

Frank turned as if to leave. He understood that he was known.

"Well—good-night, father—"

The priest turned with upraised hand.

"Brother James, just step outside."

Then he continued as the door closed.

"You needn't go, Mr.—er—Gregory. Your name shall not be mentioned to a living being without your leave."

"You know about me?"

"Of course I do.... Now be sensible, my dear fellow; go and fetch your friends. We'll manage somehow." (He raised his voice and rapped on the table.) "Brother James ... go up with Mr. Gregory to the porter's lodge. Make arrangements to put the woman up somewhere, either there or in a gardener's cottage. Then bring the man down here.... His name?"

"Trustcott," said Frank.

"And when you come back, I shall be waiting for you here."

Frank states in his diary that an extraordinary sense of familiarity descended on him as, half an hour later, the door of a cell closed behind Dom Hildebrand Maple, and he found himself in a room with a bright fire burning, a suit of clothes waiting for him, a can of hot water, a sponging tin and a small iron bed.

I think I understand what he means. Somehow or other a well-ordered monastery represents the Least Common Multiple of nearly all pleasant houses. It has the largeness and amplitude of a castle, and the plainness of decent poverty. It has none of that theatricality which it is supposed to have, none of the dreaminess or the sentimentality with which Protestants endow it. He had passed just now through, first, a network of small stairways, archways, vestibules and passages, and then along two immense corridors with windows on one side and closed doors on the other. Everywhere there was the same quiet warmth and decency and plainness—stained deal, uncarpeted boards, a few oil pictures in the lower corridor, an image or two at the turn and head of the stairs; it was lighted clearly and unaffectedly by incandescent gas, and the only figures he had seen were of two or three monks, with hooded heads (they had raised these hoods slightly in salutation as he passed), each going about his business briskly and silently. There was even a cheerful smell of cooking at the end of one of the corridors, and he had caught a glimpse of two or three aproned lay brothers, busy in the firelight and glow of a huge kitchen, over great copper pans.

The sense of familiarity, then, is perfectly intelligible: a visitor to a monastery steps, indeed, into a busy and well-ordered life, but there is enough room and air and silence for him to preserve his individuality too.

As soon as he was washed and dressed, he sat down in a chair before the fire; but almost immediately there came a tap on his door, and the somewhat inflamed face of the Major looked in.

"Frankie?" he whispered, and, reassured, came in and closed the door behind. (He looked very curiously small and unimportant, thought Frank. Perhaps it was the black suit that had been lent him.)

"By gad, Frankie ... we're in clover," he whispered, still apparently under the impression that somehow he was in church. "There are some other chaps, you know, off the roads too, but they're down by the lodge somewhere." (He broke off and then continued.) "I've got such a queer Johnnie in my room—ah! you've got one, too."

He went up to examine a small plaster statue of a saint above the prie-dieu.

"It's all right, isn't it?" said Frank sleepily.

"And there's another Johnnie's name on the door. The Rev. S. Augustine, or something."

He tip-toed back to the fire, lifted his tails, and stood warming himself with a complacent but nervous smile.

(Frank regarded him with wonder.)

"What do all the Johnnies do here?" asked the Major presently. "Have a rare old time, I expect.

I bet they've got cellars under here all right. Just like those chaps in comic pictures, ain't it?"

(Frank decided it was no use to try to explain.)

The Major babbled on a minute or two longer, requiring no answer, and every now and then having his roving eye caught by some new marvel. He fingered a sprig of yew that was twisted into a crucifix hung over the bed. ("Expect it's one of those old relics," he said, "some lie or other.") He humorously dressed up the statue of the saint in a pocket-handkerchief, and said: "Let us pray," in a loud whisper, with one eye on the door. And all the while there still lay on him apparently the impression that if he talked loud or made any perceptible sound he would be turned out again.

He was just beginning a few steps of a noiseless high-kicking dance when there was a tap at the door, and he collapsed into an attitude of weak-kneed humility. Dom Hildebrand came in.

"If you're ready," he said, "we might go down to supper."

Frank relates in his diary that of all else in the monastery, apart from the church, the refectory and its manners impressed him most. (How easy it is to picture it when one has once seen the ceremonies!)

He sat at a center table, with the Major opposite (looking smaller than ever), before a cloth laid with knife, spoon and forks. All round the walls on a low daïs, with their backs against them, sat a row of perhaps forty monks, of every age, kind and condition. The tables were bare wood, laid simply with utensils and no cloths, with a napkin in each place. At the end opposite the door there sat at a table all alone a big, portly, kindly-faced man, of a startlingly fatherly appearance, clean-shaven, gray-haired, and with fine features. This was the Abbot. Above him hung a crucifix, with the single word "Sitio" beneath it on a small black label.

The meal began, however, with the ceremony of singing grace. The rows of monks stood out, with one in the middle, facing the Abbot, each with his hood forward and his hands hidden in his scapular. It was sung to a grave tone, with sudden intonations, by the united voices in unison—blessing, response, collect, psalm and the rest. (Frank could not resist one glance at the Major, whose face of consternation resembled that of a bird in the company of sedate cats.)

Then each went to his place, and, noiselessly, the orderly meal began and continued to the reading first of the gospel, and then of a history, from a pulpit built high in the wall. All were served by lay brothers, girded with aprons; almost every movement, though entirely natural, seemed ordered by routine and custom, and was distinguished by a serious sort of courtesy that made the taking of food appear, for once, as a really beautiful, august, and almost sacramental ceremony. The great hall, too, with its pointed roof, its tiled floor, its white-wood scrubbed tables, and its tall emblazoned windows, seemed exactly the proper background—a kind of secular sanctuary. The food was plain and plentiful: soup, meat, cheese and fruit; and each of the two guests had a small decanter of red wine, a tiny loaf of bread, and a napkin. The monks drank beer or water.

Then once more followed grace, with the same ceremonial.

When this was ended, Frank turned to see where Father Hildebrand was, supposing that all would go to their rooms; but as he turned he saw the Abbot coming down alone. He moved on, this great man, with that same large, fatherly air, but as he passed the two guests, he inclined slightly towards them, and Frank, with a glance to warn the Major, understanding that they were to follow, came out of his place and passed down between the lines of the monks, still in silence.

The Abbot went on, turned to the right, and as he moved along the cloister, loud sonorous chanting began behind. So they went, on and on, up the long lighted corridor, past door after door, as in some church procession. Yet all was obviously natural and familiar.

They turned in at last beneath an archway to the left, went through a vestibule, past a great stone of a crowned Woman with a Child in her arms, and as they entered the church, the Abbot dipped his finger into a stoop and presented it to Frank. Frank touched the drop of water, made the sign of the cross, and presented again his damp finger to the Major, who looked at him with a startled eye.

The Abbot indicated the front row of the seats in the nave, and Frank went into it, to watch the procession behind go past, flow up the steps, and disappear into the double rows of great stalls that lined the choir.

There was still silence—and longer silence, till Frank understood....

(IV)

His eyes grew accustomed to the gloom little by little, and he began to be able to make out the magnificence of the place he was in. Behind him stretched the immense nave, its roof and columns lost in darkness, its sides faintly illuminated by the glimmer of single oil-lamps, each in a small screened-off chapel. But in front of him was the greater splendor.

From side to side across the entrance to the choir ran the rood-screen, a vast erection of brown oak and black iron, surmounted by a high loft, from which glimmered down sheaves of silvered organ pipes, and, higher yet, in deep shadow, he could make out three gigantic figures, of which the center one was nailed to a cross. Beyond this began the stalls—dark and majestic, broken by carving—jutting heads of kings and priests leaning forward as if to breathe in the magnetism of that immense living silence generated by forty men at their prayers. At the further end there shone out faintly the glory of the High Altar, almost luminous, it seemed, in the light of the single red spark that hung before it. Frank could discern presently the gilded figures that stood among the candlesticks behind, the throne and crucifix, the mysterious veiling curtains of the Tabernacle.... Finally, in the midst of the choir, stood a tall erection which he could not understand.

An extraordinary peace seemed to descend and envelop him as he looked—a kind of crown and climax of various interior experiences that were falling on him now—for the last few weeks. (It is useless trying to put it into words. I shall hope to do my best presently by quoting Frank himself.) There was a sense of home-coming; there was a sense of astonishing sanity; there was a sense of an enormous objective peace, meeting and ratifying that interior peace which was beginning to be his. It appeared to him, somehow, as if for the first time he experienced without him that which up to now he had chiefly found within. Certainly there had been moments of this before—not merely emotional, you understand—when heart and head lay still from their striving, and the will reposed in Another Will. But this was the climax: it summed up all that he had learned in the last few months; it soothed the last scars away, it explained and answered— and, above all, correlated—his experiences. No doubt it was the physical, as well as the spiritual, atmosphere of this place, the quiet corridors, the warmth and the plainness and the solidity, even the august grace of the refectory—all these helped and had part in the sensation. Yet, if it is possible for you to believe it, these were no more than the vessels from which the heavenly fluid streamed; vessels, rather, that contained a little of that abundance that surged up here as in a fountain....

Frank started a little at a voice in his ear.

"When's it going to begin?" whispered the Major in a hoarse, apprehensive voice.

(V)

A figure detached itself presently from the dark mass of the stalls and came down to where they were sitting. Frank perceived it was Father Hildebrand.

"We're singing Mattins of the Dead, presently," he said in a low voice. "It's All Souls' Eve. Will you stay, or shall I take you to your room?"

The Major stood up with alacrity.

"I'll stay, if I may," said Frank.

"Very well. Then I'll take Mr. Trustcott upstairs."

Half an hour later the ceremony began.

Here, I simply despair of description. I know something of what Frank witnessed and perceived, for I have been present myself at this affair in a religious house; but I do not pretend to be able to write it down.

First, however, there was the external, visible, audible service: the catafalque, a bier-like erection, all black and yellow, guarded by yellow flames on yellow candles—the grave movements, the almost monstrous figures, the rhythm of the ceremonies, and the wail of, the music of forty voices singing as one—all that is understood....

But the inner side of these things—the reverse of which these things are but a coarse lining, the substance of which this is a shadow—that is what passes words and transcends impressions.

It seemed to Frank that one section, at any rate, of that enormous truth at which he had clutched almost blindly when he had first made his submission to the Church—one chamber in that House of Life—was now flung open before him, and he saw in it men as trees walking.... He was tired and excited, of course; he was intensely imaginative; but there are some experiences that a rise of temperature cannot explain and that an imagination cannot originate....

For it seemed to him that here he was aware of an immeasurable need to which those ministrations were addressed, and this whole was countless in its units and clamant in its silence. It was as a man might see the wall of his room roll away, beyond which he had thought only the night to lie, and discern a thronging mass of faces crying for help, pressing upon him, urging, yet all without sound or word. He attempts in his diary to use phrases for all this—he speaks of a pit in which is no water, of shadows and forms that writhe and plead, of a light of glass mingled with fire; and yet of an inevitability, of a Justice which there is no questioning and a Force that there is no resisting. And, on the other side, there was this help given by men of flesh and blood like himself—using ceremonies and gestures and strange resonant words.... The whole was as some enormous orchestra—there was the wail on this side, the answer on that—the throb of beating hearts—there were climaxes, catastrophes, soft passages, and yet the result was one vast and harmonious whole.

It was the catafalque that seemed to him the veiled door to that other world that so manifested itself—seen as he saw it in the light of the yellow candles—it was as the awful portal of death itself; beneath that heavy mantle lay not so much a Body of Humanity still in death, as a Soul of Humanity alive beyond death, quick and yet motionless with pain. And those figures that moved about it, with censor and aspersorium, were as angels for tenderness and dignity and undoubted power. They were men like himself, yet they were far more; and they, too, one day, like himself, would pass beneath that pall and need the help of others that should follow them....

Something of this is but a hint of what Frank experienced; it came and went, no doubt, in gusts, yet all through he seems to have felt that sense that here was a door into that great watching world beyond—that here, in what is supposed by the world to be the narrow constraint of religion, was a liberty and an outlook into realities such as the open road and nature can but seldom give. But for my part, I can no more follow him further than I can write down the passion of the lover and the ecstasy of the musician. If these things could be said in words, they would have been said long ago. But at least it was along this path of perception that Frank went—a path that but continued the way along which he had come with such sure swiftness ever since the moment he had taken his sorrows and changed them from bitter to sweet. Some sentences that he has written mean nothing to me at all....

Only this I see clearly, both from my talks with Father Hildebrand and from the diary which Frank amplified at his bidding—that Frank had reached the end of a second stage in his journey, and that a third was to begin.

It is significant also, I think, in view of what is to follow, that the last initiation of this stage should have taken place on such an occasion as this.

CHAPTER V: (I)

There are certain moods into which minds, very much tired or very much concentrated, occasionally fall, in which the most trifling things take on them an appearance of great significance. A man in great anxiety, for example, will regard as omens or warnings such things as the ringing of a bell or the flight of a bird. I have heard this process deliberately defended by people who should know better. I have heard it said that those moods of intense concentration are, as a matter of fact states of soul in which the intuitive or mystical faculties work with great facility, and that at such times connections and correlations are perceived which at other times pass unnoticed. The events of the world then are, by such people, regarded as forming links in a chain of purpose—events even which are obviously to the practical man merely the effects of chance and accident. It is utterly impossible, says the practical man, that the ringing of a bell, or the grouping of tea-leaves, or the particular moment at which a picture falls from a wall, can be anything but fortuitous: and it is the sign of a weak and superstitious mind to regard them as anything else. There can be no purpose or sequence except in matters where we can perceive purpose or sequence.

Of course the practical man must be right; we imply that he is right, since we call him practical, and I have to deplore, therefore, the fact that Frank on several occasions fell into a superstitious way of looking at things. The proof is only too plain from his own diary—not that he interprets the little events which he records, but that he takes such extreme pains to write them down—events, too, that are, to all sensibly-minded people, almost glaringly unimportant and insignificant.

I have two such incidents to record between the the travelers' leaving the Benedictine monastery and their arriving in London in December. The Major and Gertie have probably long since forgotten the one which they themselves witnessed, and, indeed, there is no particular reason why they should remember it. Of the other Frank seems to have said nothing to his friends. Both of them, however, are perfectly insignificant—they concern, respectively, only a few invisible singers and a couple of quite ordinary human beings. They are described with a wholly unnecessary wealth of detail in Frank's diary, though without comment, and I write them down here for that reason, and that reason only.

The first was as follows:

They were approaching a certain cathedral town, not a hundred miles from London, and as the evening was clear and dry, though frosty, and money was low, they determined to pass the night in a convenient brick-yard about half a mile out of the town.

There was a handy shed where various implements were kept; the Major, by the help of a little twisted wire, easily unfastened the door. They supped, cooking a little porridge over a small fire which they were able to make without risk, and lay down to sleep after a pipe or two.

Tramps go to sleep early when they mean business, and it could not have been more than about eleven o'clock at night when Frank awoke with the sense that he had slept long and deeply. He seems to have lain there, content and quiet enough, watching the last ember dying in the brazier where they had made their fire.... There was presently a stir from the further corner of the shed, a match was struck, and Frank, from his improvised pillow, beheld the Major's face suddenly illuminated by the light with which he was kindling his pipe once more. He watched the face with a sort of artistic interest for a few seconds—the drooping shadows, the apparently cavernous eyes, the deep-shaded bar of the mustache across the face. In the wavering light cast from below it resembled the face of a vindictive beast. Then the Major whispered, between his puffs:

"Frankie?"

"Yes."

"Oh! you're awake too, are you?"

"Yes."

A minute later, though they had spoken only in whispers, Gertie drew a long sighing breath from her corner of the shed and they could hear that she, too, sat up and cleared her throat.

"Well, this is a pretty job," said the Major jovially to the company generally. "What's the matter with us?"

Frank said nothing. He lay still, with a sense of extraordinary content and comfort, and heard Gertie presently lie down again. The Major smoked steadily.

Then the singing began.

It was a perfectly still night, frost-bound and motionless. It was late enough for the sounds of the town to have died away (cathedral towns go to bed early and rise late), and, indeed, almost the only sounds they had heard, even three or four hours before, had been the occasional deliberate chime of bells, like a meditative man suddenly uttering a word or two aloud. Now, however, everything was dead silent. Probably the hour had struck immediately before they awoke, since Frank remarks that it seemed a long time before four notes tolled out the quarter.

The singing came first as a sensation rather than as a sound, so far away was it. It was not at once that Frank formulated the sense of pleasure that he experienced by telling himself that someone was singing.

At first it was a single voice that made itself heard—a tenor of extraordinary clarity. The air was unknown to him, but it had the character of antiquity; there was a certain pleasant melancholy about it; it contained little trills and grace-notes, such as—before harmony developed in the modern sense—probably supplied the absence of chords. There was no wind on which the sound could rise or fall, and it grew from a thread out of the distance into clear singing not a quarter of a mile away....

The Major presently grunted over his pipe some expression of surprise; but Frank could say nothing. He was almost holding his breath, so great was his pleasure.

The air, almost regretfully, ran downhill like a brook approaching, an inevitable full close; and then, as the last note was reached, a chord of voices broke in with some kind of chorus.

The voices were of a quartette of men, and rang together like struck notes, not loud or harsh, but, on the contrary, with a restrained softness that must, I suppose, have been the result of very careful training. It was the same air that they were repeating, but the grace-notes were absent, and the four voices, in chord after chord, supplied their place by harmony. It was impossible to tell what was the subject of the song or even whether it were sacred or secular, for it was of that period—at least, so I conjecture—when the two worlds were one, and when men courted their love and adored their God after the same fashion. Only there ran through all that air of sweet and austere melancholy, as if earthly music could do no more than hint at what the heart wished to express.

Frank listened in a sort of ecstasy. The music was nearer now, coming from the direction from which the three travelers had themselves come this afternoon. Presently, from the apparent diminuendo, it was plain that the singers were past, and were going on towards the town. There was no sound of footsteps; the Major remarked on that, when he could get Frank to attend a few minutes later, when all was over; but there were field paths running in every direction, as well as broad stretches of grass beside the road, so the singers may very well have been walking on soft ground. (These points are dispassionately noted down in the diary.)

The chorus was growing fainter now; once more the last slopes of the melody were in sight—those downhill gradations of the air that told of the silence to come. Then once more, for an instant, there was silence, till again, perhaps nearly a quarter of a mile away, the single tenor voice began da capo. And the last that Frank heard, at the moment before the quarter struck and, soft and mellow though it was, jarred the air and left the ear unable to focus itself again on the tiny woven thread of sound, was, once more the untiring quartette taking up the melody, far off in the silent darkness.

It seems to me a curious little incident—this passing of four singers in the night; it might have seemed as if our travelers, by a kind of chance, were allowed to overhear the affairs of a world other than their own—and the more curious because Frank seems to have been so much absorbed by it. Of course, from a practical point of view, it is almost painfully obvious what is the explanation. It must have been a quartette from the cathedral choir, returning from some festivity in the suburbs; and it must have happened that they followed the same route, though walking on the grass, along which Frank himself had come that evening.

(II)

The second incident is even more ordinary, and once again I must declare that nothing would have induced me to incorporate it into this story had it not appeared, described very minutely in the sort of log-book into which Frank's diary occasionally degenerates.

They were within a very few miles of the outskirts of London, and December had succeeded November. They had had a day or two of work upon some farm or other. (I have not been able to identify the place), and had run into, and, indeed, exchanged remarks with two or three groups of tramps also London bound.

They were given temporary lodgings in a loft over a stable, by the farmer for whom they worked, and this stable was situated in a court at the end of the village street, with gates that stood open all day, since the yard was overlooked by the windows of the farmer's living-house—and, besides, there was really nothing to steal.

They had finished their work in the fields (I think it had to do with the sheep and mangel-wurzels, or something of the kind); they had returned to their lodgings, received their pay, packed up their belongings, and had already reached the further end of the village on their way to London, when Frank discovered that he had left a pair of socks behind. This would never do: socks cost money, and their absence meant sore feet and weariness; so he told the Major and Gertie to walk on slowly while he went back. He would catch them up, he said, before they had gone half a mile. He hid his bundle under a hedge—every pound of weight made a difference at the end of a day's work—and set off.

It was just at that moment between day and night—between four and five o'clock—as he came back into the yard. He went straight through the open gates, glancing about, to explain matters to the farmer if necessary, but, not seeing him, went up the rickety stairs, groped his way across to the window, took down his socks from the nail an which he had hung them last night, and came down again.

As he came into the yard, he thought he heard something stirring within the open door of the stable on his right, and thinking it to be the farmer, and that an explanation would be advisable, looked in.

At first he saw nothing, though he could hear a horse moving about in the loose-box in the corner. Then he saw a light shine beneath the crack of the second door, beside the loose-box, that led into the farm-yard proper; and the next instant the door opened, a man came in with a lantern obviously just lighted, as the flame was not yet burned up, and stopped with a half-frightened look on seeing Frank. But he said nothing.

Frank himself was just on the point of giving an explanation when he, too, stopped dead and stared. It seemed to him that he had been here before, under exactly the same circumstances; he tried to remember what happened next, but he could not....

For this was what he saw as the flame burned up more brightly.

The man who held the lantern and looked at him in silence with a half-deprecating air was a middle-aged man, bearded and bare-headed. He had thrown over his shoulders a piece of sacking, that hung from him almost like a robe. The light that he carried threw heavy wavering shadows about the stable, and Frank noticed the great head of a cart-horse in the loose-box peering through the bars, as if to inquire what the company wanted. Then, still without speaking, Frank let his eyes rove round, and they stopped suddenly at the sight of yet one more living being in the stable. Next to the loose-box was a stall, empty except for one occupant; for there, sitting on a box with her back to the manger and one arm flung along it to support her weight, was the figure of a girl. Her head, wrapped in an old shawl, leaned back against her arm, and a very white and weary face, absolutely motionless, looked at him. She had great eyes, with shadows beneath, and her lips were half opened. By her side lay a regular tramp's bundle.

Frank looked at her steadily a moment, then he looked back at the man, who still had not moved or spoken. The draught from the door behind blew in and shook the flame of his lantern, and the horse sighed long and loud in the shadows behind. Once more Frank glanced at the girl; she had lowered her arm from the manger and now sat looking at him, it seemed, with a curious intentness and expectancy.

There was nothing to be said. Frank bowed a little, almost apologetically, and went out.

Now that was absolutely all that happened. Frank says so expressly in his diary. He did not speak to them, nor they to him; nor was any explanation given on either side. He went out across the yard in silence, seeing nothing of the farmer, but hearing a piano begin to play beyond the brightly lighted windows, of which he could catch a glimpse over the low wall separating the yard from the garden. He walked quickly up the village street and caught up his companions, as he had said, less than half a mile further on. He said nothing to them of his experience—indeed, what was there to say?—but he must have written it down that same night when they reached their next lodging, and written it down, too, with that minuteness of detail which surprised me so much when I first read it.

For the explanation of the whole thing is as foolishly obvious as was that of the singing that the three had heard in the suburbs of Peterborough. Obviously a couple of tramps had turned into this stable for shelter. Perhaps the girl was the man's daughter; perhaps his wife; perhaps neither. Plainly they had no right there—and that would explain the embarrassed silence of the two: they knew they were trespassing, and feared to be turned away. Perhaps already they had been turned away from the village inn. But the girl was obviously tired out, and the man had determined to risk it.

That, then, was the whole affair—commonplace, and even a little sordid. And yet Frank thought that it was worth writing down!

CHAPTER VI

An extract, taken by permission, from a few pages of Frank Guiseley's diary. These pages were written with the encouragement of Dom Hildebrand Maple, O.S.B., and were sent to him later at his own request.

"... He told me a great many things that surprised me. For instance, he seemed to know all about certain ideas that I had had, before I told him of them, and said that I was not responsible, and he picked out one or two other things that I had said, and told me that these were much more serious....

"I went to confession to him on Friday morning, in the church. He did not say a great deal then, but he asked if I would care to talk to him afterwards. I said I would, and went to him in the parlor after dinner. The first thing that happened was that he asked me to tell him as plainly as I could anything that had happened to me—in my soul, I mean—since I had left Cambridge. So I tried to describe it.

"I said that at first things went pretty well in my soul, and that it was only bodily things that troubled me—getting fearfully tired and stiff, being uncomfortable, the food, the sleeping, and so on. Then, as soon as this wore off I met the Major and Gertie. I was rather afraid of saying all that I felt about these; but he made me, and I told him how extraordinarily I seemed to hate them sometimes, how I felt almost sick now and then when the Major talked to me and told me stories.... The thing that seemed to torment me most during this time was the contrast between Cambridge and Merefield and the people there, and the company of this pair; and the only relief was that I knew I could, as a matter of fact, chuck them whenever I wanted and go home again. But this relief was taken away from me as soon as I understood that I had to keep with them, and do my best somehow to separate them. Of course, I must get Gertie back to her people some time, and till that's done it's no good thinking about anything else.

"After a while, however—I think it was just before I got into trouble with the police—I began to see that I was a conceited ass for hating the Major so much. It was absurd for me, I said, to put on airs, when the difference between him and me was just that he had been brought up in one way and I in another. I hated the things he did and said, not because they were wrong, but because they were what I called 'bad form.' That was really the whole thing. Then I saw a lot more, and it made me feel miserable. I used to think that it was rather good of me to be kind to animals and children, but I began to see that it was simply the way I was made: it wasn't any effort to me. I simply 'saw red' when I came across cruelty. And I saw that that was no good.

"Then I began to see that I had done absolutely nothing of any good whatever—that nothing had really cost me anything; and that the things I was proud of were simply self-will—my leaving Cambridge, and all the rest. They were theatrical, or romantic, or egotistical; there was no real sacrifice. I should have minded much more not doing them. I began to feel extraordinarily small.

"Then the whole series of things began that simply smashed me up.

"First there was the prison business. That came about in this way:

"I had just begun to see that I was all wrong with the Major—that by giving way to my feelings about him (I don't mean that I ever showed it, but that was only because I thought it more dignified not to!), I was getting all wrong with regard to both him and myself, and that I must do something that my whole soul hated if it was to be of any use. Then there came that minute in the barn, when I heard the police were after us, and that there was really no hope of escape. The particular thing that settled me was Gertie. I knew, somehow, that I couldn't let the Major go to prison while she was about. And then I saw that this was just the very thing to do, and that I couldn't be proud of it ever, because the whole thing was so mean and second-rate. Well, I did it, and it did me a lot of good somehow. I felt really rolled in the dirt, and that little thing in the post-office afterwards rubbed it in. I saw how chock-full I must be of conceit really to mind that, as I did, and to show off, and talk like a gentleman.

"Then there came the priest who refused to help me. That made me for a time perfectly furious, because I had always said to myself that Catholics, and especially priests, would always understand. But before I got to York I saw what an ass I had made of myself. Of course, the priest was perfectly right (I saw that before I got ten yards away, though I wouldn't acknowledge it for another five miles). I was a dirty tramp, and I talked like a brazen fool. (I remember thinking my 'openness' to him rather fine and manly!) Well, that made me smaller still.

"Then a sort of despair came on me when the police got me turned out of my work in York. I know it was only a little thing (though I still think it unfair), but it was like a pebble in your boot when you're already going lame from something else.

"And then came Jenny's letter. (I want to write about that rather carefully.)

"I said just now that I was getting to feel smaller and smaller. That's perfectly true, but there was still a little hard lump in the middle that would not break. Things might have gone crumbling away at me for ever, and I might have got smaller still, but they wouldn't have smashed me.

"Now there were two things that I held on to all this time—my religion and Jenny. I gave them turns, so to speak, though Jenny was never absent. When everything religious tasted flat and dull and empty, I thought about Jenny: when things were better—when I had those two or three times I told Father Hildebrand about (...)—I still thought of Jenny, and imagined how splendid it would be when we were both Catholics together and married. But I never dreamed that Jenny would ever be angry or disappointed. I wouldn't talk about her to anybody ever, because I was so absolutely certain of her. I knew, I thought, that the whole world might crumble away, but that Jenny would always understand, down at the bottom, and that she and I would remain....

"Well, then came her letter.

"Honestly, I don't quite know what I was doing inside for the next week or so. Simply everything was altered. I never had any sort of doubt that she meant what she said, and it was as if there wasn't any sun or moon or sky. It was like being ill. Things happened round me: I ate and drank and walked, but the only thing I wanted was to get away, and get down somewhere into myself and hide. Religion, of course, seemed no good at all. I don't understand quite what people mean by 'consolations' of religion. Religion doesn't seem to me a thing like Art or Music, in which you can take refuge. It either covers everything, or it isn't religion. Religion never has seemed to me (I don't know if I'm wrong) one thing, like other things, so that you can change about and back again.... It's either the background and foreground all in one, or it's a kind of game. It's either true, or it's a pretense.

"Well, all this, in a way, taught me it was absolutely true. Things wouldn't have held together at all unless it was true. But it was no sort of satisfaction. It seemed to me for a while that it was horrible that it was true; that it was frightful to think that God could be like that—since this Jenny-business had really happened. But I didn't feel all this exactly consciously at the time. I seemed as if I was ill, and could only lie still and watch and be in hell. One thing, however, Father Hildebrand thought very important (he asked me about it particularly) was that I honestly did not feel any resentment whatever against either God or Jenny. It was frightful, but it was true, and I just had to lie still inside and look at it. He tells me that this shows that the first part of the 'process,' as he called it, was finished (he called it the 'Purgative Way'). And I must say that what happened next seems to fit in rather well.

"The new 'process' began quite suddenly when I awoke in the shepherd's hut one morning at Ripon. The instant I awoke I knew it. It was very early in the morning, just before sunrise, but there was a little wood behind me, and the birds were beginning to chirp.

"It's very hard to describe it in words, but the first thing to say is that I was not exactly happy just then, but absolutely content. I think I should say that it was like this: I saw suddenly that what had been wrong in me was that I had made myself the center of things, and God a kind of circumference. When He did or allowed things, I said, 'Why does He?'—from my point of view. That is to say, I set up my ideas of justice and love and so forth, and then compared His with mine, not mine with His. And I suddenly saw—or, rather, I knew already when I awoke—that this was simply stupid. Even now I cannot imagine why I didn't see it before: I had heard people say it, of course—in sermons and books—but I suppose it had meant nothing to me. (Father Hildebrand tells me that I had seen it intellectually, but had never embraced it with my will.) Because when one once really sees that, there's no longer any puzzle about anything. One can simply never say 'Why?' again. The thing's finished.

"Now this 'process' (as Father H. calls it) has gone on in a most extraordinary manner ever since. That beginning near Ripon was like opening a door into another country, and I've been walking ever since and seeing new things. All sorts of things that I had believed as a Catholic—things, I mean, which I assented to simply because the Church said so, have, so to speak, come up and turned themselves inside out. I couldn't write them down, because you can't write these things down, or even put them intelligibly to yourself. You just see that they are so. For instance, one morning at mass—quite suddenly—I saw how the substance of the bread was changed, and how our Lord is united with the soul at Communion—of course it's a mystery (that's what I mean by saying that it can't be written down)—but I saw it, in a flash, and I can see it still in a sort of way. Then another day when the Major was talking about something or other (I think it was about the club he used to belong to in Piccadilly), I understood about our Lady and how she is just everything from one point of view. And so on. I had that kind of thing at Doctor Whitty's a good deal, particularly when I was getting better. I could talk to him all the time, too, or count the knobs on the wardrobe, or listen to the Major and Gertie in the garden—and yet go on all the time seeing things. I knew it wasn't any good talking to Doctor Whitty himself much, though I can't imagine why a man like that doesn't see it all for himself....

"It seems to me most extraordinary now that I ever could have had those other thoughts I told Father H. about—I mean about sins, and about wondering whether, after all, the Church was actually true. In a sort of way, of course, they come back to me still, and I know perfectly well I must be on my guard; but somehow it's different.

"Well, all this is what Father H. calls the 'Illuminative Way,' and I think I understand what he means. It came to a sort of point on All Souls' Eve at the monastery. I saw the whole thing then for a moment or two, and not only Purgatory. But I will write that down later. And Father H. tells me that I must begin to look forward to a new 'process'—what he calls the 'Way of Union.' I don't understand much what he means by that; I don't see that more could happen to me. I am absolutely and entirely happy; though I must say that there has seemed a sort of lull for the last day or two—ever since All Souls' Day, in fact. Perhaps something is going to happen. It's all right, anyhow. It seems very odd to me that all this kind of thing is perfectly well known to priests. I thought I was the first person who had ever felt quite like this.

"I must add one thing. Father H. asked me whether I didn't feel I had a vocation to the Religious Life; he told me that from everything he could see, I had, and that my coming to the monastery was simply providential.

"Well, I don't agree, and I have told him so. I haven't the least idea what is going to happen next; but I know, absolutely for certain, that I have got to go on with the Major and Gertie to East London. Gertie will have to be got away from the Major somehow, and until that is done I mustn't do anything else.

"I have written all this down as plainly as I can, because I promised Father H. I would."

PART III: CHAPTER I

Mrs. Partington was standing at the door of her house towards sunset, waiting for the children to come back from school.

Her house is situated in perhaps the least agreeable street—Turner Road—in perhaps the least agreeable district of East London—Hackney Wick. It is a disagreeable district because it isn't anything in particular. It has neither the tragic gayety of Whitechapel nor the comparative refinement of Clapton. It is a large, triangular piece of land, containing perhaps a square mile altogether, or rather more, approached from the south by the archway of the Great Eastern Railway, defined on one side by the line, and along its other two sides, partly by the river Lea—a grimy, depressed-looking stream—and partly by the Hackney Marshes—flat, dreary wastes of grass-grown land, useless as building ground and of value only for Saturday afternoon recreations of rabbit coursing and football. The dismalness of the place is beyond description at all times of the year. In winter it is bleak and chilly; in summer it is hot, fly-infested, and hideously and ironically reminiscent of real fields and real grass. The population is calculated to change completely about every three years, and I'm sure I am not surprised. It possesses two important blocks of buildings besides the schools—a large jam factory and the church and clergy-house of the Eton Mission.

Turner Road is perhaps the most hopeless of all the dozen and a half of streets. (It is marked black, by the way, in Mr. Booth's instructive map.) It is about a quarter of a mile long and perfectly straight. It is intersected at one point by another street, and is composed of tall dark houses, with flat fronts, perhaps six or seven stories in height. It is generally fairly silent and empty, and is inhabited by the most characteristic members of the Hackney Wick community— quiet, white-faced men, lean women, draggled and sharp-tongued, and countless over-intelligent children—all of the class that seldom remain long anywhere—all of the material out of which the real criminal is developed. No booths or stalls ever stand here; only, on Saturday nights, there is echoed here, as in a stone-lined pit, the cries and the wheel-noises from the busy thoroughfare a hundred yards away round the corner. The road, as a whole, bears an aspect of desperate and fierce dignity; there is never here the glimpse of a garden or of flowers, as in Mortimer Road, a stone's throw away. There is nothing whatever except the tall, flat houses, the pavements, the lampposts, the grimy thoroughfare and the silence. The sensation of the visitor is that anything might happen here, and that no one would be the wiser. There is an air of horrible discretion about these houses.

Mrs. Partington was—indeed is (for I went to see her not two months ago)—of a perfectly defined type. She must have been a handsome factory girl—dark, slender, and perfectly able to take care of herself, with thin, muscular arms, generally visible up to the elbow, hard hands, a quantity of rather untidy hair—with the tongue of a venomous orator and any amount of very inferior sentiment, patriotic and domestic. She has become a lean, middle-aged woman, very upright and very strong, without any sentiment at all, but with a great deal of very practical human experience to take its place. She has no illusions about either this world or the next; she has borne nine children, of which three survive; and her husband is almost uninterruptedly out of work. However, they are prosperous (for Turner Road), and have managed, so far, to keep their home together.

The sunset was framed in a glow of smoky glory at the end of the street down which Mrs. Partington was staring, resembling a rather angry search-light turned on from the gates of heaven. The street was still quiet; but already from the direction of the Board-school came thin and shrill cries as the swarm of children exploded in all directions. Mrs. Partington (she would have said) was waiting for her children—Jimmy, Maggie and 'Erb—and there were lying within upon the bare table three thick slices of bread and black jam; as a matter of fact, she was looking out for her lodgers, who should have arrived by midday.

Then she became aware that they were coming, even as she looked, advancing down the empty street en échelon. Two of them she knew well enough—they had lodged with her before; but the third was to be a stranger, and she was already interested in him—the Major had hinted at wonderful mysteries....

So she shaded her eyes against the cold glare and watched them carefully, with that same firm, resolute face with which she always looked out upon the world; and even as, presently, she exchanged that quick, silent nod of recognition with the Major and Gertie, still she watched the brown-faced, shabby young man who came last, carrying his bundle and walking a little lame.

"You're after your time," she said abruptly.

The Major began his explanations, but she cut them short and led the way into the house.

I find it very difficult to record accurately the impression that Frank made upon Mrs. Partington; but that the impression was deep and definite became perfectly clear to me from her conversation. He hardly spoke at all, she said, and before he got work at the jam factory he went out for long, lonely walks across the marshes. He and the Major slept together, it seemed, in one room, and Gertie, temporarily with the children and Mrs. Partington in another. (Mr. Partington, at this time, happened to be away on one of his long absences.) At meals Frank was always quiet and well-behaved, yet not ostentatiously. Mrs. Partington found no fault with him in that way. He would talk to the children a little before they went to school, and would meet them sometimes on their way back from school; and all three of them conceived for him an immense and indescribable adoration. All this, however, would be too long to set down in detail.

It seems to have been a certain air of pathos which Mrs. Partington herself cast around him, which affected her the most, and I imagine her feeling to have been largely motherly. There was, however, another element very obviously visible, which, in anyone but Mrs. Partington, I should call reverence.... She told me that she could not imagine why he was traveling with the Major and Gertie, so she at least understood something of the gulf between them.

So the first week crept by, bringing us up to the middle of December.

It was on the Friday night that Frank came back with the announcement that he was to go to work at the jam factory on Monday. There was a great pressure, of course, owing to the approach of Christmas, and Frank was to be given joint charge of a van. The work would last, it seemed, at any rate, for a week or two.

"You'll have to mind your language," said the Major jocosely. (He was sitting in the room where the cooking was done and where, by the way, the entire party, with the exception of the two men, slept; and, at this moment, had his feet on the low mantelshelf between the saucepan and Jimmy's cap.)

"Eh?" said Frank.

"No language allowed there," said the Major. "They're damn particular."

Frank put his cap down and took his seat on the bed.

"Where's Gertie?" he asked. ("Yes, come on, Jimmie.")

Jimmie crept up beside him, looking at him with big black, reverential eyes. Then he leaned against him with a quick smile and closed his eyes ecstatically. Frank put an arm round the boy to support him.

"Oh! Gertie's gone to see a friend," said the Major. "Did you want her?"

Frank said nothing, and Mrs. Partington looked from one to the other swiftly.

Mrs. Partington had gathered a little food for thought during the last few days. It had become perfectly evident to her that the girl was very much in love with this young man, and that while this young man either was, or affected to be, ignorant of it, the Major was not. Gertie had odd silences when Frank came into the room, or yet more odd volubilities, and Mrs. Partington was not quite sure of the Major's attitude. This officer and her husband had had dealings together in the past of a nature which I could not quite determine (indeed, the figure of Mr. Partington is still a complete mystery to me, and rather a formidable mystery); and I gather that Mrs. Partington had learned from her husband that the Major was not simply negligible. She knew him for a blackguard, but she seems to have been uncertain of what kind was this black-guardism— whether of the strong or the weak variety. She was just a little uncomfortable, therefore, as to the significance of Gertie; and had already wondered more than once whether or no she should say a motherly word to the young man.

There came a sound of footsteps up the street as Mrs. Partington ironed a collar of Jimmie's on the dining-room table, and laid down the iron as a tap fell on the door. The Major took out his pipe and began to fill it as she went out to see who was knocking.

"Oh! good evening, Mrs. Partington," sounded in a clear, high-bred voice from the street door. "May I come in for a minute or two? I heard you had lodgers, and I thought perhaps—"

"Well, sir, we're rather upside-down just now—and—"

"Oh! I won't disturb you more than a minute," came the other voice again. There were footsteps in the passage, and the next instant, past the unwilling hostess, there came a young, fresh-colored clergyman, carrying a silk hat, into the lamplight of the kitchen. Frank stood up instantly, and the Major went so far as to take down his feet. Then he, too, stood up.

"Good evening!" said the clergyman. "May I just come in for a minute or two? I heard you had come, and as it's in my district—May I sit down, Mrs. Partington?"

Mrs. Partington with sternly knit lips, swept a brown teapot, a stocking, a comb, a cup and a crumby plate off the single unoccupied chair, and set it a little forward near the fire. Clergymen were, to her mind, one of those mysterious dispensations of the world for which there was no adequate explanation at all—like policemen and men's gamblings and horse-races. There they were, and there was no more to be said. They were mildly useful for entertaining the children and taking them to Southend, and in cases of absolute despair they could be relied upon for soup-tickets or even half-crowns; but the big mysterious church, with its gilded screen, its curious dark glass, and its white little side-chapel, with the Morris hangings, the great clergy-house, the ladies, the parish magazine and all the rest of it—these were simply inexplicable. Above all inexplicable was the passion displayed for district-visiting—that strange impulse that drove four highly-cultivated young men in black frock-coats and high hats and ridiculous little collars during five afternoons in the week to knock at door after door all over the district and conduct well-mannered conversations with bored but polite mothers of families. It was one of the phenomena that had to be accepted. She supposed it stood for something beyond her perceptions.

"I thought I must come in and make your acquaintance," said the clergyman, nursing his hat and smiling at the company. (He, too, occasionally shared Mrs. Partington's wonder as to the object of all this; but he, too, submitted to it as part of the system.) "People come and go so quickly, you know—"

"Very pleased to see a clergyman," said the Major smoothly. "No objection to smoke, sir, I presume?" He indicated his pipe.

"Not at all," said the clergyman. "In fact, I smoke myself; and if Mrs. Partington will allow me—" He produced a small pink and gilded packet of Cinderellas. (I think he thought it brought him vaguely nearer the people to smoke Cinderellas.)

"Oh! no objection at all, sir," put in Mrs. Partington, still a little grimly. (She was still secretly resenting being called upon at half-past six. You were usually considered immune from this kind of thing after five o'clock.)

"So I thought I must just look in and catch you one evening," explained the clergyman once more, "and tell you that we're your friends here—the clergy, you know—and about the church and all that."

He was an extremely conscientious young man—this Mr. Parham-Carter—an old Etonian, of course, and now in his first curacy. It was all pretty bewildering to him, too, this great and splendid establishment, the glorious church by Bodley, with the Magnificat in Gothic lettering below the roof, the well-built and furnished clergy-house, the ladies' house, the zeal, the self-devotion, the parochial machinery, the Band of Hope, the men's and boys' clubs, and, above all, the furious district-visiting. Of course, it produced results, it kept up the standards of decency and civilization and ideals; it was a weight in the balances on the side of right and good living; the clubs kept men from the public-house to some extent, and made it possible for boys to grow up with some chance on their side. Yet he wondered, in fits of despondency, whether there were not something wrong somewhere.... But he accepted it: it was the approved method, and he himself was a learner, not a teacher.

"Very kind of you, sir," said the Major, replacing his feet on the mantelshelf. "And at what time are the services on Sunday?"

The clergyman jumped. He was not accustomed to that sort of question.

"I ..." he began.

"I'm a strong Churchman, sir," said the Major. "And even if I were not, one must set an example, you know. I may be narrow-minded, but I'm particular about all that sort of thing. I shall be with you on Sunday."

He nodded reassuringly at Mr. Parham-Carter.

"Well, we have morning prayer at ten-thirty next Sunday, and the Holy Eucharist at eleven—and, of course, at eight."

"No vestments, I hope?" said the Major sternly.

Mr. Parham-Carter faltered a little. Vestments were not in use, but to his regret.

"Well, we don't use vestments," he said, "but—"

The Major resumed his pipe with a satisfied air.

"That's all right," he said. "Now, I'm not bigoted—my friend here's a Roman Catholic, but—"

The clergyman looked up sharply, and for the first time became consciously conscious of the second man. Frank had sat back again on the bed, with Jimmie beside him, and was watching the little scene quietly and silently, and the clergyman met his eyes full. Some vague shock thrilled through him; Frank's clean-shaven brown face seemed somehow familiar—or was it something else?

Mr. Parham-Carter considered the point for a little while in silence, only half attending to the

Major, who was now announcing his views on the Establishment and the Reformation settlement. Frank said nothing at all, and there grew on the clergyman a desire to hear his voice. He made an opportunity at last.

"Yes, I see," he said to the Major; "and you—I don't know your name?"

"Gregory, sir," said Frank. And again a little shock thrilled Mr. Parham-Carter. The voice was the kind of thing he had expected from that face.

It was about ten minutes later, that the clergyman thought it was time to go. He had the Major's positive promise to attend at least the evening service on the following Sunday—a promise he did not somehow very much appreciate—but he had made no progress with Frank. He shook hands all round very carefully, told Jimmie not to miss Sunday-school, and publicly commended Maggie for a recitation she had accomplished at the Band of Hope on the previous evening; and then went out, accompanied by Mrs. Partington, still silent, as far as the door. But as he actually went out, someone pushed by the woman and came out into the street.

"May I speak to you a minute?" said the strange young man, dropping the "sir." "I'll walk with you as far as the clergy-house if you'll let me."

When they were out of earshot of the house Frank began.

"You're Parham-Carter, aren't you?" he said. "Of Hales'."

The other nodded. (Things were beginning to resolve themselves in his mind.)

"Well, will you give me your word not to tell a soul I'm here, and I'll tell you who I am? You've forgotten me, I see. But I'm afraid you may remember. D'you see?"

"All right."

"I'm Guiseley, of Drew's. We were in the same division once—up to Rawlins. Do you remember?"

"Good Lord! But—"

"Yes, I know. But don't let's go into that. I've not done anything I shouldn't. That's not the reason I'm like this. It's just turned out so. And there's something else I want to talk to you about. When can I come and see you privately? I'm going to begin work to-morrow at the jam factory."

The other man clutched at his whirling faculties.

"To-night—at ten. Will that do?"

"All right. What am I to say—when I ring the bell, I mean?"

"Just ask for me. They'll show you straight up to my room."

"All right," said Frank, and was gone.

Mr. Parham-Carter's room in the clergy-house was of the regular type—very comfortable and pleasing to the eye, as it ought to be for a young man working under such circumstances; not really luxurious; pious and virile. The walls were a rosy distemper, very warm and sweet, and upon them, above the low oak book-cases, hung school and college groups, discreet sporting engravings, a glorious cathedral interior, and the Sistine Madonna over the mantelpiece. An oar hung all along one ceiling, painted on the blade with the arms of an Oxford college. There was a small prie-dieu, surmounted by a crucifix of Ober-Ammergau workmanship: there was a mahogany writing-table with a revolving chair set before it; there were a couple of deep padded arm-chairs, a pipe-rack, and a row of photographs—his mother in evening dress, a couple of sisters, with other well-bred-looking relations. Altogether, with the curtains drawn and the fire blazing, it was exactly the kind of room that such a wholesome young man ought to have in the East of London.

Frank was standing on the hearth-rug as Mr. Parham-Carter came in a minute or two after ten o'clock, bearing a small tray with a covered jug, two cups and a plate of cake.

"Good-evening again," said the clergyman. "Have some cocoa? I generally bring mine up here.... Sit down. Make yourself comfortable."

Frank said nothing. He sat down. He put his cap on the floor by his chair and leaned back. The other, with rather nervous movements, set a steaming cup by his side, and a small silver box of cigarettes, matches and an ash-tray. Then he sat down himself, took a long pull at his cocoa, and waited with a certain apprehensiveness.

"Who else is here?" asked Frank abruptly.

The other ran through the three names, with a short biography of each. Frank nodded, reassured at the end.

"That's all right," he said. "All before my time, I expect. They might come in, you know."

"Oh, no!" said the clergyman. "I told them not, and—"

"Well, let's come to business," said Frank. "It's about a girl. You saw that man to-day? You saw his sort, did you? Well, he's a bad hat. And he's got a girl going about with him who isn't his wife. I want to get her home again to her people."

"Yes?"

"Can you do anything? (Don't say you can if you can't, please....) She comes from Chiswick. I'll give you her address before I go. But I don't want it muddled, you know."

The clergyman swallowed in his throat. He had only been ordained eighteen months, and the extreme abruptness and reality of the situation took him a little aback.

"I can try," he said. "And I can put the ladies on to her. But, of course, I can't undertake—"

"Of course. But do you think there's a reasonable chance? If not, I'd better have another try myself."

"Have you tried, then?"

"Oh, yes, half a dozen times. A fortnight ago was the last, and I really thought—"

"But I don't understand. Are these people your friends, or what?"

"I've been traveling with them off and on since June. They belong to you, so far as they belong to anyone. I'm a Catholic, you know—"

"Really? But—"

"Convert. Last June. Don't let's argue, my dear chap. There isn't time."

Mr. Parham-Carter drew a breath.

There is no other phrase so adequate for describing his condition of mind as the old one concerning head and heels. There had rushed on him, not out of the blue, but, what was even more surprising, out of the very dingy sky of Hackney Wick (and Turner Road, at that!), this astonishing young man, keen-eyed, brown-faced, muscular, who had turned out to be a school-fellow of his own, and a school-fellow whose reputation, during the three hours since they had parted, he had swiftly remembered point by point—Guiseley of Drew's—the boy who had thrown off his coat in early school and displayed himself shirtless; who had stolen four out of the six birches on a certain winter morning, and had conversed affably with the Head in school yard with the ends of the birches sticking out below the skirts of his overcoat; who had been discovered on the fourth of June, with an air of reverential innocence, dressing the bronze statue of King Henry VI. in a surplice in honor of the day. And now here he was, and from his dress and the situation of his lodging-house to be reckoned among the worst of the loafing class, and yet talking, with an air of complete confidence and equality of a disreputable young woman—his companion—who was to be rescued from a yet more disreputable companion and restored to her parents in Chiswick.

And this was not all—for, as Mr. Parham-Carter informed me himself—there was being impressed upon him during this interview a very curious sensation, which he was hardly able, even after consideration, to put into words—a sensation concerning the personality and presence of this young man which he could only describe as making him feel "beastly queer."

It seems to have been about this point that he first perceived it clearly—distinguished it, that is to say, from the whole atmosphere of startling and suggesting mystery that surrounded him.

He looked at Frank in silence a moment or two....

There Guiseley sat—leaning back in the red leather chair, his cocoa still untouched. He was in a villainous suit that once, probably, had been dark blue. The jacket was buttoned up to his chin, and a grimy muffler surrounded his neck. His trousers were a great deal too short, and disclosed above a yellow sock, on the leg nearest to him, about four inches of dark-looking skin. His boots were heavy, patched, and entirely uncleaned, and the upper toe-cap of one of them gaped from the leather over the instep. His hands were deep in his pockets, as if even in this warm room, he felt the cold.

There was nothing remarkable there. It was the kind of figure presented by unsatisfactory candidates for the men's club. And yet there was about him this air, arresting and rather disconcerting....

It was a sort of electric serenity, if I understand Mr. Parham-Carter aright—a zone of perfectly still energy, like warmth or biting cold, as of a charged force: it was like a real person standing motionless in the middle of a picture. (Mr. Parham-Carter did not, of course, use such beautiful similes as these; he employed the kind of language customary to men who have received a public school and university education, half slang and half childishness; but he waved his hands at me and distorted his features, and conveyed, on the whole, the kind of impression I have just attempted to set down.)

Frank, then, seemed as much out of place in this perfectly correct and suitable little room as an Indian prince in Buckingham Palace; or, if you prefer it, an English nobleman (with spats) in Delhi. He was just entirely different from it all; he had nothing whatever to do with it; he was wholly out of place, not exactly as regarded his manner (for he was quite at his ease), but with regard to his significance. He was as a foreign symbol in a familiar language.

Its effect upon Mr. Parham-Carter was quite clear and strong. He instanced to me the fact that he said nothing to Frank about his soul: he honestly confessed that he scarcely even wished to press him to come to Evensong on Sunday. Of course, he did not like Frank's being a Roman Catholic; and his whole intellectual being informed him that it was because Frank had never really known the Church of England that he had left it. (Mr. Parham-Carter had himself learned the real nature of the Church of England at the Pusey House at Oxford.) But there are certain atmospheres in which the intellectual convictions are not very important, and this was one of them. So here the two young men sat and stared at one another, or, rather, Mr. Parham-Carter stared at Frank, and Frank looked at nothing in particular.

"You haven't drunk your cocoa," said the clergyman suddenly.

Frank turned abruptly, took up the cup and drank the contents straight off at one draught.

"And a cigarette?"

Frank took up a cigarette and put in his mouth.

"By the way," he said, taking it out again, "when'll you send your ladies round? The morning's best, when the rest of us are out of the way."

"All right."

"Well, I don't think there's anything else?"

"My dear chap," said the other, "I wish you'd tell me what it's all about—why you're in this sort of life, you know. I don't want to pry, but—"

Frank smiled suddenly and vividly.

"Oh, there's nothing to say. That's not the point. It's by my own choice practically. I assure you I haven't disgraced anybody."

"But your people—"

"Oh! they're all right. There's nothing the matter with them.... Look here! I really must be going."

He stood up, and something seemed to snap in the atmosphere as he did so.

"Besides, I've got to be at work early—"

"I say, what did you do then?"

"Do then? What do you mean?"

"When you stood up—Did you say anything?..."

Frank looked at him bewildered.

"I don't know what you're talking about."

Mr. Parham-Carter did not quite know what he had meant himself. It was a sensation come and gone, in an instant, as Frank had moved ... a sensation which I suppose some people would call "psychical"—a sensation as if a shock had vibrated for one moment through every part of his own being, and of the pleasant little warm room where he was sitting. He looked at the other, dazed for a second or two, but there was nothing. Those two steady black eyes looked at him in a humorous kind of concern....

He stood up himself.

"It was nothing," he said. "I think I must be getting sleepy."

He put out his hand.

"Good-night," he said. "Oh! I'll come and see you as far as the gate."

Frank looked at him a second.

"I say," he said; "I suppose you've never thought of becoming a Catholic?"

"My dear chap—"

"No! Well, all right.... oh! don't bother to come to the gate."

"I'm coming. It may be locked."

Mr. Parham-Carter stood looking after Frank's figure even after it had passed along the dark shop fronts and was turning the corner towards Turner Road. Then it went under the lamplight, and disappeared.

It was a drizzling, cold night, and he himself was bareheaded; he felt the moisture run down his forehead, but it didn't seem to be happening to him. On his right rose up the big parish-hall where the entertainments were held, and beyond it, the east end of the great church, dark now and tenantless; and he felt the wet woodwork of the gate grasped in his fingers.

He did not quite know what was happening to him but everything seemed different. A hundred thoughts had passed through his mind during the last half hour. It had occurred to him that he ought to have asked Guiseley to come to the clergy-house and lodge there for a bit while things were talked over; that he ought, tactfully, to have offered to lend him money, to provide him with a new suit, to make suggestions as to proper employment instead of at the jam factory—all those proper, philanthropic and prudent suggestions that a really sensible clergyman would have made. And yet, somehow, not only had he not made them, but it was obvious and evident when he regarded them that they could not possibly be made. Guiseley (of Drew's) did not require them, he was on another line altogether.... And what was that line?

Mr. Parham-Carter leaned on the gate a full five minutes considering all this. But he arrived at no conclusion.

CHAPTER II: (I)

The Rector of Merefield was returning from a short pastoral visitation towards the close of an afternoon at the beginning of November. His method and aims were very characteristic of himself, since he was one of that numerous class of persons who, interiorly possessing their full share of proper pride, wear exteriorly an appearance of extreme and almost timid humility. The aims of his visiting were, though he was quite unaware of the fact, directed towards encouraging people to hold fast to their proper position in life (for this, after all, is only another name for one's duty towards one's neighbor), and his method was to engage in general conversation on local topics. There emerged, in this way, information as to the patient's habits and actions; it would thus transpire, for example, whether the patient had been to church or not, whether there were any quarrels, and, if so, who were the combatants and for what cause.

He had been fairly satisfied to-day; he had met with good excuses for the absence of two children from day-school, and of a young man from choir-practice; he had read a little Scripture to an old man, and had been edified by his comments upon it. It was not particularly supernatural, but, after all, the natural has its place, too, in life, and he had undoubtedly fulfilled to-day some of the duties for whose sake he occupied the position of Rector of Merefield, in a completely inoffensive manner. The things he hated most in the world were disturbances of any kind, abruptness and the unexpected, and he had a strong reputation in the village for being a man of peace.

It sounds a hard thing to say of so conscientious a man, but a properly preserved social order was perhaps to his mind the nearest approach to the establishment of the Kingdom of Heaven on earth. Each person held his proper position, including himself, and he no more expected others to be untrue to their station than he wished to be untrue to his own. There were, of course, two main divisions—those of gentle birth and those not of gentle birth, and these were as distinct as the sexes. But there were endless gradations in each respectively, and he himself regarded those with as much respect as those of the angelic hierarchy: the "Dominations" might, or might not be as "good" as the "Powers," but they were certainly different, by Divine decree. It would be a species of human blasphemy, therefore, for himself not to stand up in Lord Talgarth's presence, or for a laborer not to touch his hat to Miss Jenny. This is sometimes called snobbishness, but it is nothing of the kind. It is merely a marked form of Toryism.

It was a pleasant autumnal kind of afternoon, and he took off his hat as he turned up past the park gates to feel the cool air, as he was a little heated with his walk. He felt exceedingly content with all things: there were no troubles in the parish, he enjoyed excellent health, and he had just done his duty. He disliked pastoral visiting very deeply indeed; he was essentially a timid kind of man, but he made his rules and kept them, for he was essentially a conscientious man. He was so conscientious that he was probably quite unaware that he disliked this particular duty.

Just as he came opposite the gates—great iron-work affairs with ramping eagles and a Gothic lodge smothered in ivy—the man ran out and began to wheel them back, after a hasty salute to his pastor; and the Rector, turning, saw a sight that increased his complacency. It was just Jenny riding with Lord Talgarth, as he knew she was doing that afternoon.

They made a handsome, courtly kind of pair—a sort of "father and daughter" after some romantic artist or other. Lord Talgarth's heavy figure looked well-proportioned on horseback, and he sat his big black mare very tolerably indeed. And Jenny looked delicious on the white mare, herself in dark green. A groom followed twenty yards behind.

Lord Talgarth's big face nodded genially to the Rector and he made a kind of salute; he seemed in excellent dispositions; Jenny was a little flushed with exercise, and smiled at her father with a quiet, friendly dignity.

"Just taking her ladyship home," said the old man.... "Yes; charming day, isn't it?"

The Rector followed them, pleased at heart. Usually Jenny rode home alone with the groom to take back her mare to the stables. It was the first time, so far as he could remember, that Lord Talgarth had taken the trouble to escort her all the way home himself. It really was very pleasant indeed, and very creditable to Jenny's tact, that relations were so cordial.... And they were dining there to-morrow, too. The social order of Merefield seemed to be in an exceedingly sound condition.

(II)

Lord Talgarth, too, seemed to the lodge-keeper, as ten minutes later the gates rolled back again to welcome their lord, in an unusually genial temper (and, indeed, there was always about this old man as great a capacity for geniality on one side as for temper on the other; it is usually so with explosive characters). He even checked his horse and asked after "the missus" in so many words; although two days before a violent message had come down to complain of laxity in the gate-opening, owing to the missus' indisposition on an occasion when the official himself had been digging cabbages behind the Gothic lodge and the hoot of the motor had not been heard.

The missus, it seemed, was up and about again (indeed her husband caught a glimpse out of the tail of his eye of a pale face that glanced and withdrew again apprehensively above the muslin curtain beyond his lordship).

"That's all right," remarked Lord Talgarth heartily, and rode on.

The lodge-keeper exchanged a solemn wink with the groom half a minute later, and stood to watch the heavy figure ahead plunging about rather in the saddle as the big black mare set her feet upon the turf and viewed her stable afar off.

It was a fact that Lord Talgarth was pleased with himself and all the world to-day, for he kept it up even with the footman who slipped, and all but lost his balance, as he brought tea into the library.

"Hold up!" remarked the nobleman.

The footman smiled gently and weakly, after the manner of a dependent, and related the incident with caustic gusto to his fellows in the pantry.

After tea Lord Talgarth lay back in his chair and appeared to meditate, as was observed by the man who fetched out the tea-things and poked the fire; and he was still meditating, though now there was the aromatic smell of tobacco upon the air, when his own man came to tell him that it was time to dress.

It was indeed a perfect room for arm-chair meditations; there were tall book-shelves, mahogany writing-tables, each with its shaded electric lamp; the carpet was as deep as a summer lawn; and in the wide hearth logs consumed themselves in an almost deferential silence. There was every conceivable thing that could be wanted laid in its proper place. It was the kind of room in which it would seem that no scheme could miscarry and every wish must prevail; the objective physical world grouped itself so obediently to the human will that it was almost impossible to imagine a state of things in which it did not so. The great house was admirably ordered; there was no sound that there should not be—no hitches, no gaps or cracks anywhere; it moved like a well-oiled machine; the gong, sounded in the great hall, issued invitations rather than commands. All was leisurely, perfectly adapted and irreproachable.

It is always more difficult for people who live in such houses as these to behave well under adverse fortune than for those who live in houses where the Irish stew can be smelled at eleven o'clock in the morning, and where the doors do not shut properly, and where the kitchen range goes wrong. Possibly something of this fact helped to explain the owner's extreme violence of temper on the occasion of his son's revolt. It was intolerable for a man all of whose other surroundings moved like clockwork, obedient to his whims, to be disobeyed flatly by one whose obedience should be his first duty—to find disorder and rebellion in the very mainspring of the whole machine.

Possibly, too, the little scheme that was maturing in Lord Talgarth's mind between tea and dinner that evening helped to restore his geniality; for, as soon as the thought was conceived, it became obvious that it could be carried through with success.

He observed: "Aha! it's time, is it?" to his man in a hearty kind of way, and hoisted himself out of his chair with unusual briskness.

(III)

He spent a long evening again in the library alone. Archie was away; and after dining alone with all the usual state, the old man commanded that coffee should be brought after him. The butler found him, five minutes later, kneeling before a tall case of drawers, trying various keys off his bunch, and when the man came to bring in whisky and clear away the coffee things he was in his deep chair, a table on either side of him piled with papers, and a drawer upon his knees.

"You can put this lot back," he remarked to the young footman, indicating a little pile of four drawers on the hearth-rug. He watched the man meditatively as he attempted to fit them into their places.

"Not that way, you fool! Haven't you got eyes?... The top one at the top!"

But he said it without bitterness—almost contemplatively. And, as the butler glanced round a moment or two later to see that all was in order, he saw his master once more beginning to read papers.

"Good-night," said Lord Talgarth.

"Good-night, my lord," said the butler.

There was a good deal of discussion that night in the men's wing as to the meaning of all this, and it was conducted with complete frankness. Mr. Merton, the butler, had retired to his own house in the stable-yard, and Mr. Clarkson, the valet, was in his lordship's dressing-room; so the men talked freely. It was agreed that only two explanations were possible for the unusual sweetness of temper: either Mr. Frank was to be reinstated, or his father was beginning to break up. Frank was extremely popular with servants always; and it was generally hoped that the former explanation was the true one. Possibly, however, both were required.

Mr. Clarkson too was greatly intrigué that night. He yawned about the dressing-room till an unusually late hour, for Lord Talgarth generally retired to rest between ten and half-past. To-night, however, it was twenty minutes to twelve before the man stood up suddenly from the sofa at the sound of a vibration in the passage outside. The old man came in briskly, bearing a bundle of papers in one hand and a bed-candle in the other, with the same twinkle of good temper in his eyes that he had carried all the evening.

"Give me the dispatch-box under the sofa," he said; "the one in the leather case."

This was done and the papers were laid in it, carefully, on the top. Mr. Clarkson noticed that they had a legal appearance, were long-shaped and inscribed in stiff lettering. Then the dispatch-box was reclosed and set on the writing-table which my lord used sometimes when he was unwell.

"Remind me to send for Mr. Manners to-morrow," he said. (This was the solicitor.)

Getting ready for bed that evening was almost of a sensational nature, and Mr. Clarkson had to keep all his wits about him to respond with sufficient agility to the sallies of his master. Usually it was all a very somber ceremony, with a good deal of groaning and snarling in asides. But to-night it was as cheerful as possible.

The mysteries of it all are too great for me to attempt to pierce them; but it is really incredible what a number of processes are necessary before an oldish man, who is something of a buck and something of an invalid, and altogether self-centered, is able to lay him down to rest. There are strange doses to be prepared and drunk, strange manipulations to be performed and very particular little ceremonies to be observed, each in its proper place. Each to-night was accompanied by some genial comment: the senna-pod distillation, that had been soaking since seven p.m. in hot water, was drunk almost with the air of a toast; the massaging of the ankles and toes (an exercise invented entirely by Lord Talgarth himself) might have been almost in preparation for a dance.

He stood up at last, an erect, stoutish figure, in quilted dressing-gown and pyjamas, before the fire, as his man put on his slippers for him, for the little procession into the next room.

"I think I'm better to-night, Clarkson," he said.

"Your lordship seems very well indeed, my lord," murmured that diplomat on the hearth-rug.

"How old do you think I am, Clarkson?"

Clarkson knew perfectly well, but it was better to make a deprecatory confused noise.

"Ah! well, we needn't reckon by years ... I feel young enough," observed the stately figure before the fire.

Then the procession was formed: the double doors were set back, the electric light switched on; Lord Talgarth passed through towards the great four-posted bed that stood out into the bedroom, and was in bed, with scarcely a groan, almost before the swift Mr. Clarkson could be at his side to help him in. He lay there, his ruddy face wonderfully handsome against the contrast of his gray hair and the white pillow, while Mr. Clarkson concluded the other and final ceremonies. A small table had to be wheeled to a certain position beside the bed, and the handle of the electric cord laid upon it in a particular place, between the book and the tray on which stood some other very special draught to be drunk in case of thirst.

"Call me a quarter of an hour earlier than usual," observed the face on the pillow. "I'll take a little stroll before breakfast."

"Yes, my lord."

"What did I tell you to remind me to do after breakfast?"

"Send for Mr. Manners, my lord."

"That's right. Good-night, Clarkson."

"Good-night, my lord."

There was the usual discreet glance round the room to see that all was in order; then the door into the dressing-room closed imperceptibly behind Mr. Clarkson's bent back.

CHAPTER III: (I)

Winter at Merefield Rectory is almost as delightful as summer, although in an entirely different way. The fact is that the Rectory has managed the perfect English compromise. In summer, with the windows and doors wide open, with the heavy radiant creepers, with the lawns lying about the house, with the warm air flowing over the smooth, polished floors and lifting the thin mats, with the endless whistle of bird song—then the place seems like a summer-house. And in winter, with the heavy carpets down, and the thick curtains, the very polished floors, so cool in summer, seem expressly designed to glimmer warmly with candle and fire-light; and the books seem to lean forward protectively and reassert themselves, and the low beamed ceilings to shelter and safeguard the interior comfort. The center of gravity is changed almost imperceptibly. In summer the place is a garden with a house in the middle; in winter a house surrounded by shrubberies.

The study in one way and the morning-room in another are the respective pivots of the house. The study is a little paneled room on the ground-floor, looking out upon the last of the line of old yews and the beginning of the lawn; the morning-room (once known as the school-room) is the only other paneled room in the house, on the first floor, looking out upon the front. And round these two rooms the two sections of the house-life tranquilly revolve. Here in one the Rector controls the affairs of the parish, writes his sermons, receives his men friends (not very many), and reads his books. There in the other Jenny orders the domestic life of the house, interviews the cook, and occupies herself with her own affairs. They are two rival, but perfectly friendly, camps.

Lately (I am speaking now of the beginning of November) there had not been quite so much communication between the two camps as usual, not so many informal negotiations. Jenny did not look in quite so often upon her father—for ten minutes after breakfast, for instance, or before lunch—and when he looked in on her he seemed to find her generally with rather a preoccupied air, often sitting before the wide-arched fireplace, with her hands behind her head, looking at the red logs.

He was an easy man, as has been seen, and did not greatly trouble his head about it: he knew enough of the world to recognize that an extremely beautiful girl like Jenny, living on the terms she did with the great house—and a house with men coming and going continually, to say nothing of lawn-tennis parties and balls elsewhere—cannot altogether escape complications. He was reasonable enough, too, to understand that a father is not always the best confidant, and he had supreme confidence in Jenny's common sense.

I suppose he had his dreams; he would scarcely have been human if he had not, and he was quite human. The throwing over of Frank had brought him mixed emotions, but he had not been consulted either at the beginning or the end of the engagement, and he acquiesced. Of Dick's affair he knew nothing at all.

That, then, was the situation when the bomb exploded. It exploded in this way.

He was sitting in his study one morning—to be accurate, it was the first Saturday in November, two days after the events of the last chapter—preparing to begin the composition of his sermon for the next day. They had dined up at the great house the night before quite quietly with Lord Talgarth and Archie, who had just come back.

He had selected his text with great care from the Gospel for the day, when the door suddenly opened and Jenny came in. This was very unusual on Saturday morning; it was an understood thing that he must be at his sermon; but his faint sense of annoyance was completely dispelled by his daughter's face. She was quite pale—not exactly as if she had received a shock, but as if she had made up her mind to something; there was no sign of tremor in her face; on the contrary, she looked extremely determined, but her eyes searched his as she stopped.

"I'm dreadfully sorry, father, but may I talk to you for a few minutes?"

She did not wait for his answer, but came straight in and sat down in his easy-chair. He laid his pen down and turned a little at his writing-table to face her.

"Certainly, dear. What is it? Nothing wrong?"

(He noticed she had a note in her hand.)

"No, nothing wrong...." She hesitated. "But it's rather important."

"Well?"

She glanced down at the note she carried. Then she looked up at him again.

"Father, I suppose you've thought of my marrying some day—in spite of Frank?"

"Eh?"

"Would you mind if I married a man older than myself—I mean a good deal older?"

He looked at her in silence. Two or three names passed before his mind, but he couldn't remember—

"Father, I'm in trouble. I really am. I didn't expect—"

Her voice faltered. He saw that she really found it difficult to speak. A little wave of tenderness rolled over his heart. It was unlike her to be so much moved. He got up and came round to her.

"What is it, dear? Tell me."

She remained perfectly motionless for an instant. Then she held out the note to him, and simultaneously stood up. As he took it, she went swiftly past him and out of the door. He heard the swish of her dress pass up the stairs, and then the closing of a door. But he hardly heeded it. He was reading the note she had given him. It was a short, perfectly formal offer of marriage to her from Lord Talgarth.

(II)

"Father, dear," said Jenny, "I want you to let me have my say straight out, will you?" He bowed his head.

They were sitting, on the evening of the same day, over the tea-things in his study. He had not seen her alone for one moment since the morning. She had refused to open her door to him when he went up after reading the note: she had pleaded a headache at lunch, and she had been invisible all the afternoon. Then, as he came in about tea-time, she had descended upon him, rather pale, but perfectly herself, perfectly natural, and even rather high-spirited. She had informed him that tea would be laid in his study, as she wanted a long talk. She had poured out tea, talking all the time, refusing, it seemed, to meet his eyes. When she had finished, she had poured out his third cup, and then pushed her own low chair back so far that he could not see her face.

Then she had opened the engagement.

To say that the poor man had been taken aback would be a very poor way of describing his condition. The thing simply had never entered his head. He had dreamed, in wild moments, of Archie; he had certainly contemplated Dick; but Lord Talgarth himself, gouty and aged sixty-five!... And yet he had not been indignant. Indignation not only did not do with Jenny, but it was impossible. To be quite frank, the man was afraid of his daughter; he was aware that she would do ultimately as she wished, and not as he wished; and his extreme discomfort at the thought of this old man marrying his daughter was, since he was human, partly counter-balanced by the thought of who the old man was. Lastly, it must be remembered that Jenny was really a very sensible girl, and that her father was quite conscious of the fact.

Jenny settled herself once more in her chair and began.

"Father, dear, I want to be quite sensible about this. And I've been very foolish and silly about it all day. I can't imagine why I behaved as I did. There's nothing to go and mope about, that Lord Talgarth has been kind enough to do me this honor. Because it is an honor, you know, however you look at it, that anyone should ask one to be his wife.

"Well, I want to say what I have to say first, and then I want you to say exactly what you think. I've thought it all out, so I shan't be very long."

(He put down his cup noiselessly, as if in the presence of a sick person. He was anxious not to lose a word, or even an inflection).

"First of all, let's have all the things against it. He's an old man. We mustn't forget that for one minute. And that's a very strong argument indeed. Some people would think it final, but I think that's foolish....

"Secondly, it never entered my head for one instant." (Jenny said this quite deliberately, almost reverently.) "Of course I see now that he's hinted at it very often, but I never understood it at the time. I've always thought of him as a sort of—well—a sort of uncle. And that's another strong argument against it. If it was a right thing to do, oughtn't it to have occurred to me too? I'm not quite sure about that.

"Thirdly, it's unsuitable for several reasons. It'll make talk. Here have I been engaged to Frank for ages and broken it off. Can't you imagine how people will interpret that now? I suppose I oughtn't to mind what people say, but I'm afraid I do. Then I'm the Rector's daughter ... and I've been running in and out continually—dining with them, sitting with him alone. Can't you imagine what people—Lady Richard, for instance—will make of it?... I shall be an adventuress, and all the rest of it. That's not worth much as an argument, but it is a ... a consideration. One must look facts in the face and think of the future.

"Fourthly, Lord Talgarth probably won't live very long...." (Jenny paused, and then, with extraordinary impressiveness, continued).... "And that, of, course, is perhaps the strongest argument of all. If I could be of any real use to him—" She stopped again.

The Rector shifted a little in his chair.

It was impossible for him to conceal from himself any longer the fact that up to now he had really been expecting Jenny to accept the offer. But he was a little puzzled now at the admirable array of reasons she had advanced against that. She had put into words just the sensible view of which he himself had only had a confused apprehension; she had analyzed into all its component parts that general sense which one side of him had pushed before him all day—that the thing was really abominable. And this side of him at this time was uppermost. He drew a whistling breath.

"Well, my dear," he began, and the relief was very apparent in his voice. But Jenny interrupted.

"One minute, please, father! In fairness to—to everyone I must put the other side.... I suppose the main question is this, after all. Am I fond of him?—fond enough, that is, to marry him—because, of course, I'm fond of him; he's been so extraordinarily kind always.... I suppose that's really the only thing to be considered. If I were fond enough of him, I suppose all the arguments against count for nothing. Isn't that so?... Yes; I want you to say what you think."

He waited. Still he could make out nothing of her face, though he glanced across the tea-things once or twice.

"My dear, I don't know what to say. I—"

"Father, dear, I just want that from you. Do you think that any consideration at all ought to stand in the way, if I were—I don't say for one single moment that I am—but if I were—well, really fond of him? I'm sorry to have to speak so very plainly, but it's no good being silly."

He swallowed in his throat once or twice.

"If you really were fond of him—I think ... I think that, no consideration of the sort you have mentioned ought to ... to stand in your way."

"Thank you, father," said Jenny softly.

"When did you first think of it?"

Jenny paused.

"I think I knew he was going to ask me two days ago—the day you met us out riding, you know."

There was a long silence.

They had already discussed, when Frank's affair had been before them, all secondary details. The Rector's sister was to have taken Jenny's place. There was nothing of that sort to talk about now. They were both just face to face with primary things, and they both knew it.

The Rector's mind worked like a mill—a mill whose machinery is running aimlessly. The wheels went round and round, but they effected nothing. He was completely ignorant as to what Jenny intended. He perceived—as in a series of little vignettes—a number of hypothetical events, on this side and that, but they drew to no conclusion in his mind. He was just waiting on his daughter's will.

Jenny broke the silence with a slow remark in another kind of voice.

"Father, dear, there's something else I must tell you. I didn't see any need to bother you with it before. It's this. Mr. Dick Guiseley proposed to me when he was here for the shooting."

She paused, but her father said nothing.

"I told him he must wait—that I didn't know for certain, but that I was almost certain. If he had pressed for an answer I should have said 'No.' Oddly enough, I was thinking only yesterday that it wasn't fair to keep him waiting any longer. Because ... because it's 'No' ... anyhow, now."

The Rector still could not speak. It was just one bewilderment. But apparently Jenny did not want any comments.

"That being so," she went on serenely, "my conscience is clear, anyhow. And I mustn't let what I think Mr. Dick might say or think affect me—any more than the other things. Must I?"

"... Jenny, what are you going to do? Tell me!"

"Father, dear," came the high astonished voice, "I don't know. I don't know at all. I must think. Did you think I'd made up my mind? Why! How could I? Of course I should say 'No' if I had to answer now."

"I—" began the Rector and stopped. He perceived that the situation could easily be complicated.

"I must just think about it quietly," went on the girl. "And I must write a note to say so.... Father ..."

He glanced in her direction.

"Father, about being fond of a man.... Need it be—well, as I was fond of Frank? I don't think Lord Talgarth could have expected that, could he? But if you—well—get on with a man very well, understand him—can stand up to him without annoying him ... and ... and care for him, really, I mean, in such a way that you like being with him very much, and look up to him very much in all kinds of ways—(I'm very sorry to have to talk like this, but whom am I to talk to, father dear?) Well, if I found I did care for Lord Talgarth like that—like a sort of daughter, or niece, and more than that too, would that—"

"I don't know," said the Rector, abruptly standing up. "I don't know; you mustn't ask me. You must settle all that yourself."

She looked up at him, startled, it seemed, by the change in his manner.

"Father, dear—" she began, with just the faintest touch of pathetic reproach in her voice. But he did not appear moved by it.

"You must settle," he said. "You have all the data. I haven't. I—"

He stepped towards the door.

"Tell me as soon as you have decided," he said, and went out.

(III)

The little brown dog called Lama, who in an earlier chapter once trotted across a lawn, and who had lately been promoted to sleeping upon Jenny's bed, awoke suddenly that night and growled a low breathy remonstrance. He had been abruptly kicked from beneath the bedclothes.

"Get off, you heavy little beast," said a voice in the darkness.

Lama settled himself again with a grunt, half of comfort, half of complaint.

"Get off!" came the voice again, and again his ribs were heaved at by a foot.

He considered it a moment or two, and even shifted nearer the wall, still blind with sleep; but the foot pursued him, and he awoke finally to the conviction that it would be more comfortable by the fire; there was a white sheepskin there, he reflected. As he finally reached the ground, a scratching was heard in the corner, and he was instantly alert, and the next moment had fitted his nose, like a kind of india-rubber pad, deep into a small mouse-hole in the wainscoting, and was breathing long noisy sighs down into the delicious and gamey-smelling darkness.

"Oh! be quiet!" came a voice from the bed.

Lama continued his investigations unmoved, and having decided, after one long final blow, that there was to be no sport, returned to the sheepskin with that brisk independent air that was so characteristic of him. He was completely awake now, and stood eyeing the bed a moment, with the possibility in his mind that his mistress was asleep again, and that by a very gentle leap—But a match was struck abruptly, and he lay down, looking, with that appearance of extreme wide-awakedness in his black eyes that animals always wear at night, at his restless mistress.

He could not quite understand what was the matter.

First she lit a candle, took a book from the small table by the bed and began to read resolutely. This continued till Lama's eyes began to blink at the candle flame, and then he was suddenly aware that the light was out and the book closed, and all fallen back again into the clear gray tones which men call darkness.

He put his head down on his paws, but his eyebrows rose now and again as he glanced at the bed.

Then the candle was lighted again after a certain space of time, but this time there was no book opened. Instead, his mistress took her arms out of bed, and clasped them behind her head, staring up at the ceiling....

This was tiresome, as the light was in his eyes, and his body was just inert enough with sleep to make movement something of an effort....

Little by little, however, his eyebrows came down, remained down, and his eyes closed....

He awoke again at a sound. The candle was still burning, but his mistress had rolled over on to her side and seemed to be talking gently to herself. Then she was over again on this side, and a minute later was out of bed, and walking to and fro noiselessly on the soft carpet.

He watched her with interest, his eyes only following her. He had never yet fully understood this mysterious change of aspect that took place every night—the white thin dress, the altered appearance of the head, and—most mysterious of all—the two white things that ought to be feet, but were no longer hard and black. He had licked one of them once tentatively, and had found that the effect was that it had curled up suddenly; there had been a sound as of pain overhead, and a swift slap had descended upon him.

He was observing these things now—to and fro, to and fro—and his eyes moved with them.

After a certain space of time the movement stopped. She was standing still near a carved desk—important because a mouse had once been described sitting beneath it; and she stood so long that his eyes began to blink once more. Then there was a rustle of paper being torn, and he was alert again in a moment. Perhaps paper would be thrown for him presently....

She came across to the hearth-rug, and he was up, watching her hands, while his own short tail flickered three or four times in invitation. But it was no good: the ball was crumpled up and thrown on to the red logs. There was a "whup" from the fire and a flame shot up. He looked at this carefully with his head on one side, and again lay down to watch it. His mistress was standing quite still, watching it with him.

Then, as the flame died down, she turned abruptly, went straight back to the bed, got into it, drew the clothes over her and blew the candle out.

After a few moments steady staring at the fire, he perceived that a part of the ball of paper had rolled out on to the stone hearth unburned. He looked at it for some while, wondering whether it was worth getting up for. Certainly the warmth was delicious and the sheepskin exquisitely soft.

There was no sound from the bed. A complete and absolute silence had succeeded to all the restlessness.

Finally he concluded that it was impossible to lie there any longer and watch such a crisp little roll of paper still untorn. He got up, stepped delicately on to the wide hearth, and pulled the paper towards him with a little scratching sound. There was a sigh from the bed, and he paused. Then he lifted it, stepped back to his warm place, lay down, and placing his paws firmly upon the paper, began to tear scraps out of it with his white teeth.

"Oh, be quiet!" came the weary voice from the bed.

He paused, considered; then he tore two more pieces. But it did not taste as it should; it was a little sticky, and too stiff. He stood up once more, turned round four times and lay down with a small grunt.

In the morning the maid who swept up the ashes swept up these fragments too. She noticed a wet scrap of a picture postcard, with the word "Selby" printed in the corner. Then she threw that piece, too, into the dustpan.

Mrs. Partington and Gertie had many of those mysterious conversations that such women have, full of "he's" and "she's" and nods and becks and allusions and broken sentences, wholly unintelligible to the outsider, yet packed with interest to the talkers. The Major, Mr. Partington (still absent), and Frank were discussed continually and exhaustively; and, so far as the subjects themselves ranged, there was hardly an unimportant detail that did not come under notice, and hardly an important fact that did. Gertie officially passed, of course, as Mrs. Trustcott always.

A couple of mornings after Frank had begun his work at the jam factory, Mrs. Partington, who had stepped round the corner to talk with a friend for an hour or so, returned to find Gertie raging. She raged in her own way; she was as white as a sheet; she uttered ironical and unintelligible sentences, in which Frank's name appeared repeatedly, and it emerged presently that one of the Mission-ladies had been round minding other folks' business, and that Gertie would thank that lady to keep her airs and her advice to herself.

Now Mrs. Partington knew that Gertie was not the Major's wife, and Gertie knew that she knew it; and Mrs. Partington knew that Gertie knew that she knew it. Yet, officially, all was perfectly correct; Gertie wore a wedding-ring, and there never was the hint that she had not a right to it. It was impossible, therefore, for Mrs. Partington to observe out loud that she understood perfectly what the Mission-lady had been talking about. She said very little; she pressed her thin lips together and let Gertie alone. The conversations that morning were of the nature of disconnected monologues from Gertie with long silences between.

It was an afternoon of silent storm. The Major was away in the West End somewhere on mysterious affairs; the children were at school, and the two women went about, each knowing what was in the mind of the other, yet each resolved to keep up appearances.

At half-past five o'clock Frank abruptly came in for a cup of tea, and Mrs. Partington gave it him in silence. (Gertie could be heard moving about restlessly overhead.) She made one or two ordinary remarks, watching Frank when he was not looking. But Frank said very little. He sat up to the table; he drank two cups of tea out of the chipped enamel mug, and then he set to work on his kippered herring. At this point Mrs. Partington left the room, as if casually, and a minute later Gertie came downstairs.

She came in with an indescribable air of virtue, rather white in the face, with her small chin carefully thrust out and her eyelids drooping. It was a pose she was accustomed to admire in high-minded and aristocratic barmaids. Frank nodded at her and uttered a syllable or two of greeting.

She said nothing; she went round to the window, carrying a white cotton blouse she had been washing upstairs, and hung it on the clothes-line that ran inside the window. Then, still affecting to be busy with it, she fired her first shot, with her back to him.

"I'll thank you to let my business alone...."

(Frank put another piece of herring into his mouth.)

"... And not to send round any more of your nasty cats," added Gertie after a pause.

There was silence from Frank.

"Well?" snapped Gertie.

"How dare you talk like that!" said Frank, perfectly quietly.

He spoke so low that Gertie mistook his attitude, and, leaning her hands on the table, she poured out the torrent that had been gathering within her ever since the Mission-lady had left her at eleven o'clock that morning. The lady had not been tactful; she was quite new to the work, and quite fresh from a women's college, and she had said a great deal more than she ought, with an earnest smile upon her face that she had thought conciliatory and persuasive. Gertie dealt with her faithfully now; she sketched her character as she believed it to be; she traced her motives and her attitude to life with an extraordinary wealth of detail; she threw in descriptive passages of her personal appearance, and she stated, with extreme frankness, her opinion of such persons as she had thought friendly, but now discovered to be hypocritical parsons in disguise. Unhappily I have not the skill to transcribe her speech in full, and there are other reasons, too, why her actual words are best unreported: they were extremely picturesque.

Frank ate on quietly till he had finished his herring; then he drank his last cup of tea, and turned a little in his chair towards the fire. He glanced at the clock, perceiving that he had still ten minutes, just as Gertie ended and stood back shaking and pale-eyed.

"Is that all?" he asked.

It seemed it was not all, and Gertie began again, this time on a slightly higher note, and with a little color in her face. Frank waited, quite simply and without ostentation. She finished.

After a moment's pause Frank answered.

"I don't know what you want," he said. "I talked to you myself, and you wouldn't listen. So I thought perhaps another woman would do it better—"

"I did listen—"

"I beg your pardon," said Frank instantly. "I was wrong. You did listen, and very patiently. I meant that you wouldn't do what I said. And so I thought—"

Gertie burst out again, against cats and sneaking hypocrites, but there was not quite the same venom in her manner.

"Very good," said Frank. "Then I won't make the mistake again. I am very sorry—not in the least for having interfered, you understand, but for not having tried again myself." (He took up his cap.) "You'll soon give in, Gertie, you know. Don't you think so yourself?"

Gertie looked at him in silence.

"You understand, naturally, why I can't talk to you while the Major's here. But the next time I have a chance—"

The unlatched door was pushed open and the Major came in.

(II)

There was an uncomfortable little pause for a moment. It is extremely doubtful, even now, exactly how much the Major heard; but he must have heard something, and to a man of his mind the situation that he found must have looked extremely suspicious. Gertie, flushed now, with emotion very plainly visible in her bright eyes, was standing looking at Frank, who, it appeared, was a little disconcerted. It would have been almost miraculous if the Major had not been convinced that he had interrupted a little private love-making.

It is rather hard to analyze the Major's attitude towards Gertie; but what is certain is that the idea of anyone else making love to her was simply intolerable. Certainly he did not treat her with any great chivalry; he made her carry the heavier bundles on the tramp; he behaved to her with considerable disrespect; he discussed her freely with his friends on convivial occasions. But she was his property—his and no one else's. He had had his suspicions before; he had come in quietly just now on purpose, and he had found himself confronted by this very peculiar little scene.

He looked at them both in silence. Then his lips sneered like a dog's.

"Pardon me," he said, with extreme politeness. "I appear to be interrupting a private conversation."

No one said anything. Frank leaned his elbow on the mantelpiece.

"It was private, then?" continued the Major with all the poisonous courtesy at his command.

"Yes; it was private," said Frank shortly.

The Major put his bowler hat carefully upon the table.

"Gertie, my dear," he said. "Will you be good enough to leave us for an instant? I regret having to trouble you."

Gertie breathed rather rapidly for a moment or two. She was not altogether displeased. She understood perfectly, and it seemed to her rather pleasant that two men should get into this kind of situation over her. She was aware that trouble would come to herself later, probably in the form of personal chastisement, but to the particular kind of feminine temperament that she possessed even a beating was not wholly painful, and the cheap kind of drama in which she found herself was wholly attractive. After an instant's pause, she cast towards Frank what she believed to be a "proud" glance and marched out.

"If you've got much to say," said Frank rapidly, as the door closed, "you'd better keep it for this evening. I've got to go in ... in two minutes."

"Two minutes will be ample," said the Major softly.

Frank waited.

"When I find a friend," went on the other, "engaged in an apparently exciting kind of conversation, which he informs me is private, with one who is in the position of my wife— particularly when I catch a sentence or two obviously not intended for my ears—I do not ask what was the subject of the conversation, but I—"

"My dear man," said Frank, "do put it more simply."

The Major was caught, so to speak, full in the wind. His face twitched with anger.

Then he flung an oath at Frank.

"If I catch you at it again," he said, "there'll be trouble. God damn you!"

"That is as it may be," said Frank.

The Major had had just one drink too much, and he was in the kind of expansive mood that changes very rapidly.

"Can you tell me you were not trying to take her from me?" he cried, almost with pathos in his voice.

This was, of course, exactly what Frank had been trying to do.

"You can't deny it!... Then I tell you this, Mr. Frankie"—the Major sprang up—"one word more from you to her on that subject ... and ... and you'll know it. D'you understand me?"

He thrust his face forward almost into Frank's.

It was an unpleasant face at most times, but it was really dangerous now. His lips lay back, and the peculiar hot smell of spirit breathed into Frank's nostrils. Frank turned and looked into his eyes.

"I understand you perfectly," he said. "There's no need to say any more. And now, if you'll forgive me, I must get back to my work."

He took up his cap and went out.

The Major, as has been said, had had one glass too much, and he had, accordingly, put into words what, even in his most suspicious moments, he had intended to keep to himself. It might be said, too, that he had put into words what he did not really think. But the Major was, like everyone else, for good or evil, a complex character, and found it perfectly possible both to believe and disbelieve the same idea simultaneously. It depended in what stratum the center of gravity happened to be temporarily suspended. One large part of the Major knew perfectly well, therefore, that any jealousy of Frank was simply ridiculous—the thing was simply alien; and another part, not so large, but ten times more concentrated, judged Frank by the standards by which the Major (qua blackguard) conducted his life. For people who lived usually in that stratum, making love to Gertie, under such circumstances, would have been an eminently natural thing to do, and, just now, the Major chose to place Frank amongst them.

The Major himself was completely unaware of these psychological distinctions, and, as he sat, sunk in his chair, brooding, before stepping out to attend to Gertie, he was entirely convinced that his suspicions were justified. It seemed to him now that numberless little details out of the past fitted, with the smoothness of an adjusted puzzle, into the framework of his thought.

There was, first, the very remarkable fact that Frank, in spite of opportunities to better himself, had remained in their company. At Barham, at Doctor Whitty's, at the monastery, obvious chances had offered themselves and he had not taken them. Then there were the small acts of courtesy, the bearing of Gertie's bundles two or three times. Finally, there was a certain change in Gertie's manner—a certain silent peevishness towards himself, a curious air that fell on her now and then as she spoke to Frank or looked at him.

And so forth. It was an extraordinarily convincing case, clinched now by the little scene that he had just interrupted. And the very irregularity of his own relations with Gertie helped to poison the situation with an astonishingly strong venom.

Of course, there were other considerations, or, rather, there was one—that Frank, obviously, was not the kind of man to be attracted by the kind of woman that Gertie was—a consideration made up, however, of infinitely slighter indications. But this counted for nothing. It seemed unsubstantial and shadowy. There were solid, definable arguments on the one side; there was a vague general impression on the other....

So the Major sat and stared at the fire, with the candle-light falling on his sunken cheeks and the bristle on his chin—a poor fallen kind of figure, yet still holding the shadow of a shadow of an ideal that might yet make him dangerous.

Presently he got up with a sudden movement and went in search of Gertie.

(III)

There are no free libraries in Hackney Wick; the munificences of Mr. Carnegie have not yet penetrated to that district (and, indeed, the thought of a library of any kind in Hackney Wick is a little incongruous). But there is one in Homerton, and during the dinner-hour on the following day Frank went up the steps of it, pushed open the swing-doors, and found his way to some kind of a writing-room, where he obtained a sheet of paper, an envelope and a penny stamp, and sat down to write a letter.

The picture that I have in my mind of Frank at this present time may possibly be a little incorrect in one or two details, but I am quite clear about its main outlines, and it is extremely vivid on the whole. I see him going in, quietly and unostentatiously—quite at his ease, yet a very unusual figure in such surroundings. I hear an old gentleman sniff and move his chair a little as this person in an exceedingly shabby blue suit with the collar turned up, with a muffler round his neck and large, bulging boots on his feet, comes and sits beside him. I perceive an earnest young lady, probably a typist in search of extra culture, look at him long and vacantly from over her copy of Emerson, and can almost see her mind gradually collecting conclusions about him. The attendant, too, as he asks for his paper, eyes him shrewdly and suspiciously, and waits till the three halfpence are actually handed across under the brass wire partition before giving him the penny stamp. These circumstances may be incorrect, but I am absolutely clear as to Frank's own attitude of mind. Honestly, he no longer minds in the very least how people behave to him; he has got through all that kind of thing long ago; he is not at all to be commiserated; it appears to him only of importance to get the paper and to be able to write and post his letter without interruption. For Frank has got on to that plane—(I know no other word to use, though I dislike this one)—when these other things simply do not matter. We all touch that plane sometimes, generally under circumstances of a strong mental excitement, whether of pleasure or pain, or even annoyance. A man with violent toothache, or who has just become engaged to be married, really does not care what people think of him. But Frank, for the present at least, has got here altogether, though for quite different reasons. The letter he wrote on this occasion is, at present, in my possession. It runs as follows. It is very short and business-like:

"Dear Jack,

"I want to tell you where I am—or, rather, where I can be got at in case of need. I am down in East London for the present, and one of the curates here knows where I'm living. (He was at Eton with me.) His address is: The Rev. E. Parham-Carter, The Eton Mission, Hackney Wick, London, N.E.

"The reason I'm writing is this: You remember Major Trustcott and Gertie, don't you? Well, I haven't succeeded in getting Gertie back to her people yet, and the worst of it is that the Major knows that there's something up, and, of course, puts the worst possible construction upon it. Parham-Carter knows all about it, too—I've just left a note on him, with instructions. Now I don't quite know what'll happen, but in case anything does happen which prevents my going on at Gertie, I want you to come and do what you can. Parham-Carter will write to you if necessary.

"That's one thing; and the next is this: I'd rather like to have some news about my people, and for them to know (if they want to know—I leave that to you) that I'm getting on all right. I haven't heard a word about them since August. I know nothing particular can have happened, because I always look at the papers—but I should like to know what's going on generally.

"I think that's about all. I am getting on excellently myself, and hope you are. I am afraid there's no chance of my coming to you for Christmas. I suppose you'll be home again by now.

"Ever yours,
"F.G."

"P.S.—Of course you'll keep all this private—as well as where I'm living."

Now this letter seems to me rather interesting from a psychological point of view. It is extremely business-like, but perfectly unpractical. Frank states what he wants, but he wants an absurd impossibility. I like Jack Kirkby very much, but I cannot picture him as likely to be successful in helping to restore a strayed girl to her people. I suppose Frank's only excuse is that he did not know whom else to write to.

It is rather interesting, too, to notice his desire to know what is going on at his home; it seems as if he must have had, some faint inkling that something important was about to happen, and this is interesting in view of what now followed immediately.

He directed his letter, stamped it, and posted it in the library post-box in the vestibule. Then, cap in hand, he pushed open the swing-doors and ran straight into Mr. Parham-Carter.

"Hullo!" said that clergyman—and went a little white.

"Hullo!" said Frank; and then: "What's the matter?"

"Where are you going?"

"I'm going back to the jam factory."

"May I walk with you?"

"Certainly, if you don't mind my eating as I go along."

The clergyman turned with him and went beside him in silence, as Frank, drawing out of his side-pocket a large hunch of bread and cheese, wrapped up in the advertisement sheet of the Daily Mail, began to fill his mouth.

"I want to know if you've had any news from home."

Frank turned to him slightly.

"No," he said sharply, after a pause.

Mr. Parham-Carter licked his lips.

"Well—no, it isn't bad news; but I wondered whether—"

"What is it?"

"Your governor's married again. It happened yesterday. I thought perhaps you didn't know."

There was dead silence for an instant.

"No, I didn't know," said Frank. "Who's he married?"

"Somebody I never heard of. I wondered whether you knew her."

"What's her name?"

"Wait a second," said the other, plunging under his greatcoat to get at his waistcoat pocket. "I've got the paragraph here. I cut it out of the Morning Post. I only saw it half an hour ago. I was coming round to you this evening."

He produced a slip of printed paper. Frank stood still a moment, leaning against some area-railings—they were in the distinguished quarter of Victoria Park Road—and read the paragraph through. The clergyman watched him curiously. It seemed to him a very remarkable situation that he should be standing here in Victoria Park Road, giving information to a son as to his father's marriage. He wondered, but only secondarily, what effect it would have upon Frank.

Frank gave him the paper back without a tremor.

"Thanks very much," he said. "No; I didn't know."

They continued to walk.

"D'you know her at all?"

"Yes, I know her. She's the Rector's daughter, you know."

"What! At Merefield? Then you must know her quite well."

"Oh! yes," said Frank, "I know her quite well."

Again there was silence. Then the other burst out:

"Look here—I wish you'd let me do something. It seems to me perfectly ghastly—"

"My dear man," said Frank. "Indeed you can't do anything.... You got my note, didn't you?"

The clergyman nodded.

"It's just in case I'm ill, or anything, you know. Jack's a great friend of mine. And it's just as well that some friend of mine should be able to find out where I am. I've just written to him myself, as I said in my note. But you mustn't give him my address unless in case of real need."

"All right. But are you sure—"

"I'm perfectly sure.... Oh! by the way, that lady you sent round did no good. I expect she told you?"

"Yes; she said she'd never come across such a difficult case."

"Well, I shall have to try again myself.... I must turn off here. Good luck!"

(IV)

Gertie was sitting alone in the kitchen about nine o'clock that night—alone, that is to say, except for the sleeping 'Erb, who, in a cot at the foot of his mother's bed, was almost invisible under a pile of clothes, and completely negligible as a witness. Mrs. Partington, with the other two children, was paying a prolonged visit in Mortimer Road, and the Major, ignorant of this fact, was talking big in the bar of the "Queen's Arms" opposite the Men's Club of the Eton Mission.

Gertie was enjoying herself just now, on the whole. It is true that she had received some chastisement yesterday from the Major; but she had the kind of nature that preferred almost any sensation to none. And, indeed, the situation was full of emotion. It was extraordinarily pleasant to her to occupy such a position between two men—and, above all, two "gentlemen." Her attitude towards the Major was of the most simple and primitive kind; he was her man, who bullied her, despised her, dragged her about the country, and she never for one instant forgot that he had once been an officer in the army. Even his blows (which, to tell the truth, were not very frequent, and were always administered in a judicial kind of way) bore with them a certain stamp of brilliance; she possessed a very pathetic capacity for snobbishness. Frank, on the other side, was no less exciting. She regarded him as a good young man, almost romantic, indeed, in his goodness—a kind of Sir Galahad; and he, whatever his motive (and she was sometimes terribly puzzled about his motives), at any rate, stood in a sort of rivalry to the Major; and it was she who was the cause of contention. She loved to feel herself pulled this way and that by two such figures, to be quarreled over by such very strong and opposite types. It was a vague sensation to her, but very vivid and attractive; and although just now she believed herself to be thoroughly miserable, I have no doubt whatever that she was enjoying it all immensely. She was very feminine indeed, and the little scene of last night had brought matters to an almost exquisite point. She was crying a little now, gently, to herself.

The door opened. Frank came in, put down his cap, and took his seat on the bench by the fire. "All out?" he asked.

Gertie nodded, and made a little broken sound.

"Very good," said Frank. "Then I'm going to talk to you."

Gertie wiped away a few more tears, and settled herself down for a little morbid pleasure. It was delightful to her to be found crying over the fire. Frank, at any rate, would appreciate that.

"Now," said Frank, "you've got the choice once more, and I'm going to put it plainly. If you don't do what I want this time, I shall have to see whether somebody else can't persuade you."

She glanced up, a little startled.

"Look here," said Frank. "I'm not going to take any more trouble myself over this affair. You were a good deal upset yesterday when the lady came round, and you'll be more upset yet before the thing's over. I shan't talk to you myself any more: you don't seem to care a hang what I say; in fact, I'm thinking of moving my lodgings after Christmas. So now you've got your choice."

He paused.

"On the one side you've got the Major; well, you know him; you know the way he treats you. But that's not the reason why I want you to leave him. I want you to leave him because I think that down at the bottom you've got the makings of a good woman—"

"I haven't," cried Gertie passionately.

"Well, I think you have. You're very patient, and you're very industrious, and because you care for this man you'll do simply anything in the world for him. Well, that's splendid. That shows you've got grit. But have you ever thought what it'll all be like in five years from now?"

"I shall be dead," wailed Gertie. "I wish I was dead now."

Frank paused.

"And when you're dead—?" he said slowly.

There was an instant's silence. Then Frank took up his discourse again. (So far he had done exactly what he had wanted. He had dropped two tiny ideas on her heart once more—hope and fear.)

"Now I've something to tell you. Do you remember the last time I talked to you? Well, I've been thinking what was the best thing to do, and a few days ago I saw my chance and took it. You've got a little prayer-book down at the bottom of your bundle, haven't you? Well, I got at that (you never let anyone see it, you know), and I looked through it. I looked through all your things. Did you know your address was written in it? I wasn't sure it was your address, you know, until—"

Gertie sat up, white with passion.

"You looked at my things?"

Frank looked her straight in the face.

"Don't talk to me like that," he said. "Wait till I've done.... Well, I wrote to the address, and I got an answer; then I wrote again, and I got another answer and a letter for you. It came this morning, to the post-office where I got it."

Gertie looked at him, still white, with her lips parted.

"Give me the letter," she whispered.

"As soon as I've done talking," said Frank serenely. "You've got to listen to me first. I knew what you'd say: you'd say that your people wouldn't have you back. And I knew perfectly well from the little things you'd said about them that they would. But I wrote to make sure....

"Gertie, d'you know that they're breaking their hearts for you?... that there's nothing, in the whole world they want so much as that you should come back?..."

"Give me the letter!"

"You've got a good heart yourself, Gertie; I know that well enough. Think hard, before I give you the letter. Which is best—the Major and this sort of life—and ... and—well, you know about the soul and God, don't you?... or to go home, and—"

Her face shook all over for one instant.

"Give me the letter," she wailed suddenly.

Then Frank gave it her.

(V)

"But I can't possibly go home like this," whispered Gertie agitatedly in the passage, after the Major's return half an hour later.

"Good Lord!" whispered Frank, "what an extraordinary girl you are, to think—"

"I don't care. I can't, and I won't."

Frank cast an eye at the door, beyond which dozed the Major in the chair before the fire.

"Well, what d'you want?"

"I want another dress, and ... and lots of things."

Frank stared at her resignedly.

"How much will it all come to?"

"I don't know. Two pounds—two pounds ten."

"Let's see: to-day's the twentieth. We must get you back before Christmas. If I let you have it to-morrow, will it do?—to-morrow night?"

She nodded. A sound came from beyond the door, and she fled.

I am not sure about the details of the manner in which Frank got the two pounds ten, but I know he got it, and without taking charity from a soul. I know that he managed somehow to draw his week's money two days before pay-day, and for the rest, I suspect the pawnshop. What is quite certain is that when his friends were able to take stock of his belongings a little later, the list of them was as follows:

One jacket, one shirt, one muffler, a pair of trousers, a pair of socks, a pair of boots, one cap, one tooth-brush, and a rosary. There was absolutely nothing else. Even his razor was gone.

Things, therefore, were pretty bad with him on the morning of the twenty-second of December. I imagine that he still possessed a few pence, but out of this few pence he had to pay for his own and Gertie's journey to Chiswick, as well as keep himself alive for another week. At least, so he must have thought.

It must have been somewhere in Kensington High Street that he first had a hint of a possibility of food to be obtained free, for, although I find it impossible to follow all his movements during these days, it is quite certain that he partook of the hospitality of the Carmelite Fathers on this morning. He mentions it, with pleasure, in his diary.

It is a very curious and medieval sight—this feeding of the poor in the little deep passage that runs along the outside of the cloister of the monastery in Church Street. The passage is approached by a door at the back of the house, opening upon the lane behind, and at a certain hour on each morning of the year is thronged from end to end with the most astonishing and deplorable collection of human beings to be seen in London. They are of all ages and sizes, from seventeen to seventy, and the one thing common to them all is extreme shabbiness and poverty.

A door opens at a given moment; the crowd surges a little towards a black-bearded man in a brown frock, with an apron over it, and five minutes later a deep silence, broken only by the sound of supping and swallowing, falls upon the crowd. There they stand, with the roar of London sounding overhead, the hooting of cars, the noise of innumerable feet, and the rain—at least, on this morning—falling dismally down the long well-like space. And here stand between two and three hundred men, pinched, feeble, and yet wolfish, gulping down hot soup and bread, looking something like a herd of ragged prisoners pent in between the high walls.

Here, then, Frank stood in the midst of them, gulping his soup. His van and horses, strictly against orders, remained in Church Street, under the care of a passer-by, whom Frank seems to have asked, quite openly, to do it for him for God's sake.

It is a dreary little scene in which to picture him, and yet, to myself, it is rather pleasant, too. I like to think of him, now for the second time within a few weeks, and all within the first six months of his Catholic life, depending upon his Church for the needs of the body as well as for the needs of the soul. There was nothing whatever to distinguish him from the rest; he, too, had now something of that lean look that is such a characteristic of that crowd, and his dress, too, was entirely suitable to his company. He spoke with none of his hosts; he took the basin in silence and gave it back in silence; then he wiped his mouth on his sleeve, and went out comforted.

Dick Guiseley sat over breakfast in his rooms off Oxford Street, entirely engrossed in a local Yorkshire paper two days old.

His rooms were very characteristic of himself. They were five in number—a dining-room, two bedrooms, and two sitting-rooms divided by curtains, as well as a little entrance-hall that opened on to the landing, close beside the lift that served all the flats. They were furnished in a peculiarly restrained style—so restrained, in fact, that it was almost impossible to remember what was in them. One was just conscious of a sense of extreme comfort and convenience. There was nothing in particular that arrested the attention or caught the eye, except here and there a space or a patch of wall about which Dick had not yet made up his mind. He had been in them two years, indeed, but he had not nearly finished furnishing. From time to time a new piece of furniture appeared, or a new picture—always exceedingly good of its kind, and even conspicuous. Yet, somehow or other, so excellent was his taste, as soon as the thing was in place its conspicuousness (so to speak) vanished amidst the protective coloring, and it looked as if it had been there for ever. The colors were chosen with the same superfine skill: singly they were brilliant, or at least remarkable (the ceilings, for instance, were of a rich buttercup yellow); collectively they were subdued and unnoticeable. And I suppose this is exactly what rooms ought to be.

The breakfast-table at which he sat was a good instance of his taste. The silver-plate on it was really remarkable. There was a delightful Caroline tankard in the middle, placed there for the sheer pleasure of looking at it; there was a large silver cow with a lid in its back; there were four rat-tail spoons; the china was an extremely cheap Venetian crockery of brilliant designs and thick make. The coffee-pot and milk-pot were early Georgian, with very peculiar marks; but these vessels were at present hidden under the folded newspaper. There were four chrysanthemums in four several vases of an exceptional kind of glass. It sounds startling, I know, but the effect was not startling, though I cannot imagine why not. Here again one was just conscious of freshness and suitability and comfort.

But Dick was taking no pleasure in it all this morning. He was feeling almost physically sick, and the little spirit-heated silver dish of kidneys on his Queen Anne sideboard was undisturbed. He had cut off the top of an egg which was now rapidly cooling, and a milky surface resembling thin ice was forming on the contents of his coffee-cup. And meanwhile he read.

The column he was reading described the wedding of his uncle with Miss Jenny Launton, and journalese surpassed itself. There was a great deal about the fine old English appearance of the bridegroom, who, it appeared, had been married in a black frock-coat and gray trousers, with white spats, and who had worn a chrysanthemum in his button-hole (Dick cast an almost venomous glance upon the lovely blossom just beside the paper), and the beautiful youthful dignity of the bride, "so popular among the humble denizens of the country-side." The bride's father, it seemed, had officiated at the wedding in the "sturdy old church," and had been greatly affected—assisted by the Rev. Matthieson. The wedding, it seemed, had been unusually quiet, and had been celebrated by special license: few of the family had been present, "owing," said the discreet reporter, "to the express wish of the bridegroom." (Dick reflected sardonically upon his own convenient attack of influenza from which he was now completely recovered.) Then there was a great deal more about the ancient home of the Guiseleys, and the aristocratic appearance of Viscount Merefield, the young and popular heir to the earldom, who, it appeared, had assisted at the wedding in another black frock-coat. General Mainwaring had acted as best man. Finally, there was a short description of the presents of the bridegroom to the bride, which included a set of amethysts, etc....

Dick read it all through to the luxuriant end, down to the peals of the bells and the rejoicings in the evening. He ate several pieces of dry toast while he read, crumbling them quickly with his left hand, and when he had finished, drank his coffee straight off at one draught. Then he got up, still with the paper, sat down in the easy-chair nearest to the fire and read the whole thing through once more. Then he pushed the paper off his knee and leaned back.

It would need a complete psychological treatise to analyze properly all the emotions he had recently gone through—emotions which had been, so to say, developed and "fixed" by the newspaper column he had just read. He was a man who was accustomed to pride himself secretly upon the speed with which he faced each new turn of fortune, and the correctness of the attitude he assumed. Perhaps it would be fair to say that the Artistic Stoic was the ideal towards which he strove. But, somehow, those emotions would not sort themselves. There they all were—fury, indignation, contempt, wounded pride, resignation, pity—there were no more to be added or subtracted; each had its place and its object, yet they would not coalesce. Now fury against his uncle, now pity for himself, now a poisonous kind of contempt of Jenny. Or, again, a primitive kind of longing for Jenny, a disregard of his uncle, an abasement of himself. The emotions whirled and twisted, and he sat quite still, with his eyes closed, watching them.

But there was one more emotion which had made its appearance entirely unexpectedly as soon as he had heard the news, that now, greatly to his surprise, was beginning to take a considerable place amongst the rest—and this was an extraordinarily warm sense of affection towards Frank—of all people. It was composed partly of compassion, and partly of an inexplicable sort of respect for which he could perceive no reason. It was curious, he thought later, why this one figure should have pushed its way to the front just now, when his uncle and Jenny and, secondarily, that Rector ("so visibly affected by the ceremony") should have occupied all the field. Frank had never meant very much to Dick; he had stood for the undignified and the boyish in the midst of those other stately elements of which Merefield, and, indeed, all truly admirable life, was composed.

Yet now this figure stood out before him with startling distinctness.

First there was the fact that both Frank and himself had suffered cruelly at the hands of the same woman, though Frank incomparably the more cruelly of the two. Dick had the honesty to confess that Jenny had at least never actually broken faith with himself; but he had also the perspicuity to see that it came to very nearly the same thing. He knew with the kind of certitude that neither needs nor appeals to evidence that Jenny would certainly have accepted him if it had not been that Lord Talgarth had already dawned on her horizon, and that she put him off for a while simply to see whether this elderly sun would rise yet higher in the heavens. It was the same consideration, no doubt, that had caused her to throw Frank over a month or two earlier. A Lord Talgarth in the bush was worth two cadets in the hand. That was where her sensibleness had come in, and certainly it had served her well.

It was this community of injury, then, that primarily drew Dick's attention to Frank; and, when once it lead been so drawn, it lingered on other points in his personality. Artistic Stoicism is a very satisfying ideal so long as things go tolerably well. It affords an excellent protection against such misfortunes as those of not being appreciated or of losing money or just missing a big position—against all such ills as affect bodily or mental conveniences. But when the heart is touched, Artistic Stoicism peels off like rusted armour. Dick had seriously began to consider, during the last few days, whether the exact opposite of Artistic Stoicism (let us call it Natural Impulsiveness) is not almost as good an equipment. He began to see something admirable in Frank's attitude to life, and the more he regarded it the more admirable it seemed.

Frank, therefore, had begun to wear to him the appearance of something really moving and pathetic. He had had a communication or two from Jack Kirkby that had given him a glimpse of what Frank was going through, and his own extremely artificial self was beginning to be affected by it.

He looked round his room now, once or twice, wondering whether it was all worth while. He had put his whole soul into these rooms—there was that Jacobean press with the grotesque heads—ah! how long he had agonized over that in the shop in the King's Road, Chelsea, wondering whether or not it would do just what he wanted, in that space between the two doors. There was that small statue of a Tudor lady in a square head-dress that he had bought in Oxford: he had occupied at least a week in deciding exactly from what point she was to smile on him; there was the new curtain dividing the two rooms: he had had half a dozen patterns, gradually eliminated down to two, lying over his sofa-back for ten days before he could make up his mind. (How lovely it looked, by the way, just now, with that patch of mellow London sunlight lying across the folds!)

But was it all worth it?... He argued the point with himself, almost passively, stroking his brown beard meditatively; but the fact that he could argue it at all showed that the foundations of his philosophy were shaken.

Well, then ... Frank ... What about him? Where was he?

(II)

About eleven o'clock a key turned in his outer door and a very smart-looking page-boy came through, after tapping, with a telegram on a salver.

Dick was writing to Hamilton's, in Berners Street, about a question of gray mats for the spare bedroom, and he took the telegram and tore open the envelope with a preoccupied air. Then he uttered a small exclamation.

"Any answer, sir?"

"No. Yes.... Wait a second."

He took a telegraph-form with almost indecent haste, addressed it to John Kirkby, Barham, Yorks, and wrote below:

"Certainly; will expect you dinner and sleep.—Richard Guiseley."

Then, when the boy had gone, he read again the telegram he had received:

"Have received letter from Frank; can probably discover address if I come to town. Can you put me up to-night?—Jack Kirkby, Barham."

He pondered it a minute or so. Then he finished his note to Hamilton's, but it was with a distracted manner. Then for several minutes he walked up and down his rooms with his hands in his jacket-pockets, thinking very deeply. He was reflecting how remarkable it was that he should hear of Frank again just at this time, and was wondering what the next move of Providence would be.

The rest of Dick's day was very characteristic of him; and considering my other personages in this story and their occupations, I take a dramatic sort of pleasure in writing it down.

He went out to lunch with a distinguished lady of his acquaintance—whose name I forbear to give; she was not less than seventy years old, and the two sat talking scandal about all their friends till nearly four o'clock. The Talgarth affair, even, was discussed in all its possible lights, and Dick was quite open about his own part in the matter. He knew this old lady very well, and she knew him very well. She was as shrewd as possible and extremely experienced, and had helped Dick enormously in various intricacies and troubles of the past; and he, on the other hand, as a well-informed bachelor, was of almost equal service to her. She was just the least bit in the world losing touch with things (at seventy you cannot do everything), and Dick helped to keep her in touch. He lunched with her at least once a week when they were both in town.

At four he went to the Bath Club, ordered tea and toast and cigarettes, and sat out, with his hat over his eyes, on the balcony, watching the swimmers. There was a boy of sixteen who dived with surprising skill, and Dick took the greatest possible pleasure in observing him. There was also a stout man of his acquaintance whose ambition it had been for months to cross the bath by means of the swinging rings, and this person, too, afforded him hardly less pleasure, as he always had to let go at the fourth ring, if not the third, whence he plunged into the water with a sound that, curiously enough, was more resonant than sibilant.

At six, after looking through all the illustrated papers, he went out to get his coat, and was presently in the thick of a heated argument with a member of the committee on the subject of the new carpet in the front hall. It was not fit, said Dick (searching for hyperboles), for even the drawing-room of the "Cecil."

This argument made him a little later than he had intended, and, as he came up in the lift, the attendant informed him, in the passionless manner proper to such people, that the Mr. Kirkby who had been mentioned had arrived and was waiting for him in his rooms.

Shortly before midnight Dick attempted to sum up the situation. They had talked about Frank practically without ceasing, since Dick's man had set coffee on the table at nine o'clock, and both had learned new facts.

"Well, then, wire to go down to this man, Parham-Carter," said Dick, "the first thing after breakfast to-morrow. Do you know anything about the Eton Mission?"

"No. One used to have a collection for it each half, you know, in the houses."

"How do we go?"

"Oh! railway from Broad Street. I've looked it up. Victoria Park's the station."

Dick drew two or three draughts of smoke from his cigar-butt, and laid it down in a small silver tray at his elbow. (The tray was a gift from the old lady he had lunched with to-day.)

"All you've told me is extraordinarily interesting," he said. "It really was to get away this girl that he's stopped so long?"

"I expect that's what he tells himself—that's the handle, so to speak. But it's chiefly a sort of obstinacy. He said he would go on the roads, and so he's gone."

"I rather like that, you know," said Dick.

Jack snorted a little.

"Oh, it's better than saying a thing and not doing it. But why say it?"

"Oh! one must do something," said Dick. "At least, some people seem to think so. And I rather envy them, you know. I'm afraid I don't."

"Don't what?"

"Don't do anything. Unless you can call this sort of thing doing something." He waved his hand vaguely round his perfectly arranged room.

Jack said nothing. He was inclined to be a little strenuous himself in some ways, and he had always been conscious of a faint annoyance with Dick's extreme leisureliness.

"I see you agree," went on Dick. "Well, we must see what can be done."

He stood up smiling and began to expand and contract his fingers luxuriously before the fire behind his back.

"If we can only get Frank away," murmured Jack. "That's enough for the present."

"And what do you propose to do with him then?"

"Oh, Lord! Anything. Go round the world if he likes. Come and stay at my place."

"And suppose he thinks that's a bit too near to ... to Lady Talgarth.".

This switched Jack back again to a line he had already run on for an hour this evening.

"Yes, that's the ghastly part of it all. He's sure not to have heard. And who the devil's to tell him? And how will he take it?"

"Do you know," said Dick, "I'm really not frightened about that? All you've told me about him makes me think he'll behave very well. Funny thing, isn't it, that you know him so much better than I do? I never dreamed there was so much in him, somehow."

"Oh, there's a lot in Frank. But one doesn't always know what it is."

"Do you think his religion's made much difference?"

"I think it's done this for him," said Jack slowly. "(I've been thinking a lot about that). I think it's fixed things, so to speak ...." He hesitated. He was not an expert in psychological analysis. Dick took him up quickly. He nodded three or four times.

"Exactly," he said. "That's it, no doubt. It's given him a center—a hub for the wheel."

"Eh?"

"It's ... it's joined everything on to one point in him. He'll be more obstinate and mad than ever before. He's got a center now.... I suppose that's what religion's for," he added meditatively.

This was Greek to Jack. He looked at Dick uncomprehendingly.

Dick turned round and began to stare into the fire, still contracting and expanding his fingers.

"It's a funny thing—this religion," he said at last. "I never could understand it."

"And what about Archie?" asked Jack with sudden abruptness. (He had no continuity of mind.)

Dick brought his meditations to a close with equal abruptness, or perhaps he would not have been so caustic as regards his first cousin.

"Oh, Archie's an ass!" he said. "We can leave him out."

Jack changed the subject again. He was feeling the situation very acutely indeed, and the result was that all its elements came tumbling out anyhow.

"I've been beastly uncomfortable," he said.

"Yes?" said Dick. "Any particular way?"

Jack shifted one leg over the other. He had not approached one element in the situation at all, as yet, with Dick, but it had been simmering in him for weeks, and had been brought to a point by Frank's letter received this morning. And now the curious intimacy into which he had been brought with Dick began to warm it out of him.

"You'll think me an ass, too, I expect," he said. "And I rather think it's true. But I can't help it."

Dick smiled at him encouragingly. (Certainly, thought Jack, this man was nicer than he had thought him.)

"Well, it's this—" he said suddenly. "But it's frightfully hard to put into words. You know what I told you about Frank's coming to me at Barham?"

"Yes."

"Well, there was something he said then that made me uncomfortable. And it's made me more and more uncomfortable ever since ..." (He paused again.) "Well, it's this. He said that he felt there was something going on that he couldn't understand—some sort of Plan, he said—in which he had to take part—a sort of scheme to be worked out, you know. I suppose he meant God," he explained feebly.

Dick looked at him questioningly.

"Oh! I can't put it into words," said Jack desperately. "Nor did he, exactly. But that was the kind of idea. A sort of Fate. He said he was quite certain of it.... And there were lots of little things that fitted in. He changed his clothes in the old vestry, you know—in the old church. It seemed like a sort of sacrifice, you know. And then I had a beastly dream that night. And then there was something my mother said. ... And now there's his letter: the one I showed you at dinner—about something that might happen to him.... Oh! I'm a first-class ass, aren't I?"

There was a considerable silence. He glanced up in an ashamed sort of way, at the other, and saw him standing quite upright and still, again with his back to the fire, looking out across the room. From outside came the hum of the thoroughfare—the rolling of wheels, the jingle of bells, the cries of human beings. He waited in a kind of shame for Dick's next words. He had not put all these feelings into coherent form before, even to himself, and they sounded now even more fantastic than he had thought them. He waited, then, for the verdict of this quiet man, whom up to now he had deemed something of a fool, who cared about nothing but billiards and what was called Art. (Jack loathed Art.)

Then the verdict came in a surprising form. But he understood it perfectly.

"Well, what about bed?" said Dick quietly.

(IV)

It was on the morning of the twenty-fourth that Mr. Parham-Carter was summoned by the neat maid-servant of the clergy-house to see two gentlemen. She presented two cards on a plated salver, inscribed with the names of Richard Guiseley and John B. Kirkby. He got up very quickly, and went downstairs two at a time. A minute later he brought them both upstairs and shut the door.

"Sit down," he said. "I'm most awfully glad you've come. I ... I've been fearfully upset by all this, and I haven't known what to do."

"Now where is he?" demanded Jack Kirkby.

The clergyman made a deprecatory face.

"I've absolutely promised not to tell," he said. "And you know—"

"But that's ridiculous. We've come on purpose to fetch him away. It simply mustn't go on. That's why I didn't write. I sent Frank's letter on to Mr. Guiseley here (he's a cousin of Frank's, by the way), and he asked me to come up to town. I got to town last night, and we've come down here at once this morning."

Mr. Parham-Carter glanced at the neat melancholy-faced, bearded man who sat opposite.

"But you know I promised," he said.

"Yes," burst in Jack; "but one doesn't keep promises one makes to madmen. And—"

"But he's not mad in the least. He's—"

"Well?"

"I was going to say that it seems to me that he's more sane than anyone else," said the young man dismally. "I know it sounds ridiculous, but—"

Dick Guiseley nodded with such emphasis that he stopped.

"I know what you mean," said Dick in his gentle drawl. "And I quite understand."

"But it's all sickening rot," burst in Jack. "He must be mad. You don't know Frank as I do—neither of you. And now there's this last business—his father's marriage, I mean; and—"

He broke off and looked across at Dick.

"Go on," said Dick; "don't mind me."

"Well, we don't know whether he's heard of it or not; but he must hear sooner or later, and then—"

"But he has heard of it," interrupted the clergyman. "I showed him the paragraph myself."

"He's heard of it! And he knows all about it!"

"Certainly. And I understood from him that he knew the girl: the Rector's daughter, isn't it?"

"Knows the girl! Why, he was engaged to her himself."

"What?"

"Yes; didn't he tell you?"

"He didn't give me the faintest hint—"

"How did he behave? What did he say?"

Mr. Parham-Carter stared a moment in silence.

"What did he say?" snapped out Jack impatiently.

"Say? He said nothing. He just told me he knew the girl, when I asked him."

"Good God!" remarked Jack. And there was silence.

Dick broke it.

"Well, it seems to me we're rather in a hole."

"But it's preposterous," burst out Jack again. "Here's poor old Frank, simply breaking his heart, and here are we perfectly ready to do anything we can—why, the chap must be in hell!"

"Look here, Mr. Parham-Carter," said Dick softly. "What about your going round to his house and seeing if he's in, and what he's likely to be doing to-day."

"He'll be at the factory till this evening."

"The factory?"

"Yes; he's working at a jam factory just now."

A sound of fury and disdain broke from Jack.

"Well," continued Dick, "(May I take a cigarette, by the way?), why shouldn't you go round and make inquiries, and find out how the land lies? Then Kirkby and I might perhaps hang about a bit and run up against him—if you'd just give us a hint, you know."

The other looked at him a moment.

"Well, perhaps I might," he said doubtfully. "But what—"

"Good Lord! But you'll be keeping your promise, won't you? After all, it's quite natural we should come down after his letter—and quite on the cards that we should run up against him.... Please to go at once, and let us wait here."

In a quarter of an hour Mr. Parham-Carter came back quickly into the room and shut the door.

"Yes; he's at the factory," he said. "Or at any rate he's not at home. And they don't expect him back till late."

"Well?"

"There's something up. The girl's gone, too. (No; she's not at the factory.) And I think there's going to be trouble."

CHAPTER VI: (I)

The electric train slowed down and stopped at the Hammersmith terminus, and there was the usual rush for the doors.

"Come on, Gertie," said a young man, "here we are."

The girl remained perfectly still with her face hidden.

The crowd was enormous this Christmas Eve, and for the most part laden with parcels; the platforms surged with folk, and each bookstall, blazing with lights (for it was after seven o'clock), was a center of a kind of whirlpool. There was sensational news in the evening papers, and everyone was anxious to get at the full details of which the main facts were tantalizingly displayed on the posters. Everyone wanted to know exactly who were the people concerned and how it had all happened. It was a delightful tragedy for the Christmas festivities.

"Come on," said the young man again. "They're nearly all out."

"I can't," moaned the girl.

Frank took her by the arm resolutely.

"Come!" he said.

Then she came, and the two passed out together into the mob waiting to come in.

"We shall have to walk," said Frank. "I'm sorry; but I've got to get home somehow."

She bowed her head and said nothing.

Gertie presented a very unusual appearance this evening. Certainly she had laid out the two-pound-ten to advantage. She was in a perfectly decent dark dress with a red stripe in it; she had a large hat and some species of boa round her neck; she even carried a cheap umbrella with a sham silver band and a small hand-bag with one pocket-handkerchief inside it. And to her own mind, no doubt, she was a perfect picture of the ideal penitent—very respectable and even prosperous looking, and yet with a dignified reserve. She was not at all flaunting, she must have thought; neither was she, externally, anything of a disgrace. It would be evident presently to her mother that she had returned out of simple goodness of heart and not at all because her recent escapade had been a failure. She would still be able to talk of "the Major" with something of an air, and to make out that he treated her always like a lady. (When I went to interview her a few months ago I found her very dignified, very self-conscious, excessively refined and faintly reminiscent of fallen splendor; and her mother told me privately that she was beginning to be restless again and talked of going on to the music-hall stage.)

But there is one thing that I find it very hard to forgive, and that is, that as the two went together under the flaming white lights towards Chiswick High Street, she turned to Frank a little nervously and asked him if he would mind walking just behind her. (Please remember, however, in extenuation, that Gertie's new pose was that of the Superior Young Lady.)

"I don't quite like to be seen—" murmured this respectable person.

"Oh, certainly!" said Frank, without an instant's hesitation.

They had met, half an hour before, by appointment, at the entrance to the underground station at Victoria. Frank's van-journeyings would, he calculated, bring him there about half-past six, and, strictly against the orders of his superiors, but very ingeniously, with the connivance of his fellow-driver of the van, he had arranged for his place to be taken on the van for the rest of the evening by a man known to his fellow-driver—but just now out of work—for the sum of one shilling, to be paid within a week. He was quite determined not to leave Gertie alone again, when once the journey to Chiswick had actually begun, until he had seen her landed in her own home.

The place of meeting, too, had suited Gertie very well. She had left Turner Road abruptly, without a word to anyone, the instant that the Major's military-looking back had been seen by her to pass within the swing-doors of the "Queen's Arms" for his usual morning refreshment. Then she had occupied herself chiefly by collecting her various things at their respective shops, purchased by Frank's two-pound-ten, and putting them on. She had had a clear threepence to spare beyond the few shillings she had determined to put by out of the total, and had expended it by a visit to the cinematograph show in Victoria Street. There had been a very touching series of pictures of the "Old Home in the Country," and the milking of the cows, with a general atmosphere of roses and church-bells, and Gertie had dissolved into tears more than once, and had cried noiselessly into her new pocket-handkerchief drawn from her new hand-bag. But she had met Frank quite punctually, for, indeed, she had burned her boats now entirely and there was nothing else left for her to do.

At the entrance to Chiswick High Street another brilliant thought struck her. She paused for Frank to come up.

"Frankie," she said, "you won't say anything about the two-pound-ten, will you? I shouldn't like them to think—"

"Of course not," said Frank gravely, and after a moment, noticing that she glanced at him again uneasily, understood, and fell obediently to the rear once more.

About a quarter of a mile further on her steps began to go slower. Frank watched her very carefully. He was not absolutely sure of her even now. Then she crossed over the street between two trams, and Frank dodged after her. Then she turned as if to walk back to Hammersmith. In an instant Frank was at her side.

"You're going the wrong way," he said.

She stopped irresolutely, and had to make way for two or three hurrying people, to pass.

"Oh, Frankie! I can't!" she wailed softly.

"Come!" said Frank, and took her by the arm once more.

Five minutes later they stood together half-way down a certain long lane that turns out of Chiswick High Street to the left, and there, for the first time, she seems to have been genuinely frightened. The street was quite empty; the entire walking population was parading up and down the brightly-lit thoroughfare a hundred yards behind them, or feverishly engaged in various kinds of provision shops. The lamps were sparse in this lane, and all was comparatively quiet.

"Oh, Frankie!" she moaned again. "I can't! I can't!... I daren't!"

She leaned back against the sill of a window.

Yet, even then, I believe she was rather enjoying herself. It was all so extremely like the sort of plays over which she had been accustomed to shed tears. The Prodigal's Return! And on

Christmas Eve! It only required a little snow to be falling and a crying infant at her breast....

I wonder what Frank made of it. He must have known Gertie thoroughly well by now, and certainly there is not one sensible man in a thousand whose gorge would not have risen at the situation. Yet I doubt whether Frank paid it much attention.

"Where's the house?" he said.

He glanced up at the number of the door by which he stood.

"It must be a dozen doors further on," he said.

"It's the last house in the row," murmured Gertie, in a weak voice. "Is father looking out? Go and see."

"My dear girl," said Frank, "do not be silly. Do remember your mother's letter."

Then she suddenly turned on him, and if ever she was genuine she was in that moment.

"Frankie," she whispered, "why not take me away yourself? Oh! take me away! take me away!"

He looked into her eyes for an instant, and in that instant he caught again that glimpse as of Jenny herself.

"Take me away—I'll live with you just as you like!" She took him by his poor old jacket-lapel. "You can easily make enough, and I don't ask—"

Then he detached her fingers and took her gently by the arm.

"Come with me," he said. "No; not another word."

Together in silence they went the few steps that separated them from the house. There was a little garden in front, its borders set alternately with sea-shells and flints. At the gate she hesitated once more, but he unlatched the gate and pushed her gently through.

"Oh! my gloves!" whispered Gertie, in a sharp tone of consternation. "I left them in the shop next the A.B.C. in Wilton Road."

Frank nodded. Then, still urging her, he brought her up to the door and tapped upon it. There were footsteps inside.

"God bless you, Gertie. Be a good girl. I'll wait in the road for ten minutes, so that you can call me if you want to."

Then he was gone as the door opened.

The next public appearance of Frank that I have been able to trace, was in Westminster Cathedral. Now it costs an extra penny at least, I think, to break one's journey from Hammersmith to Broad Street, and I imagine that Frank would not have done this after what he had said to Gertie about the difficulty connected with taking an omnibus, except for some definite reason, so it is only possible to conclude that he broke his journey at Victoria in an attempt to get at those gloves.

It seems almost incredible that Gertie should have spoken of her gloves at such a moment, but it really happened. She told me so herself. And, personally, on thinking over it, it seems to me tolerably in line (though perhaps the line is rather unusually prolonged) with all that I have been able to gather about her whole character. The fact is that gloves, just then, were to her really important. She was about to appear on the stage of family life, and she had formed a perfectly consistent conception of her part. Gloves were an integral part of her costume—they were the final proof of a sort of opulence and refinement; therefore, though she could not get them just then, it was perfectly natural and proper of her to mention them. It must not be thought that Gertie was insincere: she was not; she was dramatic. And it is a fact that within five minutes of her arrival she was down on her knees by her mother, with her face hidden in her mother's lap, crying her heart out. By the time she remembered Frank and ran out into the street, he had been gone more than twenty minutes.

One of the priests attached to Westminster Cathedral happened to have a pause about half-past nine o'clock in his hearing of confessions. He had been in his box without a break from six o'clock, and he was extremely tired and stiff about the knees. He had said the whole of his office during intervals, and he thought he would take a little walk up and down the south aisle to stretch his legs.

So he unlatched the little door of his confessional, leaving the light burning in case someone else turned up; he slipped off his stole and came outside.

The whole aisle, it seemed, was empty, though there was still a sprinkling of folks in the north aisle, right across the great space of the nave; and he went down the whole length, down to the west end to have a general look up the Cathedral.

He stood looking for three or four minutes.

Overhead hung the huge span of brickwork, lost in darkness, incredibly vast and mysterious, with here and there emerging into faint light a slice of a dome or the slope of some architrave-like dogmas from impenetrable mystery. Before him lay the immense nave, thronged now with close-packed chairs in readiness for the midnight Mass, and they seemed to him as he looked with tired eyes, almost like the bent shoulders of an enormous crowd bowed in dead silence of adoration. But there was nothing yet to adore, except up there to the left, where a very pale glimmer shone on polished marble among the shadows before the chapel of the Blessed Sacrament. There was one other exception; for overhead, against the half-lighted apse, where a belated sacristan still moved about, himself a shadow, busy with the last preparations of the High

Altar—there burgeoned out the ominous silhouette of the vast hanging cross, but so dark that the tortured Christ upon it was invisible.... Yet surely that was right on this night, for who, of all those who were to adore presently the Child of joy, gave a thought to the Man of Sorrows? His Time was yet three months away....

As the priest stood there, looking and imagining, with that strange clarity of mind and intuition that a few hours in the confessional gives to even the dullest brain, he noticed the figure of a man detach itself from one of the lighted confessionals on the left and come down towards him, walking quickly and lightly. To his surprise, this young man, instead of going out at the northwest door, wheeled and came towards him.

He noticed him particularly, and remembered his dress afterwards: it was a very shabby dark blue suit, splashed with mud from the Christmas streets, very bulgy about the knees; the coat was buttoned up tightly round a muffler that had probably once been white, and his big boots made a considerable noise as he came.

The priest had a sudden impulse as the young man crossed him.

"A merry Christmas," he said.

The young man stopped a moment and smiled all over his face, and the priest noticed the extraordinary serenity and pleasantness of the face—and that, though it was the face of a Poor Man, with sunken cheeks and lines at the corners of the mouth.

"Thank you, Father," he said. "The same to you."

Then he went on, his boots as noisy as ever, and turned up the south aisle. And presently the sound of his boots ceased.

The priest still stood a moment or two, looking and thinking, and it struck him with something of pleasure that the young man, though obviously of the most completely submerged tenth, had not even hesitated or paused, still less said one word, with the hope of a little something for Christmas' sake. Surely he had spoken, too, with the voice of an educated man.

He became suddenly interested—he scarcely knew why, and the impression made just by that single glimpse of a personality deepened every moment.... What in the world was that young man doing here?... What was his business up in that empty south aisle? Who was he? What was it all about?

He thought presently that he would go up and see; it was on his way back to the clergy-house, too. But when he reached the corner of the aisle and could see up it, there seemed to be no one there.

He began to walk up, wondering more than ever, and then on a sudden he saw a figure kneeling on the lower step of the chapel on the right, railed off and curtained now, where the Crib was ready to be disclosed two hours later.

It all seemed very odd. He could not understand why anyone should wish to pray before an impenetrable curtain. As he came nearer he saw it was his friend all right. Those boots were unmistakable. The young man was kneeling on the step, quite upright and motionless, his cap held in his hands, facing towards the curtain behind which, no doubt, there stood the rock-roofed stable, with the Three Personages—an old man, a maid and a new-born Child. But their time, too, was not yet. It was two hours away.

Priests do not usually stare in the face of people who are saying their prayers—they are quite accustomed to that phenomenon; but this priest (he tells me) simply could not resist it. And as he passed on his noiseless shoes, noticing that the light from his own confessional shone full upon the man, he turned and looked straight at his face.

Now I do not understand what it was that he saw; he does not understand it himself; but it seems that there was something that impressed him more than anything else that he had ever seen before or since in the whole world.

The young man's eyes were open and his lips were closed. Not one muscle of his face moved. So much for the physical facts. But it was a case where the physical facts are supremely unimportant.... At any rate, the priest could only recall them with an effort. The point was that there was something supra-physical there—(personally I should call it supernatural)—that stabbed the watcher's heart clean through with one over whelming pang.... (I think that's enough.)

When the priest reached the Lady chapel he sat down, still trembling a little, and threw all his attention into his ears, determined to hear the first movement that the kneeling figure made behind him. So he sat minute after minute. The Cathedral was full of echoes—murmurous rebounds of the noises of the streets, drawn out and mellowed into long, soft, rolling tones, against which, as against a foil, there stood out detached, now and then, the sudden footsteps of someone leaving or entering a confessional, the short scream of a slipping chair—once the sudden noise of a confessional-door being opened and the click of the handle which turned out the electric light. And it was full of shadows, too; a monstrous outline crossed and recrossed the apse behind the High Altar, as the sacristan moved about; once a hand, as of a giant, remained poised for an instant somewhere on the wall beside the throne. It seemed to the priest, tired and clear-brained as he was, as if he sat in some place of expectation—some great cavern where mysteries moved and passed in preparation for a climax. All was hushed and confused, yet alive; and the dark waves would break presently in the glory of the midnight Mass.

He scarcely knew what held him there, nor what it was for which he waited. He thought of the lighted common-room at the end of the long corridor beyond the sacristy. He wondered who was there; perhaps one or two were playing billiards and smoking; they had had a hard day of it and would scarcely get to bed before three. And yet, here he sat, tired and over-strained, yet waiting—waiting for a disreputable-looking young man in a dirty suit and muffler and big boots, to give over praying before a curtain in an empty aisle.

A figure presently came softly round the corner behind him. It was the priest whom he had heard leaving his confessional just now.

"Haven't you done yet?" whispered the new-comer, pausing behind his chair.

"Coming in a minute or two," he said.

The figure passed on; presently a door banged like muffled thunder somewhere beyond the sacristy, and simultaneously he heard a pair of boots going down the aisle behind.

He got up instantly, and with long, silent steps made his way down the aisle also. The figure wheeled the corner and disappeared; he himself ran on tip-toe and was in time to see him turning away from the holy-water basin by the door. But he came so quickly after him that the door was still vibrating as he put his hand upon it. He came out more cautiously through the little entrance, and stood on the steps in time to see the young man moving off, not five yards away, in the direction of Victoria Street. But here something stopped him.

Coming straight up the pavement outside the Art and Book Company depot was a newsboy at the trot, yelling something as he came, with a poster flapping from one arm and a bundle of papers under the other. The priest could not catch what he said, but he saw the young man suddenly stop and then turn off sharply towards the boy, and he saw him, after fumbling in his pocket, produce a halfpenny and a paper pass into his hands.

There then he stood, motionless on the pavement, the sheet spread before him flapping a little in the gusty night wind.

"Paper, sir!" yelled the boy, pausing in the road. "'Orrible—"

The priest nodded; but he was not thinking much about the paper, and produced his halfpenny. The paper was put into his hand, but he paid no attention to it. He was still watching the motionless figure on the pavement. About three minutes passed. Then the young man suddenly and dexterously folded the paper, folded it again and slipped it into his pocket. Then he set off walking and a moment later had vanished round the corner into Victoria Street.

The priest thought no more of the paper as he went back through the Cathedral, wondering again over what he had seen....

But the common-room was empty when he got to it, and presently he spread the paper before him on the table and leaned over it to see what the excitement was about. There was no doubt as to what the news was—there were headlines occupying nearly a third of a column; but it appeared to him unimportant as general news: he had never heard of the people before. It seemed that a wealthy peer who lived in the North of England, who had only recently been married for the second time, had been killed in a motor smash together with his eldest son. The chauffeur had escaped with a fractured thigh. The peer's name was Lord Talgarth.

CHAPTER VII: (I)

On the morning of the twenty-fourth a curious little incident happened—I dug the facts out of the police news—in a small public-house on the outskirts of South London. Obviously it is no more than the sheerest coincidence. Four men were drinking a friendly glass of beer together on their way back to work from breakfast. Their ecclesiastical zeal seems to have been peculiarly strong, for they distinctly stated that they were celebrating Christmas on that date, and I deduce from that statement that beer-drinking was comparatively infrequent with them.

However, as they were about to part, there entered to them a fifth, travel-stained and tired, who sat down and demanded some stronger form of stimulant. The new-comer was known to these four, for his name was given, and his domicile was mentioned as Hackney Wick. He was a small man, very active and very silent and rather pale; and he seems to have had something of a mysterious reputation even among his friends and to be considered a dangerous man to cross.

He made no mystery, however, as to where he had come from, nor whither he was going. He had come from Kent, he said, and humorously added that he had been hop-picking, and was going to join his wife and the family circle for the festival of Christmas. He remarked that his wife had written to him to say she had lodgers.

The four men naturally stayed a little to hear all this news and to celebrate Christmas once more, but they presently were forced to tear themselves away. It was as the first man was leaving (his foreman appears to have been of a tyrannical disposition) that the little incident happened.

"Why," he said, "Bill" (three out of the five companions seemed to have been usually called "Bill"), "Bill, your boots are in a mess."

The Bill in question made caustic remarks. He observed that it would be remarkable if they were not in such weather. But the other persisted that this was not mud, and a general inspection was made. This resulted in the opinion of the majority being formed that Bill had trodden in some blood. Bill himself was one of the majority, though he attempted in vain to think of any explanation. Two men, however, declared that in their opinion it was only red earth. (A certain obscurity appears in the evidence at this point, owing to the common use of a certain expletive in the mouth of the British working-man.) There was a hot discussion on the subject, and the Bill whose boots were under argument seems to have been the only man to keep his head. He argued very sensibly that if the stains were those of blood, then he must have stepped in some—perhaps in the gutter of a slaughter-house; and if it was not blood, then it must be something else he had trodden in. It was urged upon him that it was best washed off, and he seems finally to have taken the advice, though without enthusiasm.

Then the four men departed.

The landlady's evidence was to the same effect. She states that the new-comer, with whose name she had been previously unacquainted, though she knew his face, had remained very tranquilly for an hour or so and had breakfasted off bacon and eggs. He seemed to have plenty of money, she said. He had finally set off, limping a little, in a northward direction.

Now this incident is a very small one. I only mention it because, in reading the evidence later, I found myself reminded of a parallel incident, recorded in a famous historical trial, in which something resembling blood was seen on the hand of the judge. His name was Ayloff, and his date the sixteenth century.

Mrs. Partington had a surprise—not wholly agreeable—on that Christmas Eve. For at half-past three, just as the London evening was beginning to close in, her husband walked into the kitchen.

She had seen nothing of him for six weeks, and had managed to get on fairly well without him. I am not even now certain whether or no she knows what her husband's occupation is during these absences of his—I think it quite possible that, honestly, she does not—and I have no idea myself. It seemed, however, this time, that he had prospered. He was in quite a good temper, he was tolerably well dressed, and within ten minutes of his arrival he had produced a handful of shillings. Five of these he handed over to her at once for Christmas necessaries, and ten more he entrusted to Maggie with explicit directions as to their expenditure.

While he took off his boots, his wife gave him the news—first, as to the arrival of the Major's little party, and next as to its unhappy dispersion on that very day.

"He will 'ave it as the young man's gone off with the young woman," she observed.

Mr. Partington made a commentatory sound.

"An' 'e's 'arf mad," she added. "'E means mischief if 'e can manage it."

Mr. Partington observed, in his own particular kind of vocabulary, that the Major's intentions were absurd, since the young man would scarcely be such a peculiarly qualified kind of fool as to return. And Mrs. Partington agreed with him. (In fact, this had been her one comfort all day. For it seemed to her, with her frank and natural ideas, that, on the whole, Frank and Gertie had done the proper thing. She was pleased, too, to think that she had been right in her surmises as to Gertie's attitude to Frank. For, of course, she never doubted for one single instant that the two had eloped together in the ordinary way, though probably without any intentions of matrimony.)

Mr. Partington presently inquired as to where the Major was, and was informed that he was, of course, at the "Queen's Arms." He had been there, in fact, continuously—except for sudden excursions home, to demand whether anything had been heard of the fugitives—since about half-past eleven that morning. It was a situation that needed comfort.

Mrs. Partington added a few comments on the whole situation, and presently put on her bonnet and went out to supplement her Christmas preparations with the extra five shillings, leaving her husband to doze in the Windsor chair, with his pipe depending from his mouth. He had walked up from Kent that morning, he said.

She returned in time to get tea ready, bringing with her various "relishes," and found that the situation had developed slightly since her departure. The Major had made another of his infuriated returns, and had expanded at length to his old friend Mr. Partington, recounting the extraordinary kindness he had always shown to Frank and the confidence he had reposed in him. He had picked him up, it seemed, when the young man had been practically starving, and had been father and comrade to him ever since. And to be repaid in this way! He had succeeded also by his eloquence, Mrs. Partington perceived, in winning her husband's sympathies, and was now gone off again, ostensibly to scour the neighborhood once more, but, more probably, to attempt to drown his grieved and wounded feelings.

Mrs. Partington set her thin lips and said nothing. She noticed also, as she spread the table, a number of bottles set upon the floor, two of them with yellow labels—the result of Maggie's errand—and prepared herself to face a somewhat riotous evening. But Christmas, she reflected for her consolation, comes but once a year.

It was about nine o'clock that the two men and the one woman sat down to supper upstairs. The children had been put to bed in the kitchen as usual, after Jimmie had informed his mother that the clergyman had been round no less than three times since four o'clock to inquire after the vanished lodger. He was a little tearful at being put to bed at such an unusually early hour, as Mr. Parham-Carter, it appeared, had promised him no less than sixpence if he would come round to the clergy-house within five minutes after the lodger's return, and it was obviously impossible to traverse the streets in a single flannel shirt.

His mother dismissed it all as nonsense. She told him that Frankie was not coming back at all—that he wasn't a good young man, and had run away without paying mother her rent. This made the situation worse than ever, as Jimmie protested violently against this shattering of his ideal, and his mother had to assume a good deal of sternness to cover up her own tenderness of feeling. But she, too—though she considered the flight of the two perfectly usual—was conscious of a very slight sense of disappointment herself that it should have been this particular young man who had done it.

Then she went upstairs again to supper.

The famous archway that gives entrance to the district of Hackney Wick seems, especially on a rainy night, directly designed by the Great Eastern Railway as a vantage ground for observant loafers with a desire to know every soul that enters or leaves Hackney Wick. It is, of course, possible to, enter Hackney Wick by other ways—it may be approached by the marshes, and there is, I think, another way round about half a mile to the east, under the railway. But those ways have nothing whatever to do with people coming from London proper. You arrive at Victoria Park Station; you turn immediately to the right and follow the pavement down, with the park on your left, until you come to the archway where the road unites with that coming from Homerton. One is absolutely safe, therefore, assuming that one has not to deal with watchful criminals, in standing under the arch with the certitude that sooner or later, if you wait long enough, the man whom you expect to enter Hackney Wick will pass within ten yards of you.

Mr. Parham-Carter, of course, knew this perfectly well, and had, finally, communicated the fact to the other two quite early in the afternoon. An elaborate system of watches, therefore, had been arranged, by which one of the three had been on guard continuously since three o'clock. It was Jack who had had the privilege (if he had but known it) of observing Mr. Partington himself returning home to his family for Christmas, and it was Dick, who came on guard about five, who had seen the Major—or, rather, what was to him merely a shabby and excited man—leave and then return to the "Queen's Arms" during his hour's watch.

After the amazing and shocking news, however, of the accident to Lord Talgarth and Archie, the precautions had been doubled. It was the clergyman who had first bought an evening paper soon after five o'clock, and within five minutes the other two knew it also.

It is of no good to try to describe the effect it had on their minds, beyond saying that it made all three of them absolutely resolute that Frank should by no possible means escape them. The full dramatic situation of it all they scarcely appreciated, though it soaked more and more into them gradually as they waited—two of them in the Men's Club just round the corner, and the third, shivering and stamping, under the arch. (An unemployed man, known to the clergyman, had been set as an additional sentry on the steps of the Men's Club, whose duty it would be, the moment the signal was given from the arch that Frank was coming, to call the other two instantly from inside. Further, the clergyman—as has been related—had been round three times since four o'clock to Turner Road, and had taken Jimmie into his pay.)

The situation was really rather startling, even to the imperturbable Dick. This pleasant young man, to whom he had begun to feel very strangely tender during the last month or two, now tramping London streets (or driving a van), in his miserable old clothes described to him by the clergyman, or working at the jam factory, was actually no one else at this moment but the new Lord Talgarth—with all that that implied. Merefield was his, the big house in Berkeley Square was his; the moor in Scotland.... It was an entire reversal of the whole thing: it was as a change of trumps in whist: everything had altered its value....

Well, he had plenty of time, both before he came off guard at seven and after he had joined the clergyman in the Men's Club, to sort out the facts and their consequences.

About half-past ten the three held a consultation under the archway, while trains rumbled overhead. They attracted very little attention here: the archway is dark and wide; they were muffled to the eyes; and there usually is a fringe of people standing under shelter here on rainy evenings. They leaned back against the wall and talked.

They had taken further steps since they had last met. Mr. Parham-Carter had been round to the jam factory, and had returned with the news that the van had come back under the charge of only one of the drivers, and that the other one, who was called Gregory (whom Mr. Parham-Carter was inquiring after), would certainly be dismissed in consequence. He had taken the address of the driver, who was now off duty—somewhere in Homerton—with the intention of going to see him next morning if Frank had not appeared.

There were two points they were discussing now. First, should the police be informed? Secondly, was it probable that Frank would have heard the news, and, if so, was it conceivable that he had gone straight off somewhere in consequence—to his lawyers, or even to Merefield itself?

Dick remembered the name of the firm quite well—at least, he thought so. Should he send a wire to inquire?

But then, in that case, Jack shrewdly pointed out, everything was as it should be. And this reflection caused the three considerable comfort.

For all that, there were one or two "ifs." Was it likely that Frank should have heard the news? He was notoriously hard up, and the name Talgarth had not appeared, so far, on any of the posters. Yet he might easily have been given a paper, or picked one up ... and then....

So the discussion went on, and there was not much to be got out of it. The final decision come to was this: That guard should be kept, as before, until twelve o'clock midnight; that at that hour the three should leave the archway and, in company, visit two places—Turner Road and the police-station—and that the occupants of both these places should be informed of the facts. And that then all three should go to bed.

(IV)

At ten minutes past eleven Dick moved away from the fire in the Men's Club, where he had just been warming himself after his vigil, and began to walk up and down.

He had no idea why he was so uncomfortable, and he determined to set to work to reassure himself. (The clergyman, he noticed, was beginning to doze a little by the fire, for the club had just been officially closed and the rooms were empty.)

Of course, it was not pleasant to have to tell a young man that his father and brother were dead (Dick himself was conscious of a considerable shock), but surely the situation was, on the whole, enormously improved. This morning Frank was a pauper; to-night he was practically a millionaire, as well as a peer of the realm. This morning his friends had nothing by which they might appeal to him, except common sense and affection, and Frank had very little of the one, and, it would seem, a very curious idea of the other.

Of course, all that affair about Jenny was a bad business (Dick could hardly even now trust himself to think of her too much, and not to discuss her at all), but Frank would get over it.

Then, still walking up and down, and honestly reassured by sheer reason, he began to think of what part Jenny would play in the future.... It was a very odd situation, a very odd situation indeed. (The deliberate and self-restrained Dick used an even stronger expression.) Here was a young woman who had jilted the son and married the father, obviously from ambitious motives, and now found herself almost immediately in the position of a very much unestablished kind of dowager, with the jilted son reigning in her husband's stead. And what on earth would happen next? Diamonds had been trumps; now it looked as if hearts were to succeed them; and what a very remarkable pattern was that of these hearts.

But to come back to Frank—

And at that moment he heard a noise at the door, and, as the clergyman started up from his doze, Dick saw the towzled and becapped head of the unemployed man and his hand beckoning violently, and heard his hoarse voice adjuring them to make haste. The gentleman under the arch, he said, was signaling.

The scene was complete when the two arrived, with the unemployed man encouraging them from behind, half a minute later under the archway.

Jack had faced Frank fairly and squarely on the further pavement, and was holding him in talk.

"My dear chap," he was saying, "we've been waiting for you all day. Thank the Lord you've come!"

Frank looked a piteous sight, thought Dick, who now for the first time saw the costume that Mr. Parham-Carter had described with such minuteness. He was standing almost under the lamp, and there were heavy drooping shadows on his face; he looked five years older than when Dick had last seen him—only at Easter. But his voice was confident and self-respecting enough.

"My dear Jack," he was saying, "you really mustn't interrupt. I've only just—" Then he broke off as he recognized the others.

"So you've given me away after all," he said with a certain sternness to the clergyman.

"Indeed I haven't," cried that artless young man. "They came quite unexpectedly this morning."

"And you've told them that they could catch me here," said Frank "Well, it makes no difference. I'm going on—Hullo! Dick!"

"Look here!" said Dick. "It's really serious. You've heard about—" His voice broke.

"I've heard about it," said Frank. "But that doesn't make any difference for to-night."

"But my dear man," cried Jack, seizing him by the lapel of his coat, "it's simply ridiculous. We've come down here on purpose—you're killing yourself—"

"One moment," said Frank. "Tell me exactly what you want."

Dick pushed to the front.

"Let him alone, you fellows.... This is what we want, Frank. We want you to come straight to the clergy-house for to-night. To-morrow you and I'll go and see the lawyers first thing in the morning, and go up to Merefield by the afternoon train. I'm sorry, but you've really got to go through with it. You're the head of the family now. They'll be all waiting for you there, and they can't do anything without you. This mustn't get into the papers. Fortunately, not a soul knows of it yet, though they would have if you'd been half an hour later. Now, come along."

"One moment," said Frank. "I agree with nearly all that you've said. I quite agree with you that"—he paused a moment—"that the head of the family should be at Merefield to-morrow night. But for to-night you three must just go round to the clergy-house and wait. I've got to finish my job clean out—and—"

"What job?" cried two voices simultaneously.

Frank leaned against the wall and put his hands in his pockets.

"I really don't propose to go into all that now. It'd take an hour. But two of you know most of the story. In a dozen words it's this—I've got the girl away, and now I'm going to tell the man, and tell him a few other things at the same time. That's the whole thing. Now clear off, please. (I'm awfully obliged, you know, and all that), but you really must let me finish it before I do anything else."

There was a silence.

It seemed tolerably reasonable, put like that—at least, it seemed consistent with what appeared to the three to be the amazing unreason of all Frank's proceedings. They hesitated, and were lost.

"Will you swear not to clear out of Hackney Wick before we've seen you again?" demanded Jack hoarsely.

Frank bowed his head.

"Yes," he said.

The clergyman and Dick were consulting in low voices. Jack looked at them with a wild sort of appeal in his face. He was completely bewildered, and hoped for help. But none came.

"Will you swear—" he began again.

Frank put his hand suddenly on his friend's shoulder.

"Look here, old man. I'm really rather done up. I think you might let me go without any more—"

"All right, we agree," said Dick suddenly. "And—"

"Very good," said Frank. "Then there's really no more—"

He turned as if to go.

"Frank, Frank—" cried Jack.

Frank turned and glanced at him, and then went on.

"Good-night," he cried.

And so they let him go.

They watched him, in silence, cross the road by the "Queen's Arms" and pass up the left-hand pavement. As he drew near each lamp his shadow lay behind him, shortened, vanished and reappeared before him. After the third lamp they lost him, and they knew he would a moment later pass into Turner Road.

So they let him go.

(V)

Mr. Parham-Carter's room looked very warm and home-like after the comfortlessness of the damp lamp-lit streets. It was as has already been related: the Madonna, the prints, the low book-cases, the drawn curtains, the rosy walls, the dancing firelight and the electric lamp.

It was even reassuring at first—safe and protected, and the three sat down content. A tray with some cold meat and cheese rested on the table by the fire, and cocoa in a brown jug stood warming in the fender. They had had irregular kinds of refreshments in the Men's Club at odd intervals, and were exceedingly hungry....

They began to talk presently, and it was astonishing how the sight and touch of Frank had cheered them. More than one of the three has confessed to me since that a large part of the anxiety was caused by his simple absence and by imaginative little pictures of street accidents. It would have been so extremely ironical if he had happened to have been run over on the day on which he became Lord Talgarth.

They laid their little plans, too, for the next day. Dick had thought it all out. He, Jack and Frank were to call at the lawyers' office in Lincoln's Inn Fields, and leave a message, as the office would be closed of course, immediately after the wanderer had been dressed properly in ready-made clothes. Then they would catch the early afternoon train and get to Merefield that night. The funeral could not possibly take place for several days: there would have to be an inquest.

Then they read over the account of the smash in the Star newspaper—special edition. It seemed to have been nobody's fault. The brake had refused to act going down a steep hill; they had run into a wall; the chauffeur had been thrown clean over it; the two passengers had been pinned under the car. Lord Talgarth was dead at once; Archie had died five minutes after being taken out.

So they all talked at once in low voices, but in the obvious excitement of relief. It was an extraordinary pleasure to them—now that they looked at it in the sanity conferred by food and warmth—to reflect that Frank was within a quarter of a mile of them—certainly in dreary surroundings; but it was for the last time. To-morrow would see him restored to ordinary life, his delusions and vagaries plucked from him by irresistible circumstance, and the future in his hands.

Midnight still found them talking—alert and cheerful; but a little silence fell as they heard the chiming of bells.

"Christmas Day, by George!" said the clergyman. "Merry Christmas!"

They shook hands, smiling shamefacedly, as is the custom of Englishmen.

"And to think of old Frank—" mused Jack half aloud. "I told you, Guiseley, about his coming to me in the autumn?" (He had been thinking a great deal about that visit lately, and about what Frank had told him of himself—the idea he had of Something going on behind the scenes in which he had passively to take his part; his remark on how pleasant it must be to be a squire. Well, the play had come to an end, it seemed; now there followed the life of a squire indeed. It was curious to think that Frank was, actually at this moment, Lord Talgarth!)

Dick nodded his head, smiling to himself in his beard. Somehow or another the turn things had taken had submerged in him for the present the consciousness of the tragedy up at Merefield, and his own private griefs, and the memory of Jenny.

Jack told it all again briefly. He piled it on about the Major and his extreme repulsiveness, and the draggled appearance of Gertie, and Frank's incredible obstinacy.

"And to think that he's brought it off, and got the girl home to her people.... Well, thank the Lord that's over! We shan't have any more of that sort of thing."

Dick got up presently and began to walk about, eyeing the pictures and the books.

"Want to turn in?" asked the cleric.

"Well, I think, as we've an early start—"

The clergyman jumped up.

"You've a beastly little room, I'm afraid. We're rather full up. And you, Mr. Kirkby!"

"I'll wait till you come back," he said.

The two went out, after good-nights, and Jack was left staring at the fire.

He felt very wide-awake, and listened contentedly to the dying noises of the streets. Somewhere in that hive outside was Frank—old Frank. That was very good to think of....

During these last months Frank's personality had been very persistently before him. It was not that he pretended to understand him in the very least; but he understood enough now to feel that there was something very admirable in it all. It was mad and quixotic and absurd, but it had a certain light of nobility. Of course, it would never do if people in general behaved like that; society simply could not go on if everyone went about espousing the cause of unhappy and badly-behaved individuals, and put on old clothes and played the Ass. But, for all that, it was not unpleasant to reflect that his own friend had chosen to do these things in despite of convention. There was a touch of fineness in it. And it was all over now, thank God.... What times they would have up in the north!

He heard a gate clash somewhere outside. The sound just detached itself from the murmur of the night. Then a late train ran grinding over the embanked railway behind the house, and drew up with the screaming of brakes at Victoria Park Station, and distracted him again.

"Are you ready, Mr. Kirkby?" said the clergyman, coming in.

Jack stood up, stretching himself. In the middle of the stretch he stopped.

"What's that noise?" he asked.

They stood listening.

Then again came the sharp, prolonged tingle of an electric bell, followed by a battering at a door downstairs.

Jack, looking in the other's face, saw him go ever so slightly pale beneath his eyes.

"There's somebody at the door," said Mr. Parham-Carter. "I'll just go down and see."

And, as Jack stood there, motionless and breathless, he could hear no sound but the thick hammering of his own heart at the base of his throat.

At half-past eleven o'clock Mrs. Partington came upstairs to the room where the two men were still drinking, to make one more suggestion that it was time to go to bed.

It was a dreary little room, this front bedroom on the first floor, where Frank and the Major had slept last night in one large double bed. The bed was pushed now close against the wall, the clothes still tumbled and unmade, with various articles lying upon it, as on a table. A chair without a back stood between it and the window.

The table where the two men still sat was pulled close to the fire that had been lighted partly in honor of Mr. Partington and partly in honor of Christmas, and was covered with a débris of plates and glasses and tobacco and bottles. There was a jam-jar filled with holly obtained from the butcher's shop, in the middle of the table. There was very little furniture in the room; there was a yellow-painted chest of drawers opposite the door, and this, too, held a little regiment of bottles; there was a large oleograph of Queen Victoria hanging above the bed, and a text—for some inscrutable reason—was permitted to hang above the fireplace, proclaiming that "The Lord is merciful and long-suffering," in Gothic letters, peeping modestly out of a wealth of painted apple-blossoms, with a water-wheel in the middle distance and a stile. On the further side of the fireplace was a washhand-stand, with a tin pail below it, and the Major's bowler hat reposing in the basin. There was a piece of carpet underneath the table, and a woolly sort of mat, trodden through in two or three places, beside the bed.

Mrs. Partington coughed as she came in, so tremendous was the reek of tobacco smoke, burning paraffin and spirits.

"Bless the men!" she said, and choked once more.

She was feeling comparatively light-hearted; it was a considerable relief to her that Frank actually had not come back, though she never had for one instant expected him to do so. But she didn't want any more disturbances or quarrels, and, as she looked at the Major, who turned in his chair as she came in, she felt even more relieved. His appearance was not reassuring.

He had been drinking pretty steadily all day to drown his grief, and had ended up by a very business-like supper with his landlord. There were four empty beer bottles and one empty whisky bottle distributed on the table or floor, and another half-empty whisky bottle stood between the two men on the table. And as she looked at the Major (she was completely experienced in alcoholic symptoms), she understood exactly what stage he had reached....

Now the Major was by no means a drunkard—let that be understood. He drank whenever he could, but a tramp cannot drink to very grave excess. He is perpetually walking and he is perpetually poor. But this was a special occasion; it was Christmas; he was home in London; his landlord had returned, and he had lost Gertie.

He had reached, then, the dangerous stage, when the alcohol, after having excited and warmed and confused the brain, recoils from it to some extent, leaving it clear and resolute and entirely reckless, and entirely conscious of any idea that happens to be dominant (at least, that is the effect on some temperaments). The maudlin stage had passed long ago, at the beginning of supper, when the Major had leaned his head on his plate and wept over the ingratitude of man and the peculiar poignancy of "old Frankie's" individual exhibition of it. A noisy stage had succeeded to this, and now there was deadly quiet.

He was rather white in the face; his eyes were set, but very bright, and he was smoking hard and fast.

"Now then," said Mrs. Partington cheerfully, "time for bed."

Her husband winked at her gravely, which was his nearest approach to hilarity. He was a quiet man at all times.

The Major said nothing.

"There! there's 'Erb awake again," said the mother, as a wail rose up the staircase. "I'll be up again presently." And she vanished once more.

Two of the children were awake after all.

Jimmie lay, black-eyed and alert, beside his brother, and looked at his mother reflectively as she came in. He was still thinking about the sixpence that might conceivably have been his. 'Erb's lamentation stopped as she came in, and she went to the table first to turn down the smoking lamp.

She was quite a kindly mother, a great deal more tender than she seemed, and 'Erb knew it well enough. But he respected her sufficiently to stop crying when she came in.

"Now then," she said with motherly sternness. "I can't 'ave—"

Then she stopped abruptly. She had heard steps on the pavement outside as she came into the room, and now she heard the handle of the street door turned and someone come into the passage. She stood wondering, and in that pause she missed her chance, for the steps came straight past the door and began to go upstairs. It might, of course, conceivably be one of the lodgers on the top-floor, and yet she knew it was not. She whisked to the door a moment later, but it was too late, and she was only just in time to see the figure she knew turn the corner of the four stairs that led to the first-floor landing.

"Is that Frankie?" asked Jimmie, suddenly sitting up in bed. "Oh! mother, let me—"

"You be quiet!" snapped the woman, and stood listening; with parted lips.

(II)

From that point Mrs. Partington seems to have been able to follow very closely what must have taken place upstairs.

It was a very quiet night, here in Turner Road: the roysterers were in the better-lighted streets, and the sober folk were at home. And there was not a footstep on the pavements outside to confuse the little drama of sound that came down to her through the ill-fitting boards overhead. She could not explain afterwards why she did not interfere. I imagine that she hoped against hope that she was misinterpreting what she heard, and also that a kind of terror seized her which she found it really impossible to shake off.

First, there was the opening and closing of the door; two or three footsteps, and then dead silence.

Then she heard talking begin, first one voice, then a crescendo, as if two or three clamored together; then one voice again. (It was impossible, so far, to distinguish which was which.)

This went on for a minute or two; occasionally there was a crescendo, and once or twice some voice rose almost into a shout.

Then, without warning, there was a shuffling of feet, and a crash, as of an overturned chair; and, instant upon the noise, 'Erb set up a prolonged wail.

"You be quiet!" snapped the woman in a sharp whisper.

The noises went on: now the stamp of a foot; now the scraping of something overhead and a voice or two in sharp deep exclamation, and then complete silence once more. 'Erb was sobbing now, as noiselessly as he could, terrified at his mother's face, and Jimmie was up, standing on the floor in his flannel shirt, listening like his mother. Maggie still slept deeply on the further side of the bed.

The woman went on tip-toe a step nearer the door, opened it, and peeped out irresolutely. But the uncarpeted stairs stretched up into the darkness, unlit except for the glimmer that came from the room at whose door she was standing....

There was a voice now, rising and falling steadily, and she heard it broken in upon now and again by something that resembled a chuckle. Somehow or another this sickened her more than all else; it was like her husband's voice. She recoiled into the room, and, as she did so, there came the sound of blows and the stamping of feet, and she knew, in a way that she could not explain, that there was no fight going on. It was some kind of punishment, not a conflict....

She would have given the world to move, to run to the street door and scream for help; but her knees shook under her and her heart seemed to be hammering itself to bits. Jimmie had hold of her now, clinging round her, shaking with terror and murmuring something she could not understand. Her whole attention was upstairs. She was wondering how long it would go on.

It must be past midnight now, she thought: the streets seethed still as death. But overhead there was still movement and the sound of blows, and then abruptly the end came.

There was one more crescendo of noise—two voices raised in dispute, one almost shrill, in anger or expostulation; then one more sudden and heavy noise as of a blow or a fall, and dead silence.

(III)

The next thing that Mrs. Partington remembered afterwards was that she found herself standing on the landing upstairs, listening, yet afraid to move.

All was very nearly silent within: there was just low talking, and the sound of something being moved. It was her husband's voice that she heard.

Beyond her the stairs ran up to the next story, and she became aware presently that someone else was watching, too. An untidy head of a woman leaned over the banisters, and candle-light from somewhere beyond lit up her face. She was grinning.

Then the sharp whisper came down the stairs demanding what was up.

Mrs. Partington jerked her thumb towards the closed door and nodded reassuringly. She was aware that she must be natural at all costs. The woman still hung over the banisters a minute longer and then was gone.

Jimmie was with her too, now, still just in his shirt, perfectly quiet, with a face as white as paper. His big black eyes dwelt on his mother's face.

Then suddenly she could bear the suspense no more. She stole up to the door, still on tip-toe, still listening, and laid her fingers on the handle. There were more gentle movements within now, the noise of water and a basin (she heard the china clink distinctly), but no more words.

She turned the handle resolutely and looked in.

The Major was leaning in the corner by the window, with his hands in his pockets, staring with a dull, white, defiant kind of face at the bed. The lamp on the mantelpiece lighted him up clearly. On his knees by the bedside was her husband, with his back to her, supporting a basin on the bed and some thing dark that hung over it. Then she saw Frank. It was he who was lying on the bed almost upon his face; one boot dangled down on this side, and it was his head that her husband was supporting. She stared at it a moment in terror.... Then her eyes wandered to the floor, where, among the pieces of broken glass, a pool of dark liquid spread slowly over the boards. Twigs and detached leaves of holly lay in the midst of it. And at that sight her instinct reasserted herself.

She stepped forward and took her husband by the shoulder. He turned a face that twitched a little towards her. She pushed him aside, took the basin from him, and the young man's head....

"Clear out of this," she whispered sharply. "Quick, mind! You and the Major!... Jimmie!" The boy was by her in an instant, shaking all over, but perfectly self-controlled.

"Jimmie, put your things on and be off to the clergy-house. Ring 'em up, and ask for Mr. Carter. Bring him round with you."

Frank's head slipped a little in her hands, and she half rose to steady it. When she had finished and looked round again for her husband, the room was empty. From below up the stairs came a sudden draught, and the flame leaped in the lamp-chimney. And then, once more unrestrained, rose up the wailing of 'Erb.

A little after dawn on that Christmas morning Mr. Parham-Carter sat solitary in the kitchen. The children had been packed off to a neighbor's house before, and he himself had been to and fro all night and was tired out—to the priest's house at Homerton, to the doctor's, and to the parish nurse. All the proper things had been done. Frank had been anointed by the priest, bandaged by the doctor, and settled in by the nurse into the middle of the big double bed. He had not yet recovered consciousness. They were upstairs now—Jack, Dick and the nurse; the priest and the doctor had promised to look in before nine—there was nothing more that they could do for the present, they said—and Mrs. Partington was out at this moment to fetch something from the dispensary.

He had heard her story during one of the intervals in the course of the night, and it seemed to him that he had a tolerably accurate theory of the whole affair—if, that is to say, her interpretation of the noises she had heard was at all correct.

The Major must have made an unexpected attack, probably by a kick that had temporarily disabled Frank, and must then, with Mr. Partington's judicial though amused approval, have proceeded to inflict chastisement upon Frank as he lay on the floor. This must have gone on for a considerable time; Frank seemed to have been heavily kicked all over his body. And the thing must have ended with a sudden uncontrolled attack on the part of the Major, not only with his boots, but with at least one of the heavy bottles. The young man's head was cut deeply, as if by glass, and it was probably three or four kicks on the head, before Mr. Partington could interfere, that had concluded the punishment. The doctor's evidence entirely corroborated this interpretation of events. It was, of course, impossible to know whether Frank had had the time or the will to make any resistance. The police had been communicated with, but there was no news yet of the two men involved.

It was one of those bleak, uncomfortable dawns that have no beauty either of warmth or serenity—at least it seemed so here in Turner Road. Above the torn and dingy strip of lace that shrouded the lower part of the window towered the black fronts of the high houses against the steely western sky. It was extraordinarily quiet. Now and then a footstep echoed and died suddenly as some passer-by crossed the end of the street; but there was no murmur of voices yet, or groups at the doors, as, no doubt, there would be when the news became known.

The room, too, was cheerless; the fire was long ago gone out; the children's bed was still tumbled and disordered, and the paraffin lamp had smoked itself out half an hour ago. Overhead the clergyman could hear now and again a very gentle footstep, and that was all.

He was worn out with excitement and a kind of terror; and events took for him the same kind of clear, hard outline as did the physical objects themselves in this cold light of dawn. He had passed through a dozen moods: furious anger at the senseless crime, at the hopeless, miserable waste of a life, an overwhelming compassion and a wholly unreasonable self-reproach for not having foreseen danger more clearly the night before. There were other thoughts that had come to him too—doubts as to whether the internal significance of all these things were in the least analogous to the external happenings; whether, perhaps, after all, the whole affair were not on the inner side a complete and perfect event—in fact, a startling success of a nature which he could not understand. Certainly, exteriorly, a more lamentable failure and waste could not be conceived; there had been sacrificed such an array of advantages—birth, money, education, gifts, position—and for such an exceedingly small and doubtful good, that no additional data, it would appear, could possibly explain the situation. Yet was it possible that such data did exist somewhere, and that another golden and perfect deed had been done—that there was no waste, no failure, after all?

But at present these thoughts only came to him in glimpses; he was exhausted now of emotion and speculation. He regarded the pitiless facts with a sunken, unenergetic attention, and wondered when he would be called again upstairs.

There came a footstep outside; it hesitated, then the street door was pushed open and the step came in, up to the room door, and a small face, pinched with cold, its eyes all burning, looked at him.

"Come in, Jimmie," he whispered.

And so the two sat, huddled one against the other, and the man felt again and again a shudder, though not of cold, shake the little body at his side.

Ten minutes later a step came down the stairs, a little hurriedly, though on tip-toe; and Mrs. Partington, her own thin face lined with sleeplessness and emotion, and her lips set, nodded at him emphatically. He understood, and went quickly past her, followed closely by the child, and up the narrow stairs.... He heard the street-door close behind him as the woman left the house.

It seemed to him as he came into the room as if he had stepped clean out of one world into another. And the sense of it was so sudden and abrupt that he stood for an instant on the threshold amazed at the transition.

First, it was the absolute stillness and motionlessness of the room that impressed him, so far as any one element predominated. There were persons in the room, but they were as statues.

On the farther side of the bed, decent now and arranged and standing out across the room, kneeled the two men, Jack Kirkby and Dick Guiseley, but they neither lifted their eyes nor showed the faintest consciousness of his presence as he entered. Their faces were in shadow: behind them was the cold patch of the window, and a candle within half an inch of extinction stood also behind them on a table in the corner, with one or two covered vessels and instruments.

The nurse kneeled on this side, one arm beneath the pillow and the other on the counterpane. And then there was Frank.

He lay perfectly still upon his back, his hands clasped before him (and even these were bandaged). His head lay high on three or four pillows, and he wore what looked like a sort of cap, wholly hiding his hair and ears. His profile alone showed clear-cut and distinct against the gloom in the corner behind. His face was entirely tranquil, as pale as ivory; his lips were closed. His eyes alone were alive.

Presently those turned a little, and the man standing at the door, understanding the look, came forward and kneeled too by the bed.

Then, little by little, he began, in that living stillness, to understand rather better what it was that he was witnessing.... It was not that there was anything physical in the room, beyond the things of which his senses told him; there was but the dingy furniture, the white bed, august now with a strange dignity as of a white altar, and the four persons beside himself—five now, for Jimmie was beside him. But that the physical was not the plane in which these five persons were now chiefly conscious was the most evident thing of all.... There was about them, not a Presence, not an air, not a sweetness or a sound, and yet it is by such negatives only that the thing can be expressed.

And so they kneeled and waited.

"Why, Jack—"

It shook the waiting air like the sound of a bell, yet it was only whispered. The man nearest him on the other side shook with a single spasmodic movement and laid his fingers gently on the bandaged hands. And then for a long while there was no further movement or sound.

"Rosary!" said Frank suddenly, still in a whisper.... "Beads...."

Jack moved swiftly on his knees, took from the table a string of beads from where they had been laid the night before, and put them into the still fingers. Then he laid his own hands over them again.

Again there was a long pause.

Outside in the street a footstep came up from the direction of Mortimer Road, waxed loud and clear on the pavement, and died again down towards the street leading to the marshes. And, but for this, there was no further sound for a while. Then a cock crew, thin and shrill, somewhere far away; a dray rumbled past the end of the street and was silent.

But the silence in the room was of a different quality; or, rather, the world seemed silent because this room was so, and not the other way. It was here that the center lay, where a battered man was dying, and from this center radiated out the Great Peace.

It was no waste then, after all!—this life of strange unreason ending in this very climax of uselessness, exactly when ordinary usefulness was about to begin. Could that be waste that ended so?

"Priest," whispered the voice from the bed.

Then Dick leaned forward.

"He has been," he said distinctly and slowly. "He was here at two o'clock. He did—what he came for. And he's coming again directly."

The eyes closed in sign of assent and opened again.

He seemed to be looking, as in a kind of meditation, at nothing in particular. It was as a man who waits at his ease for some pleasant little event that will unroll by and by. He was in no ecstasy, and, it seemed, in no pain and in no fierce expectation; he was simply at his ease and waiting. He was content, whatever those others might be.

For a moment it crossed the young clergyman's mind that he ought to pray aloud, but the thing was dismissed instantly. It seemed to him impertinent nonsense. That was not what was required. It was his business to watch, not to act.

So, little by little, he ceased to think actively, he ceased to consider this and that. At first he had wondered how long it would be before the doctor and the priest arrived. (The woman had gone to fetch them.) He had wished that they would make haste.... He had wondered what the others felt, and how he would describe it all to his Vicar. Now, little by little, all this ceased, and the peace grew within and without, till the balance of pressure was equalized and his attention floated at the perfect poise.

Again there was no symbol or analogy that presented itself. It was not even by negation that he thought. There was just one positive element that included all: time seemed to mean nothing, the ticks of the clock with the painted face were scarcely consecutive; it was all one, and distance was nothing, nor nearness—not even the nearness of the dying face against the pillows....

It was so, then, that something of that state to which Frank had passed communicated itself to at least one of those who saw him die.

A little past the half hour Frank spoke again.

"My love to Whitty," he said.... "Diary.... Tell him...."

The end came a few minutes before nine o'clock, and it seems to have come as naturally as life itself. There was no drama, no dying speech, not one word.

Those who were there saw him move ever so slightly in bed, and his head lifted a little. Then his head sank once more and the Failure was complete.

Made in the USA
Columbia, SC
26 September 2020